# Oneonta: The Novel

## JULIAN KOOSMAN

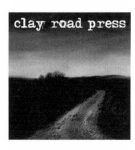 Published by Clay Road Press.

Written by Julian Koosman.
Edited by Edward Chidlington III.
Cover photograph by Julian Koosman.

Page layout and cover design by Clay Road Press.

ISBN-10: 0-9788298-2-4
ISBN-13: 978-0-9788298-2-7

First Edition, 2014

2 3 4 5 6 7 8 9 0

# FOREWORD

I was deeply saddened by word of the passing of my dear friend Julian Koosman, who is perhaps the only acquaintance I've ever had who truly knew what it meant to be alive. He died as he lived, in the midst of another adventure, this one on a fishing boat off the coast of Bora Bora. I had lost touch with Jules over the years save for the occasional letter, many of which were crinkled with beverage stains from the pub where he had written them or simply torn from one of the spiral notebooks he used as a journal.

Jules had often referenced his days at Oneonta State College in the States, which is about a four hour drive north of his childhood home of Long Island, New York. After receiving the manuscript of this work, which he referred to as his "college novel," I made it a point to visit Oneonta this past autumn and found it even more beautiful than the place I pictured from his descriptions. He often credited the experiences he had with his mates in this place as the launching point of what would become an extraordinary life that ended far too soon—although Jules may not have seen it that way, having packed so much into his forty years.

The yellow post-it note attached to the cover was a clue to his conclusion that this work would never be finished. The handwritten note simply read, "Give to Edward Chidlington, Burtlesbush UK," and below it was another post-it note with different handwriting that read, "Julian wanted you to have this." I had been Jules' editor when he wrote for me at Burtlesbush, an operation in London that shut down about a decade ago that published trade journals for the food service industry. He found the work a bore, but he considered this employment as the price of admission to experience all that London had to offer. He spent three years here before moving on to places such as Belgium, Iceland, Tierra del Fuego, and ultimately Bora Bora.

Indeed this work is raw, and I can see the struggle he had in shaping these experiences into a working narrative. Being familiar with Jules' style, I can tell which parts are pure rubbish, but I also recognize the experiences that factored into decisions he would make later in life, and, more than anything, I can see why he didn't want the amazing ride that started in this small New York town come to an end.

Edward Chidlington III
21 January 2014
Tottenham, London, UK

*To Julian, may your spirit live on forever.*
                        –ECIII

I

# 1

Tommy Austin leaned against the wall outside his room picking at the lint stuck to the suntan oil on his biceps while waiting for our complete and undivided attention. He was a short guy but built, wearing only a pair of skin tight fluorescent yellow bicycle shorts and a pair of wire framed glasses that made him look like John Denver on steroids. He was a youthful looking guy in his early thirties, but he looked much older than the new residents of Golding Hall pit lined up along the corridor walls in front of him. No one was really sure why or how he had been in college so long, but we had already heard a rumor that the guy was a sex fiend who preyed on freshman girls and that he had been living in the same room for ten years.

"Welcome to Golding Hall," he started after we had finally quieted down. "For those of you who do not yet know who I am, let me introduce myself. My name is Tommy Austin and I will be your R.A. during your stay here at Golding. 'R.A.' stands for 'Resident Advisor.' That does not mean that I am your babysitter, psychiatrist, academic advisor, tutor, counselor, bail bondsman, personal psychic, guru, mentor, shoulder to cry on, or anyone else other than your Resident Advisor. I am here primarily as a residence hall resource. If you have a problem with your room or your roommate or want to change rooms or report some illegal activity going on in this hallway, come see me. If you get arrested downtown doing something you're not supposed to be doing and need someone to bail you out, do not call me. You are your parents' problem, not mine. Speaking of things that you are not supposed to be doing, certain things will absolutely not be tolerated on my floor. This is a dry campus, so don't let me catch you with alcohol in your room. If I do, I will immediately file a report against you with our Resident Director Artie Schramm, who will in turn call you down to his office and inform you that you will have 24 hours to vacate the premises and find a new place to live. The same goes for illegal drugs. If you feel the need to smoke a fattie, go out in the woods. Do not do it on my floor. I myself am a stone sober individual. I do not use alcohol or illegal drugs to wet my whistle, so I will not have any sympathy for the trouble these things will ultimately cause you. Some of you standing before me right now will find yourself in a deep pile of shit during your stay here. It happens every year. I want to assure you right here and now that I don't give a flying fuck. I am not here to help you when you find yourself in trouble. What you do outside of this building is your own business and I am not going to hold any of that against you. But if I catch you doing something you are not supposed to be doing on my floor or anywhere else in this building, you will pay the consequences. Is that understood?"

There were a few lazy nods and mumbled yes's. Tommy looked down and flexed his biceps. Without looking back up he said with a raised voice, "I asked if that was understood!"

"Yes sir!" everyone shouted in unison.

"Come on guys, this isn't the military," Tommy laughed. "I just didn't think you heard me the first time. But I do want to make sure that you know that certain things will not be tolerated. Oh, and another thing," he said, and quickly disappeared into the open door of his room and came back out holding a thick white shoelace that was tied in a loop at the end. "If you see this shoelace hanging from my doorknob, that means that I am not to be disturbed at the moment but that I should be available in an hour or so. That means if you see this shoelace on the door, do not knock. Whatever emergency it is can wait. You do not want to disturb me when you see this shoelace. Is that understood?"

After a few mumbled "yeahs," Tommy raised his voice and said, "I asked if that was understood!"

"Yes sir!"

"You guys are pretty sharp," he said, hanging the shoelace on the knob. "Are there any questions?"

There were no questions. Tommy went into his room and slammed the door. A girl inside his room started laughing.

Most of the other new residents in the hall headed back to their rooms. The only person I had met so far was my roommate Russ, who seemed like a cool guy compared to the rest of the future frat boys of America, suburbanite cheeseballs who grew up in middle class homes but acted like they were from inner-city ghettos and spent all their money on baseball caps and sneakers. Russ and I didn't know about any parties yet or what we were going to do that night, and we were hoping to hear something at this meeting. After all, this was the night we had been awaiting since the onset of adolescence, the first night of true freedom in our lives now that we were finally beyond the range of our parents' watchful eyes and the laws that went along with living under the roofs of their homes back on Long Island.

So far, Russ and I were the only ones in this place that seemed of a like mind. Our first conversation was about Jimi Hendrix, and that was enough to cement our friendship. But judging by the rap music we had been hearing all day blasting out of the other rooms—3rd Bass, Naughty By Nature, Ice Cube, Ice-T, and an assortment of random beats and samples competing with each other—it didn't seem likely that anyone else on this floor had even heard of Hendrix.

When the hallway cleared, Russ and I found ourselves in the company of four other lost souls who clearly felt the same sense of displacement as we did. To each other, we looked like the only normal ones there—we had holes in our jeans, none of us had gel or other such substances in our hair, and our T-shirts advertised things we could relate to: Guns & Roses, Led Zeppelin, Genny beer, Sacred Reich, The Ramones, and Pink Floyd. After a day of our eardrums being pounded by electronic beats all day, it was a relief to find that there were at least a few other people there who had an appetite for beer and rock & roll. As we were introducing ourselves and shaking hands, none of us had the slightest idea that an impenetrable membrane was already forming in which we would spend the better and worse part of the next four years.

Teke and Winston lived directly across the hall from Russ and I, but it was the first time we had seen them since their door had been closed all day. Both came from small towns in upstate New York and had been in their room hiding from the cheeseball invasion from Long Island, which they had never really been exposed to. Teke was from a place called Willseyville just south of Ithaca, and Winston was from Downsville, a tired little town southeast of Walton. Having grown up on Long Island, I was under the impression that all little towns upstate were the same, but Teke and Winston couldn't have been more different.

Teke's parents were professors at Ithaca College and were a bit distant in his upbringing, focusing more on their careers and hoping to sneak in the back door of Ithaca's more famous university. He was a *Dungeons & Dragons/Star Wars* geek who dabbled in witchcraft, his head constantly buried in a fantasy novel, and he was in the process of writing his own novel full of knights and warlocks of which he had finished the first two chapters. He had *The Empire Strikes Back* bedsheets and looked like a real life version of Shaggy from *Scooby Doo*, a spindly 6'6" and easily startled. He was very easy to get along with, but he could bore you to tears with stories about a night out in Willseyville with nary a detail omitted. His declared major was "Medieval Studies," one of only six in the entire school. When asked what one could do with such a degree, he would proudly answer with a big smile, "Absolutely nothing."

Winston, on the other hand, seemed more like your traditional redneck hick except that he was an absolute genius at everything he did. He played up the good ol' boy bit as if ashamed of his gifts, telling people that he was born and raised on Genny beer and that his theme song was Lynyrd Skynyrd's "Simple Man." He looked like a young Stevie Ray Vaughn gone bad, and though he was gentle, polite, respectful, and more humane than anyone I have ever met, if you didn't know him, you might think he was an ax-murderer. At first he hardly said a word and we were a little nervous that he was going to off us and bury our bodies in the woods. Once we all got to know each other he became more talkative, but as well as we thought we had gotten to know him over time, we were always finding out things about him that we didn't know. We knew early on that he was a good guitarist because he was always playing, but it wasn't until our second semester when he declared a double major of botany and organic chemistry that we knew how smart he was. Aside from modesty, his secrecy about his gifts were a direct result of where he came from, a small town whose residents rarely ventured beyond it's borders, a place where minds are closed and artists, scholars, and anyone with the opportunity to escape to someplace better are not looked upon too kindly.

Perhaps the biggest difference between Winston and the rest of us was that he didn't use illegal drugs. He drank like a fish, but he never once took a hit of weed (though he did often catch a cheap contact high from our secondhand smoke). He said it just wasn't his thing, but I suspect the real reasons were that he had seen both his friends back home and us in college spend most of what little money we had on weed, and that he was the only one of us who took schoolwork seriously—perhaps because he was the only one who understood why we were really supposed to be there and the only one of us who was able to see far enough into the future to recognize the consequences of our actions now.

Ed and Bruno lived down at the end of the hall that always smelled like vanilla incense, across from the reclusive Doobie Brothers, who didn't show up to that first meeting with Tommy would eventually become our main drug connection during freshman year. Bruno's side of the room was decorated with a black poster with fluorescent math equations that glowed in black light and a 9-inch black & white television set with rabbit ears covered with aluminum foil on his desk. Ed had a *Never Mind the Bullocks* Sex Pistols poster on his wall, a blue lava lamp on his desk, and an Irish flag that covered his side of the window. A New York City subway map was crookedly taped to the back of their door.

Ed was from Rockaway, Queens, home of the Ramones, whom he spoke of as if he knew them personally. He was the oldest son of Irish immigrants and inherited their taste for spirits, and along with his punk rock friends, discovered the wonders of illegal drugs at a young age and had already tried just about every one of them. He spent twelve years getting kicked out of all-male Catholic schools all over New York City, claiming to have been beaten with rulers by wicked nuns but managing to escape without having been molested by a perverted priest because they were all afraid of him. Despite his behavioral issues in school, he was an honors student who could have gone to any of the more academically inclined state schools, but, having never had the opportunity to stare at girls all day like the rest of us who attended public schools, he cited Oneonta State's 2:1 female-to-male ratio as his main reason for wanting to attend here. With his rebellious charm and good looks, he would be the only one of us to truly succeeded in this department. He was one of those people who hardly ever studied or did much schoolwork but always got straight A's, which Bruno attributed to him being a sociology major (or as Bruno called it, a "Social" major, a fitting moniker because he was the only one of us who wasn't afraid to talk to girls).

Bruno was from Bay Ridge, Brooklyn, which he liked to point out was the setting of *Saturday Night Fever* as if this trivia tidbit was something to brag about. He was an unlikely conservative Republican, a tall burly guy who looked like a biker about to drive a Harley through a brick wall. He almost always wore black jeans and a leather jacket over a black T-shirt, but he conservatively pulled back his long black hair in a tight ponytail and kept his beard well-trimmed. He had originally planned to major in 3-2 Engineering, a very rare thing in Oneonta because it was supposedly the most difficult major the school offered and well over the heads of about 99% of the student body, but after he started smoking pot, he backed down and became a math major, which to him was simple. He watched six hours of television a day on his little TV even though the only station he was able to tune in was a fuzzy ABC affiliate in Binghamton that always seemed to be airing reruns of *Night Court*. He would only go down to the TV lounge if there was something he absolutely had to watch because he was uncomfortable sharing the remote with others.

My roommate Russ was a guy with dark red hair who grew up a few towns away from me on Long Island. Unlike just about everyone else who was dropped off by their parents on the first day, Russ was dropped off by his girlfriend Jennifer. They had been going out since seventh grade and had such a deep and serious relationship, it seemed more like a marriage than a teen romance. During the six years they had dated, Russ missed out entirely on the wild of his youth, which was one of the main reasons he sought the atmosphere of Oneonta, another being that it would put a couple of hundred miles between them. Unbeknownst to Jennifer, Russ had changed during his last couple of years in high school. While she was planning their wedding in her head, Russ had started reading books on Zen Buddhism and developed an interest in city planning, which he would later declare as his major. He swore to her that he would never do drugs, but during these last couple of years, he started pinching small amounts of pot from his older brother's stash and late at night would discreetly smoke one-hitters from a tiny bat pipe he picked up at a head shop in the Village. When he was with her, he had to wear the skin he had outgrown and be the same old Russ he had always been because he knew she would never accept or even understand the changes he was experiencing and would never change herself. The rest of her life was already planned out— after graduating high school, she would go to Nassau Community for two years, finish up at Adelphi, find a job, marry Russ, have kids, and live in the suburbs until she died. Russ, on the other hand, wanted to go out and experience the world and couldn't stand the thought of dying a slow painful death in the four-walled mall culture of Long Island. He was afraid that if he simply cut her loose, she might do something drastic. So, he instead headed for Oneonta knowing that she wouldn't follow because she was never going to leave Nassau County.

In high school I had acquaintances, but none of them were people I considered as true friends. I developed this deep fear that I was one of a kind and that people that I could truly connect with did not exist, and that escaping to college was my last chance to enjoy my youth. This fear lasted until the moment I met Russ and the other guys, when it became clear that I could be myself in front of them without having to choose between conforming to be accepted or, by refusing to do so, facing the exile that I ultimately experienced during my high school years.

About halfway through my first day of ninth grade, I had pretty much given up on the idea of high school. There was no point in trying to fit in with the surfers, guidos, dirtbags, jocks, freaks, and geeks; I saw no future in the suburban hell of Long Island and didn't plan on staying there after I graduated. All I wanted was to get out, and it was quite obvious to me that the quickest way of doing so was to become a famous rock star. I figured that if I practiced guitar at least eight hours a day every day, by the end of high school I would be at least as good as Jimmy Page, if not better. I kept at it for a couple of years and took weekly lessons at a nearby music store and got pretty good until I reached a plateau where it became apparent that I wasn't going to get much better.

In the meantime I had developed more of an interest in writing songs than performing music, and after discovering the joys of my parents' liquor cabinet, the lyrics seemed much more interesting, at least until I looked at them the next day. Soon the songs gave way to angry essays driven by teen angst and hard liquor, and while the music eventually faded away, the desire to live the rock star lifestyle only grew stronger.

By eleventh grade I finally realized that the only way out would be to go away to college. I had always hated school—I had difficulty sitting still and fought myself to stay awake in class and struggled to maintain my 82 overall average by doing as little schoolwork as possible. As the S.A.T.'s neared, I realized that this might not be good enough to get into a faraway school and that I was in danger of starting my post-secondary life pumping gas for minimum wage to pay the rent my mother was threatening me with if I didn't go to college, or, even worse, winding up at Nassau Community College.

I picked up a copy of the *Princeton Review* S.A.T. preparation book and threw myself into it with even more of a fervor than I had for the guitar. Getting out was my only hope. I took practice test after practice test, but the night before the actual exam I couldn't sleep, so I went downstairs and threw down three big screwdrivers to knock myself out. While I succeeded at the task, I woke up the next morning with a hangover. I still managed to pull an 1190, which was good enough to get me into six of the eight S.U.N.Y. schools I applied to on the handy multi-application my guidance counselor had given me. After having heard the stories, however, there was only one institution I wanted to attend.

During the 1970's, Oneonta cemented it's reputation as New York State's premier party school and was commonly referred to by high school students as "Stoneonta", while the school itself touted itself as "S.U.C.O.", the acronym for "State University College at Oneonta". By the time we got there, the school was years into a campaign attempting to transform its image from party school to academic institution. The local cops were helping out by declaring war on college students, constantly raiding the bars and open house parties hunting for underage drinkers. By then, however, the legacy had been cemented. Every fall a couple of thousand high school graduates like myself with little academic interest or any idea what they want to do with their lives show up at Oneonta looking to get away from their parents and spend four years getting drunk and laid before graduating into the oblivion of reality. The result was a staggering 43% of freshmen failing out by the end of their first year, and only 29% surviving all four years and graduating.

Oneonta's reputation had become so far-reaching that even my grandmother had heard a few stories about it at her senior living community. My mother had wanted me to attend one of the more academically inclined state schools that I had been accepted to, but I managed to come up with an excuse for each one: Oswego, too far; Albany, too big and impersonal; Stony Brook, way too close to home; Buffalo, would you really want to spend four years in Buffalo? But, after receiving the official Oneonta State Open House Weekend brochure in the mail one day, my mother decided that maybe it wouldn't be such a bad idea to go up there and check it out.

After driving to the foot of the Adirondacks in the height of autumn color, seeing the street signs and quaint downtown gift shops, taking the tour of campus and one of the newer dorms given by a sophomore student who seemed like she had better things to do, my mother was sold. My stepfather was sold after we attended a horrifically boring two hour financial presentation in the Hunt Union ballroom that showed what a bargain Oneonta State was for residents of New York State compared to the outrageous expense of sending your child to a private school. I been sold before we even got there, but seeing the place in person only made me want it more.

With *Animal House* as my model for what college is supposed to be like, Oneonta seemed to be a perfect match. The town is tucked away in the foothills pretty much in the middle of nowhere between a long stretch of Interstate 88 between Binghamton and Albany, and the only reason it is even there at all is because of the college. It is an old railroad town, once boasting a large locomotive turnstile, but now only long freight trains only pass through without stopping.

The houses in town are old timberboxes, some with fraternity letters crudely nailed to them, many with empty beer kegs littering their front porches. Down on Main Street are sooty old four and five story brick buildings with street level shops and apartments on the floors above. A block south of Main there is Water Street, which is more of a paved alley running between the three-story parking garage and the legendary strip of sixteen bars squeezed into vacant spaces on the backsides of the Main Street buildings. Bars such as the Alley, Paradise, the Sip & Sail Tavern, Sports On Tap, the Black

Oak—their neon signs glowing in the windows like beacons signaling the real beginning of my life.

The campus was situated on top of the big hill overlooking town. Only a couple of the original buildings remained from when it began as a "normal" school in 1889 that trained women to become teachers. The other buildings on campus were haphazardly built as the college expanded after becoming a founding member of the State University of New York (SUNY) system in 1948, many of them constructed to the utilitarian standards of 1950's architecture. It wasn't exactly ivy covered bricks, but it was just as beautiful to me.

In the spring, after receiving all the other letters from the schools I had applied to, the one from Oneonta finally arrived. It was really going to happen—I was going to escape from Long Island. A welcome packet came in the mail a few weeks later that included a four page questionnaire asking about my habits, goals in life, if I smoked cigarettes (which at the time I didn't, but that would change soon after I got there), what kind of music I listened to, what type of dorm I would like to live in (a three bedroom suite with a common room and it's own bathroom, a two bedroom quad with a common room but no bathroom, or a double with no common room and no bathroom). Since I had no idea what the difference was, I checked that I had no preference, and like most of the other incoming freshman who did the same, I was assigned to live in the freshman dorm. That was fine with me, as I thought it might be easier if everyone else there didn't know what the hell they were doing either.

Like the other two "specialty" dorms (the all-female dorm and foreign exchange student dorm being the others), Golding Hall was an unaesthetic brick building with two separate three story wings connected by a main lobby in the middle and TV and study lounges down in "the pit" below. Each floor was segregated by gender because there was only one bathroom per hallway. The rooms were all doubles, square boxes of space with faded yellow walls that hadn't been painted in years, each with two metal spring cots underneath stained mattresses, two desks, two chairs, two mirrors, two closets, and a single floor lamp that provided insufficient light.

"This doesn't look like the rooms we saw on the tour," my mother said when we first got there, but to me it didn't matter. As long as it wasn't my bedroom back home, it was paradise.

**2**

"Well, ah, does anyone know if anything is going on tonight?" Teke asked with his nasally voice after the introductions and handshakes were over.

"According to everything I've heard about this place, I would assume so," Russ said.

"I think Teek is having a party," Ed said. "The fraternity 'Teek', not you, I assume."

"Well, ah, yeah," Teke said.

Teek, or Tau Kappa Epsilon, was a huge national fraternity and the biggest frat on campus.

"Many kegs and major snatch," Ed said. "That's all we need to know. Just don't listen to those frat cheeseballs when they try to recruit you. You might wind up on your knees being paddled by a Greek."

A little while later we set out towards the TKE house on Center Street via Golding Path, a steep asphalt trail behind the dorm that wound down through a section of woods and led to a gravel parking lot that nobody ever used. At the end of the lot there were two guardrails with a space between for pedestrians that separated the lot from a dirt path that cut through a small patch of woods and let out at the top of Maple Street, one of several roads that ran from the lower border of campus to Main Street a mile down at the base of the hill.

As we emerged from the woods, we heard voices and laughter nearby. Upon reaching the sidewalk on Maple Street, we were spotted by several guys hanging out on the porch of a beat up house with the Greek letters for Phi Epsilon crudely nailed to the shingles between two upstairs windows. They were wearing T-shirts with the same Greek letters on the house and drinking cans of Milwaukee's Best, a low-budget brew affectionately known in Oneonta State circles as "The Beast". They looked like seniors, and it was obvious to them that we were freshmen. We were content to keep on going until one of them stepped off the porch and asked how we were doing. He was a short skinny guy with a fake tan and a pair of Ray-Ban sunglasses pushed up on his head, a pair of Dockers shorts, and deck shoes without socks, a look that, on the cusp of the fashion revolution known as "Grunge", seemed pathetically dated. Unlike the others guys drinking out of plastic keg cups, he was holding a bottle of Heineken.

"Alright," Ed answered. He tried to keep walking, but the guy stepped in front of us on the sidewalk.

"Where are you guys headed?"

"The Teek party."

"The Teek party?" A few of the other frat guys laughed. "Teeks are geeks, man. You don't want to go there. You want to be where all the chicks are gonna be, and in a little while they'll all be here. We have three kegs on ice downstairs, and I'm sure there will be more before the end of the night."

"What kind of beer is it?" Bruno asked.

"Cold beer," the guy said. "My name is Fred, by the way."

"The Beast," some other frat guy said and held up his can for us to see. "Finest goddamn brew in the world!"

"That's right," Fred said. "Best goddamn beer in the world. So why don't you guys come on in and have a few while we wait for the chicks to show up?"

Ed asked him to give us a minute and we walked across the street. A total freshman move for sure, but these guys were intimidating to all of us except for Ed. The rest of us were ready to keep going to what we thought we a sure thing, but Ed had other ideas and was the only one of us who seemed to know what the hell was going on.

"Think about it," he said. "We could have three kegs all to ourselves."

"This could be a trap," Bruno said. "I don't want to get caught in some sausage party."

"There'll be snatch," Ed said. "Wall to wall maüs in a little while."

"What the hell is a maü?"

"Chicks. Tits. Gams. A fucking snatchfest. It'll be mint!"

Back across the street, Fred led us around to the back of the house. At the door he had us sign a disclaimer in a marble composition notebook affirming that we were of the legal drinking age of 21. All of us except Ed were naïve enough to use our real names (he went with the old standard "Mike Hunt"). After signing in, a fat guy collected three bucks from each of us in exchange for a plastic cup and directed us down a set of rickety wooden stairs.

The basement was hot and humid and smelled of stale beer and must. The small windows just below the ceiling were covered with couch cushions to muffle the noise and block the view from outside just in case any curious cops decided to take a peek. In one corner a piece of plywood that served as a bar had been laid across two empty beer kegs, and in another corner there was an old Sears Kenmore washer and dryer with laundromat-style coin slots. Several pinup posters were duct-taped to the walls, including one of Samantha Fox that I remembered seeing in seventh grade.

We helped ourselves to the keg and toasted to the first night of college. A little while later Fred came down with a fresh bottle of Heineken.

"I'm glad to see that you guys are making yourselves at home," he said. "Say, let me ask you something. Do you guys like beer?"

A couple of us nodded weakly. Ed said "Yeah."

"We drink a lot of beer in this fraternity," Fred continued. "A lot of beer. That's what this fraternity is all about. Of course, it's a lot more. Girls, for instance. No chick can resist a man wearing letters."

"Is that so?" Bruno said.

"Damn straight. And aside from that, when you're in a fraternity, you have a hundred brothers who are like your best friends who will do anything for you. If someone fucks with you on the street, a hundred brothers will be right there to back you up in an instant. We're all family. That's why we call each other brothers."

"Well, ah, what fraternity is this again?" Teke asked.

"Phi Ep," Fred said. "Are you guys thinking about pledging?"

"Not really," Russ said.

"You should really give it some thought," Fred said. "It's the only way to go."

Over the next hour, more people who had likely taken the same route we had started to trickle in, and soon the basement was wall-to-wall freshmen. We had a good buzz going, and there were a lot of chicks—or maüs, as Ed kept calling them—so we went from feeling relieved that our risky decision to come in turned out well to patting ourselves on the back for being ingenious enough to be the first ones to arrive and secure a prime position near the keg. Our cups were kept filled while everyone else had to fight for a beer on the keg line, and we started referring to everyone else as "suckers" for showing up late.

At some point in the evening, some little guy named Anson who looked like he had just stepped off a school bus glommed on to our little circle but was largely ignored until we started making fun of his blond mullet of hair that he looked like he cut himself. That didn't seem to bother him, but when we started calling him "Potsie" (a reference to Anson Williams, who played Warren "Potsie" Weber on *Happy Days*), he got mad and told us to go fuck ourselves. After he finished his first beer—which took about four times longer than the pace that the rest of us were drinking—his face turned purple and he puked in the washing machine, which, fortunately for him, none of the frat guys seemed to notice.

Upstairs, the bathroom line was ridiculous, so guys were just going outside and pissing in the backyard. During one trip Russ and I were out there, and while we were zipping up, we heard someone say that the kegs were kicked. We were pretty drunk at this point, so Russ suggested that we head down to the Teek party, so we headed out front without bothering to go back in and tell the other guys.

Out in front of the house, the muffled noise from the party was faint and we were the only people out there except for the Doobie Brothers, the two long-haired burnout guys who lived across the hall from Bruno and Ed. They were across the street packing weed into a corncob pipe and didn't notice us. Russ suggested we ask them for a hit, which I didn't really want to do since I had only smoked pot once in my life and was afraid I would make a fool of myself, but Russ was persistent and we went over.

"Do you mind if we get a hit?" he asked them.

The guy wearing the Rasta hat answered in a friendly manner, "Sure, man." The other guy was still packing the pipe from a cellophane bag and greeted us with a mistrustful glance.

"Were you guys just at the party?" the one with the Rasta hat asked. He sounded a little like Jeff Spicoli.

"Yeah," Russ said.

Suddenly a bright light appeared out of nowhere down the road and an engine roared.

"Cops!" the other guy said. He hastily shoved the bag of weed down his pants and tossed the pipe into the neighbor's bushes while the rest of us tried to look as if we had some legitimate reason for being there.

The cruiser screeched to a halt in front of us. There was only one officer in the car, a burly guy in his forties with dark hair and a thick mustache. He wearily stepped out of the car, leaving the engine running and the high beams shining in our faces, and walked right by us towards the bushes. He found the pipe and held it up for us to see.

"Does this belong to you guys?" he said.

"No sir," the friendly long-hair said.

"Alright. All of you put your hands on the hood and spread your legs."

While we were being patted down, I couldn't help but wonder if my college career was coming to an end before it even began. I hadn't even registered for classes yet and I was already being frisked by a cop. Fortunately he did not find the bag of weed, and after finishing his search, he said we could stand up straight.

"This belongs to me now," he said, tapping the pipe on the hood. "You guys can go, but I don't want to see any more of this garbage. Understood?"

"Yes sir," we mumbled.

"Now get the hell out of here and go home. I don't want to see you again tonight."

Just like that he was gone. The Doobies headed towards Golding Path while Russ and I went back to the party and found the other guys hanging out next to the washer and dryer. Anson was sitting on the washing machine with his short arm reaching as far as it could around the shoulder of a fat biker chick sitting on the dryer next to him. She was wearing tight leather pants, a loose-fitting black blouse that covered a pair of enormous breasts, and high-heeled boots that didn't look like they could possibly support her weight. Her hair was teased high above a puffy face covered with dark makeup, and she had long red fingernails that looked like manicured claws. She appeared to be our age, but next to Anson she looked old enough to be his unwed mother. She wriggled free of Anson and looked right at me when we came over.

"Hey, Hank, this chick says she wants to have your children," Ed laughed.

To a pair of sober eyes she was probably less than appealing, but my beer goggles were thick and she looked like an easy lay.

"Get lost, Hank, this one's mine!" Anson scowled.

"I hear that you want to have my children," I said to her, ignoring Anson.

"Maybe I do," she said and held out her hand. "I'm Patty."

"Hank," I said, shaking her hand.

"I know. Your friends were telling me about you."

"My friends hardly even know me."

"I thought you said you liked me!" Anson whined to Patty. He tried to put his arm around her again, but she pushed him away, which caused him to knock over his beer. A couple of the frat guys yelled "Alcohol abuse!"

"I saw her first!" Anson said to me. "There are plenty of other chicks at this party, go find one of them!"

"No!" Patty said.

"I don't think that's what she wants," I said.

"That's so cute that you boys are fighting over me," Patty said and giggled.

"Come on, let me have this one," Anson pleaded to me. "I'll owe you one."

"I believe that's up to me," Patty said. "And Hank's the one I want."

"You heard the lady," I said.

"I'm gonna marry her," Anson said.

"Ewww," Patty squealed. She slid off the washing machine and began rubbing her thigh against my crotch.

"Do you want to go somewhere a little quieter?" I asked in her ear.

"Hell yeah," she said.

I took her hand and led her through the crowd. Upstairs the guy at the door snickered as we went by, but I pretended not to notice. Out in the yard a few guys were pissing in the bushes and against trees. We held hands as we walked through the wooded path but stopped at the guardrail when we noticed Anson staggering behind us. We waited for him to catch up.

"I'm not into threesomes," he said when he caught up. He looked like he was about to collapse. "None of that ménage à trois shit for me."

"Get rid of him," Patty said in my ear.

"Why don't you go back to the party," I said. He didn't seem to hear me and staggered backwards a few steps before regaining his balance. Patty and I continued on our way and he did his best to keep up with us, but he was having difficulty walking straight. His face was purple and he looked like he was going to puke again. About halfway up the hill we encountered a group of ten or so people heading down the path.

"Excuse me," I said. "Are you guys heading down to the party?"

"Yeah we are," one of the girls said.

"Can you do us a really big favor and take this guy down with you?" I asked, pointing at Anson.

"Is he alright?" one of the guys asked.

"He's fine. He just needs another beer to get him going again."

"Sure, we'll take him," one of the other guys said and laughed. The girls assumed worried expressions.

"Thanks a lot," I said. "I really appreciate it."

"No problem," the guy said.

I took Patty's hand and we continued up the path. At the top of the hill we stopped to rest and leaned side-by-side against the iron handrail listening to the voices and laughter below. Patty ran the tip of her fingernails up and down my thigh and I became aroused.

"I want you," she whispered in my ear. "I'll do anything you want."

"Let's get out of here," I said.

"I don't want you to get the wrong impression," she said. "I'm not a slut."

"No. Of course not. Let's go."

Up in the room, she threw herself on me as soon as the door was closed and started kissing me wildly. I guided her to the bed and fell on top of her, reaching up her blouse and slipping my fingers underneath her metal-framed bra. I felt my way across the sea of breast searching in vain for a nipple, and, after not being able to find one, I unbuttoned her blouse, exposing a frayed pink bra of which the metal frame was visible in several of the sections that had been worn away. I had to use all of my reach to get my hands around her body to try and unclasp the industrial strength hooks that were pinned underneath our weight. I struggled with it for a minute or so before she finally undid it herself and tossed it on the floor at the foot of the bed.

Her body was like a waterbed, her skin pale as if it hadn't seen daylight in years. Her breasts sagged on both sides of her body, the nipples dark in contrast to the rest of her flesh. I tried to focus on the leather and heels to maintain my arousal, but it was fading fast. I unzipped her pants and struggled to pull them off with her panties, and even though I was clearly having difficulty, she remained motionless and offered no assistance. Sensing her second thoughts and racing my deflation, I sprang off the bed, kicked off my shoes, and removed my pants. I gave my erection a couple of quick strokes to get it going again before rifling through the official Oneonta State College Orientation Kit, which was nothing more than a shoebox full of sample sized things such as Vivarin, Advil, Nyquil, Breath Savers, Pizza Hut coupons, a campus directory, a list of emergency phone numbers, a pamphlet explaining what safe sex was, and a lubricated red condom in a clear unmarked wrapper. I unwrapped the condom and stroked myself a couple of more times before strapping it on.

I jumped on top of her and slid my hand down her body feeling for her muff. When I finally found it she let out a low moan, which at first I took for an expression of pleasure. After sticking my finger in the wet spot, however, she pushed me off and turned away.

"What's the matter?" I asked. "I'm covered."

She looked up at me with glassy eyes.

"Would you be mad if I said no?" she asked.

I thought about it for a minute.

"No," I said.

"Are you sure?"

"Yes."

"I really like you, Hank."

"You don't even know me."

I looked at the poster of Jimi Hendrix on his knees squirting lighter fluid into the flames of his burning guitar that Russ has taped to the wall earlier in the day.

"You're mad," she said.

"I'm not mad."

I rolled over and pretended to fall asleep. She took up most of the space on the bed and left me hanging precariously on the outer edge desperately trying to think of a way out of this situation. Ten agonizing minutes later I caught my break when she started snoring. I quietly rolled off the bed, grabbed my clothes and boots, and slipped out into the hallway with the red condom still dangling from my penis. I gently closed the door and headed towards the bathroom, ignoring the cheers of a couple of drunk chicks who happened to be down at the end of the hall. I locked myself in one of the stalls and quickly got dressed and flushed the condom down the toilet.

The girls were still out in the hall and cheered again when I emerged from the bathroom. I gave them a thumbs-up and headed towards the staircase at the opposite end of the hall and exited the dorm through the side door.

I thought the party might still be going on, but when I got to Golding Path I heard a drunken crowd heading up towards me. I went down anyway, and towards the bottom of the hill I ran into the other guys hovering over Anson passed out under the handrail.

"What the hell happened?" I asked.

"Well, ah, we're not sure," Teke said, sounding really drunk. "We were just heading back to the dorm and found him here."

"What happened at the party?"

"It just broke up," Russ said. "What the hell happened to *you*?"

"Nothing," I said. "She shot me down."

"Where is the little lady?" Ed asked.

"She's passed out in the room."

"In *our* room?" Russ said.

"Yep."

I nudged Anson with my foot. "Hey, Potsie, this is your lucky day!" He stirred and slowly started to regain consciousness. There were dead leaves in his mullet and he was covered with dirt.

"Do you still want Patty?"

"Patty," he slurred and tried to push himself to his feet. I helped him up and threw my arm around him.

"She's waiting for you, man. She's naked."

"I didn't need to hear that," Russ said. "I have to sleep in that room tonight."

"Seriously," I said to Anson. "She told me that you're the one she really wanted."

"She said that?"

"I even got her warmed up for you. She told me to go find you and bring you to her."

"Bullshit."

"You don't believe me? I'll take you to her. She's up in my room."

The plan was for Anson to quietly enter the room and slip into bed with Patty as if he had been there the whole time. I realized that Patty wasn't drunk enough to believe that she actually went to bed with Anson, but he was drunk enough to believe that she would fall for it. By the time we got to the room, however, she was already gone, though her bra was still on the floor. When Anson thought nobody was looking, he swiped the bra and stuffed it up his shirt. Ed let out a loud laugh when he noticed the pink straps hanging out.

"Whatcha got there, Potsie?" Ed asked. Anson's face turned purple and it took him a moment to figure out what he was going to say.

"This belongs to my future bride and I'm keeping it! Fuck you all!" He stormed out with bra in hand and disappeared into the stairwell at the end of the hall. We never saw him again.

A large crowd of those who had been to many of the parties going on that night but lacked the false identification to continue partying downtown at the bars gathered in front of the dorm. We went down there and stood off to the side staring at girls, but I was preoccupied with my concern of seeing Patty. After scanning the crowd a few times and convincing myself that she wasn't there, I started to relax and forget about her.

A little while later a Pizza Hut car pulled up and honked. The hazard lights started blinking and the driver stepped out, opened the back door, and pulled out a box of pizza covered in a cozy with the Pizza Hut logo on it. As he made his way through the crowd, a few people offered him money for the pie, but, like a true professional, he stoically ignored them and disappeared into the building.

"Someone should check the back of his car to see if he's got any extras," Bruno said jokingly. I hadn't eaten since early that morning, and seeing the logo on the side of the car made me realize how hungry I was. Not fully aware of what I was doing, I started casually walking towards the car. At first I was just going to look, but the other guys started cheering me on, and the next thing I knew I was opening one of the rear doors. I dove into the back seat, tossing empty pizza cozies over my shoulder hoping to find anything edible, but all I found were empty cassette cases, pens, coupon books, candy wrappers, and a frisbee, all of which wound up on the street. By now it sounded like the whole crowd was cheering me on, and after the back seat was cleaned out I came back from oblivion and asked myself, *What the fuck am I doing?*

20

When I got out of the car, Winston standing in front of me.

"You should probably get out of here for a while," he said. "The guy came out and saw you and started yelling that he was gonna call the cops."

"Shit," I said, suddenly recalling my earlier encounter with the law.

"If anyone asks, we'll tell them we don't know you. Just get the fuck out of here."

As I made my way through the crowd towards Golding Path, people were patting me on the back and calling me "Pizza Hut Guy." Behind the dorm the crowd noise suddenly sounded distant, and since no one was back there, I started running and didn't stop until I reached Maple Street. The lights were still on at Fred's house, but no one seemed to be there. I didn't know where else to go, so I walked the entire length of Maple all the way down to Main Street, which at this hour was desolate with the stores and restaurants all closed.

When I turned onto Water Street around the block, however, it was like walking smack into the middle of Mardi Gras. It was after 2:00 AM and everyone down there was bombed, bouncing from bar to bar along the strip while a cop cruiser slowly rolled down the street. Everyone looked so much older and I began to feel as if I had the word "FRESHMAN" tattooed to my forehead. I jumped when someone behind me yelled "FRESHMAN!" in my ear and I turned to see Fred and a couple of his frat buddies laughing. Soon several people in the immediate area started yelling "FRESHMAN!" so I picked up the pace and tried not to make eye contact with anyone until I was standing at the bus depot on the other side of the parking garage.

Those waiting to catch a bus up to campus were mostly sophomores, so it wasn't as obvious to them that I was a freshman and nobody bothered me. I took the bus back up to the top of Maple Street near Fred's house so I could walk up Golding Path and wind up behind the dorm just in case the cops were out front.

There were no entrances in the back of the dorm, and the ones at the far sides of each wing were locked because if was after midnight. The dorm was built on a slope so that the back side of the pit was on ground level, so I was able to see who was in the TV lounge through the window. The TV was on, and to my good fortune I saw Teke and Winston inside watching *Headbanger's Ball* on MTV. I tapped on the window and signaled them to let me in through the side door, where I met them a couple of minutes later.

Our floor was quiet, and Tommy's shoelace was hanging from his doorknob. Russ had been asleep but woke up when we got there, and Bruno and Ed came over. They told me about how the campus

Public Safety rent-a-cops showed up and started questioning people, but since nobody else knew who I was, they were unable to determine my identity. To make it more confusing for the cops, Ed started a rumor that quickly circulated through the crowd about how I was a local high school kid who didn't even go to school here. Since nothing was stolen and nobody one got hurt, they didn't stay long but instructed people to notify them if they happened to see me.

After telling them about my trip downtown, we popped *Playing With Fire* into the VCR, an old porno I had stolen from my stepfather. The film was about a guy who sleeps with his stepdaughter behind his wife's back while his wife is doing the same with her stepson, and all the while the stepbrother and stepsister are sleeping together behind both of their parents' backs. We were lost in the movie until a pounding on the door jolted us back to reality. I knew it was probably someone looking for me, but at this point I had nowhere to run or hide, so I told Russ that he might as well answer it because whoever it was already knew we were in there.

Russ opened the door and a female voice shrieked, "Where's Hank?"

In my flight downtown I had forgotten all about Patty, and she had worked herself into a rage. Russ attempted to block her entrance, but she was too much for him and threw him aside like he was a child. Her face was red and her nostrils were flaring, the leather and heels having been replaced by a faded pink sweatsuit and bunny slippers.

"There you are, you fucking loser!" she yelled. "Where's my bra?"

"Anson took it."

"What do you mean Anson took it? Why does that little fucker have my bra? And what the hell happened to you before?"

"I had to take a shit, so I went to the bathroom and when I got back you were gone!"

"Bullshit!" she yelled. "You're such a fucking pig!"

"Look who's talking," Ed muttered from his seat on my bed.

"What did you say?" she yelled, and without waiting for an answer took a swing at him and struck him in the eye. Losing her balance on the follow-through, she landed on top of him and he struggled and cursed at her to get off of him until a shirtless Tommy Austin appeared in the doorway.

"What the fuck is going on in here?" he asked. No one answered. He looked around the room and stopped at me, staring at me for what seemed an eternity and worrying me that he was on the verge of realizing that I was Pizza Hut Guy. I managed to keep my fear somewhat in check by repeatedly telling myself *he doesn't know*, and my case was helped by the confusion of the current situation. Patty was struggling to remove herself from Ed, whose left eye was swollen and on it's way to becoming a nice shiner. Tommy was then further distracted when he saw what was on TV.

"Hey, *Playing With Fire*," he said with a big smile. "This is a classic."

He watched the movie silently for a few moments before his face turned angry again.

"If I here another peep out of this room," he said, "I will write each and every one of you up and file a report with Artie Schramm."

He looked around at all of us and momentarily stopped at me before heading out and slamming the door. Patty called us "ass holes" and turned to leave as well, but just as she was reaching for the knob, the door flew open and hit her in the face.

"Did you just call me an ass hole?" Tommy screamed at Patty, not realizing what he had done until he noticed the blood tricking out of her nose.

"I was talking about them!" she cried and stormed out. Tommy chased her down the hall yelling that he was sorry and that it was an accident, but she told him to go to hell and kept going. A couple of minutes later we heard his bare feet thumping back in our direction and thought we were done for, but instead he went back to his room and slammed the door, leaving the hallway suddenly silent.

**3**

At the beginning of the semester there were plenty of open house frat parties to keep us occupied on Friday and Saturday nights, which kept us nice and drunk for the price of admission—which was usually no more that three bucks. Little did we realize at the time was that the abundance of parties was because the frats where merely showcasing their Greek lifestyles and telling drunk freshmen how pledging such and such fraternity was the greatest decision of their lives. They pretty much left us alone, however. We must have seemed a bit off to them, whether it was because we showed up to the parties long before anyone else—sometimes while they were still eating dinner, and often before the kegs even arrived—and would then just crowd ourselves around the keg and gawk at all the girls. They knew that we weren't the slightest bit interested in pledging, and when the rush period began, we even got thrown out of a couple of parties because of it. At one point we resorted to feigning interest in pledging, but that usually led to annoying sales pitches that quickly became very awkward when the frat guys saw that we were biting our lips in attempting not to laugh in their faces. At a Sigma Nu party, Ed flat out told one of the brothers, "Sure, we'll pledge. What frat is this again?" We were quickly shown the door and told never to show up at one of their parties again.

When the rush period was over and pledging began, the open house parties suddenly ceased. Since none of us had fake IDs, we had to resort to waiting outside the supermarket like a bunch of high school kids to find a grownup to buy us beer. We would then have to lug the cases up to the parking lot below Golding Path and drink there, which at first was fun, but with no girls hanging out with us and the autumn air starting to get a little chilly, it got old pretty quick.

Most of the other guys on our floor were pledging, and despite often coming home covered in mud or condiments or not coming home at all, they seemed to at least have something going on. Though none of us were willing to admit that we had thought about pledging, we started to wonder if life did exist outside the Greek world in Oneonta.

Then one morning I was greeted by the following notice taped to the door of one of the toilet stalls:

**OPEN HOUSE PARTY**
**4 CENTER STREET**
**FRIDAY OCTOBER 11, 8:00 PM-???**
**JELLO SHOTS**
**GIRLS DRINK FREE**
**THIS IS NOT A FRAT PARTY!!!**
**J.F.P.**

Much to the amusement of the pledges and other fraternal-minded residents of Golding Hall, these notices had been posted all over the building. To them it was unfathomable that anyone other than a fraternity or a sorority would even consider attempting an open house party. Things such as "LOSERS," "NERDS," and "RUSH PHI KAP AND SPARE YOURSELF THE PAIN OF PARTYING WITH GEEKS" were written on the few notices that hadn't been torn down in a fit of laughter.

I removed the notice on the stall door and showed it to the other guys. It was intriguing that it specifically indicated that it was not a frat party, and by going to this party, we might perhaps catch a glimpse of our independent futures and see how much better our lives would be without all the Greek bullshit.

A telltale sign that the hosts of this party were rank amateurs were the photocopied signs stapled to telephone poles all over Center Street that said "PARTY" and "J.F.P." with arrows directing partygoers to the house. Seeing as most people who attend college open house parties are underage and that the cops were cracking down on such gatherings, most open houses were held in basements so the noise was muffled and the upstairs would look empty and quiet. The Oneonta Police Department had the authority to place a residence on probation and even had the power to evict upon further incident. If you got evicted, you were put on a black list by all the real estate companies in town that rented to students, and then you had to either move back up to the dorms or rent from

Oneonta's reputed underworld leader Old Man Giuseppe Gambaro, who would charge you an arm and a leg to live in a place that would have otherwise been condemned if anyone other than him had owned it—not to mention that not paying the rent on time might literally cost you an arm or a leg.

The arrows on the signs directed us up a staircase along the side of a duplex that had separate apartments on each floor. It sounded quiet inside, which was normal to us because we were usually the first ones to show up at parties anyway. But this one already felt different. Ed started knocking on the door, and before he even finished knocking the door swung open to reveal two guys who looked old enough to be in grad school staring back at us.

Despite one of them being a beanpole and the other being obese in the neighborhood of 400 pounds, they looked very much alike. They looked like time travelers from 1986, both wearing thick gold necklaces and metal-framed glasses with Coke-bottle lenses, and their hair meticulously blow-dried down to the last strand. The fat one was wearing an Adidas Run/DMC sweatsuit, and the skinny one was wearing a black and white striped sweater over a pair of Cavaricci slacks like the guidos used to wear when we were in junior high. Neither said anything until Bruno announced that we were there for the party.

"Are you guys ready to party?" the skinny one asked.

"I'm ready to get fucked up and get laid," Ed said. "Where's the keg?"

The skinny guy said it would be three bucks each. He collected our money while the fat guy handed us plastic cups, which were 12 ouncers instead of the standard 16 ounce cups usually handed out at parties, which seemed like a rookie mistake because it would lead to shorter refill intervals and longer keg lines. Winston let out a laugh when he saw that they had picked up a keg of Genny, which was an upstate thing that none of us suburban and city natives were familiar with and had us wondering if we would need an extra dose of Kaopectate in the morning.

The skinny guy introduced himself as Eliot. He said the other guy was his brother, but he didn't tell us his name.

"Well, you guys are the first ones here, but you're early. In a little while this place is going to be crawling with hot babes."

"I couldn't help but notice on your flyer that you guys made a point of mentioning that you were not affiliated with a fraternity," Russ said to Eliot.

"Yeah, who the hell are you guys?" Ed asked.

"You'll know soon enough. You guys are lucky to be getting in on the ground floor."

"The ground floor of what?" Bruno asked.

"You'll see. Peace out, brothas. I have to finish getting ready. Just make yourselves comfortable, but please don't drink all the beer." He snickered and went into a room down the hall and closed the door.

"Fuck that," Winston said and laughed. "I'll drink this whole fucking keg myself!"

"Did he say *peace out*?" Russ asked.

"Well, ah, I think he called us *brothers*," Teke said.

They had prepared for the anticipated crowd by moving all of their furniture into Eliot's bedroom, which was stuffed to the ceiling with chairs and tables and everything else that had been in the apartment. There was no living room, so we situated ourselves in an empty room at the end of the hall that we assumed was the Big Guy's room—the walls were bare and the room smelled like deviled ham. The beer went down easily, which had more to do with the situation than the quality of the brew, and after several rounds and a quickly achieved buzz it dawned on us that we were going to be the only ones who showed up.

"No music?" Russ asked.

"We're probably better off," I said. "I don't even want to venture to guess what they would consider party music."

"This is so gross!" Ed shouted and laughed.

Hearing Ed's shout, Eliot suddenly shot into the room and asked if everything was alright. He looked exactly the same as he had before except now he reeked of cheap cologne.

"When are the girls gonna get here?" Ed asked.

"They should be here shortly," Eliot said. "Would you fellows care for a Jell-o shot? Two bucks each, three for five."

"Fuck that," Bruno said.

"No, really," Ed said. "When are the girls going to get here? You said this place was going to be crawling with hot babes."

"I know, I know," Eliot said, looking at his watch. "They should have been here by now. Did you guys hear anyone else in the dorms talking about coming?"

"No."

"Why do you think no one else showed up? I thought this was a happening party school."

"Maybe you didn't put up enough flyers," I said.

"I knew it!" Eliot yelled down the hall to the Big Guy. "I told you we should have put up more flyers!" Eliot turned back to us. "Well, this is ridiculous. I'm going to go up to campus and cruise for some babes."

"How do you propose to do that?" Russ asked.

Eliot pulled a set of car keys out of his slacks and started jingling them in front of Russ' face. "Brand new fucking Monte Carlo," he said. "Killer sound system, sub-woofer and everything. The babes can't resist. It's my secret weapon."

By the time we hit double-digit beers, we were still the only ones there. It's amazing how fast and how much one can drink when there are no women about. After Eliot had been gone nearly an hour, the Big Guy was still sitting in a chair next to the door with package of cups in hand as if the crowd was going to show up any minute. He wasn't drinking, and every couple of minutes he peeked through the blinds to see if anyone was coming up the stairs. At one point Ed and I were in the kitchen refilling our beers when he asked us if we wanted to smoke some pot.

"I've been saving this one for the party," he said, extracting an enormous Bob Marley size joint from the inside pocket of his sweatjacket and holding it in his palm for us to see. After the others were summoned, he sparked the joint and took a tremendous hit that he held in his lungs until his face turned red and he started tottering. When he finally exhaled, the whole kitchen fogged up like a winter morning in San Francisco. After the joint went around, he sat on the floor Indian-style declining to smoke anymore and started slumping down until he was flat on his back and unconscious. We asked him if he was alright, and Teke started tapping his face but he didn't answer.

"Well, ah, should we do something?" Teke asked.

"We could leave," Russ said.

"Not with a full keg to ourselves," Ed said. "Besides, he's fine. He's breathing, see? The excitement was just a little too much for him."

He was still passed out when Eliot got back. There were two girls with him who couldn't have been a day over fifteen, and when they caught their first glimpse of what they had just walked into, they looked as if about ready to turn and run.

"Hi, ladies!" Ed said.

They sheepishly said "hi" and avoided eye contact.

"Is he alright?" one of them asked, looking down at the Big Guy.

"Did he smoke dope?" Eliot asked us.

"He did," Russ said.

"He'll be fine in a minute. He does this every time he smokes. He has a valve problem or something."

"Isn't that serious?" Russ asked.

"Yeah. But he's alright as long as he takes his pills."

"What kind of pills does he have?" Ed asked, suddenly interested.

"I don't know. Nothing you can get stoned from, I assure you."

Eliot went into his room and came back with another joint. "Would anyone like to smoke?" he asked.

"You'll have to show us how to inhale," one of the girls said. They were still visibly nervous, but they were definitely interested in the weed.

"That won't be a problem," Ed said. Winston started laughing so hard at Ed's remark that he had to leave the room.

"What's his problem?" the other girl asked.

"He's just a hick," Bruno said.

Eliot sparked the joint, took a hit, and passed it to one of the girls. She was a skinny brunette with undeveloped breasts, while the other was a skinny blond with slightly larger breasts. Both were wearing jeans and tight bodysuits with big unbuttoned flannel shirts and work boots. The brunette looked at the joint and sniffed it before lifting it to her lips, and Eliot talked her through the process of inhaling. After a couple of false starts, she finally got it right and passed it to her friend, whom Eliot had to talk through the process as well.

The blond then handed the joint to Ed and he took a quick hit, exhaled, and took a long hit before passing it along. The joint was passed around the circle, and when it got to me at the end, instead of passing it back to Eliot, I took another hit and then reversed the direction and handed it back to Russ so that it was heading back in the direction from which it had just come. The brunette protested, but Eliot didn't seem too concerned. By the time it got back to Ed, it was just a roach, so he pulled out the brass pipe he always carried around ("for just such occasions"), dropped the roach in, took a big hit, and passed it to the girls, who had an easier time smoking from that than they did the joint. Eliot declined his turn and passed the bowl to me, but by then it was kicked—not that I needed any more because I was very fucked up.

When Eliot finally realized that no one else was going to show up, he offered us free Jell-o shots. Every shelf and rack in the refrigerator was filled with peach flavored Jell-o mixed with Barton's vodka in little white condiment cups as if they had been expecting an army. Ignoring Eliot's protests not to take them all, we grabbed as many as we could hold in our arms and ran back to the room at the end of the hall. Like hungry animals we slurped one after the other and tossed the empty cups on the floor. The shots were pretty strong and I started feeling nauseous during my fourth, but Teke managed to down seven or eight before dropping the rest of his stash and hauling ass to the bathroom with hand over mouth.

He made it as far as the kitchen before a streaming projectile of peach vomit shot out of his mouth and landed on the girls' work boots. They screamed as he stumbled into the bathroom and started puking again, missing the toilet entirely and covering the floor, walls, and sink with Jell-o chow.

"Oh my God!" Eliot yelled frantically over the girls' screaming. "Should we call an ambulance?"

"Relax," Ed laughed. "He does this all the time."

"He looks like he's going to die!"

Eliot's concern for Teke was immediately forgotten when the girls ran out the door. He chased after them as the Big Guy slowly regained consciousness and watched with childlike amusement as Teke emerged from the bathroom with strings of vomit drooling from his chin. I was still standing in the middle of the room at the end of the hall surrounded by gelatinous refuse, paralyzed by fear that if I made the slightest movement, I was going to fall through the floor and wind up in the apartment below. I took a deep breath every time the floor creaked beneath my feet until Winston came back and asked me what I was doing.

"Don't move," I said.

"Are you alright, man?"

"No."

"Are you gonna puke?"

"I don't know."

After unsuccessfully trying to lure the girls back, Eliot returned and started yelling that the party was over.

"No it's not," Ed said. "There's still beer in that keg!"

"C'mon, guys, don't do this to me," Eliot whined. "You guys had a good time, it was a good party. Hell, it was a J.F.P., man."

"A what?" Russ asked.

"J.F.P. Jolly Fucking Party." Eliot slowly started chanting "J.F.P." and tried to get us to chant with him, but we stared at him until he stopped.

"The party isn't over until the keg is kicked or the cops show up," Ed said.

"C'mon, you guys. I want to go downtown and get some babes."

"If you guys go down there, do you mind if we stay here with the keg?" Ed asked.

"I can't let you guys stay here by yourselves!"

"He'll be here," Ed said, pointing to the Big Guy.

"He's coming with me."

"He doesn't look like he's going anywhere."

"He'll be alright in a minute. He just needs another pill."

"Well, bring the keg outside then. We'll drink in the yard."

"I can't let you do that."

"It wouldn't be very J.F.P. to kick us out while there's still beer left," Russ said.

"Listen, I'll give you the rest of my pot if you just go."

"What about the beer?" Ed asked.

"Let's just take the pot and get the hell out of here," Russ said, and it was settled. We waited in the kitchen staring at the Big Guy on the floor, his eyes now closed behind his glasses and snoring loudly while Eliot went down the hall to get the bag of weed. When he came back he handed the bag to Russ and we left, Ed patting Eliot on the shoulder and saying "Thanks for the memories" on our way out. We went down to the corner and staked out the house until we saw Eliot and the Big Guy get into the Monte and pull away. After they were gone, Ed and Winston went back up the stairs and started throwing their shoulders against the door until it finally opened and they fell inside. Moments later they came back out with the keg, which we covered with our jackets and carried up the side streets all the way up to Golding Path, planting it triumphantly in the gravel of the parking lot, which is about when we realized that we didn't have any cups. We drank straight from the tap and did keg stands until foam finally started shooting out somewhere around 4:00 AM. Ed removed the tap for us to keep since they were a valuable commodity, and we carried the keg out to the top of Maple Street right in front of Fred's house and let it roll down the sloped street and bolted when it slammed into a parked car halfway down the block.

**4**

"I'm sick of this shit," Ed said one night in mid-November. We were in his and Bruno's room just after returning from smoking a bowl in the woods.

"Well, ah, what shit would that be?" Teke asked.

"We go to a school where there are twice as many girls as there are guys, yet in the three months we've been here, the closest any of us have come to getting laid is Hank's little exploit with that fat sow on the first night."

"Please don't remind me," I said.

"And now we've become complacent to the point where we don't even fucking try."

"What the fuck are we supposed to do?" Bruno said. "There haven't been any parties lately, we don't have any ID to get into the bars, and most of the chicks around here are either in sororities or pledging, so they don't want anything to do with you unless you're a cheeseball frat guy."

"You see, this is what I'm talking about. We sit around here making excuses, blaming chicks for having the bad taste to fall for frat cheeseballs and not having high enough standards to hook up with us. So what if they have bad taste? I just want to get laid. Our principles aren't gonna get us any pussy."

"What are you getting at?" Russ asked.

"I'm just saying that we're never gonna get laid if we don't try. And if that means setting aside some bullshit principles in exchange for some pussy, so be it."

"I ain't pledging no frat, if that's what you're trying to say," Winston said.

"I don't think we have to go to that extreme. I think that there are plenty of chicks out there who aren't in sororities."

"You mean the ones on the Womyn's Rugby Team?" Bruno laughed.

"No, not the Womyn's Rugby Team or the fat chicks in the service fraternity. I'm talking about the ones outside the boundaries of the masses. They're out there, but we're just not trying very hard to find them."

"Well, where the hell are they?"

"The Aquarium."

"Oh no," Winston said.

"This is a crisis, gentlemen. I don't know about you, but I for one am tired of jerking off in that bathroom in the geography section of the library."

"What?" Bruno laughed.

"What I'm saying is that I need to get laid. So in the strict pursuit of snatch, I am proposing an 'anything goes' night at the Aquarium. What I mean by that is that no matter who or what any of us happens to come home with, as long as she doesn't have a penis, no one has the right to make any snide comments. Agreed?"

The Aquarium was one of those cheesy 18-to-get-in-21-to-drink dance clubs that those of us from the suburbs had been to once or twice and vowed never to step foot in again. It was owned by Old Man Giuseppe Gambaro, who, in addition to his real estate ventures, also owned a pizza place next door locally famous for it's "cold cheese" pizza (which is a regular slice of pizza with shreds of cold mozzarella sprinkled on top). If you were under 21, you had to pay a $5.00 cover charge to get in and have the back of your hand stamped "UNDER 21," but once inside, the bartenders didn't care how old you were as long as you were willing to pay $2.00 for an 8 ounce draft of Busch, which is what a six pack of it cost at the Red Barrel mini-mart down the street. And though the majority of it's clientele was clearly under 21, the Aquarium seemed to be the only bar in Oneonta that the cops never raided.

The Aquarium attracted a few high school kids who grew up in Oneonta and the surrounding towns, but it was mostly the bottom of the barrel college leftovers who had been rejected by the fraternities and sororities and the losers like Eliot and the Big Guy who saw this place as a prime meat market. The fraternities and sororities supposedly all had ways of obtaining fake identification (which was another one of the perks of pledging), so there were hardly ever any Greeks there, which is one of the few things this place had going for it—but that was hardly enough. It was the kind of place I swore I'd never go again after having experienced a couple of clubs like it back on Long Island, but Ed was right. It was desperation time.

To avoid paying the exorbitant alcohol prices and not having to endure the booming dance music at the Aquarium for a lengthy amount of time, we had planned what would essentially be a guerilla raid of the Aquarium. We would pick up a few cases of Beast and drink down at the Golding Path lot before proceeding downtown armed with the condoms Ed had plundered earlier in the day from the complimentary condom basket on the reception counter at the Health Center.

The bus ride downtown was one of Beast-fueled determination to get laid. This felt like a serious mission, and together we were heading into uncharted territory for the sake of snatch. Upon our arrival at the bus depot downtown, the thumping dance beat grew louder with each step we made across the dirt parking lot that led to our destination. The Aquarium was by far the largest bar in Oneonta and was set apart from the more intimate taverns clustered together on Water Street, and a large sea-themed mural that spelled out "The Aquarium" painted on the brick façade was illuminated by large floodlights as if to indicate to strangers in town who didn't know any better that this was the place to be on a Saturday night. The grand entrance along with the very large bouncers stationed at the door, who were rumored to be Old Man Gambaro's hit men, made it a very intimidating sight, especially for a bunch of rock & rollers like ourselves who didn't feel comfortable at the very thought of entering a place that offended every fiber of our sense of taste.

About twenty yards from the door, Winston stopped and suggested we just pick up another case or two of Beast and head back up to the path. This didn't sound like such a bad idea to me and probably everyone else besides Ed, but he was quick to remind us that this place was now our only realistic chance at getting any pussy and that he was going in regardless of what the rest of us decided to do. With that said, there seemed no other option than to follow him inside.

The bouncers checked our IDs to make sure all of us were 18—which we were since Bruno had just turned 18 the week before—and we reluctantly handed over our five bucks each to one of the bouncers and had our hands stamped with a stamp that said "UNDER" by the other—which merely meant that we had to pay double for a beer. Once inside the dance music became exponentially louder, and the long passage that led towards the main part of the club felt like we were making the inevitable trek into the mouth of hell.

The inside of the club was dimly lit with blacklights that made the fluorescent palm trees painted on the walls and the white on our clothes and teeth glow. The bar itself was made of plastic bamboo, and behind the rack of liquor bottles was an enormous tropical aquarium filled with exotic fish. Gambaro's staff of bouncers, more pumped-up thugs wearing Hawaiian shirts who looked like out-of-work professional wrestlers, were stationed throughout the club. The Old Man himself was doing his rounds looking like he wanted to kill someone and gave us a long cold stare as he went by. He was a short guy who looked old but powerful in a Jack LaLanne kind of way, with blow-dried iron gray hair that peered over his forehead like a visor and a crevasse on the right side of his face that ran from the end of his eyebrow down his cheek to the base of his chin. He was wearing a half-buttoned short-sleeve brown polyester dentist shirt that exposed a glint of gold from a medallion buried in a prairie of steel wool chest hair, and his Popeye-like forearms hung at his sides like torpedoes. Up in the DJ booth overlooking the dance floor, sixteen year old Giuseppe Jr. was spinning records and trying to get more people on the dance floor other than the four overweight high school girls wiggling out there now. The rest of the crowd sat at their tables looking anxious to go out there but waiting for more people to go out there in order not to draw too much attention to themselves.

We went to the bar and spent all the money we had on two pitchers of Busch, which worked out to be just slightly more than a beer each. After that was gone, Ed invited himself to sit down at a table with two girls who were nearly as big as Bruno and started making small talk with them as he helped himself to their pitcher. He just kept on talking while the girls sat there not sure what to make of him and listened with puzzled smiles as he bullshitted his way to the bottom of their pitcher. After refilling his cup with the rest of their beer, he wished them a pleasant evening and headed for the dance floor.

Giuseppe Jr. put on Marky Mark's "Good Vibrations", a popular number at the time that attracted a crowd of people to the floor. There was, however, still plenty of room for Ed to remove his shirt, swing it over his head, and slide on his knees while howling like a wolf. The other dancers formed a circle around him and started clapping to the beat while Ed did his best *Saturday Night Fever* impersonation, and when the song was over he got a round of applause. Naughty By Nature's "O.P.P." came on next, and even more people crowded the floor, amongst them the two girls from Eliot's party. Ed started dancing with one of them and soon had his groin pressed against hers and their hands on each other's asses. While everyone else was flailing around them, the two of them slow danced like they were at the junior prom to 3rd Bass' "Pop Goes the

Weasel" and then Public Enemy's "Bring tha Noize" before leaving the club holding hands.

A couple of songs later Giuseppe Jr. broke into his rock segment with AC/DC's "You shook Me All Night Long"—Winston's least favorite AC/DC song, but an AC/DC song nonetheless—so he *had* to go out there. His idea of dancing was standing nearly still and slightly bending his knees to the rhythm while looking at the floor. The other dancers slowly drifted away from him until he had his own little pocket of space in the corner, but he was oblivious.

The next song was Nirvana's "Smells Like Teen Spirit." Teke led our charge to the floor and we started moshing, getting in a good 30 seconds before the Hawaiian shirts swarmed and yanked us away. We offered no resistance as they dragged us towards the exit and shoved us out into the parking lot. While we were dusting ourselves off, Old Man Gambaro came out and said with a heavy accent that he never wanted to see us in his club again, but then added we could still buy pizza from him at the restaurant. He gave us a long look as if committing our faces to memory before heading back inside while the bouncers waited with arms folded until we left.

Back at the dorm, Bruno's pillow and blankets were on the floor outside his and Ed's room and there was a piece of notebook paper taped to the door with "DO NOT DISTURB" written on it in purple crayon. We took turns putting our ears against the door but couldn't hear anything before Bruno finally gathered his things and set up camp on our floor. After Russ and I climbed into our own beds, I was just about to fall asleep until I was jolted awake by what sounded like a tractor-trailer racing through the room that Russ and I soon realized was Bruno snoring. It was so unbearable that Russ and I gathered our pillows and sheets and trudged down to Teke and Winston's room, where we spent the night camped out on their floor trying not to get to close to one another in the cramped space and hardly getting any sleep at all.

The next morning, while sitting in one of the stalls in the men's room suffering the consequences of drinking both Beast *and* Busch in the same evening, two guys came in and started shaving at the sinks. One asked the other if he was going out that night, but the other said he couldn't get into any of the bars because he lost his ID and was waiting for one of his frat brothers to get him a new one. The first guy suggested he go see this girl who lived upstairs named Holly who would chalk his real driver's license for a couple of bucks.

"She's an artist," the guy said.

She was cute too, but unfortunately a sorority pledge. Since she was still pledging, she had yet to achieve full snobdom like the veteran sisters of Epsilon Pi Tau and was rather friendly, if not only because I told her that I was seriously thinking about pledging Phi Ep next semester. But, more importantly, she *was* an artist. With a white pencil, a finely sharpened #2 pencil, a can of Aqua Net, and a hairdryer, she was able to add some lines to and remove others from the block print digits of the date of birth on the license to turn me from 18 to 21 in a matter of minutes. She then sealed the flawless alteration with the hairspray (apparently the old ozone-killing aerosol spray cans worked the best) and flopped it back and forth to let it dry a bit without smudging before shooting it with the hairdryer on low power for a few seconds to make it permanent. She suggested that I keep it in a plastic ID holder and never take it out for a bouncer because if they look at the license while shining a flashlight behind it, they might be able to see the lines of the original numbers that had been blocked out with the white pencil. I gave her the $2.00 and told her that she did wonderful work and referred her to the other guys. By that afternoon we were all 21 and in possession of the keys to the promised land.

Despite our hangovers, we made our first trip down to the strip later that night. We were too intimidated to go to any of the bars on Water Street with the big bouncers watching us from the doors as if they knew we were freshmen and daring us to even try to get into their bar, so we eventually wound up in the little shopping center across Chestnut Street standing outside of The General Clinton Pub, Oneonta's infamous townie bar, where most college students fear to tread. A black P.O.W./M.I.A. flag hung over the entrance and there was no bouncer.

"I don't know about this," Russ said.

"Well, you guys didn't want to go to any of the other bars," Ed said.

"What's the big deal?" Winston said. "I've been hanging out in places like this since I was thirteen. I bet they don't even check our ID."

We pondered it for another couple of minutes before Winston finally said "fuck it" and went inside, followed by Ed. After a few more moments of indecision, the rest of us finally decided to go in.

The place was small and had some wobbly tables and chairs scattered about, but no one was sitting in them. There was a pool table in the corner where a couple of townie guys wearing "West Nesbitt Feed & Seed" T-shirts stopped playing for a moment and looked at us when we came in before resuming their game. There were a few old guys sitting at the bar staring off into space with shots of whiskey in front of them who didn't notice us, and a woman with hardened facial features who didn't take her eyes off of us the whole time we were there. The only person in there close to our age was the girl behind the bar, a gorgeous brunette with a heavy Southern accent who looked a little like Daisy Duke in her prime.

"Boy am I glad to see you guys," she said. Her name was Georgia. Winston was right, she didn't bother to card us. She told us it was her second night on the job and she had been a little bored but mostly frightened of the patrons she had liquored up thus far. We ordered a couple of pitchers of Beast and pushed three of the little tables together in the dark corner near the pinball machine.

Aside from the occasional curious look, the townies pretty much left us alone. Later, Georgia gave us three dozen complimentary hot wings and only charged us for every other round as if doing everything she could to keep us from leaving. After we had been there for a couple of hours, a fight broke out over at the pool table. Two guys who were playing against the West Nesbitt guys started pushing them and suddenly every guy there except us jumped into the fray and started throwing punches. Behind the bar Georgia pleaded for them to stop, and when they didn't, she put her hands over her face and started crying. Ed said he wanted to jump in and break a chair over someone's head, but we were able to restrain him.

Suddenly a door next to the bar opened and a fat biker guy emerged. He was wearing black jeans and a leather vest over a Harley Davidson T-shirt, and behind his thick black beard and eyebrows his eyes looked groggy. As he made his way across the bar, he mumbled something to Georgia about how he thought it was supposed to be his night off and very casually walked right into the fracas. He tossed the combatants aside until he got to the nucleus and grabbed one of the guys who had been playing pool against the West Nesbitt guys by the back of the collar, shoving him hard against the wall with a forearm on his throat.

"You know you're not supposed to be in here," the bouncer calmly said. The music had been turned down and everyone was quiet. "Now what the fuck are you doing here?"

The guy tried not to look at the bouncer's face.

"You thought it was my night off, didn't you?" the bouncer continued. "Well it is my night off, but you failed to realize one thing, dude. I live here. You're trespassing in my home. And if I ever catch you in my home again, I am personally going to take every one of these pool cues and shove 'em up your ass sideways. Now, am I ever going to see your ugly face in here again?"

"No sir."

"Good answer."

The bouncer pulled the guy by the collar to the door and shoved him out into the parking lot, where he suddenly found his guts and started calling the bouncer a "fat fuck" amongst a slew of other profanities. The bouncer paid no attention and headed back to his room, telling Georgia on his way to holler if there was any more trouble and suggesting that she give everyone a round on the house.

Later while I was at the bar ordering another pitcher, the townie woman who had been staring at us the whole time knocked over a glass of beer and watched the spillage flow towards me. She appeared to be in her 40's and was a bit skanky, her face covered with sloppily applied makeup, her outfit looking like it had been taken off the rack at a thrift store for prostitutes, and her stringy dyed-blond hair a disheveled mess of dark roots and split ends. Georgia hurried over and wiped the spilled beer before it reached me and poured the woman another one, which she deliberately knocked over. She was staring at me and paid no attention to Georgia wiping the bar again.

"And just what the fuck do you think you're looking at?" she slurred at me.

"Be nice," Georgia said to the woman.

"Quiet, you little hussy," she said to Georgia without taking her eyes off of me. "I asked you a question, sugar. I asked you just what the fuck you think you're looking at."

"Nothing," I said and turned away.

The woman stumbled off her stool and came over, getting right in my face so I could smell the beer and cigarettes on her breath.

"Can I tell you something, sugar?" she asked me, her tone suddenly sweet.

"What's that?"

"You remind me of a dead friend."

"Is that so?" I tried to pay Georgia for the pitcher, but she said it was on the house. I left a couple of singles on the bar as a tip.

"You remind me of a dead friend," the townie woman repeated and moved closer. "Someone I was very close to a long time ago."

I tried to go back to the table, but she grabbed my arm.

"You really are something special," she said.

"Thanks." Again I tried to walk away, but she tightened her grip.

"Leave him alone," Georgia said.

"Shut up, you little tramp," the woman said.

"Listen," I said, "why don't you get the hell away from me, alright?"

The woman let go of my arm and slapped me hard across the face. The other guys laughed while the West Nesbitt guys stopped playing pool to watch. Georgia knocked on the bouncer's door. The woman slapped me again.

"That's for what you done to me before," she said.

Suddenly the bouncer's door opened. Georgia said something to him while pointing towards us.

"How can a guy get any sleep around here?" the bouncer laughed as he made his way over. "What seems to be the problem here?" he asked the woman.

"Stay out of this!" she screamed at him. "This is between me and him!"

"Not in my house," he said. "I'm afraid I'm going to have to ask you to leave."

"I'm not going anywhere until this is settled."

"It's settled now," he said and looked at Georgia. "If she's not out of here in ten seconds, go ahead and call the cops." He turned to me. "Why don't you go have a seat with your buddies. Drinks are on the house for you guys the rest of the night. I'll take care of this."

"Thanks," I said.

The woman still refused to leave and Georgia picked up the phone.

"She's calling the cops," I said to the other guys.

"Bottoms up!" Ed announced and hastily filled everyone's glass with the pitcher I had just brought over. We quickly slammed our beers, and as we were scurrying towards the door, Georgia asked where we were going and reminded us that drinks were on the house for the rest of the night.

"We have a big test tomorrow," Bruno said, never mind that the next day was Sunday. The bouncer gave us a look as if he knew why we were leaving, but he still wished us a good night and told us to come back soon.

Out in the parking lot Ed said he wanted to go to The Novelty Lounge, the town's tittie bar conspicuously located right on the middle of Main Street. Local officials had been trying to shut the place down for decades or at least move it outside city limits, but there was some kind of grandfather clause that legally allowed it to stay open right where it was. It was owned by a woman who appeared to be at least in her 90's who had been managing strip clubs since the Great Depression and was still running the day-to-day operations while tending bar at night.

Above the front door there was a huge vertical sign with blinking neon red letters that spelled out "TOPLESS" except that the "P" didn't light up, so that when it blinked, it said "TO LESS." Below the letters a blinking arrow pointed to a crudely painted sign advertising "GO-GO GIRLS." Inside the place looked like something right out of the height of Burlesque—the walls were covered with yellow and black striped wallpaper accentuated by burgundy velvet curtains, several chandeliers that looked like they were about to come crashing down dangled from the high ceilings, and behind the antique bar there was an elevated stage complete with a full-sized wall mirror and brass fireman's pole.

The old woman gave us a sharp look when we came in. She was tiny, barely tall enough to see over the bar, and had a head of blazing red hair that appeared to be a wig. Her face was shriveled like a raisin and she was wearing a pair of granny glasses with a little chain that went around the back of her neck. Up on stage a fat wrinkled woman of at least 50, wearing nothing but a barely visible G-string buried in rolls of stretch-marked flesh, tattoos, and pubic hair, was swinging her sagging breasts to Aerosmith's "Same Old Song and Dance" for the benefit of an elderly man sitting at the bar, the only other patron there.

The old lady immediately demanded to see our identification and scrutinized our licenses under a banker's lamp behind the bar. After she was satisfied that we were of legal age, she asked what we were drinking.

"A pitcher of the cheapest beer you've got," Ed said.

"We don't have pitchers!" she snapped.

"Then we'll settle for the cheapest domestic brew you have in a longneck."

Winston laughed when she pulled six bottles of Genny Cream Ale (or, as he referred to them, "Genny Screamers") out of the cooler and charged us an outrageous $3.00 each. After the beer was paid for, we used our remaining dollar bills for a round of "pussy basketball," crumpling the bills into wads and attempting to shoot them into the "basket" formed by the dancer holding out the front of her G-string with her thumbs. None of us even came close. When we were out of money, I stood up and shouted "Take it all off, baby!" and the old lady gave me a stern look.

"Watch it, young man," she said. "This is a class establishment."

"I was just having a little fun," I said.

"If I hear any more suggestions like that I'll call the police!"

"Jeez!"

"I mean it! I'll call the cops!"

When the show was over, we were informed that the next one wouldn't be for another 45 minutes. The dancer put on a robe and started talking to the old guy down the bar, and a few minutes later they disappeared behind a curtain towards the back.

"I haven't seen you boys in here before," the old lady said while wiping down the bar. "Are you from around here?"

"No," I said. "We're just passing through."

"Where are you from?"

"Schenectady," Ed said.

"Really? I used to run a club up there many years ago. Great town."

"It sure is," Ed said and slid off his barstool. Facing the old lady, who could only see his head across the bar, Ed unzipped his pants and started pissing on the buttoned leather padding covering the partition.

"Have you ever been to the Pink Pussycat?" she asked Ed.

"The Pink Pussycat?" Ed said, still pissing. "No, I'm afraid not." When he was finished, he attempted to coolly zip his pants and pick up his beer at the same time, but in the process he knocked his Screamer on it's side. A stream of cream ale ran across the surface that the old lady had just wiped down.

"You watch it!" she snapped. "Do that again and you're all out of here!"

"It was an accident!" Ed said. "It won't happen again."

"It better not!"

"Well, ah, were you a dancer?" Teke asked the old lady as she wiped up the spillage.

"Oh, no," she laughed. "I just ran the clubs."

"That's a shame," Bruno said. "You must have been something in your day."

She looked at him as if trying to decide if he was being a wise ass.

"I have an idea," I said and leaned over the bar. "Since the next show doesn't start until one, why don't you get up there and give us a little number."

"Don't get fresh with me, young man!"

"It was just a thought."

"You were being a wise aleck!"

"Please accept my apologies. I must now use the restroom."

Above the urinal at eye level, an old vending machine advertising cock rings, glow-in-the-dark condoms, and "Pussy Photos" for 50¢ stared back at me while I pissed. After I was done, I plugged in two quarters and turned the dial for the Pussy Photos, but nothing happened.

"That damn machine in there ripped me off!" I yelled on my way back to the bar. "I put in two quarters for the Pussy Photos and the fucking thing took my money!"

"There is nothing wrong with that machine!" she yelled back. "I just serviced it last week!"

"I'll be you did!" Ed said, prompting a sharp death glance.

"The thing stole my money!" I shouted. "I want my Pussy Photos!"

"Don't get fresh with me, young man!"

I pounded my fist on the bar. "I want my Pussy Photos!"

"That's it!" she yelled. She picked up the receiver of an old rotary phone behind the bar and started dialing. By the time the second "1" came back around, we were already out the door.

Back up at campus, Russ, Teke, and Bruno decided to call it a night while Ed and Winston were ready to keep the party rolling. I wasn't ready to go to bed yet and was content with the idea of going downstairs and watching a little TV before turning in, but Ed suggested the three of us go on a panty raid.

"Come on, Gardner," Ed said. "What would college be without a panty raid?"

"All I can see is our asses getting hauled away by the campus rent-a-cops and a brief meeting with the Dean of Student Affairs telling us that we have 24 hours to vacate the premises."

"Panties, Hank, panties that smell like fresh autumn snatch," Ed said.

"Or tuna," Winston said and laughed.

"Or some chick who thinks we're there to gang rape her."

"Jesus, Gardner, lighten up," Winston said.

Against my better judgment, I decided to go with them. We headed through the woods towards the deepest, darkest corner of campus, where Littell Hall, the all-female dorm, was located. At the time we still had our schoolboy fantasies of what an all-girls dorm would be like—horny hot chicks in bras and panties having pillow fights and wishing that some drunk guys would show up and steal their panties—and were completely unaware that this was the home of the undergraduate members of the Womyn's Rugby Team and the girls in the service fraternity who referred to themselves as 'brothers'.

The building was the same style as Golding Hall, but only one of the wings of this dorm was occupied. Ed led us around to the side door at the far end of the vacant wing only to find it locked, but around back he found an unlocked bedroom window on the first floor that he slid open. We climbed into the room and Ed started opening the dresser drawers to see if anything had been left behind.

"This would be a cool hideout," he said as he searched. "No one would ever find us here. It would even be good to bring chicks here."

"Oh yeah," I said. "They'll just love climbing through the window."

"I could climb through the window and then let them in through the side door."

The power had been cut on this side of the dorm and the hallway was dark except for the red "EXIT" signs lit up at both ends. Ed led us down to the pit so we could get to the other side of the building without being detected, our only obstacle being the TV/recreation room, but it was empty. On the other side we climbed the stairs to the second floor, Ed's logic being that we shouldn't go to the first floor because we could be seen from the lobby, and on the second floor we could make a quicker escape if need be than we could from the third floor.

"Now what?" I asked after we emerged from the stairwell and stared down the corridor full of closed doors.

"Will you relax, Gardner?" Ed said.

"What are we supposed to do, just barge into someone's room and start rifling through the dressers?"

"Let's just walk to the other end and see what happens."

Halfway down the hall, the R.A's door opened just as we were passing it. Knowing we were busted, we stopped. A cute blond wearing a silk robe poked her head out the door and smiled at us.

"I thought I heard some guys in here," she said.

"Hi," Ed said.

"Are you guys lost?"

"In a way," Winston laughed.

"We're looking for Maü's room," Ed said. *Maü* was a word Ed used whenever he saw an attractive female, a Rockaway slang adaptation of the Chinese word for 'cat.' "Do you know where she lives?"

"Maü?"

"Yes. Maü."

"Is that her first name or her last name?"

"First. Her full name is Maü Schneider."

"Maü Schneider."

"Correct."

"There's no one by that name on this floor."

"See, I told you," Ed said and smacked Winston's arm with the back of his hand. "It must be the third floor. Thanks for your help."

Ed and Winston started to walk away, but I stayed and shrugged my shoulders.

"Were you guys downtown?" she asked.

"Yeah."

"I can smell the beer on you. Where did you go?"

"The Clinton. A couple of other places."

"The Clinton?" she said as Ed and Winston turned the corner at the end of the hall and disappeared. "Isn't that a redneck bar?"

"Kind of. It's not so bad."

"Alright, what are you guys really doing here?"

I let out a deep breath. "You wouldn't happen to have any extra pairs of panties, would you?"

"What?"

"We're pledging a fraternity and we were supposed to go on a panty raid, but it's not exactly going very well. I know it's childish, but if we come back empty-handed, we'll get in trouble."

"How perverted."

"I know."

"I like it."

"You do?"

"Hell yeah. You have no idea how boring this fucking place is. These girls are such fucking losers that they go to bed at 9:00 on weekends. All they ever do is watch movies and make snacks except for the rugby girls, but they're all dykes and they're never here."

"What are you doing here then?"

"I became an R.A. so I could get a discount on room and board, but I signed up late and they stuck me here because no one else wanted it. I'm not doing this again if I have to stay here. I'll take out a fucking loan if I have to. I don't care, I'm not getting stuck here again."

"That sucks."

"Yeah it does. What frat are you pledging?"

"Phi Ep," I said.

"Ooh, I like Phi Ep," she said. "Do you know Chuck Flarney?"

"Sure, I know them all. I have to or else I'll get in trouble."

She laughed. "I might be able to help you."

She went back inside her room and pulled open a dresser drawer. I couldn't believe she was actually going to give me some panties, or better yet, if I was really, lucky invite me in. At the very least I would try to get her number.

While I was fantasizing, there was a sudden popping flash like someone had dropped a big light bulb. Moments later the fire alarm sounded. A cloud of thick white smoke started consuming the end of the hall where Ed and Winston had turned the corner.

I knew immediately that the two of them were somehow responsible for whatever was happening and that I should get the fuck out of there, but for a split second I considered staying before making a run for it. Without any regard for my physical well-being, I ran straight towards the smoke, thinking it was the safer of the two alternatives since everyone else would be headed towards the lobby in the opposite direction. Bedroom doors were opening all around me and girls were screaming, the lessons of a lifetime of orderly fire drills having quickly been forgotten in the face of the real thing. As I entered the stairwell, I was surprised by the lack of heat that I thought would normally accompany smoke and fire, but my train of thought was interrupted when I tumbled down the unseen stairs to the landing between floors. I was dizzy and all I could see around me was white, but I managed to feel my way down the rest of the stairs using the handrail and make it safely out the side door.

A floodlight above the door that had probably been triggered by the alarm brightly lit the immediate vicinity. With no darker route available, I had to make a dash across the spotlight of grass towards the woods. My drunken legs were heavy like running in a dream, and I fell several times. When I finally reached the cover of the woods, I felt safe enough to slow down to a brisk jog. After a few minutes I wanted to stop to catch my breath, but there were sirens racing up towards campus from all directions and I kept thinking that I heard something rustling nearby, so I kept going and didn't stop until I reached Golding Path. Streams of sweat were pouring down my face and I could hardly breathe, yet I managed to keep it together long enough to make it by the night host sitting at his little table in the lobby despite him greeting me as "The Pizza Hut Guy." I nodded politely and headed upstairs, where I found Ed and Winston telling Teke about what they had just done.

I was ready to kill them, but when they saw me they started laughing. After I caught my breath, I started laughing with them. Ed began the story again, starting where Winston lit the smoke bomb he had concocted during a quiet moment in the science lab and had been carrying around ever since and Ed putting one of his socks over his hand to protect it from the ink that squirted out when he pulled the fire alarm. After we stopped laughing, we listened to the sirens in the distance until they finally died down and left behind an unsettling silence that kept me up half the night thinking that at any moment someone was going to break down the door and haul my ass to jail. Even more unsettling, however, was the thought that I very well could have gotten laid with a very cute girl if those other two ass holes hadn't gotten in the way.

**5**

St. Patrick's Day is the biggest holiday of the year in Oneonta, a day when people who normally don't wake up before noon start drinking at 8:00 AM and don't stop until they either pass out or get arrested. Every year so many students cut class on St. Pat's that some professors canceled their lectures, while others purposely scheduled midterms on that day, or, even worse, the day after, to make some futile point that we were in college for academic reasons, not to indulge in debauchery, especially when a majority of the student body was not old enough to legally consume alcohol.

That morning Ed and I were on the 7:30 bus surrounded by a large crowd of green-clad revelers with FUCK ME I'M IRISH buttons pinned to their sweaters who were obnoxiously blowing New Year's horns in each other's faces. The other guys said they would meet us downtown later in the day, but they didn't bother and spent the day running around in the woods getting stoned. Ed, however, as the only Irishman among us, would have none of it. He declared "St. Pat's Rules," meaning that since this was a drinking holiday, we should stick to alcohol only, which was fine with me since I had been pretty burnt out lately from smoking too much weed out in the woods, which had become the routine on those off nights when we didn't go out and get piss drunk.

The Sip & Sail Tavern was giving away free T-shirts to the first 100 people in the door. By the time we got down to Water Street, however, the line to get in was two blocks long, so we went over to The Clinton instead. Georgia was tending bar and fed us a breakfast of green eggs and ham and schlepped us pitchers of green Beast for the next six hours until her shift was over at two. We sat in there so long we didn't know how drunk we were until we emerged from the dusty gloom into the blinding overcast daylight holding each other up as we stumbled down Water Street. Ed suggested that we take a breather before we started drinking again because we had another twelve hours until last call, so we stopped at Gambaro's and each had a slice with cold cheese.

There were parties going on all over town, but none bigger than the annual St. Pat's bash at the Philanthan sorority house. The Philanthans were a local sorority, and unlike most of the national sororities that attracted the princesses from Long Island, they were not stuck up. They accepted almost any girl who rushed, which made them by far the biggest sorority on campus. They owned a blue and yellow Victorian mansion on the corner of Center and Maple that looked like a castle, each corner of the house having attic towers with cone-shaped roofs that served as single bedrooms and fifteen other bedrooms that accommodated two or three girls each. The property was surrounded by a moat of flowers, and on the front of the house there were three enormous Greek letters that were illuminated at night by blue and yellow floodlights. The sorority had been founded well over a century earlier when the college was still a normal school, and the house had been passed down through the generations of Philanthan sisters. Several decades earlier, the City of Oneonta declared the house a local historical landmark, a decision that somewhat hampered the current administration's efforts to improve the school's image because they could pretty much get away with anything without worry of being evicted.

The house was right in the middle of town and perhaps the easiest place in all of Oneonta to find, especially since it was right on the bus route and only a ten minute walk from Main Street, but it still took Ed and I well over an hour to find it in broad daylight. Along the way we had to make a couple of backyard pit stops to empty our bladders, and on one sidestreet I peeled a magnetic sign off the side of a pickup truck that said *ROSCOE'S TAXIDERMY SERVICE—WE DELIVER!* When we finally did find the house and were in the living room paying to get in, I presented the sign as "a gift to the sisters of Philanthan" to the two pledges sitting behind a table with an antique cash register on top.

"It'll look great on the fridge!" I said. They looked at each other as if telepathically contemplating whether or not they should even let us in, but finally one of them accepted it with a 'thank you' and rang us up for $4.00 each while the other handed us green plastic cups and directed us down the stairs.

Compared to the spider-infested dungeons we had become accustomed to at open house parties, this basement was

immaculate. Everything was white—the walls, floor tiles, ceiling—
and the fluorescent lighting made the room painfully bright. There
were stoves, microwave ovens, refrigerators, cabinets, long dining
hall tables folded up against the wall (all covered with sheets of
clear plastic), and enough counter space to prepare food for the
entire sorority of over a hundred members. Green, white, and
yellow streamers adorned the ceiling, and cardboard clovers that
said "Happy St. Patrick's Day!" were taped to the plastic sheets
covering the appliances. A makeshift wait station was set up in one
of the corners where several pledges wearing white T-shirts with
their pledge names written diagonally across the front in blue and
gold glitter were filling pitchers from several kegs for the other
pledges to pick up and serve the guests. All you had to do was hold
out your cup and one of them would come over and fill it.

A pledge named Azalea came over to fill our cups and said hello
to me by name. It took me a moment to recognize her as Maria
Viola, a girl I had gone to high school with who appeared now
much more attractive than I remembered her. She had been in my
ninth grade Spanish class, but I don't think we ever said a word to
each other and I don't recall ever seeing her again after that. Back
then she was one of those pre-goth alt-rock chicks who listened to
Depeche Mode and Erasure and who wore black makeup and had
shaved part of her head save a bob of dyed black hair on top. Now
her hair was grown out in long brown curls and she was wearing
hardly any makeup. She had lost weight since I saw her last and
had developed a nice pair of breasts that I probably stared at a
moment too long before looking her in the eye.

"I was wondering when I was going to run into you," she said,
sounding a little drunk.

"Me too," I lied. "So, you're pledging, huh?"

"Yeah. I wasn't going to at first, but I changed my mind."

"How come?"

"I don't know. I wanted to meet some new people, I guess."

"Do they make you do stupid stuff at lineups?"

"Sometimes."

"Like what?"

"I've been sworn to secrecy."

"Why did they name you 'Azalea'?"

"I'm not really sure. Our big sisters gave us pledge names and
we're supposed to try and figure them out, but I have no idea what
mine is supposed to mean."

I introduced her to Ed, but he was staring blankly into his beer
and didn't seem to hear me.

"Is he alright?" she asked.

"He's fine. He gets this way around beautiful women."

I realized that it sounded cheesy right after I said it, but she smiled as if she appreciated it.

"I have to get back to filling cups," she said. "I'll talk to you later when I get a chance."

Unfortunately the only bathroom in the house available to the general public was way up on the second floor. After an agonizingly long wait on a line monitored by two pledges assigned to make sure that only one person at a time went in to prevent the typical frat-house scenario where ten guys go in at once and piss all over the place, I finally got to relieve myself and felt so good afterwards that on my way back down the basement stairs I became lightheaded and lost my balance. I thumped down the stairs on my ass and at the bottom was swarmed by several Philanthans asking if I was hurt. To show them I wasn't, I jumped to my feet and said "I'm alright!" with both hands in the air, but in the process I lost my balance and fell back down against the wall.

"Hank, oh my God!" Maria said, fighting her way through the crowd. "Are you alright?"

"Yeah, I'm fine," I said as she helped me up. "I do that when I'm sober too."

"I'm cutting you off," she said in a way that I wasn't sure if she was kidding or not.

"You wouldn't cut off an old friend, would you?"

"I could if I want."

"Please don't."

She filled my cup while I attempted to reacquaint myself with balance.

"Can I tell you something?" she asked, handing me the beer.

"Tell me anything, Azalea."

"I used to have the biggest crush on you."

"That's interesting."

"I'm serious, Hank. All I ever did in Señora Garcia's class was sit there and stare at you. I daydreamed so much that I never paid attention, and every time she called on me she had to repeat the question. She hated me."

"This is quite a revelation. I had no idea I was even your type. I was kind of a rock & roll loner back then, and you had that new wave thing going."

"I kind of liked that you were a loner. You didn't seem to care about impressing other people or wearing the same clothes or listening to the same music as everyone else. I liked that because I hated just about everyone else we went to high school with."

"So did I. But still, I never would have guessed."

"Do you remember the note your 'secret admirer' wrote inside your locker door?"

"That was you? I always thought it was Denise Pepperwitz!"

"Nope."

"All along I thought Denise left that note because she was always flirting with me before class. I really didn't want anything to do with her, so I never said anything about it. But how the he hell did you get my locker open?"

"My father taught me how to pick locks when I was a kid. Don't even ask. But yeah, I remember *Denise*, and I don't blame you for not wanting anything to do with her. I hated that girl. Whenever I saw her talking to you I wanted to beat the shit out of her. I had some rage issues in high school."

"You never did look very happy."

"I wasn't."

Ed suddenly emerged from his trance and took a long sip of his beer. He finished what was left in the cup but kept his mouth on the rim, and suddenly it began to fill slowly with chunky green fluid. He was so subtle about it that Maria and I probably wouldn't have noticed had the cup not overflowed and the fluid started splattering on the sparkling white floor tiles. When he was finished he casually placed the cup on the floor and moved over a couple of steps, where he stood trying not to look like it was his although he was the only person anywhere near it.

"You should probably get your friend out of here," Maria said to me just before one of her pledge sisters saw the mess and screamed.

"The nerve of some people!" Ed said, looking down at the cup and shaking his head. "Pogue mahone!"

I told Maria that I would see her later and kissed her on the cheek, which I could tell she hadn't expected. I threw Ed's arm over my shoulder and helped him towards the stairs, both of us stumbling several times before finally making it up to the living room, where the taxidermy sign was sticking out of a wastebasket. Ed insisted that he was alright and left the house under his own power, only to trip and fall down the porch steps and into the moat of flowers.

After helping him up, I assumed that we were going back up to campus and started walking in that direction, but Ed didn't follow.

"Where the hell do you think you're going?" he slurred. "We still got a long way to last call!"

"Ed, you can't even walk! I can barely walk!"

"That's not very Irish of you—we still got a lot of drinking to do! Pogue mahone!"

"I don't know if we can even make it downtown," I said, which is the last thing I remember until Ed was trying to prop me up in front of the bouncers at the Black Oak. After being shot down there, we went down the line and were rejected at every bar until Ed offered the bouncer at Paradise ten bucks to let us in, never mind that he only had two dollars on him. The bouncer agreed, so Ed retrieved my wallet from the back pocket of my pants and gave the guy the rest of the cash I had and helped me inside.

The bar was crowded and hot and Ed leaned me against a wall before disappearing into the crowd. I vaguely remember staring with quadruple vision at the neon Old Milwaukee sign behind the bar until the heat and smoke became too much and I started sinking to the floor. The next thing I remember was being escorted towards the exit by a couple of bouncers and Ed jumping in front of us. He assumed a punch-drunk Muhammad Ali pose and said, "I'm tellin' you motherfuckers that I sting like a butterfly and float like a bee!" They shoved him aside and tossed me out onto Water Street, where I sat waiting for Ed to come out. After several minutes I forgot what I was waiting for, so I got up and stumbled towards Chestnut Street.

It was dark by now and I was under the impression that I had been booted from the bar because it was after last call and the bars were closing. The bank clock up the road tried to tell me it was only a few minutes after six in the evening, but I was oblivious and thought it was a few minutes after four in the morning, long after the buses had stopped running. Walking up Chestnut I thought that each bus that went by was the last one of the night, so I didn't wait for the next one at any of the stops I passed even though they were going by on a regular basis.

Rather than taking the more direct route straight up the hill to campus, I unconsciously followed the circuitous bus route along Chestnut and turned onto West Street. The temperature had dropped below freezing, and though I was not consciously aware of the dangerous predicament I would find myself in if I failed to make it back to Golding Hall, some sort of dormant survival instinct kicked in and pushed me all the way up past Center Street, where the buses turned and headed back across town before turning on East Street and heading up the hill to campus. Here West Street becomes a steep winding road that cuts through the woods that border the west entrance of campus, which is pretty much only used by the tenured professors and administrative big shots who live in this semi-exclusive area since most of the buildings are located on the eastern half of campus and the other entrances are far more convenient.

There were no streetlights and I recall feeling like I was walking on a treadmill in the dark. As I unknowingly neared the campus entrance, I spotted the small orange glow of a fire burning down in the woods to my right. I veered off the sidewalk into the snow and immediately duffed it, tumbling down a steep hill thinking I was going to hit a tree, but the next thing I knew I was standing over the fire rubbing my nearly frostbitten hands together while two guys sitting on a fallen tree several feet away stared into the flame.

I remember saying, "Campus," and without looking at me, one of the guys pointed towards a hill that turned out to be just below Ravine Parkway. After another blackout, I found myself crawling up the embankment of mud and snow and reaching for an exposed tree root near the top that I used to pull myself up the rest of the way to the sidewalk.

Back on level ground I staggered along the desolate stretch of road, sticking my thumb out at the lone car that went by and giving it the finger after it didn't stop. When I reached the library, there were several people emerging from the building who stopped on the steps and stared when they saw me. I snarled and asked them what the fuck they thought they were looking at and then continued on my way. About halfway down Golding Path I tripped and tumbled all the way down the slope, acquiring several more cuts and bruises, none of which I would feel until awaking from my slumber the following evening.

Fortunately the night host wouldn't be on duty for several more hours and I made it inside without a hassle. After finding my way to my bed, I passed out for nearly 24 hours, a long deep death sleep of which my mind completely shut down while my body fought off the massive amount of alcohol I had consumed. When I finally woke up it was dark and a hard rain was pattering the windows. The room was hot and smelled like vomit. During my first few moments of consciousness I didn't know where I was. I was still wearing my mudcaked clothes and boots and it took me a couple of minutes to move my painfully stiff body.

"I was starting to worry about you," Russ said.

"What happened?"

"You don't remember?"

"No."

"Well, I'm not exactly sure what happened before you got here, but you came home cursing like a longshoreman and demanding to know where Ed was and then demanding to speak to Maria—"

"Maria. Fuck. Roscoe's Taxidermy."

"Do you remember talking to her on the phone?"

"What?"

"Before you passed out."

"Last night? What day is it?"

"Wednesday. Last night was Tuesday, St. Patrick's Day. You called the Philanthan house and asked to speak to Azalea, but you were so drunk you couldn't pronounce or spell 'Azalea,' so finally you asked to speak to Maria."

"Fuck. I don't remember any of this."

"You kept telling her that you loved her."

"What?"

"You also said something about your locker and tried to count to ten in Spanish."

"Did I curse at her?"

"No, you were nice to her. You took a swing at Teke, though, for giving you bad directions home from downtown. He tried to explain that he hadn't even been downtown, but you were belligerent."

"Did I hit him?"

"You weren't even close. You knocked over your desk lamp and made this hideous face and puked all over the radiator. And then you passed out."

**6**

On the last Saturday night of our freshman year, Russ and I smoked a bowl of Doobie Brothers weed in our room for the first time. Before then we had only smoked out in the woods, or, if it was really cold, down at the Golding Path lot, but as much as a prick Tommy Austin had been, we figured that with only five days left in the school year he wasn't going to bother us. Even so, we took all the precautions—packing the door with a wet towel, lighting incense, opening the window, turning the fan on, and exhaling into an empty paper towel tube stuffed with Bounce dryer sheets to mask the smell by making the room smell like a fresh load of laundry. We even smoked cigarettes to cover any lingering marijuana smell and discovered that nicotine made us lightheaded, the trigger that would eventually lead Russ, Teke, and I to become full time cigarette smokers during the upcoming summer.

After the pot and nicotine we were feeling pretty good until a knock on the door brought on a wave of paranoia. At first we didn't move, but after the second knock we hid the bowl and bag underneath the dirty laundry in my closet.

"Dude, it's me," a voice said through the door.

"I think it's one of the Doobie Brothers," Russ said. He opened the door and Glen the friendly Doobie was standing in the hallway.

"Dudes, can I come in?" he asked.

"Sure," Russ said and closed the door after he came in.

"Listen, dudes, we got a sheet of acid we're trying to unload and figured you guys would want some. It's pretty mild stuff, nice light trip. We'll give you a deal if you buy some quantity."

Russ and I looked at each other. I could tell he wanted to, but I wasn't so sure that I did. While I was curious about acid after hearing Ed tell his tales of tripping, I was afraid it would make me do something crazy like bite my tongue off or jump out a window.

"Can we get back to you on that?" Russ finally said. "The other guys might want some, but I don't know yet."

"Yeah, that's cool. We'll be around until midnight, but then Denny and I have to split."

We went across the hall and asked Teke if he was interested. Having absorbed all of Ed's tales about how amazing LSD was, he was all for it. Down the hall Ed said that it was about time we scored some acid, but Bruno gave us a firm no.

"The stuff makes you crazy," he said.

"But that's the point," Ed said.

"I'll stick to the weed, thank you very much."

We wound up buying six tabs for ten bucks. Ed bought three tabs because of his high acid tolerance while the rest of us each bought one. Ed popped the tabs in his mouth like they were candy and laughed as Russ, Teke, and I inspected the little white squares closely. The tabs were about quarter inch in length and were stiff like they had been wet at one point and dried, and each had a mysterious blue telephone receiver printed on them. I asked Ed if the phone was an indicator of what kind of acid it was or if the acid was actually in the ink of the symbol, but he said that the manufacturers usually just printed miscellaneous symbols so they could keep track of what batch it was and that the acid itself not visible.

"Are you sure you want to go through with this?" I asked Russ and Teke.

"You'd better," Ed said, sticking out his tongue with the three tabs on it.

"Well then, here goes nothing," Russ said. He popped his tab and Teke did the same. I continued to hesitate until the three of them mockingly stuck their tabbed tongues out at me, so I finally popped mine. It had no taste and I didn't hear or feel the little hiss I thought I would when acid hit saliva, but I did suddenly become nervous about stepping over the line. Now there was no turning back. During the next eight hours I was going to have to endure whatever was going to happen until the acid wore off, and then I was going to have to live with the synaptic consequences for the rest of my life.

"Just remember," Ed said like a mentor, "whatever crazy shit seems to be happening is really happening behind your eyes, not in front of them."

"How is that different than usual?" Russ asked.

"You tend to forget that when you're on acid."

Ed said we should keep the tabs on our tongues for half an hour before swallowing them and that it would be an hour or so before we felt anything. In the meantime we went down to the TV lounge and watched *Saturday Night Live* for a while. About 45 minutes later the back of my head became numb and my jaw felt like it was locking up.

"I'm beginning to think that the people on TV are talking directly to me," I said to the other guys. A couple of girls sitting on the couch in front of us turned around and gave me a look. I suddenly became paranoid that the ten or so other people in the room besides us knew that we were tripping and I suggested that we get out of there. The other guys didn't want to go back upstairs, and I wasn't too keen on the idea on going out in the woods in the dark because I usually bugged out after smoking weed and figured that on acid it would be far worse, so we decided to take a bus ride downtown to watch the drunks on Water Street before we started peaking. Ed said the peak usually started two or three hours into the trip and lasted two to three hours before the crash.

The bus stop was crowded with an unusually late Saturday night crowd, many of whom had been studying for finals and needed to let off some steam. We waited at the back fringe of the crowd and I became paranoid whenever someone looked in our direction, yet it was difficult to look away even when someone was staring at us. The random conversations going on around us started drowning my own thoughts in a cesspool of confusion. The longer we waited, the less I wanted to go, but the other guys seemed calm and I didn't want them to think I was on the verge of losing it, so I kept my mouth shut.

When the buses pulled up we were among the last to get on and had to stand in the aisle holding on for our lives. It occurred to me that we were the only ones *on the bus* who knew what was *really happening*, that we were trapped in a large vehicle sailing through the universal void towards our inevitable doom. While the other passengers were casually talking and laughing like everything was fine, I was on the verge of a serious panic attack. The other guys looked like they knew what was happening, but their cool courage in the face of peril helped me keep it together just long enough to make it downtown.

Since we had been standing between the front and back doors, we were amongst the last to get off. I waited impatiently for the naïve fools surrounding us to get off before the bus pulled away and imploded into the forever of the past. With each passing moment the tension was building towards a climax that would release me from the precarious grip I had on reality.

We got off just in time before the doors closed and the bus pulled away. The level asphalt under my feet steadied my sea-legs, and the dazzling lights on Water Street brought me down from the ledge. The crowd noise was comforting as long as individual conversations remained indistinguishable. We were disconnected from everything around us as if watching live entertainment being performed solely for our benefit. Every weekend since getting our licenses chalked we had been a part of the scene in front of us, but now it seemed so distant and unfamiliar that we were content to observe rather than participate.

The top of the parking garage served as our balcony for the stage below. We watched with our forearms leaning against the wall and occasionally pointed out something of interest to one another. Nobody seemed to notice us. We had been up there for about twenty minutes when right below us a couple of guys started throwing punches at one another. One of them was wearing Lambda Beta letters, the local fraternity of brutes that had once been national but had had so many infractions over the years with the IFC (Intra-Fraternity Council) that they lost their affiliation and had to drop a letter, while the other guy was from Delta Zeta Nu, a bunch of harmless hip-hop pretty boys who for whatever reason Lambda Beta had a serious problem with. A circle quickly formed around the combatants and frat guys started streaming out of the bars until Water Street was clogged. A couple of skirmishes on the outskirts broke out, but everyone taking swings was too drunk to land a good punch, and a couple of minutes later the cops pulled up. The officers fought their way through the crowd yelling at people to get out of their way while we became mesmerized by the flashing red and blue lights on top of the cruisers. When they got to the nucleus they arrested the two guys who started the fight and the crowd headed back to the bars. Suddenly Water Street was calm, but several bike cops stayed behind to make sure there wasn't any further trouble. One of the cops looked up at us and stared for a few moment. Russ, Teke, and I became noticeably paranoid.

"Relax," Ed said. "We're not doing anything wrong. Hell, we're not even drunk."

"I still think we should go back," I said.

"I do too," Russ said. "The show's over down here and I don't want to be in a public place when we start peaking."

By the time we were back on the bus I was really fucked up. This crowd was smaller but rowdier than the previous one, everyone talking loudly and some singing while we stood in the aisle with our sweaty palms gripping the overhead handrails trying not to topple over. My teeth were clenched so tight I wasn't sure if I could open my mouth until I made eye contact with a girl who was staring at me. She looked familiar, but I didn't recognize her.

"Hey!" she said. "You're the guys who tried to burn my dorm

down!"

"Hi there," I said. "How are you?"

"Oh my God! Can I tell you that they're still trying to find you guys? They bring it up every week at the R.A. meeting!"

"Well, you know. Just trying to liven things up a little bit."

"Don't worry, I didn't say anything. They have no idea who you guys are."

"That's good," I said.

"Where did you guys go tonight?"

"Downtown. Bars."

"What bars?"

"What?"

"What bars did you guys go to?"

"I don't know."

"You don't know?"

"I don't even know where I am now!"

At first she laughed, but when she finally noticed how fucked up I was she looked away and spent the rest of the ride staring out the window. Meanwhile in front of me Teke was standing underneath one of the emergency hatches on the ceiling that the driver had opened a crack to get some air circulating in the stuffy bus and was reaching up with his long bony arms to take hold of the edges. At first I thought he was just trying to keep his balance, but then he started pulling himself upwards. When the drunken crowd noticed what he was doing they started cheering him on while I yelled at him to get down, but he paid no attention. When it became clear that he might actually get his Popsicle stick body through the small crack of space and onto the roof, I gave his dangling legs a bear hug and with all my weight pulled him down. Both of us crashed hard to the floor and the crowd started booing and throwing stuff at us until the bus driver jammed on the brakes and said that he wouldn't go any farther until every single piece of trash was picked up. After a ten minute delay he was finally satisfied and continued up towards campus. The drunks were considerably more subdued than before and stared at us for the rest of the ride while we pretended not to notice.

At the bus stop up on campus several of our fellow passengers laughed and jeered at us. One girl repeatedly asked what we were on, which made my paranoia ascend to a whole new level. I overheard another girl say that the one who had tried to climb out of the bus was kind of cute, and her friend ridiculed her for being attracted to a psychopath. My hearing had become so acute that other people's voices sounded like they were actually emitting from inside my own head.

The peak had begun. I was now incapable of communicating with anyone who wasn't as fucked up as I was. As we passed through the Golding Hall lobby I tried not to make eye contact with anyone, particularly the night host, who gave us a look that made me very paranoid as we went by. The only thing that kept me going was that the other guys seemed perfectly calm, especially Russ, who hadn't said a word in the past hour and had hardly seemed to notice Teke trying to climb out of the bus even though he had been standing right in front of him.

Russ and I went back to our room while Ed and Teke went into the bathroom. I wanted to ride out the peak by listening to some music, but while I was looking at my CD's, Russ very calmly announced that the door was breathing.

"What's that?" I said, hardly paying attention.

"The door is breathing," he repeated, staring intensely at the door.

"That's fucked up, man."

"No. Really. The door is breathing. Look."

To my surprise the door did actually appear to be breathing, repeatedly bending inwards and returning to its original position. At first it seemed rather innocent and humorous, but after a while I wasn't sure if I should appreciate it as my first psychedelic hallucination or take it as a sign that we were on the verge of losing our minds.

"I don't know if it's more fucked up that the door is breathing or that we're having the same hallucination," I said.

"I'm getting out of here," Russ said. He closed his eyes and held his breath like he was about to jump off the high diving board and yanked the door open. He ran next door to the bathroom while I stayed behind to see if the door breathed while it was open. It didn't. I closed it and it started breathing again, so I went out into the hall to see if it breathed from the outside, but from there it was just a plain old dead door.

I was distracted when I heard yelling in the bathroom. I ran in and found Teke sitting on the windowsill with his legs on the outside looking down at Ed fifteen feet below.

"Come on, you pussy," Ed said. "Jump! It's nothing!"

"Well, ah, alright," Teke said, but didn't move.

"What the fuck are you doing?" I asked him.

"Jumping out the window."

"Why?"

"Ed says it will enhance the trip."

"First you try to climb out of a moving bus, and now you're going to jump out the bathroom window?"

"He won't do it," Russ said.

I had always heard that one of the things you're not supposed to do when trying to talk down a potential jumper is challenge him.

Not that Teke was attempting suicide, but he had a head full of acid and a frail body that would snap like a twig if he landed the wrong way. Without warning he pushed himself off the ledge. Russ and I watched him fall and it seemed like it was happening in slow motion. There was nothing artistic or athletic about his descent, gravity simply did it's job. Fifteen feet below he hit the ground with a thud, landing in a crouch and doing an awkward tuck and roll before winding up flat on his back. He repeatedly groaned, "Ow, ow, ow," while Ed stood over him and said, "Get up, you fucking hick."

"Are you alright down there?" I asked.

"Well, ah, kind of, but not really," Teke answered.

"Is anything broken?"

"No, I don't think so. But it hurts like hell."

"What hurts?"

"Well, ah, I'm not really sure."

Ten minutes later he finally got up and came back upstairs with Ed. The four of us went into Ed and Bruno's room and lined up next to Bruno's bed like we were visiting a coma patient while he snored like a beast. It was such a hideous noise that after a couple of minutes I started getting paranoid again.

"How do you sleep at night?" Russ whispered to Ed.

"It took a couple of weeks to get used to, but he got used to me waking up screaming in the middle of the night, so I guess anything is possible. I don't think anyone else would be able to live with either of us."

A little while later we took a walk to the other side of the building, which was a nerve-wracking journey through a parallel universe. As we were approaching the lobby on our way back, Ed suddenly halted us. Ten yards ahead and practically busting out of a white T-shirt several sizes too small with the words "Tau Tau Tau" written diagonally in magic marker across the front stood the Big Guy from Eliot's house. His head was bouncing around like a bobblehead doll while the rest of his mammoth body remained perfectly still. He looked even bigger than we remembered, his head nearly reaching the ceiling and his body looking like it had put on a couple of hundred more pounds.

"It looks like he ate Eliot for lunch," I said quietly.

"It looks like he ate *Bruno* for lunch," Ed said. "But what the fuck is he doing here? He doesn't even live on campus."

"I don't think he knows where he is."

We approached cautiously. He didn't notice us until we were a few feet away.

"How's it going," Ed said.

"You guys are dosing," he said with a twisted smile.

"So are you," Ed said.

"Were you guys at the Acid Meet?"

"What's the Acid Meet?"

"It's like the Bong Olympics, except everyone takes acid. I took ten hits."

"Jeez," Ed said. "That would probably kill any one of us."

"What?" he said, suddenly panicked. He looked at Ed and then at the rest of us like a cornered animal.

"Nothing," Ed said, slowly backing away towards the staircase on our side of the building. When we reached a safe distance, the Big Guy's head started bouncing around again and we ran up the stairs.

Safely back in our room with the door locked, Russ said, "Think about it. The only reason that even happened is because we're on acid. He could be in that same exact spot at that exact same time doing the exact same thing every night, but we never would have known if we didn't take the acid. Can you imagine all the shit we've already missed out on? There's probably things happening at this very moment that would blow our minds! We would have never seen the Big Guy all fucked up like that if we had gone through our normal routines! Did you see him reading our minds? He knew exactly what every one of us was thinking!"

"I don't think he even knew what he was thinking," I said.

"That's just it! Our collective thought was inside his head and he was trying to make sense of it! That's why he was looking around like that!"

"Easy, killer," Ed said. "If you're not careful you're gonna blow your mind."

"Think about it," Russ continued as if he hadn't heard Ed. "Wouldn't you be confused if his thoughts were going through your head?"

"Oh definitely. Who knows what's going on in that guy's head even when he's not on acid."

"Exactly. Now he had all of our psychedelic thoughts going through his head all at once that he was trying to interpret simultaneously! I think I saw smoke coming out of his ears!"

"I think he was just hungry."

"But didn't you see the look on his face? It was the look that all of us had on our faces!"

"I think smoke is starting to come out of *your* ears," Ed said to Russ.

"I can't make it stop!" Russ said, and then he stopped talking.

In fact no one said anything for a while. We stared out the window, the sky no longer black but a deep indigo that became a shade lighter with each blink. Eventually Ed, Teke, and I came out of our meditations and started looking at each other on the verge of laughing while Russ continued to stare.

"Well, ah, is everyone alright?" Teke asked. "Russ?"

He didn't answer. We calmly said his name repeatedly trying not to spook him, but he was catatonic.

"I think that last train of thought derailed him," Ed said. "The best thing we can do for him right now is leave him alone and let him ride it out on his own. In the meantime, I suggest we go up to the fields and watch the sunrise."

"I don't like leaving him here alone like this," I said.

"Well, ah, me neither," Teke said.

"All he's going to do is sit there and stare out the window," Ed said. "Staying here with him isn't going to do him any good. In fact, it might even make it worse."

Teke asked Russ if he wanted to go up to the fields but got no response. We waited a couple of more minutes until we decided that Ed was probably right. We told Russ that we would be back in a little while and headed out.

We took the trail through the wooded area between the Hunt Union and East Street. The daylight and fresh morning air burned off the fear and paranoia that had been lingering from the darkness, which looking back on now seemed unfounded and silly. Everything around us looked crisp and clear as if we were seeing it all for the first time. Several deer munching on their breakfast stopped eating and looked at us like they knew what was going on in our minds. It felt like we had become one with nature, that we were actually a part of it as opposed to simply inhabiting and destroying it.

Up on the third tier of fields we sat Indian-style and waited. When the first rays of the sun appeared over the eastern hilltops I felt like I had been reborn, except this time I was fully conscious of it. All the events of my life seemed to have led me to that very moment and everything in the universe became perfectly clear. For the first time in my life I understood what it meant to be alive, and I still had an entire lifetime ahead of me to appreciate it.

After the sun had cleared the hills we headed towards the woods behind the tennis bubble. This section of campus was new to us, and as we approached the property line we heard a stream running somewhere ahead that we couldn't see until we reached the edge of a cliff. A muddy path led down to a rust-iron footbridge that spanned only halfway across the stream about a hundred feet below. It looked like it would have been a pretty nice bridge had it been completed, but it appeared as if the construction was suddenly abandoned one day many years earlier and hadn't been touched since.

The path was slick and we had to hold on to the tree roots jutting out of the growth beside the path on our way down. Even with this assistance, however, each of us slipped several times before reaching the stream. Since there was nothing on the other side and no other trails in the area, it was unclear as to what the original purpose of the bridge was supposed to be. We went out to the end of it where the running water below us drowned out all other noise in the woods. Rays of sunlight beamed through the tiny spaces between the leaves above that blocked out most of the sky.

"This is very Zen," Ed said.

"Russ would have appreciated this."

Later we separated and did some exploring along the bank. About a hundred feet from the bridge I stepped across several flat stones that were level with the water's surface to the middle of the stream. With my arms spread like wings I faced the current as it rushed through me like life itself. Time halted to show me what I had been missing, and a surge of euphoria passed through my soul. When it was over I felt like a hollow log waiting in vain for it to come back. Little did I realize at the time that this was one of those once-in-a-lifetime highs that you spend the rest of your drug-taking days chasing but never catch.

Ed meanwhile had been walking along the bank but stopped when he saw me and assumed an expression of horror. At first I thought he was horsing around, but after he dropped to his knees and started crossing himself, I became concerned.

"Are you alright?" I called over, but he remained on his knees staring at me with mouth agape.

"Ed, don't look at me like that. You're scaring me."

I asked him several more times if he was alright, but he didn't answer. I stepped back over the stones to the bank and when I got there he was still on his knees. I touched him on the shoulder and he shuddered violently.

"Are you alright?" I asked him.

"I don't know. You scared the shit out of me."

"How?"

"For a second I thought you were Jesus Christ with a blue face walking on water."

"Well, ah, you were in Catholic school too long, Cafferty," Teke said as he approached.

"My face was blue?"

"Yeah. It still is a little bit, but when you spread your arms out, it was glowing. That was the most fucked up thing I've ever seen in my life."

"Glad I could be a part of it," I said.

Back at Golding Hall Russ had come out of his coma and greeted us like saviors.

"When I came out of it and you guys weren't here, I almost freaked out," he said rapidly. "I don't really remember what was going on in my head while I was gone, but I know it was some pretty fucked up shit. Now it's like a dream that I can't quite remember. All I know is that when I came out of it, I thought I was dead and I was afraid to open the door because of what might be on the other side."

"Well, ah, damn," Teke said. "I wish I was having a trip like that."

"I don't," I said.

"It's too fucked up," Russ said.

"I think we should get you out of the room for a while," Ed said. "Let's walk downtown. Some fresh air will do you good, and it's gorgeous outside."

On our way down Golding Path it seemed hard to believe that nine months had already passed since that first night we came this way down to Fred's house. At the time we were all still strangers, but now we knew each other so well that we remembered it as if we had already known each other. The time since had gone so fast that it felt like the morning after that very first night, and in the ignorant bliss of our youth, it felt like there was so much more ahead of us that it didn't matter how fast it was going.

Fred's front lawn was littered with plastic cups, tipped over lawn chairs, and a couple of bras, a scene similarly repeated in several front yards along with the occasional splotch of dried vomit on the sidewalk. It was the first time any of us had been up at that hour on a Sunday morning to see the aftermath of a Saturday night in Oneonta, especially at the end of the school year when the seniors were getting their last licks.

"Well, ah, it must be awesome to be a senior in this place," Teke said.

"I don't know," I said. "Sure, you'd party like crazy, but by then it'll all be over, and then what? Going back home to find a job and working the rest of your life? It's too depressing to even think about. Who would ever want to leave this place?"

By the time we got to Main Street, Russ and Teke were crashing and decided to begin their walk back up to campus since it was only seven and the buses didn't start running until nine on Sundays. I was still flying high and didn't want it to end, and Ed was still going strong too, so we took a seat on one of the sidewalk benches and watched the old people going about their business. There were so many of them that it seemed as if they planned it this way knowing that there wouldn't be any college students around at this hour on a Sunday morning. Some gave us inquiring glances while others tried not to look. After sitting there a while I started getting paranoid and suggested that we move on.

We walked up Chestnut Street and stopped in front of the giant cathedral next to the P&C supermarket. It was the town's architectural marvel, a huge structure made of carved stone and stained glass with a bell tower on the roof that could be heard every hour on the hour all the way up to campus. I wanted to see what the inside looked like, but Ed was still a little spooked from the Jesus incident back at the stream, not to mention the sacrilege of a brainwashed Catholic boy strolling into the house of the Lord with a head full of acid. I, on the other hand, not being much of a religious fellow after having been halfheartedly brought up a Lutheran in the Catholic and Jewish world of Long Island, had no concerns regarding the spiritual implications of taking a peek.

"Look," I said, pointing to the sign on the front lawn that said *ALL ARE WELCOME*.

"It's still not right," he said.

"What could happen? You're Catholic. This is a Presbyterian church."

"That's true," he said.

The front doors were locked, so we followed an asphalt path around back that led to the entrance of the Sunday school wing. This door was unlocked, and once inside we found ourselves in a hallway decorated with Crayola drawings and construction paper montages depicting scenes from the Bible, several of which were rather gory. The lights were on, but the classrooms were empty. Every so often we heard a metal door close in a distant part of the building that scared the shit out of Ed and normally would have scared the shit out of me, except I was determined to find out once and for all if God really did exist, not to mention get back at Ed for all the times we were smoking out in the woods at night and I wanted to turn back because I was bugging out but he kept leading us deeper and deeper into the darkness, so I pressed on.

After several twists and turns, the corridor eventually led us to the clergyman's entrance at the front of the main cathedral. I pulled the door and went in, and, after hesitating, Ed said, "I'm going to hell anyway" and followed.

We were greeted by a larger-than-life model of the Crucifix suspended by wires from the ceiling that probably looked impressive from the back of the church, but up close looked like a cheap prop from the local theater group. There were fresh flowers and lit candles all over the place, and both walls were adorned with enormous stained glass windows depicting colorful religious figures that on the east side were brightly illuminated by the morning sun. Ed wandered over to look at the windows and didn't notice me step up to the podium and switch on the microphone.

"Ed, this is God!" I boomed. He immediately dropped to his knees and covered his head. After recovering from the shock, he got up and stormed the altar.

"Careful, you're in God's house," I said, but he grabbed my collar and shoved me against the wall.

"I ought to knock your fucking teeth out for that!"

"Take it easy, I was only kidding! I didn't know you were gonna freak out!"

"If you spent twelve years of your life being tortured by nuns with rulers, you would freak out too!"

He let go and headed down the aisle towards the back of the church. In the lobby he signed the guest register and left through the main doors that we had to tried to get in earlier that were apparently only locked from the outside.

I was still at the podium.

"You're not here," I said into the mike. "You have a beautiful house, but You don't even live here."

Suddenly a heavy door just outside the clergyman's entrance slammed shut. I took off down the aisle expecting that at any moment a man of the cloth would start yelling and threatening to call the cops, but by the time I reached the last row of pews and it hadn't happened, I looked over my shoulder and no one was there. Out in the lobby I signed the register under Ed's entry and found him outside sitting on the front steps watching the cars go by on Chestnut Street.

The crash came swiftly and hit hard. As exhausted as I was, by the time my head finally hit the pillow, my mind continued to race and I couldn't fall asleep, which Ed attributed to the acid being loaded with speed. After a while the film of sweaty grime coating my body became unbearable and I jumped in the shower before spending a painful half hour on the toilet and another hour lying in bed before the acid finally let go and allowed me to drift off to sleep. When I woke up later that afternoon I felt fine, but something was different.

II

# 1

After spending the summer temping at the shipping department of a major Japanese camera company's U.S. distribution center and having the freedom I had become accustomed to in Oneonta squashed under the roof of my parents' home, all I could think about was going back. Freshman year had been the greatest year of my life, but sophomore year promised to be even better.

For one thing, the six of us signed up to live in a three bedroom suite in Matteson Hall, which meant no more Tommy Austin and Golding Hall. And now that we knew our way around, now that we had reliable ID to get into the bars, and now that we had a steady drug connection in the Doobie Brothers, we would be living on Easy Street.

I thought that once we got up there we would pick up right where we left off. When I stepped into our new suite for the first time, however, I knew right away that this wasn't going to happen. Something had changed. It wasn't so much the new living arrangements, it was something more subtle. Over the first couple of weeks I began to realize what it was. The anticipation was gone. When we were freshmen, everything was new and we didn't know what was going to happen next. This year we did. Everything we did we had done before. Going to a keg party or a bar or smoking a bowl was now old hat, and Oneonta wasn't big enough to be continually experiencing new things. In one year we had pretty much covered all the bases, and our lives began to settle into routine.

Regardless of our youth wafting away like pot smoke out an open window, we had it pretty good in our new home. The suite kept us isolated in our own little world, which was fine, though it would have been a lot better if there were chicks in it with us. In the far interior of the suite there were three double bedrooms, the six of us retaining our original roommates, and in the middle there was a common room with a connecting hallway that led to the main door. Perhaps the best feature of living in a suite, however, was that we not only had our own bathroom, but once a week an old lady named Helga showed up and cleaned it for us. She was a grumpy old hag who always had a cigarette dangling from her lips and was constantly muttering under her breath, but she did nice work. Also, as an incentive for students to live on campus, the school had wired the dorms with free basic cable over the summer. Since my old TV was busted and Bruno's little black & white set was inadequate, we found a place where we were able to rent a brand new 23 inch set with built-in VCR for $120 for the entire year. We bought an old flower-print couch from the Salvation Army for $50 and decorated the common room with psychedelic wall coverings and pictures of naked women torn out of *Playboy* and *Penthouse*. Teke had a funky old sheet with a wavy yellow and orange pattern that we used as a curtain to cover the hallway entrance. After our decorating was finished the place truly felt like ours, a feeling we never had living under the tyranny of Tommy Austin's Golding Hall. In fact, we didn't even know where our R.A. lived for the first couple of months. The building was so sprawling and asymmetrical that it took me a couple of weeks before I was able to find our room from the lobby without getting lost in the maze of corridors, of which the walls were painted like the Partridge Family bus. The exterior of the building was some architect's way-off vision of the future from 25 years earlier that made it look like a federal penitentiary.

Now that we had the luxury of smoking weed in our room without worry, gone were the days of going out in the woods to smoke a bowl. With the common room and hallway entrance buffering our bedrooms from the main corridor, we usually didn't even bother toweling the door cracks when we smoked. Over the summer Russ, Teke, and I had become full-time cigarette smokers, so the room Russ and I wound up with became the designated smoking room since Bruno and Ed didn't want people smoking butts in their room and Winston didn't want anyone smoking pot in his. Every night we gathered in our room to smoke and play cards for one-hitters, and while it was nice not having to go on an adventure in the woods just to smoke a bowl, it made us lazy.

Our only concern was that the Doobie Brothers were nowhere to be found. Fortunately Ed brought up an ounce from home that held us in check for the first several days, but after that was gone, we were back to square one. Then, after I had just returned to the suite from my first day of classes, there was a knock on the door. I was the only one home at the time so I answered it and a 6'6" Delta Zeta Nu brother wearing Tommy Hilfiger urbanwear and several gold chains around his neck stuffed a dime bag into my shirt pocket.

"Welcome to the building, neighbor," he said with a gleaming smile.

At the time I didn't know who he was, but it didn't take me long to realize that Brooklyn Valentino was the biggest drug dealer on campus. He had several guys on his payroll and was paranoid that the DEA, FBI, and CIA were watching him. Despite his kingpin status, however, he seemed like a rather down to earth guy.

"Normally I only deal with fraternity representatives," he explained, "but I got a tip that I could get some steady business from you guys, so I'm willing to make an exception. I can get you guys anything you need."

"How did you hear about us?" I asked.

"I can't reveal my sources. Let's just say I hear things."

"You're not a cop, are you?"

"Hell no!" he said and laughed loudly. "Would a cop give you unsolicited drugs?"

"Probably not," I said.

"Like I said, I can get you guys anything you need. The only thing I ask is that I deal with only one of you, and since you answered the door—you da man! Nothing against your crew, I just don't want six different guys showing up at all hours, know what I'm sayin'? But anything you need, I'm right upstairs in 421."

While it was convenient having a dealer who was always plentiful in supply living right upstairs, it quickly became a hassle because the other guys were constantly asking me to run up there to pick up a nickel of hash or a dime of weed for themselves in addition to the communal eighths and quarter-ounces we bought for our nightly sessions. After a while it got so bad that I had to limit my trips upstairs to once a day, but even then someone was always asking me to make an exception "just this once." I always complied, but it really started to annoy me that they made no effort whatsoever to coordinate their purchases and took my exceptions for granted. As much as I was tempted, I knew that the moment I decided to enforce the rule, all the exceptions would be forgotten and the rejection is what would be remembered.

A couple of weeks later I had another surprise visitor. It was during the four day Rosh Hashanah weekend when most of the students on campus go home even though the dorms remain open. This year Russ, Bruno, and I stayed and spent the first three days locked in the suite smoking weed without pause out of contraptions that Russ had devised out of soda bottles, copper plumbing pipes, beer funnels, and coffee cans. Then late on Saturday night there was a knock on the door. Usually we didn't answer the door when we smoked, but things had gotten so stale by then I jumped up and answered it without even considering who it could be. When I opened the door Maria Viola was standing there wearing a makeshift toga and a drunken smile. I hadn't seen her since St. Patrick's Day six months earlier, and after my performance at the Philanthan house that day and the drunken phone call I made afterwards that I still couldn't remember, I didn't think she wanted to talk to me again, so I had pretty much forgotten about her.

"I saw your name on your mailbox down in the lobby the other day and had been meaning to stop by," she said.

"I didn't even know you were living here," I said. "Nice toga."

"Thanks. We had a toga party down at the house with Phi Ep."

"Would you like to come in?"

"I can't stay because we're having a little after-hours party up in our suite, which is actually why I'm here now. There's still some leftover punch we brought home from the party if you and your roommates are interested."

We were sluggish and burnt out, not exactly prime condition for socializing, but we badly needed to get out of the room for a while, and it wasn't every day that we had the opportunity to party with drunk sorority girls in togas.

Maria lived upstairs on the other side of the building with five of her sorority sisters, all of whom were on the waiting list to live down at the Philanthan house. When we got there, several toga-clad people were on their way out and we were left alone in the common room with Maria and one of her suitemates, who was snoring on one of the couches unaware that one of her breasts was hanging out of her toga with nipple in full view. Of course we couldn't help but gawk, yet as blatant as six bloodshot eyes staring at the same exact spot was, Maria didn't notice what we were looking at. She ladled the last of the punch into paper cups for us and invited me to sit next to her on the vacant couch. Russ and Bruno seated themselves on desk chairs.

"Are you guys high?" Maria asked.

"Very much so," Bruno said.

"You guys are funny when you're high."

Maria's roommate Kathy, a short, chubby Italian girl with guttural voice and heavy Long Island accent, emerged from one of the bedrooms as if on cue and went right into an excruciatingly embarrassing rendition of Joe Pesci's "funny guy" routine from *Goodfellas*.

"Funny? You think I'm funny? What the fuck is it about me that makes me so funny?" When the scene was over she ran back into her room and puked in the wastepaper basket, violently masculine hurls that made us shudder with each turn. She stopped momentarily to slam the door shut and it was quiet for a moment before she started puking again.

"I'm so sorry about that," Maria said.

"That's alright," I said. "We do it all the time."

Maria playfully kicked my leg with her bare foot. I kicked her back with my boot a little harder than I had intended and she said 'ouch.' Russ and Bruno were preoccupied with the nipple and didn't notice us.

Suddenly the bedroom door flew open again and Kathy stumbled out, her face red and her tight curly hair kinky and wild. Her eyes landed right on the nipple and she yelled, "Oh my God! Her breast is showing!" She ran over and shook the girl until she started moaning. When the girl's eyes came into focus and she saw Kathy's wild face, she started laughing and then looked over at us.

"Hey, it's *those* guys," she said, pointing weakly. "*Those* guys are in our room! Hi, burnout guys!"

"Hello," Bruno said with a deep formal voice.

"Let's get you to bed," Kathy said while trying to fix the breast girl's toga.

"How come you guys weren't at our party?" the breast girl asked.

"We weren't invited," Russ said.

Kathy pulled the girl to her feet and helped her to the bedroom at the other end of the suite. Before going inside, the breast girl turned and waved, saying, "Bye, you guys! Smoke a fatty for me!" Kathy pushed her into the room and slammed the door.

"I think I'm going to head back," Bruno said, stretching his arms above his head.

"Me too," Russ said.

The two of them got up and said good night. I told them I would be down in a couple of minutes.

"How did that girl know who we were?" I asked Maria after the other guys were gone.

"Everybody knows who you guys are," she said.

"What do you mean *everybody knows who we are*?"

"You guys are campus celebrities."

"*Us?*"

"Sure. You guys are always hanging out in a pack—out in the quad smoking cigarettes, in the dining hall, downtown at the bars. Some people think you guys are in some secret fraternity."

"That's fucked up. I didn't think anyone knew who we were."

"Everybody knows."

While I was mulling over this revelation, Maria started running her bare foot up and down the side of my leg. I was still really stoned and started to get paranoid. She ran her fingers through my hair and had a look on her face that I had never seen yet immediately recognized, the look of a girl who truly wanted me. Unfortunately I was pitted against Maria Viola's 9th grade fantasy version of Henry Gardner, a perception that the Henry Gardner sitting next to her now could never possibly live up to.

"I think I'm going to get going too," I said, letting out a fake yawn and stretching.

"You can stay," Maria said.

"I think I'm going to hit the sack soon," I said, realizing how lame it sounded but too burnt to come up with anything better. "I'm pretty beat."

"You can stay up here with me if you want."

"I don't know if that's such a good idea."

"Why not?"

"You seem pretty drunk."

"I am pretty drunk," she said. She looked away suddenly embarrassed. "And now I feel like a total idiot."

"No, don't say that. What I meant is that I'm really stoned, and you're really drunk. I just don't think it would be a good idea right now."

"You're right."

"We should talk about this."

"Alright, let's talk."

"When we're sober."

"Yeah," she said as if she thought I didn't mean it.

"I'm serious," I said.

"Why can't we talk right now? We can always talk when we're sober too."

"I don't have the words right now. My mind is fried."

I got up and she followed me to the door. "I know I'm making a mistake letting you go. I'm afraid you won't come back."

"I'll be back."

"When?"

"Soon."

"How soon?"

"I don't know."

"Tomorrow?"

"Maybe."

She pressed her body against mine and I became aroused. She kissed me and I kissed her back, a long, passionate kiss that was on the verge of becoming something more before I pulled away.

"I wish I would have known you in high school," I said.

"You know me now."

I couldn't stop thinking about what had happened with Maria, so a few days later I made a surprise visit to her room. She and her roommate Kathy were sitting on their beds cutting construction paper into the shapes of leaves. Kathy said "Hey, sexy" when I came in, and seeing her there made me consider coming up with an excuse to make it look like I had only dropped by for a minute until she got up and said she was going to the dining hall.

"What are you working on?" I asked Maria after Kathy was gone.

"We're having a mixer on Friday night with Rho Sig with a 'changing of the season' theme. Kathy and I were put in charge of decorations."

"Lucky you."

"Yeah, really. I don't even want to go to the stupid thing."

"Can I help?"

"Actually, I think I've had enough of this for one day, but thanks anyway. So what brings you by these parts?"

"Just came for a visit, say hello, maybe hang out for a while if you're not busy."

"No, not at all. Come, sit down."

She cleared a space on the bed and dumped some of the arts & crafts supplies on her desk. I took off my shoes and we both sat Indian-style on the bed facing each other.

"I'm sorry I ran out on you the other night the way I did," I said. "I was a little fucked up."

"That's alright. I was pretty fucked up too. I felt like an idiot after you were gone."

"There was no reason to feel way."

She looked down and let out a little laugh. I wanted to continue the conversation but was under the impression that she didn't. I started looking around the room for something to comment on.

"Do you mind if I put some music on?" she asked.

"No, not at all."

"Do you like Enya?"

"I don't know."

"It's very mellow. I'm sure you'll appreciate that."

"I'm not stoned."

"Relax, I'm only kidding. You're so defensive."

I picked up one of the paper leaves she had cut out and inspected it. "I used to love arts & crafts in kindergarten."

"You don't seem like the arts & crafts type."

"I used to love to draw. I used to be kind of wild when I was a little kid and my kindergarten teacher learned that the best way to get me to behave was to give me some paper and crayons."

"What did you draw?"

"Baseball stadiums, mostly. And football."

"How exciting."

"Well, I was too young to appreciate fine art like I do now."

"Would you like to color? Kathy's got a box of Crayolas. 64 colors."

"I never could resist a box of 64 colors."

She grabbed the crayons, paper, and some folders to lean on from Kathy's desk. I started drawing an LSD-inspired piece I titled *Sunrise at the Fields* while Maria drew a garden of colorful flowers. Enya's soothing "Caribbean Blue" made the room feel like a sanctuary from the smoky haze and hardened candle wax of my own bedroom. Though I hadn't smoked all day, I started feeling a little high.

We worked on our drawings in quiet comfort until we were interrupted by an uncertain knock on the door. Maria said 'come in' and the door slowly opened. The toga-breast girl cautiously stuck her head in as if worried that she was disturbing us and said that there was someone there to see me.

"Me?" I asked incredulously. I hadn't told anyone where I was going and didn't think anyone would even know where to look for me.

Bruno and Teke were waiting out in the common room. I knew exactly why they were there and it pissed me off that they would disturb me at Maria's room of all places, but I kept my cool. Maria knew that I smoked weed, but I didn't want her to think that I was a drug runner for my roommates, which lately was exactly what I had felt like.

"I'll be back down in a few minutes," I said in a way meant for them to know that I was annoyed. They left without saying anything.

Knowing that the other guys were waiting for me, I wouldn't have been able to stay there and enjoy myself, so I told Maria that I had to go. She said nothing and I became worried that she might think I would rather be downstairs smoking dope with my roommates than hanging out with her.

"Well, thanks for stopping by," she finally said. "I hope I didn't bore you."

"No, not at all. I like coloring."

"Are you going to visit me again?"

"Definitely."

She walked me to the door. I didn't know if I should kiss her, and after an uncomfortable moment, I chickened out and said, "See you later."

As pissed as I was when I first saw Bruno and Teke standing in Maria's common room, I realized on my way back to the suite that it wasn't their fault. They didn't know. The two of them showing up there was merely an indication that unless I completely alienated myself from my friends and devoted myself to live in Maria's sorority sister world, it would never work between us. Days earlier I couldn't have even imagined this scenario and certainly would have never considered stepping outside the blissful world my friends and I had created for myself, but now the thought of doing so had entered my mind and I wasn't trying to make it leave.

## 2

On Halloween Teke, Ed, and I spent the better part of the day waiting impatiently for Brooklyn Valentino to show up at his suite. We wanted to buy some acid for later that night and it was going to be just the three of us since Russ had gone home for his anniversary with his girlfriend Jennifer, and Bruno declined again, though he did actually consider it this time. Every hour on the hour I went upstairs to see if Valentino had returned, but at 9:00 we finally gave up hope and went downtown.

After spending the evening at the bars, we got back to the suite at around 2:00 AM and ordered a pizza. Teke said he didn't want any and spent the next twenty minutes in the bathroom stall puking before staggering into his room and passing out. Winston was already asleep, having spent a quiet evening alone in his room with his textbooks and guitar. Bruno planted himself in front of the television and waited for the pizza to arrive.

Ed and I were ready to keep the party rolling and he suggested that I go upstairs to see if Valentino was home. When I got up there it sounded like they were having a party inside. I knocked and some girl yelled to come in. The room was packed with cute little sorority girls wearing pajamas and there were sleeping bags all over the floor. I asked no one in particular if Valentino was around, and one of his suitemates asked what my name was and went into his room.

While I was waiting the sorority girls did their best not to acknowledge my presence. These were the really cute ones, Phi Pi chicks, but they were also the most spoiled assortment of daddy's little Long Island girls you will ever meet, the kind that made me suffer acute sexual frustration in high school by giving me boners all day long that would never see the light of day or dark of night. There were so many of them in the room that it was difficult not to make incidental eye contact, and every time I did I made a scary face, frightening them even more than they probably already were at the sight of a long-haired burnout in a tattered denim jacket who showed up in the middle of the night at their little slumber party with the pretty boys of Delta Zeta Nu.

After several minutes Valentino's door finally opened and the guy who had asked my name emerged and said I could go in. As tempted as I was, I did not step on any of the sorority girls as I maneuvered across the minefield of sleeping bags. Before going in I had to wait for five girls being sent out of the room, Valentino ever-so cautious to never let anyone witness a transaction apart from the parties involved.

When I was inside he closed and locked the door. He was wearing only a pair of silk boxer shorts and a gold necklace with a Crucifix pendant.

"Sorry to disturb you," I said.

"That's alright," he said. "My clients come first. Besides, I needed a break anyway, know what I'm sayin'?"

When he started putting on a pair of latex gloves, he noticed my expression and laughed.

"Don't worry, I'm not going to ask you to bend over," he said. "I just don't wanna touch the stuff because it goes in right through the pores and I don't want to be trippin' tonight, know what I'm sayin'?"

He opened the minifridge and pulled out a sheet of tabs loosely wrapped in cellophane moist with condensation.

"This stuff is home-brew," he said, removing the cellophane from the sheet. "My boy in Flatbush blots this shit in his basement."

He picked up the sheet with a pair of tweezers and held it in front of my face. It looked nothing like the stuff we bought from the Doobie Brothers. This sheet was soggy and stained with dark green splotches as if someone had spilled absinthe on it.

"Bakery fresh," he said, cutting off four tabs with a pair of surgical scissors and dropping them into an empty stamp bag. "You guys are gonna get off on this shit."

I wasn't sure what to make of it, but Ed said blotter was better than that "low-grade commercial shit" the Doobies sold us. Ed took 2½ tabs and I took 1½, and as soon as we popped them the pizza showed up. I accidentally swallowed my tab with my first slice, but Ed said it probably wouldn't make much of a difference if it was good acid.

Halfway through my second slice the phone rang. Normally I would have never answered the phone right after swallowing acid, but I was still drunk and sociable so I picked it up. It was Maria.

"Hank," she said, sounding as if she was crying. "I'm so glad you're home."

"What's the matter?" I asked.

"I'm seriously considering throwing myself out the window."

"What?"

"Hank, can you please come up here? I'm all alone and I'm really upset and I need someone to talk to."

"Alright, I'll be right up."

I told Ed that I had to run upstairs for a few minutes and that I would be right back. When I got up there the door was wide open, so I knocked and went in without waiting for an answer. She greeted me in the common room with tears running down her reddened cheeks.

"Where is everybody?" I asked.

"They're all downtown," she said, taking my hand. "Come talk to me."

She led me to her room and closed the door. When we were seated on the bed, she started crying and hugged me. She cried into my chest for a long time before finally calming down and saying she was sorry. She pulled me down with her so that we were both on our backs holding hands and staring at the ceiling.

"I saw him," she finally said and sniffled.

"Who?"

"*Him*, Hank, I saw *him*! I know I didn't tell you about this before and I'm sorry that I didn't, but when I saw him, I wanted to kill him! We were downtown and when I saw him and I told my roommates that I wanted to leave before I did something crazy, but they said they were staying and I had to come home by myself. That's when I called you."

"Who is this *him*?"

She took a deep breath. "He," she started and stopped. "Last year I lived in a quad with these two girls first semester, Doris and Ashley, real fucking bitches. I had my own room and they shared the other bedroom. One weekend one of them, Doris, had some friends up, some guys she knew from back home. They all went downtown and I stayed in and went to bed early because I wasn't feeling well. I usually didn't lock my bedroom door thinking that there was no reason to, but I always made sure the main door of the quad was locked—I guess it didn't matter anyway because Doris gave that animal the key. But I still should have locked my bedroom door..."

She sat up and looked away. I sat up next to her and looked at the Monet print on the wall, autumn in the woods, the ground covered with fallen leaves, and realized that I was having difficulty focusing my eyes.

"Anyway," she continued, "my door opened quietly and I thought it was just Doris or Ashley poking their head in, but then the door closed gently and locked. I was suddenly wide awake because I knew someone was in the room with me. I asked who was there, but there was no answer. I reached to turn the light on and saw him for a split second before he leaped on top of me and started punching me in the face. I tried to scream, but no sound came out. The next thing I knew I was in a hospital room and Ashley was standing next to my bed."

"God, I'm so sorry."

"He fucking raped me, Hank!" she cried. "And those fucking bitches covered the whole thing up! They said that he was downtown with them the whole time and never left their sight and that they all came home together and found me crying in my room all bruised and cut up and that I was too fucked up to know what really happened! Those bitches said I had a drug problem and that I was unstable!"

"What did the police say?"

"They couldn't prove anything. No evidence, no witnesses, nobody in the dorm even heard anything. It was their word against mine."

"I'm so sorry."

"I really wanted to kill him when I saw him downtown, but I didn't know what to do. My so-called sorority sisters were no help either. They were too busy trying to get laid. I thought I was going to have a breakdown and collapse right in the street, but I just got on a bus and came back here and called you. I feel bad for laying this on you, Hank, but I really had nowhere else to turn. Thank you so much for coming up here."

"That's okay," I said. "I'm glad I could be here for you."

"You're like the only person in this whole goddamn school that I can talk to. After it happened I was going to drop out, but my parents convinced me to stay. That's the main reason I pledged last semester, to keep my mind off of it and to make some new friends who will be there for me. Now I can see how that worked out."

"Well, I'm here for you."

"Thank you, Hank. I really appreciate it. You're so nice. That's why I liked you so much in ninth grade—you seemed like such a nice quiet boy."

"Well, I don't know about that. I was kind of a low-key badass back then. I was pretty good at not getting caught, except that time I got suspended for fighting."

"I remember that! In class that day Señora Garcia asked if anyone knew why you were suspended. She was so shocked that it happened because you were such a smart, quiet boy. I remember sitting there wishing that I could tell her everything there was to know about you, and it killed me that I couldn't because I didn't know you. But I loved you! You were my first crush. I still love you now. I don't think you have the slightest idea how much I love you."

"You still barely know me."

"I *do* know you, Hank, better than you realize. I've known you for a long time. I realize that I don't know much about you, but I *know* you. I don't know what I'm trying to say. I must sound like an idiot. But I love you, Hank. *I love you!*"

"Are you sure you're not in love with a perception?"

"Maybe. But the perception is still you."

For a moment neither of us said anything.

"Hank, do you want to go to my sorority formal with me?"

"What?"

"Do you want to go to my sorority formal?"

"When?"

"In two weeks. I'll understand if you don't, but you would make me so happy if you do. Otherwise, I probably won't even go. I really don't even care about the stupid formal or even about the sorority at this point, but if you go with me it'll be different. You don't have to give me an answer right now, but I need to know soon because the tickets will only be on sale for another week…"

Maria's voice faded into an echo as if I was moving away from her into a world of white where the Monet print was suspended in the air and undulating like an old rabbit-eared television with bad reception. I didn't know what was happening until I heard Maria's voice suddenly up close again and remembered the acid.

"Hank, are you alright?"

The room was back to normal, but I was terrified. I looked around not sure exactly what to do, only that I had to get out of there as soon as possible.

"Are you going to be sick?"

"I think I am."

Maria pulled me off the bed and led me towards the bathroom, but I stopped her before going in.

"I have to leave," I said.

"It's alright. You certainly won't be the first person who ever puked in this room."

"I have to go home."

"Home?"

"Back to my…"

"Hank, what's the matter with you?"

"I'm really sick. Very…"

"Well, let's get you into the bathroom so you don't make a mess out here."

She pulled me in and I froze when I saw myself in the mirror. My face was a deep shade of aquamarine that was gradually getting darker and starting to boil. After the initial shock wore off, I noticed Maria worriedly looking over my shoulder. Her face was normal, but when I looked back at mine it was bubbling purple and strands of flesh were dangling from my chin and cheeks like melted cheese. I shut my eyes tight, but not being able to see only made me paranoid. When I opened them again my face had returned to a more normal fever red, which may have been it's actual color.

"Hank, you're really starting to make me nervous," Maria said.

"Okay," I said as calmly as I could. I came to my senses just long enough to realize that if she knew I was tripping, she would probably think I was some kind of acid freak and would no longer want anything to do with me. I assumed the role of a drunk on the verge of puking, feeling my way into the stall and hovering over the toilet. I repeatedly spit into the bowl and dry-heaved a couple of times of times to make it look convincing, but after a while I started feeling dizzy and was worried that I was going to fall in and get sucked away. The stall walls started closing in and the paranoia became unbearable.

Finally I turned around. With a weak smile and a voice that sounded nothing like mine I said, "False alarm."

"Do you feel better?" she asked.

"No. Have to go. Don't want to sicken your room. Very... soon... mess..."

"Hank, please don't leave. I want you to spend the night here. Don't worry about making a mess."

My face in the mirror was beginning to change colors again, this time a rainbow sherbet swirl that mixed together to form a shade of olive vomit. During a brief moment of clarity I realized that leaving now would severely damage any chance I had with Maria, if not end things altogether, but staying would be even worse.

"I can't," I said. "I have to go. I'm really sick."

"Please don't leave," she said and hugged me. "I'll take care of you. Please don't leave."

"I have to."

"I'm not letting you go."

"I have to. I'm sorry that you don't understand, but I have to leave."

"Make me understand."

"I can't now. I'll explain later, but I really have to leave. I *must* leave."

Before she had a chance to say anything more I was gone. I walked swiftly down the hall and broke into a full sprint after turning the first corner. I felt like I was being chased, but it wasn't

Maria who was after me.

Back at the suite the door was locked and it took me a couple of minutes to get the key into the liquid doorknob. Inside Ed was staring at the television, which was not turned on. When he looked up at me I knew I was looking at Ed, yet I wasn't thoroughly convinced it was him.

"We have to get out of here," I said.

He smiled and looked like he was about to ask why, but before he had a chance I told him there was no time to explain. We grabbed our coats and hurried down the stairs to the service entrance.

Outside the fog was so thick that we couldn't see five feet in front of us. We walked briskly through the quad towards the fields without saying anything. I badly needed a cigarette but had smoked my last one when we got back from downtown.

After stepping off the asphalt of the Hunt Union parking lot, our feet sank deep into the mud. Ed said it was probably just that spot and that it couldn't all be this bad, so we continued up towards the baseball field. It was like walking on pudding. Ed didn't help matters by telling me to imagine that the squishing noise our boots were making in the mud was actually worms and that we were walking on a mountain of bloodsuckers trying to slither inside our pants and suck the blood out of our bodies and come back out through the empty sockets of our skulls. I thought I was going to be sick.

Next to the leftfield foul pole there was an opening in the fence and we stopped on the gravel warning track. Our feet had become cinder blocks of mud, our boots no longer visible, and my back hurt from supporting the extra weight. We found a couple of sticks and attempted to scrape the mud off, which at first seemed futile because there was so much of it, but it kept my mind occupied and I actually started to enjoy it until Ed asked me what happened up in Maria's room.

"Nothing," I said, continuing to scrape. "Some fucked up shit. I don't want to talk about it."

"Did you bang her?"

"I don't want to talk about it."

After managing to get most of the mud off of our boots, we walked towards home plate along the warning track. There was a parking lot behind the batting cage, and beyond that East Street, which led back down to the main part of campus. The fog was now so thick that we could hardly see each other even though we were only a couple of feet apart. Down at the road I thought I heard footsteps that weren't ours, dress shoes clacking on concrete that didn't seem to be getting any closer or farther away, but Ed said he didn't hear anything. At this point all I wanted to do was lock myself in my room and ride out the rest of the trip.

The main entrance to Matteson Hall was quiet, but it felt like we were being watched by unseen eyes behind every darkened window. The acid was coming at us from every direction. My only consolation was that there were no ambulances or crowds that would have assembled had there been a suicide. Hopefully Maria had just cried herself to sleep and had already forgotten that this night ever happened, but somehow I doubted it.

Ed's bedroom door was open and the suite was glowing blue from the lava lamp on his dresser. Suddenly everything seemed calm. Ed lit the candle on top of the big concrete Buddha in the common room that he had stolen from a neighbor's front lawn in Rockaway. A rainbow of candle wax had streaked from his bald head down to his puffy cheeks and made it look like he was wearing a clown wig. For the first time all night I did not feel the immediate need to be somewhere else.

I followed Ed into his room. A breeze coming through his open window made the Irish flag covering it look like a ghost. On the other side of the room Bruno was making vicious snarls in his sleep that after a minute or so frightened me back out to the common room.

It seemed calm again until I noticed that the walls were breathing kind of like the door visual from the first trip, but now all four walls were bending outwards and inwards as if I was inside a lung. The Buddha was silently laughing as if enjoying the role of perpetrator. I told him to shut up, but he only started laughing harder.

I went into my room and locked the door. I put on Pink Floyd's *Wish You Were Here* CD to mellow me out and sat at Russ' desk with my acid journal. I attempted to write down every thought racing through my head, but there were too many and they were moving too fast, so I went back next door to borrow Ed's crayons. The door was still open and Bruno was still snoring loudly, but Ed wasn't there. I was going to check and see if he was in the bathroom, but when I pulled the hallway curtain aside I found the main door of the suite wide open. I thought maybe he just went to the water fountain down the hall so I waited, but after several minutes I went out and looked for him. After turning the first corner I started bugging out, so I hurried back to the suite and locked the door.

I really wanted those crayons, but I was afraid to go in there by myself with Bruno snoring and the Irish ghost haunting the window. The Buddha was laughing at my cowardice and I did my best to ignore him, but after a while he started to piss me off. To show him that I was no coward, I went in and successfully grabbed the box from Ed's desk. While I was in there, Bruno snarled as if subconsciously realizing that there was an intruder, but he didn't wake up. On the way back to my room I gave Buddha the finger, but he had already stopped laughing and pretended not to notice.

Back at Russ' desk I opened a fresh pack of loose leaf paper and started drawing lines that corresponded to the music, creating angles with the sharp changes in the song and curves for the more gradual changes. I was actually *seeing* the music appear on the paper as translated by 62 of the 64 colors except white, which didn't show up on the paper, and burnt sienna, which had been lost somewhere in the couch cushions. My conscious played no part in the matter; my drawing hand existed independently while I sat back and watched the patterns and figures appear on the paper before me. After *Wish You Were Here* ended, I tried it with *Sgt. Pepper* and the Dead's *American Beauty*, but it only seemed to work with Pink Floyd, so I put on *Dark Side of the Moon* and it came right back. I used nearly all of the 200 sheets in the package before my newfound ability started to wane in proportion to the sky getting lighter.

My tranquility was jolted when the door to the suite suddenly slammed shut. Ed came in and said he had taken a long walk around the perimeter of campus and sat in the quad for a while writing in his journal. He looked at my drawings scattered all over the room as if someone had stacked them in front of a fan and turned it on high power.

"Are you alright?" Ed asked. "It looks like you're going schizo or something."

"It's that damn Buddha out there," I said.

I really needed a cigarette, but the Hunt Union wouldn't be open for several more hours. The thought crossed my mind to sneak into Teke's room and try to find one in there, but then I remembered that he had run out while we were downtown, and I didn't want to run the risk of catching a glimpse of Winston sleeping in his tightie-whities.

We spent the hours before the crash staring blankly at the television. It was going to be a bad one, both of us still wired and numb from the acid and hung over from the alcohol, which now seemed like days ago. Some time after 9:00 we felt the first cracks of the crash like a polar thaw that would leave us both puddles. Ed started moaning and ran into the bathroom. Moments later I heard a splash that sounded like someone dropping a car engine into the toilet followed by a scream.

Soon it would be my turn. The beer, acid, and pizza was rumbling in my stomach, but after hearing Ed, I held it in as long as I could. I was afraid that as soon as I sat down, all my internal organs were going to fall into the bowl. When I couldn't hold it any longer I took baby steps to the bathroom and spent the next 45 minutes wiping and sweating. When I was finished I finally felt tired enough to attempt sleep. After spinning its wheels all night, my subconscious was so exhausted that I was able to fall asleep as soon as my head hit the pillow, lapsing into a deep coma that temporarily prevented me from thinking about what I wouldn't be able to stop thinking about as soon as I regained consciousness.

**3**

After I ran out on Maria I thought that there was no way in hell she would want anything to do with me. Yet I couldn't stop thinking about her. I wanted to call her and tell her how horrible I felt about it and that I would be honored to go to the formal with her and that I was willing to toss aside everything to be with her, but my embarrassment was too great. Not surprisingly, she didn't call me either.

I tormented myself trying to forget about her. The day of the formal came and went and I thought that the finality of this date passing combined with large quantities of alcohol would help me forget and move on, but it only got worse. I had to do something or else I was going to crack up, so one night I picked up a six pack of Bud tallboys to catch enough of a buzz to give me the nerve to go upstairs without getting too drunk to say what needed to be said.

The other guys were taken aback when I said I wasn't going to smoke with them that night, but I couldn't go up there stoned. They knew something was up, but seeing that I didn't want to talk about it, they refrained from asking questions. After I was gone, however, I'm sure I was the main topic of conversation.

Heading upstairs I felt confident and determined, but by the time I got up there I found myself staring at her door having serious second thoughts. I managed to convince myself that regardless of what might happen I had to do this, if only to stop thinking about her. Finally I knocked. A few moments later she answered wearing a pair of white silk pajamas.

"Hank," she said. "This is a surprise."

"Yeah. I just thought I'd stop by because there's something I need to talk to you about."

"Okay."

"Can I come in?"

"Sure."

I followed her into the common room and she invited me to sit next to her on one of the couches.

"It's quiet in here," I said.

"Everyone went to a meeting down at the house. I would have gone too, but I'm not feeling very well."

"Sorry to hear it. I can come back another time."

"That's alright. I was getting a little bored up here by myself anyway."

While I was trying to figure out what to say next, the phone rang in her bedroom. She went in and answered it and asked whoever it was if it was alright if she called back later before hanging up.

"Sorry about that," she said after coming back. "So, what did you want to talk about?"

"Well, I feel really bad about how I ran out of here that night a few weeks ago."

"You feel bad about it *now*?"

"I've felt bad about it since it happened, but I've been too embarrassed to come up here and talk to you about it until now."

"And you needed to have a few beers before you came up here."

"Well, I was having a few beers when I decided to come up here."

"How flattering. You need to be drunk to come up here and talk to me."

"I'm not drunk. It just so happened that I had a few beers in me when the time felt right to come up here."

"I see."

"Listen, Maria, I don't want you to think that you were the reason I ran out of here that night."

"It's alright. I understand. I dumped something heavy on you and you couldn't handle it. I don't blame you for running away."

"That's not why I ran out of here."

"Hank, it's alright. That's why I didn't tell you about it before—I didn't want to scare you away."

"But the reason I ran out of here is that *I* didn't want to scare *you* away."

"What are you talking about?"

"I was really drunk that night. We were downtown drinking, and when we got back to the room Ed and I decided to take some acid. We popped the tabs a few minutes before you called. It was pretty strong stuff. When I came up here I had forgotten about it until the posters on the wall started moving, which was when I ran into the bathroom. When I saw myself in the mirror, my face was blue and it started melting. I was a fucking mess. At first when you called I thought I was only going to be up here for a couple of minutes and would be back before it started kicking in, but I guess with what you were telling me, I had forgotten about it until it did. That's why I was so anxious to get out of here. I was afraid to tell you because I didn't know what you would think, and there was no way I could have spent the night here without you finding out."

"Why were you afraid to tell me?"

"I don't know. I was fucked up and paranoid. I guess we just never talked about acid and I didn't know how you felt about it."

"I've taken acid."

"Really?"

"Yeah, a couple of times in high school. I wasn't crazy about it."

"I wasn't crazy about it that night. The first time it was amazing, but this time the stuff was too strong. After I left here I was bugging out for the next eight hours. Ed and I wound up walking through fields of mud because I was afraid that if I stayed in the room I was going to freak out. After we got back I was finally able to calm down by drawing lines with crayons on loose leaf paper for the rest of the night."

"Hank, you could have told me. I would have understood."

"But I didn't know that! When I was in the bathroom I was totally freaking out. All I knew was that I had to get out of there. I didn't want you to see me like that. I knew that by running out of here like that you would probably never want to speak to me again, but I thought that staying would only be worse. I like you, Maria. That's why I was so worried about you seeing me like that. I didn't know how you would react."

There was a long silence. I playfully nudged her foot and she nudged mine back, which I interpreted as a signal. I moved a little closer and she started fidgeting with one of the buttons on her pajama shirt. I leaned in and kissed her. She kissed back for a moment but then pulled her head away.

"I shouldn't," she said. "I have a really bad cold and I don't want to get you sick."

"I'm sorry," I said.

"There's no need to apologize."

I was too embarrassed to look at her.

"I should get going," I said.

"You can stay if you'd like," she said unconvincingly.

"No, I really should get going. I have a lot of shit to do tomorrow."

I couldn't get out of there soon enough. On my way out I heard her say "Bye, Hank," but I didn't acknowledge it. I threw the door open and didn't bother to close it. I walked swiftly through the maze of corridors trying to get away as quickly as I could.

About halfway back to the suite I started feeling relieved. I didn't have to think about her anymore. I could go back to my nest and get drunk and stoned and trip acid as I pleased without worry. By the time I was back in the suite sitting with the other guys and a fresh bowl was being packed, I had already forgotten why I wanted to leave in the first place.

**4**

Life was good again. We were drinking and smoking more dope than ever, and I had finally found a way to utilize the shrinking yet increasingly intolerable gaps of sobriety that spotted our days— schoolwork. During freshman year my academic motivation had been the fear of flunking out, but now that I had briefly been exposed to life outside the circle and realized that life inside it was mortal, I started thinking about the future. I still had no idea what I was going to do with my life, so I declared my major in English.

Also during that semester we finally found a bar we could call our own. The Black Oak was the 'artsy' bar in town, the usual crowd consisting of artists, musicians, burnouts, bisexuals, actors, and pretty much everyone else not in a fraternity or a sorority who wasn't a total recluse. The fraternities steered clear of this place because they thought it was a gay bar, as the reputation goes with such types regarding places reputed as 'artsy'. With our long hair and earrings we looked like the typical Oak patrons, but amongst the regulars we were conspicuous because we were usually by far the drunkest ones there. We fit in because this was the drug crowd, and we probably took more drugs than anyone, but what made us stand out in this crowd is that we also drank as much and perhaps even more than the frat boys. To the Oakies we were drunks, and to the frats and sororities we were dope fiends. In our eyes we had it all, and we loved every second of it.

On the last night of the semester we went down there and secured what had become our usual booth in the back corner. Even Winston, who had only gone out a couple of times during the semester and who didn't exactly feel comfortable at the Oak, came out with us ready to drink. With finals being over and the thought of going home the next day for a much needed break from Oneonta fresh on our minds, everyone was in good spirits.

Many of the college students had already gone home for the holidays, so the place was relatively quiet. The night was uneventful until I noticed Maria Viola being carded by the bouncer at the door. I had never seen her nor any other Philanthans at the Oak before, and not having given her a thought since that night I went up to her room a month earlier and that by all indications whatever had happened between us was seemingly over for good, it didn't occur to me that she would be there looking for me. By the wild look on her face I thought at first that she may have seen the rapist again, but she didn't look upset in that kind of way. She looked lost, fumbling through her pockets for her ID, perhaps so drunk that she didn't know what bar she was trying to get into.

Once inside she spotted me immediately and headed straight for our booth. I was sitting on the outside and she slid right in next to me with one cheek hanging off the edge, and without saying hello or anything she started kissing me. Not just an innocent little peck on the lips, mind you, but a full-fledged attempt to get me to swallow her tongue. Before I realized what I was doing, I started kissing her back and the other guys started cheering us on. Suddenly everything that had happened between us didn't seem to matter. No more 9th grade crushes, no more sorority formals, rapists, or bad trips. I was finally going to get laid in Oneonta, and that's all there was to it.

I stopped kissing and suggested that we go somewhere else. She got right up and I followed while the other guys gave us a round of applause, to which I responded by giving them the finger.

It was 10 degrees Fahrenheit outside, and since it was after midnight on a weeknight, the buses had stopped running. We held hands as we walked up the quiet streets and didn't say anything, but it was not an uncomfortable silence; it felt like we were the only two people in the world, perhaps the only scenario in which we could thrive. Without realizing where we were, I stopped at the corner of Center and Maple, right across the street from the Philanthan house, and kissed her, pressing my crotch against hers, but she pulled back and said, "Let's get back to my room where it's warm."

We continued up Maple, past Fred's old house, up Golding Path, and finally across campus to Matteson Hall. I tried not to think about anything beyond sex, but the phrase **FEAR OF COMMITMENT** kept popping in my head like a bumper sticker. Fortunately I still had the yellow condom that I picked up from the Health Center at the beginning of the semester, and hopefully it hadn't dried out after spending four months in my wallet.

Maria's suitemates had already gone home and we had the place to ourselves. She led me by the hand to her bed and pulled me down on top of her. I started kissing her passionately to show her that this time I wasn't going to run away, my erection pressing against her crotch and practically fucking her through our clothes, but suddenly she stopped. I attempted to keep the momentum going by unbuttoning her jeans and slipping my hand inside her panties, but she grabbed my wrist.

"Hank, I don't think we should do this right now."

I rolled off her body and nestled my head between her breasts. She started running her fingers through my hair.

"Why not?" I asked.

"We're too drunk."

"Sobriety is overrated," I said.

"We should talk about this when we're sober."

"Where have I heard that before?"

"I just don't think this is such a good idea right now."

"Is this about…"

"The rape? No, that has nothing to do with it. It's just something I don't want to talk about when we're drunk."

"What is there to talk about? I'm not going to run out on you again, I promise. Believe me, I have regretted running out of here that night since the moment it happened. I thought you hated me after that, and I don't blame you for kicking me out the last time I was here. All I can say is that I'm sorry and I promise that it will never happen again."

"Hank, I can never hate you. The only person in the world I hate is *you-know-who*."

"Then what is it?"

"I don't want to talk about it when we're drunk."

"I'm not that drunk."

"Well, I am, and my instincts are telling me that we shouldn't be doing this right now. Besides, I'm leaving very early tomorrow morning and I haven't even finished packing yet. We'll get together back home. I'll call you after Christmas, but you have to go now."

I thought it would be easy seeing Maria at home. No college buddies, no sorority sisters, no interruptions, just Maria and I spending every day of winter break together doing the things that normal couples do—going to the movies, going out to dinner, drinking hot cocoa on the Jones Beach boardwalk at sunset. I figured that by the time we got back to Oneonta we will have already forgotten what had kept us apart before. More important, we would finally know each other. No more uncomfortable lulls, no more awkward moments. By then she would be my *college sweetheart*.

When she called the day after Christmas, however, the fantasy revealed itself to be exactly what it was.

"Do you still want to hang out?" she asked.

"Sure," I said, though suddenly I didn't feel so sure at all. In my sober state, in this place that had become a mere rest stop from the months long drug and alcohol fueled binges up in thar yonder foothills, years removed from the ghost of myself that this person remembered better than I remembered him myself, in a past that I didn't know until recently had even existed, I didn't know who I was talking to or what I was trying to accomplish. I was stuck in this cycle of dreaming about how nice it would be to be in love and have a real girlfriend and a real relationship, but every time I was with Maria I didn't know what I wanted, and then when I was back in my drunken state I would start thinking that I can't keep getting fucked up like this and would long for Maria, which was actually a longing of the idea of being in a relationship rather than being in love with this person who I really didn't know but who seemed to remember a time in my life I was more than happy to forget. I had no fucking idea what I wanted to do.

"What do you want to do?" she asked.

"What? Oh, I don't know. What do you want to do?"

"I don't know."

"…"

Since I didn't have access to a car at the moment, I eventually suggested that she come pick me up and we could figure out what to do from there. I gave her directions to my house and she said she would be there in an hour.

When I saw her standing on the front steps, she looked like she didn't why she was there. Though we had both grown up in this very town and went to the same high school, she looked totally out of place outside of Oneonta.

I opened the door and we said hello, but we didn't hug or kiss. My whole family was home, so I didn't invite her in. I grabbed my coat and followed her out to her car, a beat up 1985 Buick Century that used to belong to her parents.

We silently drove in no particular direction until we hit Sunrise Highway. The quiet quickly became unbearable, so I turned on the radio and flipped through the stations. She headed east on Sunrise for a while and probably would have kept going until we were in the Hamptons if I hadn't suggested that she pull into a diner coming up on the right.

It was only four in the afternoon, but it was already almost dark. The sky was filled with cold winter clouds that had kept the sun hidden all day. We were seated at a booth overlooking the traffic on Sunrise and the elevated tracks of the Long Island Rail Road across the street. I took out my cigarettes and offered one to Maria, but she said she had been trying to quit and declined. The waitress came over with glasses of water and asked if we wanted anything to drink while we decided what to order.

"I'm just going to have coffee," Maria said.

"I'll have a cheeseburger deluxe with mozzarella fries and a large Coke," I said.

The waitress went away and came back a couple of minutes later with the coffee and soda. I stubbed out my cigarette and looked at Maria, who seemed to be waiting for me to say something. I tried to recall the many simulated conversations I had been having with her in my head over the last several days, but I drew a blank.

"So," she finally said.

"So."

"Are we actually going to talk or was your plan just to drive around and go to the diner?"

"I like driving around and going to diners. But yes, we should talk."

"Alright."

I lit another cigarette and tried to think of something to say, but all I came up with was, "That was pretty wild the other night."

"Yeah," she said. "I still can't believe that I just went up to you like that in the bar."

"Me neither."

There was a long pause.

"Hank, do I mean anything to you?"

"Of course."

"What do I mean to you, Hank?"

I thought about it for a minute.

"To be honest, I'm not really sure," I said. "I consider you a friend, but at the same time I feel like I don't know you very well since we haven't spent that much time together. I guess what I'm trying to say is that I'm just not used to being around you. And you have this knack for coming out of the blue when I least expect it."

When she didn't respond I got worried that I had said something wrong.

"Don't get me wrong," I said. "I want to hang out with you and get to know you better. It's just kind of weird being where we are now without having had that gradual process of getting to know each other first."

"You're right," she said.

"What about you?"

"I like you, Hank. I think about you all the time. But when we actually spend time together, I never know what to say or do. It's like I know you so well but don't know you at all."

"I wish it could be like that day we were coloring in your room."

"Me too."

I watched a train go by. I was tempted to light another cigarette, but I didn't want her to think I was nervous. The waitress came back with my food and refilled Maria's coffee cup.

"Are you sure you don't want anything to eat?" I asked Maria after the waitress was gone. "I'll pay."

"No, thanks. I'm fine. I'm having dinner with the family later."

"How is the family?"

"They're alright. Crazy as usual, but alright. What about yours?"

"They're fine. Crazy too."

"I think most families are."

"Yeah."

Not realizing that I was making it look like a hurry to get out of there, I wolfed down my burger and fries while Maria sipped her coffee and stared out the window. After I finished eating I lit another cigarette and joined her in staring out the window.

"Home sweet home," I said.

"I hate Long Island," she said.

"So do I."

"Someday I will be far from here… far from everywhere."

I liked the way that sounded, but I wasn't sure if she was including me in 'everywhere', so I said nothing.

The waitress took my plate and asked if there would be anything else.

"Just the check," I said.

She scribbled the total on the slip and tore it off the pad, thanking us as she placed it face down on the table. I dropped a couple of singles down as a tip and we went over to the cashier. Maria offered to put in a few dollars to cover the coffee and the tip, but I said it was on me.

Outside it had gotten considerably colder and darker. I felt exhausted. Maria didn't ask if I wanted to go home. During the ride we didn't say a word and the radio volume was low enough to distinguish our silence. When she pulled into my driveway I told her I would call in a couple of days and she nodded.

## 5

With the assistance of my journal, an eighth of weed, and late night television, I spent the rest of winter break pushing Maria Viola into the past and went back to Oneonta determined not to let her ruin another semester. My new resolve was immediately put to the test when, on my way to the very first class of the semester, I spotted her in the quad heading right towards me. My initial reaction was to make a sharp turn or duck into a nearby building, but I stayed my course. While I didn't want to get stuck in an awkward conversation with her, I didn't want to be on alert every time I stepped out of the suite.

There were a lot of people walking in both directions and I lost her in the crowd until she was five feet in front of me. With a friendly smile I said, "Hey, Maria," as she went by, but, to my astonishment, she didn't say hello back or even look at me. I stopped in disbelief and watched her join a group of her sorority sisters at the Philanthan section of the wall where the Greeks hung out between classes. For a moment I was tempted to go over there and give her a piece of my mind, but I was supposed to be over her, so I said fuck it and continued on my way.

That winter Oneonta was being slammed by record snowfalls. The buses couldn't get up or down the hill to take us to the bars, leaving us holed up in the suite night after night hovering over our milk crate and cardboard card table playing hands of our favorite new card game '99' for one hitters. While it was fun most of the time, there were moments when I thought I was going to go mad if I had to sit through another night of smoking, coughing, and playing cards, and during those moments I would wonder what I might be doing instead had that day back home with Maria gone differently.

Russ, meanwhile, was having problems of his own. He had spent his winter break being badgered by his girlfriend Jennifer about transferring to a school closer to home and had reached his breaking point.

"I'm tired of pretending to be someone I no longer am," was all ever he said about it, perhaps thinking that we wouldn't be interested in his relationship problems, unaware that when he wasn't around I was dishing out the gossip like an old lady at a bridge game. For six long years he had been with her, the only girl he had ever been with, and had remained completely faithful to her until he met Rosanna.

On the surface Rosanna seemed like the complete opposite of Jennifer. She was a retro- hippie-chick from Manhattan who smoked dope, read books on Zen Buddhism, and listened to pre-*Dark Side of the Moon* Pink Floyd, with Syd Barrett's *The Piper at the Gates of Dawn* being her favorite. Jennifer, on the other hand, was taking real estate sales classes on Long Island and listening to pop divas on the Top 40 stations. It was Jennifer who made Russ wait several agonizing years before finally spreading her legs for him after the junior prom; Rosanna put out the first night. They did, however, have one thing in common; they both believed that they owned Russ.

During his first night with Rosanna, Russ thought he was getting into a liberating affair that would finally break the chains of his former life. After being swallowed whole by his relationship with Jennifer, however, he had not learned how to date casually, and the next morning he woke up and found himself in the belly of not one, but two overbearing relationships. To make matters worse, Rosanna was not the sexually uninhibited girl he thought she was; she had been saving herself until she met the right man, and she knew right away that Russ was that man.

It didn't take long for Rosanna to find out about Jennifer. When Russ tried to explain what a delicate situation it was, she said, "Be a man and dump her ass already." Two hundred miles away Jennifer sensed that something was wrong and started calling more than she usually did. Since Russ was now spending all of his free time in Rosanna's room, I was stuck answering the constantly ringing phone. Jennifer may have believed me the first time I told her that he was at the library, but after that one was used up and I ran out of other plausible excuses, I had to stop answering the phone. Yet this only seemed to encourage her to call even more. She started leaving long soliloquies on the answering machine about how she couldn't go on like this and threatening to leave him, only to call back five minutes later crying that she didn't mean it, completely unaware that she was entertaining a room full of guys sitting around smoking dope. Winston even started hanging out during our smoke sessions just to hear the nightly drama, which served as a much needed diversion from the monotony of playing cards. Instead of playing hands for one-hitters, we started wagering on how long she would wait before she called back and whether she would be screaming or crying.

"I'm really sorry about this," Russ said to me during one of his now rare visits to the room. He hadn't shaved or changed his clothes in days and appeared to have lost a few pounds. "I promise this is going to stop soon. I just need a little more time."

"Are you alright, man?" I asked.

"Not really."

"Is there anything I can do?"

"Just be patient with me for a little while longer. I know what I have to do, I just don't know yet how I'm going to do it."

Russ managed to juggle his lives between the whips and a full courseload for a few weeks until early February when Teke invited us to accompany him on a weekend road trip to Binghamton. A friend of his from back home was going to school there, and while most of us weren't the least bit interested in spending the weekend with one of his old *Dungeons & Dragons* buddies, Russ jumped at the chance to get away from Rosanna and the answering machine. He didn't tell anyone outside of our suite that he was going.

A few days earlier, Valentino told me that he was expecting a sheet of acid that his Flatbush connection said was his best batch ever. After telling the other guys about it, Bruno's fledgling conservatism was dealt another blow when he said he was finally ready to go the way of Dr. Timothy Leary, a deviation only added fuel to the fire that he was really a closet liberal.

On my way to class Friday afternoon I spotted Valentino walking across the quad holding a FedEx envelope. When he saw me he waved the envelope in the air with a big smile. After class I hurried back to the suite and collected the money from Ed and Bruno, each of whom wanted 1½ tabs. I asked Bruno if he was sure he wanted to take that much his first time, especially since Valentino said this stuff was stronger than the last batch, but he said that he was bigger than Ed and I so it would take more to get him off, and if he was going to do it at all, he wanted to experience it in full. After the last trip, Ed and I were content to stray towards the mellow side; his 1½ was rather moderate for him, and I only wanted one, figuring that my tolerance had probably risen a bit after last time and that one would be just right.

The sheet was soggy like the last one, except this batch was dark gray instead of green. Valentino put on his latex gloves and cut four tabs from the sheet with his surgical scissors.

"You guys are the guinea pigs," he said, dropping the tabs into an empty nickel bag with his tweezers. "Usually I try everything I get before I sell it, but I know you guys are gonna get your money's worth with this shit. My boy said he used Timothy Leary's personal recipe."

After we popped the tabs I went up to the dining hall for a quick dinner. I was gone only twenty minutes, but by the time I got back I was already feeling fucked up. The other guys seemed fine and Ed suggested we smoke a bowl to hold us over until the acid kicked in, which I agreed to so they wouldn't suspect what a mess I already was.

After the bowl was kicked, Bruno went out to the common room and planted himself in front of the television while Ed and I stayed in my room and I put on Neil Young's *Ragged Glory* CD. Ed was sitting on Russ' bed with his back leaning against the wall and I was doing the same on mine, both of us feeling sickeningly mellow as if we had taken too much valium. During the first song, "Country Home," the instruments started isolating themselves into individual waves of highs and lows that I found myself attempting to surf. Every time I wiped out, I got back on the board and caught another wave until the end of the song when ol' Neil gently brought me back to shore by letting the last chord hang and fade out.

"That Neil is a wacky guy," Ed said during the silence between tracks. He seemed to be looking at me mistrustfully, and I began to question whether he was friend or foe until the next song started and took me back out to sea.

Each song took me out deeper and deeper and it became increasingly more difficult to come back in when the music stopped. After the CD ended and left us in silence, Ed and I stared at each other like wild animals ready to strike at the first flinch. I didn't recognize him and he didn't recognize me, and I was starting to lose track of who I was.

Suddenly Winston burst into the room with Bruno's walking stick draped over his shoulders.

"Hark, thou trippers!" he said. "I am Jesus Christ, here to sacrifice myself for the sins of the potheads and acid freaks of the world!"

With his long hair and unshaved face, Winston actually did look a little like Jesus Christ, which horrified Ed, who slid off the bed and got on his knees in front of Winston, worshipping his feet and begging for forgiveness.

"I command thou Cafferty to get off the floor and resume thou art original position," Winston said. Ed obeyed and climbed back onto the bed without taking his eyes off him.

"Okay, men!" Winston suddenly commanded. "I am your commander General George Washington, father of your beloved country and champion of freedom in the New World! We are now crossing the Delaware River to get those Redcoat bastards, but I need your complete cooperation, each and every one of you! So row, men, row!"

Ed and I sat up and started rowing the beds through the chunks of ice floating on the river that moments ago had been my bedroom. Above us the sky was clear, the moon and stars shining bright, and the air was bitterly cold. General Washington, in full Colonial garb, had his foot up on the bow of his boat, a first class rowboat moving of its own accord, and pointed us towards the dark shore.

"Faster, men! Faster!" he yelled. Ed and I started rowing our beds frantically. At one point I dropped my paddle in the water but was able to retrieve it before the General noticed. As we got closer to the shore, I was able to make out the black outline of a huge fort.

"Stop!" the General commanded, holding his hand out like a crossing guard. We stopped paddling and awaited further instruction, but the General only laughed maniacally. "Alright, men, you may now return to your regularly scheduled programming."

In the blink of an eye the room returned to its normal state and the General left. Ed was looking at me again like a wild animal ready to attack, so I slowly got off my bed and backed up towards the door. Our eyes were locked on each other and I was careful not to make any sudden movements. After making it safely out of the room, I gently closed the door.

The common room was cold and dim. A large man with a pony tail and a beard was sitting in front of the television playing with the tint button on the remote. The screen going from one end of the spectrum to the other made me feel like I was on a ship in stormy seas. With sea-legs I attempted to sneak by without him noticing, but as I neared the hallway curtain he suddenly turned and snarled. I managed to slip behind the curtain and into the bathroom without further incident, and for a moment I felt safe until I looked at the mirror.

I didn't recognize the face staring back at me; it was like looking at someone else entirely. It had the same savage expression as the guy in the bedroom and the guy with beard. I tried to regroup and figure out who I was, where I was, and what I was doing, but I couldn't keep my mind on a single thought for more than a second. The grout lines between the sea-green wall tiles were tying themselves in knots, but I hardly noticed.

The face in the mirror started bugging me out, so I sneaked back into the bedroom without attracting the attention of the bearded guy. The other guy was still in there, but he didn't seem to notice as I tentatively took a seat on the edge of my bed as if it wasn't my own. Moments later General Washington exploded into the room and announced, "Have I got a tape for you guys!" While he was putting the cassette into the deck, he explained, "It's Marty Friedman's solo album. It's surprisingly like Pink Floyd."

"Who the hell is Marty Friedman?" the other guy asked like an old barfly.

"He's the guitarist for Megadeth. I bought this tape for a buck from one of my buddies in Downsville when he was fiending for weed."

The music faded in, droning keyboards layered with a soft guitar solo. Washington watched us for a reaction but got none. Again I started riding the music, but unlike the raunchy feedback of Neil Young and Crazy Horse, this was a peaceful ride that lifted me out of the room and deep into outer space. Behind me the earth got smaller and smaller until it became a distant star that I could no longer distinguish from the others. I started floating faster, passing huge colorful planets and moons, and soon forgot the world that I had left behind. I continued accelerating until the spiral arms of the Milky Way became a single point of light. I was overcome with euphoria, and the concrete Buddha from the common room floated by and said, "Congratulations, you have attained Satori," and started laughing before veering off in a different direction and exploding.

Suddenly I hit something that made a sound like a mosquito zapper and sent a painful electrical surge through my body. Everything turned white until the nurse pulled the blanket from my eyes. She handed my infant body over to my mother, and, looking up at her young face, I beheld for the first and perhaps only time in my life pure love, love that exists only within the bond connecting mother and child, love so intense that I could only withstand it for a few seconds before passing out.

I didn't know how long I was out, but when I opened my eyes I was back in my room sitting on the edge of my bed. I felt feverish and my face was covered with sweat, so I got up and opened the window. The cold air felt good and I stared at the snow glittering in the dorm lights. My entire body started tingling and everything around me ground to a halt. The tingling became a tearing at the fiber of my physical being and a solid glass sculpture shaped like my body fell out of me. I made a fumbling attempt to catch it, but I missed. When it hit the floor it shattered into a million tiny pieces except for two bleeding red chunks on top of the pile.

Like a guilty child I looked around to see if anyone had noticed, but no one was there. The lights were out and several candles were burning in wax-streaked beer bottles. Bob Marley's fluorescent cartoon head inside one of the posters on the wall started laughing, and next to him a miniature Jimi Hendrix was sitting Indian-style loudly chewing a wad of gum and strumming a scorched Stratocaster.

"Look at da mess you made, mon!" Marley said and let out a baritone belly laugh. "You got to clean up dat mess, mon! But firss, let us smoke da bowl."

"I hear that, cat," Jimi said, strumming a chord that sounded awful.

"Come *on*, mon, get wid it! Smoke da bowl!" Marley pointed with his head to the desk where a bowl was already packed, the weed charred from someone having already taken a hit before abandoning it. I picked it up and Marley let out another laugh. "Dat's it, mon! Torch dat bowl! Ha ha!"

"Pass that sucker along, let's not keep us cats waiting," Jimi said.

"Come *on*, mon!" Marley said impatiently.

I picked up the lighter and took a small hit. After exhaling, I looked at Marley for approval.

"Dat's it, mon!" he laughed. "Pass it along now!"

I held the bowl out to Marley and waited.

"No, mon, can't you see dat I don't have arms! I'm all head, mon! Hold it to my lips!" I held the bowl to his lips and lit it for him. Jimi stopped strumming and watched Marley take an enormous hit.

"Save some of that shit for us cats," Jimi said. When Marley finally couldn't inhale anymore, he exhaled a cartoon cloud of smoke that filled the room. I took the bowl from him and tried to hand it to Jimi, but when he reached for it he dropped it and it fell under the bed.

"Shit!" Jimi said. "Don't worry about it, cat, I got my own stash. Thanks anyway, you're an alright cat."

"Tank you, mon!" Marley boomed. "Now you got to clean up dat mess you made! Ha ha! Good luck, mon!"

The posters became still again. Somewhere in the room a girl was crying, but I didn't see her. I sat on the edge of the bed and picked up the two red chunks from the top of the pile of broken glass. I held them in my open palms and watched them bleed through my fingers. Upon closer inspection, the two pieces appeared to have originally been a single object that when fitted together formed the crude shape of a heart.

Suddenly I was startled by a noise at the door and dropped one of the pieces. A large bearded figure in a green felt vest and matching knickers was standing in the threshold of the doorway thudding a walking stick on the floor with one hand and holding a plastic bottle of Canada Dry ginger ale with the other. He was wearing white stockings up to his knees, pointy shoes with tiny bells on the tips, and a green felt hat that matched the rest of his outfit.

"Glad to have you back," he said. "I was starting to worry."

"Are you The Merry Woodsman?" I asked.

"Am I the Merry Woodsman?" he laughed. "No, it's me, Bruno. Don't you know me? Well, I'm sure it'll come back to you. I'm just relieved to see you up and around again. You were a zombie for a while."

He took a cautious step towards me. When I wasn't startled, he slowly approached like someone trying not to spook an animal until he was standing right above me.

"You seem to have broken that rock," he said.

"It's my heart," I said. "It fell out and broke."

"This?" he said, taking the piece from my hand and inspecting it. "This is Russ' rock, the one his girlfriend gave him. I don't imagine he will be too pleased when he sees this."

"Who's Russ?"

"Oh boy," he said and picked up the other piece. He looked at them for a moment before putting them down on the desk. "I can see we have some work to do here. But first we have to get you out of this deathly room and get your blood flowing again. Come on, there's something I have to show you."

He triumphantly marched out the room expecting me to follow. When he realized that I hadn't, he turned around and commanded, "Come on, let's go!"

Out in the common room a very tired looking George Washington, now decked out in a tattered Genessee Beer T-shirt, was sitting on the couch watching television.

"Is he alright?" he asked the Woodsman.

"He will be once I get through with him!" he said without breaking stride, thumping the walking stick on the floor as he walked.

I followed him past the curtain and into a brightly lit corridor with white walls and highly buffed floor tiling that gave it the antiseptic look of an old hospital. Every ten feet or so on both sides were unmarked doors, and up ahead there was no visible end to the hallway. The fluorescent tube lights in the ceiling buzzed sharply and the rubber on my boots squeaked on the tiles as I walked. The Woodsman walked swiftly and every so often had to stop and wait for me to catch up.

I thought for sure that I was dead and that the hallway was a corridor inside my mind being powered by the last kilowatts of energy left over from my life. I thought the rooms behind the doors each contained a different memory of my life, but I couldn't remember any of them and it frightened me. I didn't know who I was, but I thought that my mind had created this Merry Woodsman to help guide me through the part of death where your whole life pass in front of your eyes, or, in this case, behind them. After passing by many doors, I began to think that he was looking for something in particular, something bad, that he was going to torture me with. I was too afraid to ask any questions, especially the one where I ask if I was really dead, because I was afraid he was going to confirm it.

Finally he stopped at a door that, unlike the others, had a small rectangular window above the handle.

"Are you ready?" he asked before opening it.

I nodded and looked away. He turned the handle and held it open for me to go in first before following me in.

The room was filled with tables, chairs, and cubicle desks. Two beautiful angels were sitting at one of the tables staring into open textbooks. Both had glowing halos hovering over their heads and wings on the back of white silk gowns that in the front revealed major cleavage. They looked annoyed when we came in.

The door slammed shut and I nearly jumped out of my skin.

"Sorry about that," the Woodsman said. "That door gets me every time. Come on, let's have a seat at that table over there in the corner."

The Woodsman slid a chair out for me and went around to the other side of the table. He rested his walking stick against the wall and took a sip of his ginger ale before putting it down and taking a seat.

"So, how do you feel?" he asked after I sat down.

"I don't know," I said.

"Do you know where you are?"

"No."

"Well, I'll tell you. You're *here*."

"Here?"

"*Here*."

"You're *here*."

"I'm *here*."

"That's right," he said with a pleased smile. "That's good. You know you're *here*." He slid the ginger ale across the table. "Take a sip."

I thought this might be a trick. I sniffed the bottle and it did smell like ginger ale, and inside the soda looked normal.

"Go ahead," the Woodsman said. "It's good."

I looked at him and then at the angels.

"You do feel the bottle in your hand, right?" he asked.

"Yeah."

"And you know what it's made out of."

"Plastic."

"What does it say on the side?"

"Canada Dry."

"Good. Now, why don't you go ahead and take a sip to see if you can taste it."

"Is this a trick?"

"No, it's real. Trust me. I'm trying to help you."

I took a small sip and put the bottle back down.

"How was it?"

"Alright, I guess. A little flat. And warm."

"Good, good. And you felt it go down your throat?"

"Yes."

"And into your stomach?"

"Yes."

"So it was definitely real to you."

"I guess."

"Fucking freaks," one of the angels said and slammed her textbook closed. The other did the same and the two stormed out of the room.

"Their wings don't flap when they move," I said, not realizing that the Woodsman wasn't seeing their wings.

"What's that?"

"Their wings—they didn't flap when they walked."

"Take another sip. I think I'm losing you again."

I did as he said and waited for his approval.

"How was it?"

"Alright. But I don't think I want any more."

"That's fine, that's good. You seem to have found *it*."

"Found what?"

"Reality."

"Reality?"

"Yes, *reality*. You were aware that you were drinking ginger ale and that there were other people in the room. Tell me, where do you think you are? Be specific."

"I don't know."

"You don't recognize this place? Well, actually it wouldn't surprise me if you didn't because I know you don't spend much time here."

"Where?"

"The study lounge."

"Study lounge?"

"Third floor study lounge. Matteson Hall."

I thought about it for a moment and everything started to come back. I took another sip of the ginger ale. When I looked back at the Woodsman, he was no longer wearing his green outfit but a plain old V-neck undershirt with huge sweat stains on the chest and armpits. Bruno. I felt dizzy for a moment and nearly blacked out.

"Are you alright?" he asked.

"I think so," I said.

Back at the suite Winston was sitting in front of the television and asked Bruno if I was alright, but he didn't answer and went into his room.

"I think I'm alright," I said.

"If I had known you guys were this fucked up I wouldn't have done the Jesus Christ thing," Winston said. "I don't know what the fuck happened. You guys seemed fine, but when I put on the Marty Friedman tape all of a sudden you lost it."

"What did I do?"

"You just sat there on your bed for hours staring at the floor like you were in a coma or something. I said your name and waved my hands in front of your face, but you had no fucking idea I was even there. Same thing with Ed. He's still out of it. He's just standing in his room holding a broomstick with this crazy look on his face. Are you guys sure that you only took acid?"

"Yeah, it was acid, I think. Valentino said it was Timothy Leary's personal recipe."

Bruno wandered out of his room and closed the door. I asked him how Ed was doing, but he didn't answer. Like a blind man he felt his way to the lounge chair in front of the television and sat down.

"Are you alright, man?" I asked him, but he still didn't answer.

"Looks like we got another one," Winston said.

"He'll probably be alright as long as he stays in front of the TV."

"That shouldn't be a problem," Winston laughed.

I went in to check on Ed and found him standing near the window in the dark, his hands wrapped tightly around a broomstick that he was moving in a slow circular motion like he was churning butter. He was wearing his flannel nightshirt and his green-knit flatcap with gold clover sewn on it, and he was looking at me as if aware of my presence but not threatened by it. I turned for a moment and closed the door, and when I looked up again I was standing under a brightly moonlit night sky dotted with stars in a landscape of rolling green hills as far as the eye could see. At first I feared that I was having a relapse, but I was still holding the ginger ale bottle and I knew who I was. Though it didn't make sense, I realized that I was inside of Ed's hallucination.

"How are you doing, Ed?" I asked, but he didn't answer. I looked around at the scenery before turning back to him. "Is this Ireland?"

Again he didn't answer. I took a couple of steps forward, but I got too close and he assumed a defensive stance with the broomstick. His blank expression made him seem all the more dangerous since he clearly wasn't aware of what was happening. I held my hands out in front of me and slowly backed away, slipping out of the room and gently closing the door.

Back in the common room, Bruno's face was flushed with sweat and he was breathing heavily. His breaths steadily became more rapid until it sounded as if he was about to start hyperventilating.

"If this doesn't get any better soon I think we should consider calling 911," Winston said.

"No!" I said more loudly than I intended. Fortunately Bruno wasn't startled.

"Listen, Hank, this is pretty serious. He could die if something happens and we don't act quickly enough."

"He's not gonna die. Besides, there's nothing they can do for him at the fucking hospital anyway. All we can do is sit here and let him ride it out and make sure he doesn't do anything stupid until he comes down."

I tried to hand Bruno the ginger ale bottle, but he viciously yanked it from me with a snort and crushed it before tossing it aside. His breathing started getting louder until it sounded like he was about to explode.

"Hank—" Winston started, but I cut him off.

"I know, I know," I said, but suddenly Bruno's breathing stopped. For a moment I feared the worst and was just about to tell Winston to call 911 when Bruno let out a low moan and said, "Water."

"He wants water!" I said. I picked up the bottle and uncrushed it. "Alright, Bruno, let's go to the water fountain." He made no move to get up. "Don't you want water?" I said loudly, almost yelling. "Water, Bruno, water! We need to get you some water! Reality calling, Bruno, *reality*!"

"Why don't you just get it for him?" Winston said.

"Because he needs to do it himself! Trust me. He brought me back this way earlier."

After waiting several minutes, I was about to get the water myself until he slowly pushed himself out of the chair and took the bottle from my hand. His eyes were fully dilated and streams of sweat were running down his face and dripping off his beard. He took baby steps towards the hallway and I held the curtain open for him. He felt his way along the walls to the door and I went out into the corridor to make sure the coast was clear.

"Can you see?" I asked him.

"The light..." was all he said.

The water fountain was about twenty yards down the hall, but it was worth the trip because it had a much higher quality of drinking water than our bathroom sink. I went ahead and took a long drink before Bruno got there and held the button down for him so he could fill the bottle. He had trouble holding it still under the stream of water, but I wasn't about to try to take it from him and waited patiently until it was nearly full.

He followed me slowly back to the suite, walking stiffly like the Tin Man before the oil was applied. About halfway back to the room he started drooling, thick streams of clear fluid running down of both sides of his mouth and dangling from his whiskers that suddenly turned into chunks of vomit. He was completely unaware of what was happening and continued his mechanical march without breaking stride. His T-shirt became streaked with melon-colored stains and he left a trail of puke puddles on carpeting behind him. I took his forearm and tried to get him to pick up the pace, but he was obliviously resistant. By the time we got back to the room he had stopped puking, but he was still drooling. I parked him in front of the television and got him some wet paper towels that he had no idea what to do with, so I wiped his chin and shirt for him. I then grabbed some more wet paper towels and went out into the corridor and did my best to clean up the evidence that led directly to our door, but the stains had already started to set.

"Did he drink any of the water yet?" I asked Winston when I got back.

"No."

"Bruno," I said. "Drink the water." He still wasn't hearing me, so I took his wrist and lifted the bottle to his mouth. He didn't know what to do and started mumbling something, but we couldn't tell what he was trying to say.

"Maybe give him a pen and he can try to write it," Winston said.

I handed him a pen and a notebook open to a fresh page. He scribbled something but immediately crossed it out. He did this repeatedly with increasing intensity until his face turned crimson and he jumped out of the chair. He started violently stabbing the notebook with the pen until Winston and I managed to wrestle them away. He suddenly became calm and we sat him back down in front of the television. Winston started flipping through the channels until he found *Saturday Night Fever* playing on TBS.

"There you go, Bruno," Winston laughed. "Home sweet Brooklyn."

"Home," Bruno mumbled.

After he was settled in we looked at the notebook. He had repeatedly written *I JUST DIED and I AM DEAD* before scribbling it out each time.

Suddenly Ed wandered out of his room wearing only his flatcap and a pair of boxer shorts.

"I have to shit," he announced with a big smile. "Where do I shit?"

"In the bathroom, Ed," I said.

"What do I do?" he said.

"Well, you have to go to the toilet, and when you get there, pull your shorts down and take a seat."

"Like this?" Ed said and dropped his shorts to his ankles.

"I don't want to see this," Winston said. "I'm going to bed. Good night and good luck." He went into his room and locked the door.

"No, Ed, not here. Pull your shorts up."

He crouched into a squatting position.

"Not here!" I yelled. I noticed that the blinds were open, so I hurriedly closed them and pulled him up by the armpits.

"But I have to shit!" he cried.

"Not here! In the fucking bathroom!"

With his boxer shorts still at his ankles, I led him into the bathroom and managed to get him seated on the toilet. I leaned against the other side of the stall wall and waited with arms folded.

"How do I shit?" he asked.

"Just let it flow, buddy."

"But how?"

"Just sit there until it comes out. Don't force it."

"I don't get it."

"Just sit and wait. If you really have to go, it will happen by itself. Just stay seated."

We waited in silence for a couple of minutes.

"Nothing's happening," Ed said.

"Sometimes it takes a while."

He started moving around. There was a big splash that sounded too big to be a turd.

"Are you alright in there?" I asked.

"I'm shitting!" he said. I looked under the stall and saw only one foot. The toilet flushed and he cheered. I pushed the stall door open and found Ed with one foot in the bowl.

"I'm shitting!" he yelled and let out a big laugh.

"Ed, stop!"

"I figured it out! I'm the shit!"

"No, the shit comes out of you!"

"My life is shit!" he cried. He flushed again and water splashed all over the stall.

"Sit down!" I yelled. His wild-eyed look was suddenly replaced by fear.

"What do I do?" he asked, his voice cracking a little.

"Just sit like you were before and wait."

He looked down at the wet seat. After staring at it for a moment, he sat and buried his head in his hands and started crying.

"Ed, you're not shit," I said.

"Yes I am. I'm a shitty person, I'm a shitty friend, I'm a shitty son— my whole life is shit."

"Come on, Ed, you are not. What's my name?"

"Hank."

"Where are you?"

"I'm in the bathroom trying to flush my fucking life down the toilet. What the hell does it look like I'm doing?"

"Alright, just stay right there and don't move."

"Where am I gonna go?"

"Don't go anywhere. Just stay there and wait for the shit to come out of your ass hole."

I went back to my room for a cigarette. When I came back I waited until there was a plunk in the toilet. Moments later Ed started recklessly spinning the roll of toilet paper on the dispenser.

"The paper is stuck!" he yelled. It was a new roll and the first square was still stuck to the rest of the paper and he was spinning it around. There were several more new rolls on top of the mirror light, so I grabbed one of those and started it for him before handing it to him under the stall.

"Make sure you're thorough," I said. "I'm not letting you back in the common room with a dirty ass hole."

I waited while he wiped. A few minutes later the toilet flushed and he emerged from the stall with his shorts pulled up. He looked like he had just been beaten up.

"Did you see any shit on the paper on your last wipe?" I asked him.

"Nope. Clean as a whistle."

"Good. Now wash your hands."

Ed washed his hands and then splashed cold water on his face.

"Acid always gets me in the gut," he said while splashing.

After fifteen hours we finally started crashing, but having to come down from so high we would still be wired for a while. Ed and I joined Bruno in front of the television and we watched "CHiPs." It was the episode where Ponch inhales some toxic fumes from a truck they were attempting to pull over and starts tripping.

Bruno said that while *Saturday Night Fever* was on he thought he was in a car driving through Bay Ridge and going to discos.

"I know one thing," he said. "I've done acid once and I sure as hell won't do it again."

"That wasn't a trip," Ed said. "That was psychosis. We now know what insanity is like. We lost our fucking minds."

"At least we found them," I said.

"That remains to be seen."

"Did you really think you were dead?" I asked Bruno.

"Dude, I *was* dead for a while. Everything around me was dark except for a light in front of me. It was like what those people say who die on the operating table and come back. The light kept getting bigger and bigger and when I finally got there, I was suddenly driving around Bay Ridge. I didn't know what the fuck was going on."

After "CHiPs" was over I went to my room. The window was still open and the room was freezing. While I was sliding the window closed, I noticed the two pieces of rock on the desk. I picked one of them up and for a moment it came back—the room dark, glass all over the floor, candles burning, blood running through my fingers. I put it back down next to the several unfinished bowls and took a small hit from one of them. My head immediately started throbbing, so I put the bowl down and lit a cigarette instead.

The light on the answering machine was blinking and I hit the button. There were several messages from Jennifer in which she didn't say anything and only cried, and then there was one from Rosanna: *Running off to Binghamton, are you? You are a fucking coward, Russell Delvecchio! Don't even bother calling me back, ass hole!* There were several more crying messages from Jennifer, but at the end of the very last one, in a barely audible whisper, she said, "It's over. And this time I mean it." She never called again.

I was exhausted, but my mind was still racing as if I was having a normal acid trip after the psychotic episode. I knew it would be several hours before I would be able to sleep, so I put on Pink Floyd's *Wish You Were Here* and started writing in my acid journal. When that CD ended I put in Enya's *Shepherd Moons* and got into bed, but when that one was over I was no closer to sleep than when it started. I listened to several more CDs and finally, by 11:00 AM, eighteen hours after we popped the tabs, I started drifting off to *The John Lennon Collection*. When the track "Love" came on I mercifully fell into the arms of sleep, my subconscious fading out with the music at the end of the song. But, as if the knowing John Lennon was trying to fuck with my head from beyond the grave, the music drifted back in for several more seconds and I started tripping again, riding up and down one last little hill before finally fading into silence.

**6**

Five days later, ten minutes before the midnight that would mark my twentieth birthday, Ed asked me what my last act as a teenager was going to be.

"I don't know," I shrugged. "Smoke a bowl, I guess."

"Come on," he said. "You have to do something crazy."

"Like what?"

"I don't know. Why don't you run through the dorm naked?"

"I don't think so."

"Why not?"

"I'm shy."

"Don't give me that bullshit."

"Alright, I don't want to."

"I don't think you realize the significance of this moment. This is something you'll remember for the rest of your life, and now that the idea is in your head, you'll come to regret it later if you don't do it. Come on, I'll do it with you."

On the opposite side of the building, down on the second floor where we were less likely to be recognized, Ed and I stood in the stairwell wearing nothing but our boxer shorts. My watch said 11:57.

"This is it," Ed said. He removed his shorts and I tried not to look, having already seen enough of Ed's genitals for one week. "Say good-bye to your childhood."

"I think I did the other night," I said.

I was still balking until we heard someone heading down the stairs above us. I hastily removed my shorts and Ed let out a yell as he took off running. I ran after him, sprinting like an Olympian down the straightaway before the first turn and passing him around the corner. By the second straightaway I was exhilarated, uninhibitedly flapping in the breeze as my watch beeped at the passing of midnight and the pains of my childhood were breaking up into irrelevant pieces and falling off behind me. I ran faster towards a new freedom that would carry me fleet of foot to the rest of my life until we made the last turn, where we were stopped cold by a large black man.

"Whoa whoa whoa," he said, blocking our path. He had been unlocking the door of his room and looked down at us with a laugh. "I guess it's true what they say about white boys."

We laughed nervously trying to cover ourselves with our boxers.

"Y'all know I'm an R.A., right?" he said.

"It's his twentieth birthday," Ed said.

"Is that so? It's his twentieth birthday and y'all figured that's a good excuse to run around naked on my floor. That's fucked up, man. Normally I'd write your asses up in a heartbeat for pulling shit like this on my floor, but to be honest, this is the first laugh I've had all day, so I'm gonna let it slide. But if you don't have those motherfuckin' shorts on in five seconds, I will personally make sure you never run through these hallways again."

Two nights later we were down at the Oak celebrating my birthday. Everybody seemed to be having a good time, but I couldn't get into it. The hollow feeling that I had since the trip was even worse under the influence of alcohol. I was a walking chasm. Whatever that thing was that fell out of my body had not been replaced. There I was surrounded by the best friends I ever had, buying me drinks and shots and toasting our friendship, yet I never felt more alone in my life.

All night I kept looking towards the door hoping to see her come in. I didn't even realize I was doing it until I was suddenly overcome by the uncontrollable urge to tell her everything at that very moment. I put my drink down and headed towards the door, ignoring everyone else asking me where I was going. I went in and out of every bar on Water Street but couldn't find her. I caught the next bus to campus and went up to her suite, but no one was home. I considered going down to the Philanthan house, but I was overcome by a wave of exhaustion that knocked some sense into me and made me realize that going down there in that condition was perhaps not the best course of action. Instead I went back to the suite and passed out.

The next morning I woke up at around eight. It was the day before Valentine's Day and I was still a little drunk. The determination from the night before was still there and I didn't want to lose it, but it was way too early to go upstairs. I went up to the Hunt Union instead.

The gift shop was just opening. They had a display of Valentine's cards and I bought one with a rose on the cover that was blank inside and a red Oneonta State College pen. I went into the dining hall, where, over a three-cheese omelet and a large orange juice, I wrote the following inside the card:

*Dear Maria,*

*I know it's been a while, and for that I apologize, but I have been miserable ever since that day we spent together back home when I was unable to express my true feelings for you. I have now reached the point where I cannot hold it in any longer, so I will come right out and say it—I LOVE YOU. I want nothing more than to start over and begin a relationship with you that I am sure will make both of us happy. Your absence in my life has left a void that only you can fill. I am now ready to walk away from everything to be with you and not look back. I hope you can forgive me for my past behavior and be assured that I will not run away again.*

*HAPPY VALENTINE'S DAY!!!*

*Love,*
*Hank*

After breakfast I crashed and spent the rest of the day in bed. Later that night everyone went downtown again, this being the first weekend in a month we weren't snowed in and the other guys were anxious to make up for lost drinking time, but I told them I was too hung over and stayed in. I smoked a couple of quiet bowls and refused to look at the card, which was sealed and buried in my underwear drawer. I was afraid that if I even looked at the envelope with her name neatly written on it, I would change my mind.

The next morning I woke up at around ten. I shat, shaved, and showered, and went up to the dining hall for breakfast with card in pocket. After I finished eating, I sat at the table looking out at the frozen pond next to the building and cleared my head of all clutter in order to focus on what I had to do while trying not to think about what I was going to say. I was just going to go up there and honestly pour my heart out, and whatever happened, happened. The moment of discomfort would be far less than the burden of regret.

I went right up to her door and knocked without hesitating. No one answered, so I knocked again. I hadn't considered that she might not be home and wasn't sure if I should just slide the card under the door or come back later. Before I had a chance to decide, however, the door flew open and the toga-breast girl gave me a big smile.

"Hey stranger!" she said.

"Hey."

"I haven't seen you in these parts for a while."

"Yeah, how are you?" I said, realizing that I didn't know her name.

"I'm alright. Are you looking for Maria?"

"Uh, yeah. Is she around?"

"Actually she went away for the weekend."

"Oh. Do you know when she'll be back?"

"I think she's coming back tomorrow."

I pictured the card torn in tiny pieces on the floor with the two pieces of rock bleeding all over them. I didn't realize how obvious the flashback was until she asked me if I was alright.

"Yes, I'm fine. Thank you."

"Whatcha got there? Is that a Valentine for me?"

"Uh, actually it's for Maria," I said, suddenly embarrassed. "Can you do me a favor and give it to her when she gets back?"

"Sure," she said and took the card. "That's so sweet. I wish somebody would give me a card or some flowers or candy or something, but I guess nobody loves me."

"Don't say that," I said, and then added, "Somebody loves you."

"Then how come they haven't sent me any stupid flowers?"

"It's still early. You might get some."

"I really don't know what to say," Maria said. It was Monday afternoon. She had called as soon as she read the card and I was now sitting next to her on her bed with the card resting between us. "I'm totally at a loss."

"I meant every word of it," I said. "Maria, I love you. I'm determined to do anything to be with you. I admit that at first I wasn't so sure about how I felt about you, but now I know. I've had a revelation."

"A revelation?"

"I don't want to sound like some religious freak or something. Let me just put it to you this way. My soul fell out of my body and smashed on the floor into a million little pieces. My heart fell out with it and it broke in half. I've been trying to put it back together ever since, and this is the only way I know how."

"I've never heard you talk like this," she said, looking down at the card.

"Well, I mean it. I've done some growing up in the past few weeks. I'm twenty years old now and I'm tired of acting like a child. I wasn't ready for a relationship before, but I am now, if you'll give me a chance."

"Don't you think you're rushing into this? I haven't seen you in almost two months and now all of a sudden you show up out of the blue and say you want to start a relationship? Alright, I know it sounds a little familiar, but I think you're moving just a little too fast for me right now."

"I'm not asking you to marry me. I just want to start a relationship. It doesn't have to be a heavy relationship, not at first anyway. Come on, it'll be fun!"

She looked at me like I was crazy and then turned away. She took a deep breath.

"Hank, there's something I have to tell you."

"I'm listening."

"You're not going to like it."

"Try me."

"Well, I'm kind of seeing someone."

"Kind of?"

"I am seeing someone."

"I see."

"No, Hank, I don't think you do."

"No, I understand. I feel like an idiot now, but at least I understand. I shouldn't have expected you to sit around brooding over me. Is it anyone I know?"

"I don't think so. He's in Zeta Beta. His name is Dale. We have this casual relationship thing going and I kind of like it. It's nothing serious."

"How long have you been seeing him?"

"Since November."

"November?"

"I went to the formal with him."

"You mean this was going on when we hung out back home?"

"We were in a fight at the time."

"Did you decide to go to the formal with him before or after you asked me?"

"After. I really wanted to go with you, but after the way you reacted when I asked you and then when you didn't call me, I didn't think you wanted to go. I wasn't even going to go, but at the last minute Kathy talked me into going with Dale and we hit it off."

"Hit it off? Then why the hell did you attack me at the Oak that night?"

She looked away for a moment and took a deep breath.

"You're probably going to hate me for this," she said, still looking away, "but since you are being honest with me, I am going to be honest with you. All that I ask is that you hear me out."

"I'm listening."

"You're mad already."

"I'm not mad. I'm listening."

"Hank, this is really difficult to say."

"So just say it and get it over with."

"Alright. Fine." She took another deep breath and looked down at the card. "Just before I went into the Oak that night, I caught Dale kissing one of my sorority sisters at Sports On Tap. I got really pissed, and that's when I went looking for you."

"So you were just using me to get back at him."

"No, let me finish. I went looking for you, Hank, *you*. If I wanted to get back at him like that, I would have kissed some guy at Sports On Tap right in front of him, which wouldn't have been too difficult because almost all the guys who hang out in that place are a bunch of horny animals."

"Like Dale."

"No, not like Dale. He's really not like that."

"Could have fooled me."

"You don't even know him."

"And that's a good thing."

"Would you please let me finish! Anyway, I was really drunk and I didn't know what to do, so I just left. Without even realizing where I was going, I went into the Oak because I knew you would be there. It was kind of like the night I saw that scumbag who raped me downtown and I didn't know what to do, so I went looking for you. I was being controlled by my raw emotions, and that's where you are because you're the one I truly love. I do love you, Hank. I'll probably always love you, even if I never understand why. Dale has nothing to do with how I feel about you."

"You know, I'm really tired of playing games with you," I said. "That's why I'm here now. That's why I gave you that card. I wanted to lay it all out plain and simple, and if you want to start a relationship with me, great, then let's do it. But if not, let's just put it out of our heads."

"Hank, please don't do this." She was starting to cry. "I'm not ready right now. After what happened with Dale that night I thought that casual relationships weren't my thing, but when I saw you back home I realized I wasn't ready for a relationship with you because I know that once it starts, it won't stop. You're my one, Hank. I just need some time."

"Why didn't you tell me this back home?"

"I was too embarrassed. I felt like an idiot for going up to you like that in the bar, and that day back home you really didn't want to seem to be there either and I didn't want you to feel like I was pressuring you into something. I figured it would be best to let it breathe, and even though it was a bad day together, I didn't want to make a big deal about it because I didn't think either of us were ready. The timing wasn't right. But that's what I like about what I have with Dale. I eventually realized that it wasn't a big deal that he was kissing another girl. It couldn't be that way with you. Dale and I have a relationship without a major commitment hanging over our heads. This is the first time I've been happy since I got to this goddamn place, and I didn't want to risk losing that and at the same time risk losing you by getting into a relationship that I didn't think either of us were ready for."

"So you just want to keep banging *Dale* until you're ready for me."

"That hurt, Hank."

"Well, how the hell do you think I feel?"

"Honestly, I had no idea how you felt until about an hour ago when I read your card. Quite frankly, I'm shocked. Since I've gotten to know you these past few months, you gave virtually no indication that you felt this way, and then all of a sudden you give me this card and an ultimatum. I thought you needed some time and I realized that I needed some too."

"I'm tired of waiting, Maria. I'm tired of thinking about being with you and it not being real. I can't wait any longer."

"Dale is transferring at the end of the semester."

"Oh yeah?"

"Yeah. He won a partial scholarship to play on the water polo team at Notre Dame."

"Well la-di-da. Go Irish."

"After he's gone I'll probably never see him again."

"That's too bad."

"It's only a few months, Hank."

"So you're suggesting that I wait for him to transfer to Notre Dame and then we can start seeing each other."

"The reason we're seeing each other in the first place is that you didn't want to go to the formal with me."

"I did want to go."

"Why didn't you tell me?"

"After I ran out on you that night I thought you hated me."

"I can never hate you."

I didn't want to talk anymore. I got up and looked at the Monet print on the wall and for a moment it started undulating again.

"Have a nice life, Maria."

"What is that supposed to mean?"

As I headed towards the door she told me to wait, but I didn't stop. Her voice faded to echo until I could no longer hear it. Suddenly I was back inside the circle, where the harsh winds outside were drowned out by the whir of a plastic fan turning it's head from side to side. Here the wonder of something better was gently suppressed by the warm comfort of familiarity, the pain of life numbed by the freedom of apathy, the light of day eclipsed by the drawn blinds, the dark of night illuminated by the glow of a burning candle stub that was about to become a lump of wax at the bottom of an empty beer bottle.

# III

**1**

The following evening after folding quickly in a hand of 99, I just happened to be on my way to the bathroom when there was a knock on the door. Thinking I knew who it was, I decided to answer it before someone else did. If it was who I thought it was, I would calmly ask her to leave. If she wanted to talk, I would tell her that I had nothing to say and that anything she had to say didn't matter to me at all. If she still wouldn't leave, I would suggest she go play some water polo before slamming the door in her face.

I had never believed in love at first sight. Lust maybe, but not love. Yet when I opened the door there it was staring back at me with hazelnut eyes, and just like that I immediately forgot about old what's-her-name.

She was the most beautiful girl I had ever seen. Her beauty was unassuming in that only a discerning eye could fully appreciate it. She was tall, perhaps a shade under six-feet, and had long wavy hair that fell past her shoulders and matched the color of her eyes. She had sweet water lily lips and a small constellation of faint freckles on each side of her dainty nose. She wore no makeup, which would have only hid how naturally beautiful she was. Her unbuttoned coat revealed breasts like ripened pears and nipples hard from the cold pressing against her tight black bodysuit without the interference of a bra. Oh, how I loved her!

"Hi," she said sheepishly, letting out a little laugh.

"Hi," I mumbled back, still in shock. I tried to think of something clever to say, but I was distracted by the nipples.

"This is so embarrassing," she said, "but I was wondering if you guys can do me a favor."

"Sure. Whatever you need."

"Do you know where I can get some weed?"

"Weed? Sure. Maybe. Are you a narc?"

"No," she laughed.

"Are you in a sorority?"

"God no."

"Good. Good good. Glad to hear it."

"I'm not really even looking to buy. I'm just jonesing really bad right now because the guy I buy from ran out a few days ago and I want to get high. My name is Virginia, by the way."

Virginia Duvall was the only child of Chester and Priscilla Duvall, whom she once referred to as 'the boringest people in the world.' Chester had met Priscilla at Putnam Valley High School (Home of the Tigers) and they married at the ripe old age of 18, just prior to Chester shipping off to Vietnam. He fought in the Army for nearly three weeks before contracting a nasty case of cerebral malaria that nearly killed him and was released from the military on a medical discharge.

When Chester got home he moved in with Priscilla and her parents and spent nearly a year recovering from his illness before landing a job at a nearby toothpick factory. In the meantime Priscilla earned her teaching certificate and got a part-time job as a home economics teacher for two years before becoming pregnant with Virginia. After the baby was born she went back to work full-time, and with Chester being promoted to foreman that same year, things went pretty well for the Duvalls until the toothpick factory closed down a few years later. He was out of work for nearly two years before finally landing a sales job with a toothpick dispenser company that had just relocated to the area, where he worked his way up to Executive Vice President of Global Sales and got a corner office.

Chester and Priscilla knew early on that Virginia was a gifted child—they just couldn't figure out exactly what that gift was. She was smart and did well in school, but she didn't seem interested in anything except staying home and reading. Despite these clues, they had no idea that her secret passion was writing, a talent that blossomed when she was introduced to some very fine hydroponic cannabis sativa in tenth grade. She discovered that when she smoked, she could hardly write fast enough to get all the thoughts racing through her mind down on the college-ruled pages of her spiral five-subject notebook. Every night after Chester and Priscilla went to bed at ten o'clock sharp, she would light up and write until her mind was purged, leaving herself physically and mentally on the brink of collapse. She kept this up until her senior year of high school when she had finally written all she could about her parents, kids at school, and life in Putnam County. There was an entire world out there waiting for her to write about, and it wasn't long before the itch became unbearable.

She got a job at Barnes & Noble and started saving money. The plan was to have enough money by graduation to spend the summer backpacking through Europe and eventually wind up in Amsterdam, where she would do the starving expatriate artist thing until she was published. She got her passport and Youth Hostel International Card without telling anyone of her intentions, and on the night of commencement while her fellow graduates were partying with friends and family, she was sitting on a plane to London. The note left on her pillow was not read until the following afternoon.

After spending her first night abroad at a sleazy hostel in North Camden, she changed her mind about the backpacking thing and the next day skipped over to Paris, where she caught a train to Amsterdam. As soon as she got there she planted herself in a café near Dam Square and spent the next three days scribbling in her notebook under the influence of some very powerful and expensive Lebanese hashish. When she ran out of money she wandered the streets begging for change, resisting the call of the red glow that would make her some quick cash to take back to the café, until she caught pneumonia and nearly died in a Dutch hospital.

Not trusting her enough to wire the money, her father caught the next flight over and claimed her at the hospital. Back home she eventually got her old job back at Barnes & Noble and spent her nights high on good old hydroponic, hashing through the hundreds of pages she had written in her notebook during her adventure overseas. Life at home wasn't so bad as long as she was busy, but once that project was finished she was right back where she started, except this time she had nothing to look forward to. It wasn't long before what her parents had been saying all along about college suddenly didn't sound so bad. Before her flight across the Atlantic she had wanted the education that life had to offer rather than the one attained sitting in a classroom for four years, but now, if it got her out of Putnam County, she was all for it.

The other guys looked confused. We had never had a girl sit in with us during one of our smoke sessions and had never really hung out with one in the year-and-a-half we had been at Oneonta. It was always just us, there were never any outsiders. I thought she might be a little intimidated meeting all of us at once, but when I introduced her to everyone she seemed perfectly at ease.

"Virginia is in need of our help," I said. "It seems that her connection is out of commission and she has come to us to accommodate her smoking needs. I told her that we couldn't sell her any, but that she was more than welcome to sit in with us."

"We're always willing to help a damsel in distress," Ed said. He got up and kissed the back of her hand, which prompted Bruno to roll his eyes. I was a little annoyed by it myself but even more annoyed when he invited her to sit next to him on Russ' bed.

"How do you guys know each other?" Russ asked after he finished packing the bowl.

"We don't," I said.

Russ was about to spark the bowl but checked himself.

"So you just showed up here looking to get high?"

"Well, yeah," she said, letting out a nervous laugh.

"Well, ah, do you live here in Matteson?" Teke asked.

"No, I live in Ford Hall."

"How did you know where we live?" Bruno asked.

"This is so embarrassing," she laughed. "I kind of followed a couple of you guys home the other day. You and you to be exact," she said, pointing to Teke and Ed.

"Hey, our first stalker!" Ed said.

"I wasn't stalking you guys! Actually, I've been curious about you guys ever since that day last semester when you were smoking weed in the quad with your jackets over your heads right in front of everybody. There were like hundreds of people around and you guys were sitting right in the middle of them smoking up. Professors were walking by! It was the funniest thing I've ever seen!"

"I thought we were being cleverly discreet," Ed said.

"Ha! There goes your theory about people not noticing something they wouldn't expect to see," Bruno said.

"Everybody noticed! I heard some girl call you guys 'those fucked up guys in the woods.' She said she always used to see you going in and out of the woods from her dorm room. I heard someone else say that one of you guys tried to climb out of a moving bus."

"Well, ah, that would be me," Teke said.

"The whole time I've been here I haven't met anyone even remotely interesting. My quadmates are freaks, and just about everyone who goes to school here is in a sorority or a fraternity or they're just losers. You guys seem like the most interesting people here and I just thought it would be cool to hang out and smoke with you guys. You always look like you're having fun."

Unaccustomed to smoking with outsiders, much less someone as attractive as Virginia Duvall, everyone curiously watched her take each hit from the many bowls that went around over the course of the evening. After a while she became self-conscious and asked why everyone was staring at her, and Ed told her that we weren't used to taking drugs with beautiful women. All of us rolled our eyes at that one. When we weren't staring she seemed totally comfortable and fit right in, contrary to the impression I was under that most any chick would feel totally out of place inside our little circle. But Virginia was different. Here was a cool, interesting, attractive girl that I wouldn't have to give up my life to be with. She laughed at our jokes, she laughed at us making fun of each other, and she laughed at us making fun of our own campus celebrities, which made me wonder if at that very moment others were sitting around smoking dope and making fun of us.

At one point she noticed the picture of Eddie Vedder with his arm around Russ' sister. It had been taken at the Jones Beach Theater the summer before at a concert that had been cancelled due to inclement weather. The bands were hanging out in the parking lot signing autographs when she spotted Vedder and asked if she could get a picture with him. He took the camera from her, put his arm around her shoulder, and held it out in front of them as he snapped the picture.

"You know, Russ is Eddie Vedder's second cousin," Ed said.

"Really?" she said. She was very high, her eyes bloodshot and tearing, and she was laughing at nearly everything we said whether it was meant to be funny or not.

"Yeah," Ed continued. "That picture was taken at a family reunion out in Seattle last year."

"Are you from Seattle?" Virginia asked Russ.

"Actually, I grew up with Ed in San Diego," Russ said, recalling the article about Pearl Jam in the crinkled copy of *Rolling Stone* in our bathroom. "But I haven't seen much of him since he became famous."

"Russ is a little bitter," Ed said. "He was actually in a band with him in high school."

"Really? What did you play?"

"Bass."

"He wrote a bunch of songs for the band," Ed said. "Then they put out that album and Vedder took all the credit for Russ' songs. Didn't even give him a mention in the liner notes."

"Bastard," Russ said.

"Well, ah, it was Russ' mother Pearl who was Eddie's aunt who made the psychedelic jam they named the band after," Teke said.

"My mama liked to trip," Russ said.

"Oh my God," Virginia said to herself, believing every word of it.

"And Jeremy was in Russ' kindergarten class!" Bruno said, which is when Virginia realized. She looked around the room at us trying to hold in our laughter and finally cried, "You guys are so mean!"

She covered her face in embarrassment as everyone burst out laughing, but moments later she was laughing as loudly as we were.

Later that night I couldn't fall asleep. I replayed the entire evening in my head over and over from the moment I opened the door to the moment she left. I knew I was getting ahead of myself, but I didn't care. This was destiny. All I had to do get to know her and allow her to get to know me, and especially be careful not to scare her away by moving too fast. As long as I was patient and didn't do anything to fuck it up, nothing could stand in our way.

**2**

It had been 91 hours and 23 minutes since my last cigarette, but now, on the day after St. Patrick's Day, my willpower was steadily waning and the teeth-grinding stress of the past several days left me looking for any excuse at all to have one. I had decided to quit after experiencing shortness of breath for several consecutive nights while trying to fall asleep, and I was tired of waking up every morning hocking up globs of green phlegm and spitting them into the metal wastepaper basket that had become my bedside spittoon. Either the pot or the cigarettes had to go, and I wasn't about to give up the pot. The final straw was waking up to a forty-five minute coughing fit on Sunday morning. When I was finally able to stop coughing long enough to have one last smoke, I gave the rest of my pack to Russ and hadn't had one since.

I had not gone out on St. Pat's Day because my priggish History of English Grammar professor purposely scheduled the two-part midterm that counted as 50% of our final grade on the Thursday and Friday after the holiday, because, as she put it, "You are here to learn, not to get drunk." Meanwhile Ed had gone down to the bars at eight in the morning and was this time accompanied by Bruno, who made it until three in the afternoon before puking all over himself and his leather jacket on Water Street and coming home by himself. As of the time I got back to the suite after the first part of my midterm the following day, Ed had still not returned.

"I'm this close to calling the hospital," Bruno said, sitting in his easy chair watching *Saved By the Bell*. "Who knows what the hell that drunk Irish idiot has gotten himself into."

"Maybe you should try the police station first," Winston laughed.

A moment later the door opened and Ed emerged from behind the curtain looking like he had been in a train wreck.

"What the hell happened to you?" Bruno asked.

"I couldn't even begin to tell you," he answered, heading right for his room without stopping.

"Where were you?"

"At Virginia's." He slammed the door and fell hard onto the springy bed.

"Did you bang her?" Bruno yelled at the closed door.

"Yes," the door answered.

The next thing I knew I was storming towards the quad. Russ and Teke had been at class and I was hoping to run into one of them so I could bum a cigarette, but they were nowhere to be found. I needed nicotine immediately and thought it would be quicker to try and grub one from someone rather than go all the way up to the Hunt Union, take out a twenty from the cash machine, break it at the gift shop into smaller bills (if they had any), and go to the change machine at the arcade to get $3.00 worth of quarters to plug into the cigarette machine.

It was a nice day and there were plenty of smokers hanging out. I scanned the crowd for someone who probably wouldn't say no and spotted a cute hippie girl sitting on the steps of Schumacher Hall who looked like something right out of Haight-Ashbury circa 1967. She had long straight dirty-blond hair that fell halfway down her back, and she was wearing a tie-dye dress, several beaded necklaces, and sunglasses with purple lenses. I was so fixated on her cigarette that I barely noticed her bare feet.

She was already looking at me as I approached.

"Do you have an extra cigarette?" I asked.

"I sure do," she said and handed me one. "I was watching you look around and hoped that you would ask me. You look like you could really use one."

"Thank you," I said, a little embarrassed at how obvious I was. I put it between my lips and she lit it for me. "You're a lifesaver."

"I don't know about that. By giving you a cigarette I just shortened your life by five minutes."

"This five minutes is worth more to me now than when I'm an old man dying of cancer." I became really lightheaded after the first drag. "This is definitely worth it. Thank you again."

"Don't mention it," she said, tossing her butt away and getting up. "Enjoy." I watched her climb the stairs and disappear into the building as I smoked, and after I was finished I headed up to the Hunt Union.

At the time I had no idea that the hippie girl was Virginia's roommate.

Her name was Sandy. She was a lost child who had grown up on a farm in Chenango County and currently resided in her own little world of hippie dreams and psychedelic skies. She was a quiet girl, not so much because she was shy but that she was usually on something and didn't know where she was half the time. The world outside herself didn't concern her because she was completely oblivious to it. Her disposition was sweet, but her apathy towards her excessive drug use was a little disconcerting, especially since the excess was wasted because she was never sober long enough to appreciate it. She didn't seem to care that if she maintained her pace she wasn't going to make it to twenty-five, and that quality in her made you think about your own mortality.

Virginia and Sandy shared a quad with two other girls, Zoë and Hannah.

Zoë was a bisexual goth from Brooklyn who liked to think of herself as the second coming of Madonna. She had short black hair and wore black makeup, leather shorts, and fishnet stockings. She had several body piercings and tattoos, including a large Star of David with a snake slithering through it on her thigh that she was not shy about showing off. She smoked Newports and the only alcohol she drank was Sambuca. Virginia said she often Fed-Exed her homework to her father, a big shot in the garment industry, and he would complete it for her and Fed-Ex it back the next day with large sums of cash in the envelope. Bruno took an immediate liking to this girl, and she was not shy about using it to her advantage.

Zoë's roommate Hannah was from Schenectady. She dressed like a slutty schoolgirl, often wearing little girl dresses or Catholic school uniforms with Mary Jane shoes and white stockings, and she wore her hair in French braids. It probably would have been sexy if she didn't dress like this all the time and hang out with Zoë and Sandy, the three of them together looking like they were on their way to a Halloween party. She followed Zoë around like a sidekick, laughing at all of her jokes and agreeing with everything she said while rarely expressing opinions of her own.

Not long after St. Pat's Day we met them as a group for the first time. Much to Virginia's chagrin, they soon became regulars at our nightly smoke sessions. Russ was inwardly annoyed about this as well, but he didn't complain since they often supplied the weed. Everyone else seemed to enjoy having them around, and I didn't really mind as long as Virginia was there. She and Ed had been sleeping together on a regular basis, but that's all it was. Both of them seemed content to keep their relationship on a physical level, which led me to believe that it would end as soon as Ed found someone else to fuck who wouldn't burden him with a relationship.

In the meantime I just had to deal with it and stick to my plan. With her hanging out with us nearly every night, I took full advantage of the opportunity to show her how much fun I was, and it seemed to be working. Without there being a sexual tension between us we became friends, and I was hoping to be the one she turned to when Ed dropped the bomb.

Just before the last weekend of the semester Zoë suggested that we have a group acid trip. At first I didn't want anything to do with this and didn't think Bruno and Ed would either, but Bruno didn't want to miss out on a chance to trip with Zoë and Ed decided it was "time to get back on the horse." Russ and Teke were also in, leaving me as the only tripper who didn't want to partake. Up until the last minute I wasn't going to do it, but then Virginia told me that it wouldn't be any fun without me and that she would be disappointed if I didn't. Finally I relented, telling her that I would do it this one last time so that we will have at least tripped together once, because after this I was done with acid for good.

After suffering a severe anxiety attack from the same acid that caused our psychotic episodes, Valentino retired from drug dealing and began a new, less stressful career working at the front desk of the Howard Johnson's just outside of town in order to keep up the insurance payments on his Ferrari. So, as had been the case with our dope supply since his retirement, Virginia got the tabs through her connection. She said it was pretty mild stuff, but Ed, Bruno, and I were still only going to take one tab each. Teke, Russ, and Virginia were going to take two, Zoë and Hannah three, and Sandy was going to take an astounding five tabs, saying that she had a "very high acid tolerance" and taking that much was the only way she could get off.

The girls showed up at around noon on Saturday and we popped the tabs before heading up to the fields. It was a beautiful afternoon, the first day it really felt like summer after an unseasonably cold spring, and there was not a cloud in the sky. Sandy brought a blanket and laid it on the grass before taking a seat and staring off at nothing in particular for the first hour or so. I found my own little spot about twenty yards away from everyone else and went through my bookbag packed with my acid journal, Ed's crayons, two oranges, and a can of Coca-Cola. I opened the journal and looked at the entries from the last couple of trips, not having looked at them since, and vividly recalled the horror of those two nights before turning to a clean page and drawing the fields and surrounding hills with the crayons, a piece I titled "A New Day."

Virginia was right about the acid not being strong, but it was loaded with speed and my mind started racing. After I finished my drawing I started writing down everything that came into my head, mostly reflections on my previous trips. Virginia came over and asked what I was writing and I told her I was just rambling. She asked if she could look at the book and I handed it to her. We sat Indian-style next to each other and I explained as well as I could what each entry meant as she flipped through the pages.

After she was finished looking at it she told me about the novel she had written based on her journal entries and about how she escaped to Amsterdam because she needed material for the ending. Her dedication to writing made my own literary attempts seem pathetic, but at the same time it inspired me. She told me about how Jack Kerouac had influenced her and that I should read *On the Road*, the book that got her out of her room and into the world.

"I just want to get in a car and drive in no particular direction, she said. "I want to see every state and experience everything this country has to offer."

"Are you ever going back to Amsterdam?"

"Probably not. It was pretty sleazy over there, and I want to stay in the States. I do want to go to Vancouver, though. They're pretty open-minded about weed up there."

I would have been content sitting there all day talking to her, but the others called us over to smoke a bowl and she didn't want to miss out. They were sitting in a circle and Sandy invited me to sit next to her on the blanket. I wanted to sit next to Virginia, but Ed had saved a spot for her next to him, so I accepted Sandy's invitation.

Russ had carved a bowl out of a carrot stick and put a screen in it. It worked surprisingly well but didn't hold much weed, and with so many of us smoking we had to pack it several times.

"I can't believe we're smoking pot out of a carrot," Zoë said.

"This isn't pot," Russ said. "It's actually 100% pure grade rabbit shit."

Suddenly I started laughing uncontrollably. It got so bad that I fell back on the blanket, not realizing that Sandy had just removed her sunglasses and placed them right behind me. She screamed "My glasses!" a second too late. I landed on them before leaping to my feet and doing a little dance that made everyone else start laughing, but I felt bad and apologized to Sandy.

"These are my favorite glasses," she said, almost crying. The purple lenses had fallen out and the frames were badly bent.

"Can you fix them?" I asked.

"Maybe." She popped the lenses back in and attempted to straighten out the frames before putting them back on. "I think they're alright," she said.

"I'm so sorry," I said, not mentioning that they were a bit crooked on her face.

"Well, ah, I know it's probably just the acid talking," Teke said, "but I could have sworn that a just saw a huge purple condom fly across the sky."

"That was a frisbee," Virginia laughed, looking at the people across the field tossing it to one another.

"I think there was some rabbit shit on that frisbee," Russ said. He let out a maniacal laugh that caused the frisbee tossers to look over. His face was almost as red as his hair. "Rabbit shit on a shingle!"

"Is he alright?" Zoë asked Bruno while pointing at Russ with her head. Bruno shrugged.

"Like the big fat Buddha said," Russ said, "*Life is one big shit of rabbit.*"

"Well, ah, that's pretty heavy," Teke said.

"You guys are foaming rabbit shit at the mouth," Ed said.

Hannah had to pee and headed off towards the bushes beyond the fence. She was wearing her Mary Ann from *Gilligan's Island* outfit, a pair of short cutoff jeans and a tight red and white checkered blouse tied in a knot just above her belly button that looked like it had been made from a tablecloth at an Italian restaurant. A few minutes later she came back with a big wet spot on the front of her shorts. When Ed noticed he yelled "Holy rabbit shit!" and started laughing loudly. It was obvious to everyone what he was laughing at and the girls pretended not to notice, but all the rest of us could do was make it look like we were laughing at something else.

"Purple rabbit shit looks red if smeared against linoleum!" Russ said.

"I was walking in the rain and I stepped in a pile of rabbit shit!" Ed laughed.

"Are you guys losing your minds again?" Virginia asked.

"Peter Frampton has a rabbit shit head!" Russ said.

"This is getting weird," Zoë said.

"It's not weird," Russ said calmly. "It's Introductory Fundamentals of the Theory of Rabbit Shit Evolution 101 taught by Brother Bruno."

"Hey, leave me out of this," Bruno said.

"Oh, Hank," Ed said with a really bad imitation of a chick. "You have the most rabbit shit blue eyes I have ever seen."

"I beg your pardon, madam," I said, "All I have is left-handed rabbit shit tonsils in my right hand."

"Oh yeah? What are you going to do about it?"

"I'm gonna rabbit shit all over you!"

"The rabbit shit has hit the fan!"

"Rabbit shit splatters, so you might as well wear it!"

"Enough!" Zoë yelled.

"Quick doctor, we need the rabbit shit vaccine!"

"Pack it!"

"It looks like you're packing more rabbit shit into that rabbit shit toilet!"

"I don't want any rabbit shit, but you can't have any!"

"I'll have a hoot of rabbit shit, hold the mayo."

"Guys, stop it!" Virginia yelled. "You're freaking me out!"

"Have another rabbit shit, Larry, she's just kidding."

"What came first? The rabbit or the rabbit shit?"

"The rabbit shit vaccine isn't working! I can't stop!"

"That's it!" Zoë yelled and jumped to her feet.

"Alright!" Ed yelled. "Someone has to take control of this mess! I have an idea to end this madness. Let's get our rabbit shit together and take a nice long walk on the trail."

"I don't know if I want to go out in the woods with you guys after that," Zoë said.

"I'll go!" Sandy said.

"I will too," Virginia said, "but only if you guys stop with the rabbit shit."

By the time we finally hit the trail the sun was getting low in the sky. We walked quietly in a single line absorbing the serenity of the woods, looking around at the trees and giant moss-covered rocks beside the path or down at our feet traversing the path as if they were not our own. Sandy in particular seemed really out of it, weaving from side-to-side while looking up at the rays of sunlight slicing through the new spring leaves. She was walking very slowly, and every so often we had to stop and wait for her to catch up.

The sun was just about to dip behind the hills to the west when we reached the sticky vines of 'Blackberry Hill,' which was our name for the clearing made for the power lines that cut through the hills and valleys visible for miles in both directions. We took a seat on the path and Russ packed the carrot bowl. After everyone got a hit we silently watched the big orange ball in the sky mechanically descend towards the hill across the valley. When it touched the summit the sky changed colors, blending into a mural of purple, orange, and blue swirl. After it was over we sat there for a good fifteen minutes hoping it would come back, but when it didn't Ed got up and started picking blackberries.

A little while later everyone was ready to go except Sandy, who was still sitting and staring off in the direction where the sun had disappeared. The others were coming down from their peaks and in their own little worlds, but I felt fine and was the only one who noticed that Sandy was still sitting there while everyone else had already started walking. I asked her if she was ready to go and she answered by looking up at me with a jaw-lock smile. I offered my hand and she took it, allowing me to help her up but having difficulty keeping her balance. When she was finally standing under her own power I tried to pull my hand away but she wouldn't let go, so I held it and led her back to the trail.

The rest of the group was well ahead of us but didn't stop to wait. Sandy walked slowly and unsteadily, constantly stopping to look at something—a flower, a branch, a long blade of grass—and we soon lost sight of the others. Every time she stopped I asked her if she was alright and she would look at me with that smile, which had a childlike innocence that was cute in a way but also starting to concern me.

By the time we got back to Matteson it was dark. Up in the suite I held the hallway curtain open for her and she went right into Ed and Bruno's room as if drawn like a moth to the blue light emanating from Ed's lava lamp. My Enya CD was in Ed's CD player and I played "Caribbean Blue" while she stared wondrously at the lamp. I stood next to her and for a moment felt like a guy trying to pick up a chick at a museum until I got lost in the lamp myself. The bubbles oozed and floated in perfect harmony with the music and I felt like I was floating naked in the warm blue sea, uninhibited by the petty concerns of the cold cruel world above the surface.

"It's beautiful," Sandy whispered without taking her eyes off the lamp. "I wish it could last forever."

"Me too," I said.

"This is what it must have been like in the womb. If I had known better I would have never come out."

"But this is better because we're conscious of it."

"We were conscious of it then too. We just don't remember."

When the song was over, Sandy wandered out of the room and out of the suite. Everyone else was in my room smoking a bowl, so I followed her out and caught up to her down the hall.

"Where are you going?" I asked.

"I don't know," she said.

"Do you mind if I join you?"

"You are welcome to."

We left the building and wandered aimlessly around campus for about an hour before she finally came down. We started talking and she told me she was dropping out of school after finals and moving to Colorado at the end of the summer. She had been there once before to see a Dead show with her friends, some of whom liked it there so much that they stayed and moved to a nearby commune they heard about from the Deadheads. She had regretted ever since not staying out there and had been living for the day that she would return for good. After finals she was going to get a job at home for a couple of months to save some money, and then at the end of the summer head back out there and never come back.

We eventually wound up in front of Ford Hall and she invited me upstairs. It was the first time I had been up to their quad and the common room was empty except for the chairs that came with the room. I commented on how I was impressed that they had already finished cleaning out their common room when we hadn't even started on ours, but she said it had been that way all year.

She led me into her and Virginia's room and it was immediately obvious as to whose side of the room was whose. On one side there was a bed with tie-dye sheets and a panoramic poster of Woodstock at daybreak covering two walls that managed to squeeze in all 500,000 people and the tiny stage in the distance, and scattered over the rest of the wall space and ceiling were colorful psychedelic posters and pictures of Jerry Garcia that had been torn out of magazines. The other side of the room had only a few posters that looked like they had been bought at the same place—Pearl Jam, REM, Nirvana, U2, and the same exact Monet print that Maria Viola had on her wall. The bed was neatly made with sheets that looked like they had been purchased from an old Sears catalog, and unlike the filthy drug den on the other side of the room, this side was impeccably tidy.

Sandy invited me to sit next to her on the tie-dye bed.

"I want to show you something," she said, rifling through a pile of miscellaneous junk on the floor while I stared at the other side of the room. She found a plastic egg covered with paisley designs and tiny beads inside that she rattled to the rhythm of "Not Fade Away," and after a couple of minutes of this I grabbed her wrist to make her stop because the room was starting to spin. She laughed and kissed me, pushing me gently down on my back and my head landing on the pillow. She removed my boots and pulled off my pants and boxer shorts before getting up and taking off her dress. She had been wearing neither bra nor panties.

I was crashing hard, and with my head on the pillow it became increasingly difficult to keep my eyes open. Sandy stroked my forehead and pulled my eyelids up.

"Don't fall asleep," she whispered.

"I won't," I said, though I wasn't sure how much longer I could stay awake. I woke up a little when she slipped her tongue into my ear, which sent a chill through my entire body. She kissed me down my neck and across my chest, stopping to suck my nipples before continuing on to my stomach, where she stuck her tongue in my navel. From there she went down a little farther and started sucking my dick, taking it all the way in to the base and swirling her tongue around until it was hard, but with the acid still flowing through my system and being on the verge of a major crash, I couldn't quite reach full arousal.

I still had the yellow condom that had been in my wallet all year. After struggling to open the wrapper I was relieved to discover that it hadn't crusted. By the time I was ready to put it on, however, I had lost my erection and frantically started jerking myself off to get it back up. Sandy sat up and asked if I would like her to do that for me.

"No, I'm alright," I said. "Just strapping one on."

"Here, let me."

She started blowing me again and in a couple of minutes I was aroused. I put the condom on and she gently pushed me back down on the bed. She climbed on top of me, but while she was guiding me inside her I heard the door open and close out in the common room. Sandy didn't seem to notice and started moaning as she began to thrust, but after hearing Zoë laugh and Virginia say something, I went into a panic and lost my erection.

"I'm sorry," I said. "I got a little distracted."

"That's okay."

She slid off and started pumping my member like she was taking my blood pressure, but after a while her arm got tired and she needed a break. By now I had a load built up inside me that was going to have to come out, so I took over and got it back up. The lubrication on the condom had dried up, so I started massaging her muff to get her moist and then had to get myself back up before climbing on top.

I started slow and gradually picked up the pace until my balls started to hurt. I couldn't hear anything out in the common room, but the bed was squeaking so loudly it was hard to tell. After a while it felt like my skin was being rubbed raw inside the condom. At this point Sandy had pretty much lost interest, but for my benefit she let out a little moan to let me think that she was still into it.

"I'm getting close," I said.

"You're trying too hard," she said. "Just relax. You'll get there."

When I finally did get there it suddenly didn't seem worth it. All that painstaking effort for three seconds of pleasure that would leave me sore for the next three days and most likely ruin any chance I had with Virginia. Sandy carefully removed the condom and tied a knot at the end like a balloon. She put on a tie-dye terrycloth robe and dropped the condom into one of the pockets, looking at me with a smile before heading out of the room. I rolled over and stared at Max Yasgar's farm and a few moments later heard the industrial flush of a dorm toilet down the hall.

Soon after the flush someone came into the room. At first I thought it was Sandy, but after hearing the springs creak on the bed across the room I rolled over and saw Virginia lying on her bed fully clothed with her back to me. As quietly as possible I slipped under the sheets, and when Sandy came back she slipped under with me, her warm naked body pressing against mine as I drifted into unconsciousness oblivion.

I dreamed that I was at Woodstock wandering through the muddy crowd when the announcement came from the stage not to take the brown acid. I started to panic because I had swallowed a couple of brown tabs not fifteen minutes earlier and thought I was going to have a trip even worse than the psychotic episode. I spotted Sandy dancing naked in a puddle of mud being cheered on by some other hippies and ducked behind the crowd hoping that she wouldn't notice me go by. Closer to the stage I saw Virginia sitting naked by herself on a blanket. She had a wreath of yellow flowers in her hair and was the most beautiful vision my eyes ever had the fortune to behold, so much so that she was actually glowing. I started walking towards her but was suddenly tackled from behind and taken down into a puddle of mud. I struggled to get up, but my assailant was relentless and kept pushing me back down until I finally gave up. Looking down at me with arms folded, head eclipsing the sun, face shadowed and covered with mud, I couldn't tell who it was until I looked into the eyes.

"You're not getting away this time," Maria said and started laughing wickedly.

I woke up with a start. The sun was shining brightly through the blinds right into my eyes and it took me a few moments to realize where I was. Across the room Virginia's bed was vacant and neatly made. Sandy woke up and started massaging my back while I stared blankly at the other bed.

"I have to go," I said. I sat up, but Sandy pulled me right back down. She started kissing me but stopped when she realized I wasn't kissing back.

"What's wrong?" she asked.

"Nothing. I have to go."

I got out of bed and got dressed. While I was putting my boots on she asked me to stay a little longer, but I told her that I had to study for finals. Just before I left I kissed her quivering lips, and we briefly made eye contact when we realized that we were never going to see each other again. She looked like she was about to start crying, so I said good-bye and hurried out.

The other bedroom door was open and no one was inside. I slipped out of the quad and walked swiftly down the hall hoping not to run into the other girls, eventually finding my way to the service entrance at the back of the building. I pushed open the heavy door and wandered across campus in a daze, my mind burnt like it had been gutted by fire, and for the first time since I had been in Oneonta I wanted to be somewhere else. But right now I was willing to settle for sleep, sweet uninterrupted sleep.

**3**

A few nights later while I was packing, Virginia called and asked if I wanted to smoke a joint with her. Upon hearing this unprecedented invitation, my heart stopped for a moment until I realized that Sandy probably put her up to it to find out why I hadn't called. But then again, so what? This was my first chance to be alone with Virginia and my first opportunity to assess the damage I had done by sleeping with Sandy, who, as far as I was concerned, might as well have already been in Colorado. I suggested that we meet at the tennis bubble in an hour and from there go down to the bridge.

It was a pleasant evening, the sun just about to set and the campus quiet. Though I was ready to put the year behind me and get away for the summer, I was somewhat depressed by the thought that college was already half over. When I got to the bubble I waited fifteen minutes and smoked three cigarettes. When Virginia finally showed up, she didn't look at all thrilled about being there.

As we walked through the woods we made small talk and I told her about the last time I was there when Ed thought I was Jesus Christ. When we arrived at the cliff and she saw how steep the path was, she didn't want to try it. I offered to help her down, but she said where we were was good enough.

She took the joint out of her shorts pocket and handed it to me to light.

"I don't care for joints," she said. "I like bowls and bongs better."

"Then why did you roll it?"

"I didn't. I got it from Zoë."

I lit it and we passed it back and forth. The pot and the sound of the stream running below relaxed me somewhat, but I had no idea where I stood with her and didn't know what to say. When the joint was down to a roach she said she didn't want any more and that I could keep it. I extinguished the berry and stuffed the roach into my cigarette pack and took out butts for both of us.

"You guys were pretty loud the other night," she said, exhaling her first drag from the cigarette.

"What?"

"You and Sandy."

"Oh."

"I was trying to sleep out in the common room, but the springs on the bed were squeaking really loud. And it went on for so long."

"Sorry about that."

"I still can't believe you hooked up with her."

"Neither can I."

"Then why did you do it?"

"I was fucked up."

"She's really upset that you haven't called her."

"Why? She seems more like a carefree child of the sexual revolution than a lonely romantic."

She laughed. "Zoë and Hannah tried talking her into calling you last night, but she was too upset. She was crying."

"I didn't realize she was upset. I thought we both understood that this was a one night thing that just happened, especially considering how fucked up we were. And she can't possibly expect to start something more if she's planning on moving to Colorado."

Neither of us said anything for a while and I looked down at the stream.

"Did she put you up to this?" I finally asked.

"Actually, Zoë and Hannah did. At this point Sandy doesn't want to think about you, but those two won't leave it alone. I just wanted to get high, so I agreed to it."

"I didn't mean to upset her."

"She really likes you, Hank. She said she's liked you since that day in the quad you asked her for a cigarette."

"She doesn't even know me."

"She said she didn't think you were like that."

"Like what? Does she think I'm a pig?"

"She didn't say that. She just said she thought you were a nice guy."

"Do you think I'm a pig?"

"No."

"God damn," I said to the stream.

"Hank, I wouldn't worry about it too much. The girl's a freak. She thinks she's Janis Joplin. I think she puts mushrooms on her

Cheerios every morning. You've seen our room—she doesn't even know what year it is!"

"I didn't mean for it to happen. It never even occurred to me that it would until it actually did. As soon as I woke up the next morning I knew it was a mistake."

There was a long silence.

"It's getting dark," Virginia said. "I still have some studying and packing to do."

"Me too."

We walked back through the woods in silence, but upon reaching the quad we became more relaxed and started talking about what we were going to do over the summer. She said she was going to try to get her job back at Barnes & Noble and do some writing, and I told her about my job at the camera warehouse and that I was going to read *On the Road*. Before we knew it we were standing in front of Ford Hall, where I suddenly became worried that we would encounter the other girls.

"So, you're leaving right after your final tomorrow?" I said.

"Yeah."

"I guess we're not going to see each other until the fall."

"I guess not."

"I can't believe how quickly this year has gone."

"I know. It feels like we just got here."

We arrived at our awkward moment. The voice in my head was screaming at me to kiss her, so, after a brief hesitation, I leaned in to kiss her on the cheek. Just before my lips were about to make contact, however, she turned her head towards mine and our lips met. Suddenly my tongue was in her mouth and hers was in mine. We kissed sloppily like lovesick teens until some guy coming out of the dorm told us to get a room. When it was over we were both embarrassed, but neither of us shied away. We looked at each other as if to say this would be continued in the fall and parted with something to think about, which, for the next three months, is exactly what I did until it became something that was no longer real.

4

Since the days of Tommy Austin and Golding Hall we had been looking forward to moving off campus and into a house of our own. Back then the thought of living downtown produced visions of keg parties, after-hour orgies, and life without R.A.'s, but by the end of sophomore year it was simply a matter of having our own rooms, which you couldn't do on campus unless you were willing to pay double. For two years we had lived without privacy, but now it had become a necessity for each of us to have our own little pocket of space to retreat and hide during those moments when life inside the circle became suffocating. If we had to share rooms for another year, it would be only a matter of time before we started turning on each other.

The only holdout was Teke, whose college professor parents were a little less naive about student rental houses than the rest of ours and wanted him to remain on campus. He was too lazy to argue with them about it and was willing to concede without a fight, but we had already found the house we wanted, a six-bedroom duplex on Center Street, and we badgered him until he finally agreed to write them a letter. He refused to show it to us before mailing it, but he said that he eloquently informed them that he was no longer a child, that he had proven his responsibility in a college atmosphere, that it was time to learn how to run a household, and that living on campus was only cheaper because you had to share a room with someone and he needed his own room to study in without distraction. Whatever he wrote worked because they finally relented, which was a damn good thing because we had already gone down to the real estate office and signed the lease before someone else beat us to it.

The house looked like an abandoned chapel, tall and narrow with flecking white paint and built on an upward slope so that it towered over the other houses on the block. It was divided right down the middle into two addresses. Each side had three upstairs bedrooms and a bathroom, and downstairs there was a large living room, dining room, and kitchenette. There was a shared attic that both sides had access to from the upstairs hallways, and out front there was a small porch. While the two sides were structurally identical, years of slipshod patchwork had given each a distinct personality.

Ed and Bruno agreed to live together on one side as did Russ and I on the other, and the hicks didn't mind at all being split up. Winston said he didn't want Ed taking a shit on his living room floor and decided to room with Russ and I, leaving Teke to shack up with Ed and Bruno. A coin was flipped to determine who got to pick which side, which Ed, Teke, and Bruno won. They chose the homier side, which Winston, Russ, and I wouldn't have selected anyway.

The other side was a wood-paneled dungeon with creaky hardwood floors and thick green curtains covering the windows that when drawn blocked out all traces of sunlight. The ceiling looked like what you would find in an office or a classroom, asbestos speckled Styrofoam panels covered with faded stains and fluorescent tube lighting. The previous tenants had left behind a rickety old foosball table that we kept in the dining room since we didn't have a table. We didn't have much else to decorate with— Winston brought up an old coffee table and a door from a Downsville Police car that he found at the county dump, Russ brought up a couple of old Archie Bunker easy chairs, and I brought up the old family television that my mother and stepfather were willing to part with since they had just bought a new one. We retained the old Salvation Army couch from Matteson Hall, which was now missing all four of it's legs and was extremely uncomfortable to sit on since it was wobbly and so close to the floor. Throughout the year we added various items that we picked up on our way home from the bars, including plastic patio chairs, a *New York Times* vending machine, and a bright orange traffic barrel with blinking yellow reflector on top.

In contrast, the other side was bright and cheery—they had pea-green shag carpeting, yellow and white wallpaper, and thin white curtains that only veiled outside light. Ed's parents had given him a nice oak dining room table and matching chairs, and Teke had secured two couches and a love seat from his grandparents. Like our side the place was pretty beat up, but they managed to fix it up enough to make it feel more like a home than the cold dark cave on the other side of the wall.

Up on campus there was no way in hell Virginia was going to live with Zoë and Hannah again. With Sandy gone and no other friends to room with, she signed up to live in a suite with five strangers, all of whom turned out to be freshman princesses whose only concern in life was which sorority to pledge. Zoë and Hannah meanwhile signed up to live together in Littell Hall, but they didn't spend much time there as they were constantly down at our house. Virginia did her best to avoid showing up at the house when they were there, but that proved difficult since they were there *all the time*.

During our first weekend in the new house Virginia called the other side and told Ed that she could get mushrooms. Zoë and Hannah were already there, and within minutes the money was collected. Ed and Teke caught the next bus up to campus to pick up the bags and returned an hour later with Virginia. It was the first time I had seen her since *the kiss*, and after spending the entire summer thinking about what I would say and what she would say when we finally saw each other again, all we did was give each other an awkward hello.

The mushrooms tasted like the cow shit they were grown in, so we ordered a couple of pizzas and used them as a topping to make them go down easier. After dinner we smoked a bowl up in Ed's room and played with the vintage transistor radio he had found in the attic and named Beatrice, tuning in AM stations from as far away as Cleveland, Detroit, Toronto, Pittsburgh, Chicago, and Indianapolis, all of which seemed like exotic locales compared to Oneonta. After an hour and three trips to the bathroom, jaw-lock set in and I started getting paranoid. I had to get away from everyone else, so I slipped out and went up to the attic.

The space was cluttered with dusty junk that had probably been there since the Great Depression—broken chairs, bed frames, dressers, an antique sewing machine that may have actually been worth something, and some other stuff that was so old we didn't know what it was or what it was used for. The room was dimly lit by the light from the street coming in through the two middle windows that overlooked the front yard and Center Street. I admired the view for a couple of minutes until I heard a noise coming from the staircase on our side of the house. I turned and froze when I saw a shadowed figure climbing the stairs.

"General Washington," I said.

"I am not General Washington," he said, stopping at the head of the stairs.

"We crossed the Delaware together," I said.

"I am not General Washington."

150

"Are you Winston?"

"I am not Winston."

"Then who are you?"

"I am acid."

"What?"

"I am acid."

Suddenly he vanished, only to return a moment later and say "Riboflavin!" before vanishing again. I waited for him to reappear, but after he didn't I went down the stairs on our side of the house. Winston's door was closed and he was playing along to the crunching electric version of Neil Young's "Hey Hey, My My (Into the Black)." I stood outside his room listening for a couple of minutes until I realized that it really wasn't him up in the attic. I took a deep breath and told myself not to panic before heading down the hall to my room.

I smoked a cigarette and listened to the others talk and laugh in Ed's room on the other side of the wall. After my smoke I put on the Stones' *Beggar's Banquet* CD and lay in bed staring up at the ceiling. My mind was racing and I got dizzy trying to slow it down, and when it became clear that the brakes were out I just let go and allowed it to take me wherever it was going.

My pinup poster of Linda-Jo the Topless Cowgirl floated up the wall and across the ceiling. She stopped directly above me and with a wicked smile whispered "riboflavin" before floating back down to her original place. A river of the word "riboflavin" written in different fonts and sizes started flowing across the ceiling with several objects floating in the current—a rubber chicken, little foosball men, my hash pipe, Canada Dry ginger ale bottles, and a teddy bear I had when I was a kid, among other things. At first I was afraid that I was having another psychotic meltdown, but when it didn't get any worse and my mind finally accepted what my eyes thought they were seeing, I started enjoying it until there was a soft knock on the door.

Virginia was standing in the doorway. I sat up quickly as if I had been caught doing something. I was drenched with sweat and wiped my forehead with my T-shirt sleeve. Riboflavin River disappeared.

"Hi," she said, looking around the room.

"Hey," I said, trying to act as if everything was normal.

"I like your room."

"Thanks."

Suddenly the room rotated 180°. The window wound up where the door was, and Virginia was outside peering in. She slid the window open and whispered "riboflavin" before the walls shifted another 180° back to their original position.

"What the fuck!" I said loudly. "Did you see that?"

"See what?" Virginia asked, nervously looking around.

"The room just went around in a circle! You saw it! I saw you!"

"I didn't see anything!"

"But I saw you! You were outside the window! I know you saw it!"

"Are you alright, Hank?"

"I know you saw it! You said 'riboflavin'!"

"You're scaring me, Hank."

"What does that mean? Why does everyone keep saying 'riboflavin'?"

Virginia looked terrified. She turned and hurried down the hall.

"What does it mean?" I called after her, but by then she was already thumping down the stairs. *"What does it mean?"*

After several minutes I managed to calm down and have a cigarette before resuming my former position staring up at the ceiling with my hands clasped across my chest.

A little while later *Beggar's Banquet* ended and all was quiet until thunder started rumbling in the distance. Within minutes the sky was flashing and a torrential rain was pounding the roof. The sound was so soothing that it paralyzed me. Every so often I heard someone come down the hall and peek their head in the room, but I didn't look. Eventually they went away, and after they were gone I wasn't sure if anyone had really been there. It felt like I was in a coffin at my own wake.

Suddenly Bruno barreled into the room and asked if I was alright.

"Yeah, I guess," I said. "I just have a bad feeling."

"A bad feeling? About what?"

"I'm not sure." I didn't know what I was talking about, but I was convinced that it was real. "I just have a real bad feeling. Do you know anything about 'riboflavin'?"

"What?"

"Nothing. Forget it."

Bruno eventually left and the others continued to peek their heads in, but I ignored them and focused on trying to anticipate the thunder after the lightning. The storm eventually passed and the house got quiet, but the feeling grew louder and sounded like static. Soon I could see it above me, little spores swirling faster and faster like heated molecules until they exploded in every direction, spreading all throughout the house and embedding themselves in the walls and floor, tinting everything yellow like an old photograph before eventually crumbling to dust and settling in the dark.

**5**

It wasn't long before the other side of the house belonged to Zoë as much as, if not more than, the three guys who had signed the lease. Her coup was rapid, three nights of sharing a twin-sized bed hardly big enough for Bruno alone that culminated in a blow job she tactfully left unfinished. He worshipped her and she ate it up, cruelly teasing him with sexual implications that would never be satisfied. After her position as queen was secure, she no longer had to subject herself to sharing a bed with her lovesick subject and reigned from the comfort of the living room couches, one of which she began to refer to as hers.

The girls usually stayed on the other side of the house, but occasionally Russ, Winston, or I would go downstairs and find Zoë and Hannah making themselves at home in our living room. If they were there long enough, Bruno would eventually show up, followed by Teke, then Ed, and at that point it became a party and we wouldn't be able to get rid of them. I wouldn't have minded so much if Virginia was there, but the only times she had been to the house aside from the night we shroomed were the already several occasions that Ed brought her home from the bars.

We got into the habit of locking the front door when we were home. One day in October, however, someone forgot. It was just before the first pitch of Game 3 of the World Series between the Blue Jays and Phillies when Winston and I simultaneously emerged from our rooms and headed downstairs. We found Zoë on the couch watching *Beaches*, and without even saying hello she gave us a look as if she was annoyed that we were there. Winston and I marched right through the living room and convened in the kitchen.

"What the fuck?" Winston said.

"I guess we forgot to lock the door," I said.

"No fucking way am I missing the World Series for some fucking Bette Midler movie."

"It looks like she's on the rag. Zoë and PMS might be a dangerous combination."

Winston thought about it for a moment.

"Fuck it," he said. "I haven't missed a pitch of the World Series since I was in diapers, and I'm not about to break that streak because some Madonna wanna-be bitch is having her period on my couch." With that he marched back out to the living room and changed the channel from the cable box on top of the TV.

"Hey!" Zoë yelled.

Winston looked at her and very calmly said, "In my house, when the World Series is on, we watch it."

"I was just leaving anyway," she said angrily. She got up and stormed out, never again to step foot in our house again or even acknowledge us on the rare occasions we were on the other side of the house.

A few days later Ed found a micro-tape recorder under Zoë's couch. He rewound it a little and heard part of a conversation him and Teke had the night before about the difficulty they had been having trying to find the hidden bunny on the cover of the latest issue of *Playboy*. He rewound the tape to the beginning and heard Zoë and Hannah saying good-bye just before they left that same night, which at the time struck him as odd because it was the first time in a couple of weeks they weren't going to spend the night, but he had been so glad they were leaving that he didn't given it much thought. He listened to a little more before pulling the ribbon out of the cassette and marching into a wooded area of Wilber Park, where he dug a hole with his hands, buried the tape recorder and cassette, and spit on the grave. Later he told Russ and I about it and made us promise not to tell Bruno, who a few days later asked if we had seen a tape recorder lying around.

The following weekend Virginia made a rare trip home, and it didn't take long for Hannah to find her way into Ed's bed. The next day he said that "she was amazing, by far the best lay I ever had," but refused to get into specifics, saying only that she knew what she was doing and was willing to try anything. From then on the rest of us weren't able to look at her the same way. If she was anywhere near us, we found ourselves in a daze trying to imagine what it was she did that made Don Juan Cafferty say she was his best ever.

I thought for sure that this was my chance. If Virginia had any dignity at all, she would never look at Ed again. When she found out, however, and the initial disgust wore off, she became obsessively jealous. Before it happened she never knowingly came down to the house when Zoë and Hannah were around, but now all of a sudden she was there whenever they were. She became a zealous participant in our barroom speculation about what Hannah did that made Ed say she was so good in bed and scoffed at the idea that he was actually interested in her. I hadn't pictured Virginia as the jealous type and at first thought this was some knee-jerk reaction to Ed tossing her aside for someone she hated, but I failed to see how much the two of them had in common.

After two weeks of sleeping with Hannah, however, Ed started to crack. While the sex was "fantastic," the girl couldn't get enough. He started sneaking over to our side of the house through the attic and we often found him the following morning asleep in our living room with the TV on. Occasionally Virginia or Hannah would try our front door, but we were diligent about locking it and had even put up a sign to remind ourselves to do so as soon as we came in. Sometimes they knocked, but no one ever answered. They could have got in through the attic, but either they didn't know that we left the attic door open for Ed or were afraid of encountering Winston in our upstairs hallway, who at this point they truly believed was psycho.

"They're there *all the time*," Ed said to Russ and I one night while we were smoking a bowl in my room.

"You play, you pay," I said. Ed shot me a look.

"Have you said anything to the other guys?" Russ asked.

"Teke will sit there complaining to me what a wanna-be Zoë is because she doesn't even know what the five points of the Pentacle stand for and that for her being a goth is just some fashion statement. But he's not going to do anything because Bruno is more generous with his weed when they're around and they're always bringing their own stuff over, so he's constantly getting stoned for free. And Bruno, for whatever reason, still seems to think that he's got a chance with Zoë, so he sure as hell isn't going to do anything. But something has to be done."

"Like what?"

"I don't know. All I know is that I'm through with the whole lot of them. We need some new flesh around here anyway."

"No more Hannah?"

"No more Hannah, no more Zoë, no more Virginia—no more!"

"No more Virginia?" I asked.

"They all have to go."

The following Tuesday Ed reached his breaking point. Zoë, Hannah, and Virginia had been there every night for the past two weeks and he couldn't take it anymore. He put on his jacket and shoes and stormed down to the living room.

"Do you want to go downtown?" he asked Teke, who was sitting next to Virginia on one of the couches with smoking bowl in hand.

"I don't have any money," he said. Virginia looked like she was about to say something, but Ed didn't give her a chance.

"That wasn't the question. I asked if you want to go downtown."

"Well, ah, yeah. I guess."

Ed hardly had any money himself, but the bars had good specials on Tuesday nights and he had just enough to get both of them to last call. By the time they got home, the lights were out and Zoë and Hannah were sleeping on their couches and Virginia was in a sleeping bag on the floor.

"I like it when a man comes home to his own house and it's nice and quiet like this," Ed said loudly. "A man's home is his castle. He can do whatever the fuck he wants whenever the fuck he wants, and he doesn't have to tolerate freeloaders."

"Well, ah, okay Ralph Kramden," Teke said.

"I am not the prince of a flophouse! I am the king of this fucking castle!"

"He's a fucking maniac," Zoë whispered to Hannah.

"What was that?" Ed yelled and flipped on the light. The girls sat up and rubbed their eyes. "Do you goddamn freeloaders have something to say? You spend more time in *my home* than you do in your own fucking rooms and you have the gall to call me a 'fucking maniac' in my own goddamn living room?"

He went into the kitchen and ripped the fire extinguisher off the wall.

"Get out!" he yelled. He pointed the extinguisher and started spraying the girls. "Get out, you five-cent whores!"

The girls screamed and tried to get away, but Ed chased them while yelling, "Be gone, whores! Get out!" Teke looked on helplessly, and moments later Bruno was thumping down the stairs in his boxer shorts demanding to know what was going on. When he saw what was happening, he grabbed Ed from behind and tried to wrestle the extinguisher away. During the struggle Ed lost his balance and fell backwards, pushing both him and Bruno into the long mirror on the wall next to the kitchen entrance. The mirror fell from it's hook, hit the floor, and shattered. A shard of glass cut into Bruno's hip and he roared as the blood ran down his leg and formed a big stain on his boxers. Ed ran upstairs through the attic with extinguisher in hand to the other side of the house.

"I'm getting out of this fucking nuthouse," Zoë said.

"Don't leave!" Bruno pleaded, but the girls were already putting their shoes and coats on and he was too concerned about his wound to further attempt convincing them to stay. Teke handed him several moist paper towels that he pressed against the cut.

"I think I'm going to need a ride to the emergency room," he said to Teke.

"Well, ah, I'll start the car," Teke said.

Teke's parents had loaned him the LaRoche family K-car, which he dubbed the *Karbon Monoxide Kruiser*. In high school he and a friend attempted to use the *Kruiser* to sacrifice themselves to Wee Jas, Goddess of Death Magic, by locking themselves in the garage and turning the ignition, but it wouldn't start. It was the only K-car any of us had ever seen that had a stick-shift, and in fact all of the LaRoche family vehicles had standard transmission in models you would normally not find it, including the Astrovan and the old Grand Torino station wagon that Mr. LaRoche used to get around town.

After Bruno was dressed, they headed out to the running car that had already fogged half the block with exhaust.

"That Irish idiot has gone too far this time," Bruno muttered on his way out.

Meanwhile Ed was busy dousing our side of the house with the remaining contents of the fire extinguisher. Winston, Russ, and I, didn't even try to stop him. When the canister was finally empty, Ed opened the basement door and tossed it down the stairs. The entire house was left in a haze, and a film of fine yellow powder covered the furniture and floors.

"You're a real ass hole, Cafferty," Winston said.

"It had to be done," Ed replied.

In order to get him out of the house and let him cool off, Russ suggested we go to the park and smoke a bowl. Ed responded by saying, "Yes! Drugs!"

He was quiet as we walked, and Russ and I didn't say anything that would get him going again. We headed over to the south side of the park and went halfway up a large wooded hill before stopping at a moonlit clearing. We took a seat on the ledge of a big boulder protruding through the hillside and Russ packed a bowl.

"We don't do this enough anymore," Ed said. "Remember freshman year when we used to go out in the woods every night? Now all we do is sit around and get stoned and do nothing."

"We're getting old," Russ said and took the first hit before passing it to Ed.

The sky was clear and the moon was three-quarters full. No one said anything until the bowl was kicked and Russ and I were lighting cigarettes.

"It had to be done," Ed said, more to himself than to us.

A couple of hours later the *Kruiser* was parked in front of the house. The other side was dark, but our side was lit. Inside Winston was sitting on the stairs with an open textbook on his lap.

"Bruno went to the cops," he said when we came in.

"He what?" Ed said.

"After he got stitched up at the hospital, he ordered Teke to drive him to the police station. He filed a report against you, Ed."

"That fucking bastard!" Ed yelled.

"He didn't press charges, he just filed a report. But all he has to do is pick up the phone and they'll come down here and arrest you."

"I can't believe this," I said.

"How many stitches did Bruno need?" Russ asked.

"Just a couple. It wasn't too bad. But he was mighty pissed at you, Cafferty."

"That fat fucking bastard!" Ed said. "I can't believe he ran to the fucking police over a fucking boo-boo! Motherfucker!"

"Maybe you should have thought of that before you went on your little rampage," Winston said, shutting his textbook. "In a matter of minutes you sent your best friend to the hospital, cost him any chance he had with the woman he loves, wrecked the house, and most likely ruined one of the biggest tests I have to take all year, which is now only a few short hours away."

"It had to be done!" Ed said. "That cunt was using him!"

"He didn't seem to think so."

"I did him a fucking favor! I did us all a favor! Nice fucking gratitude!"

"Well, even if he didn't have a chance with her, she was still his friend. And so was Hannah."

"And Virginia," I said.

"They all had to go!" Ed said. "We needed a good housecleaning."

"We still do," Russ said, looking around.

"I'll clean it tomorrow," Ed said. "I can't believe that fucker went to the cops!"

"It tastes lemony in here," I said.

"I wouldn't worry about it too much," Winston said to Ed. "I don't think he's going to press charges unless you pull another stunt like this."

"I should tip the fucking pigs off about that stash he's got up in his room," Ed said.

"But that would make you as bad as him," Russ said.

"Yeah, maybe. I wouldn't do that to one of my friends. But then again, I no longer consider Bruno Sebastian a friend."

"What are you going to do about living with him?" Russ asked.

"I'm not going anywhere. If that fat bastard wants to leave, let him. It's not my fucking problem."

"Do you think he's going to move?"

"I have no fucking idea," Ed said. "But I'm not gonna worry about it right now. I've had enough excitement for one evening and I'm gonna take full advantage of finally being able to get a good night's sleep. Well, boys, it's been a pleasure."

"Make sure you clean this shit up tomorrow," Winston said. Ed let out a sarcastic laugh on his way out.

The next day Ed and Bruno wouldn't even look at each other, and no one mentioned the incident in front of Bruno. While the rest of us felt bad for Bruno, Ed was right in that something had to be done, though the means in which it had been accomplished was left in question. Bruno slipped into denial, refusing to believe that Zoë had been stringing him along, and he continued to blame Ed even after she stopped returning his calls and started hanging out with a skinhead guy we often saw down at the Oak, who she more than anyone used to make fun of because he was always talking to God out loud, referring to Him as "My Man G." As obvious as her shallowness was in casting Bruno away now that he could no longer provide her with a place to crash and her sudden befriending of this skinhead guy who just happened to have an apartment with a coveted Main Street address, he still held Ed responsible and wouldn't accept that she had been using him and that he never had a chance with her to begin with.

Meanwhile, I was highly pleased that Virginia just happened to be there during Ed's rampage. After being jilted for someone she loathed and then being called a 'five-cent whore' and thrown out of the house in the dead of night, I figured there was no way in hell she would want anything to do with him.

It was a couple of weeks before I saw her again. She was down at the Oak by herself and seemed to be looking for someone while trying not to make eye contact with any of us, but as soon as I saw her I made my way towards her through the crowd. She didn't see me coming and practically walked right into me.

"Hey, Virginia," I said.

"Hi, Hank."

"How are you?"

"Alright, I guess. I was supposed to meet my friend Barb here, but she hasn't showed up yet."

"Listen, Virginia, about what happened—I'm kind of glad that Ed threw Zoë and Hannah out, but I was a little upset that he threw you out too."

"So was I. He was crazy."

"Hell yeah he's crazy. He sent Bruno to the hospital."

"I heard."

"It's still kind of a mess down at the house. Ed and Bruno haven't said a word to each other since that night. But I don't want you to think that I don't like you anymore, and I don't want either of us to feel awkward when we see each another. I can't blame you if you don't want to talk to us, but after it happened, everyone was shocked about you being included in that mess. Zoë and Hannah had to go, but everyone said that he shouldn't have thrown you out too."

"They said that?"

"Yeah. Well, everyone except Ed. But I just wanted to let you know that you're always welcome in my house. Not that you ever visited me anyway."

"Your door was always locked. And you never answered your phone."

"Well, that's because we were trying to keep Zoë and Hannah out."

"Honestly, I don't think I'm going to be down at your house for a while. But you can come visit me. You haven't been to my room once this semester."

"You're right, I'm sorry I haven't. I'm not even sure where you live."

"Hays Hall. Room 205."

"Well, that should be easy for me to remember, I just have to remember the room number. Hays Hall 205, Hays Hall 205, Hays Hall 205—"

"It's in the campus directory if you forget."

"Yes, the campus directory. Very good. I'm going to visit you soon. I promise. You mean a lot to me."

"What?"

"You mean a lot to me."

"You mean a lot to me too."

"Do you really mean that, or are you just saying it because I said it first?"

"I really mean it, Hank. I consider you a good friend."

"That's not what I meant."

"What do you mean then?"

Before I had a chance to answer, Barb showed up. I had never seen or heard of Barb before and wondered if Virginia was trying to distance herself from us by making new friends.

"I have to go," Virginia said.

"I understand."

"Are you mad at me?"

"No. Of course not."

"I want to continue this conversation. I'll come back in a little while, alright?"

"Sure. I'll be here."

She left with Barb and I found an empty stool at the end of the bar. While I was waiting I drank several whiskey & Cokes, and about an hour later she came back alone. I got up to go meet her, but as she was making her way through the crowd she ran into Ed. I sat back down and watched, hoping to witness her telling him to go to hell and then go racing across the bar into my arms, but instead they just talked and then they hugged. With the whiskey flowing through my veins I felt like hitting someone, but instead I picked up my empty glass from the bar and smashed it on the floor. I was gone before the bouncer had a chance to throw me out and stormed across Chestnut Street towards The Clinton, where I spent the rest of the night drinking with all the other pathetic souls in Oneonta who had nothing better to go home to.

**6**

At first we thought Ed and Bruno would make amends and everything would get back to normal. Perhaps they thought so too, but the days stretched into weeks, and it began to sink in that things might not ever go back to the way they were regardless as to whether they made up or not. The rest of us did our best to remain neutral, but because Ed and Bruno were both well aware of how we felt about the girls being gone, we were able to openly discuss the situation with Ed while with Bruno a conscious effort had to be made to avoid the topic altogether.

Russ and I had no idea how much our relationship with Bruno had changed until a few days later when he invited us to smoke a bowl in his room. It didn't occur to us that he might be feeling us out and we gladly accepted the invitation, but as soon as we got over there we were greeted with an overwhelming awkwardness as if Zoë herself was in the room. As the bowl went around, the initial small talk quickly died, and the pot only amplified the tension. After it was kicked, we couldn't get out of there soon enough and used the excuse of leaving our cigarettes on the other side of the house to flee.

"I feel really bad about what just happened," Russ said after lighting his cigarette. "I still consider him a good friend, but I couldn't stay in that room another second."

"Neither could I," I said. "After that, it's hard to believe he's the same guy we smoked with nonstop for three days last year. It feels like that was just last weekend, but at the same time it seems like lifetimes ago."

With the girls gone and Ed continuing to spend most of his time on our side of the house, the once lively atmosphere on the other side of the house decomposed into an inhospitable reminder of *the incident*—bits of broken mirror in the shag carpeting, dirty ashtrays with Zoë's stubbed out Newports still in them, yellow dust from the fire extinguisher, pizza boxes, Chinese food cartons, empty beer cans. Even Teke, who had been the only one to express any sympathy at all to Bruno and the only one who at least appeared neutral on the surface, started avoiding Bruno so he could easily slip over to our side of the house. The card-playing smoke sessions like those in the good old days of Matteson Hall were revived in my room and the dark side of the house came to life, leaving Bruno abandoned in front of his television with bowl in hand and bag of weed on the coffee table. It may have sounded like his ideal scenario, but we knew it wasn't; and though we felt bad about it, we were no longer willing to subject ourselves to the awkwardness of hanging out with him. Nobody wanted to see him go, and deep inside neither did Ed; but this was between the two of them, and both were unwilling to apologize.

And then came the call. It was late on a Sunday night a couple of weeks before finals. Russ and I were up in my room scraping resin from our bowls when Teke came in through the attic door.
"Well, ah, I have some bad news," he said.
"Trouble in Paradise?" Russ said.
"Bruno's father passed away."
"What?"
"Bruno's father passed away. He had a massive heart attack."
"Oh my god," Russ said.
"How did Bruno take it?" I asked.
"I don't know yet. Ed's in his room now breaking the news."
"*Ed's* breaking the news?"
"Well, ah, yeah. He answered the phone and Bruno's brother Mike told him what happened and that he was leaving immediately to come up here and bring Bruno home. Ed told me about it first and I offered to tell Bruno, but he said that he should do it. He had to take a couple of shots from that of that emergency bottle of Jameson's he keeps stashed away just before he went in there. He was pretty shaken up."
Teke took a seat and we just sat there for a while. After the initial shock subsided, Russ asked if we wanted to smoke the resin. I gave him what I scraped from my bowl and he rolled it together with his to form a decent sized ball. The bowl went around once before Ed came in from the attic.
"Did you tell them?" he asked Teke.
"Well, ah, yeah," he said.

"I can't believe you fucking guys! You just find out that Bruno's father died and you're sitting up here smoking dope?"

"What the hell are we supposed to do?" I said. "Teke said you were in his room breaking the news to him. And besides, didn't you do a couple of shots before you went in there?"

"You're right," he said. "I'm sorry. I'm just a little freaked out that the first words I've said to Bruno in weeks were that his father died."

"How did he take it?" Russ asked.

"Not too well. I wasn't in there long. He just sat there for a minute or so and then said he wanted to be left alone. Does Winston know?"

"Not yet."

Ed went down the hall and came back with Winston a couple of minutes later. I went downstairs and retrieved the dusty bottle of Four Roses whiskey that we found in one of the kitchen cabinets when we moved in and an armful of stolen shot glasses. Back upstairs I poured the shots and we toasted to the life of Mr. Sebastian and threw back the shots, which went down about as easily as turpentine.

The smokers finished off the resin and then we all headed to the other side of the house via the downstairs route so that Bruno wouldn't hear a parade going by his room. We situated ourselves in front of the TV and watched one infomercial after another, wishing there was something we could do for him and frustrated that we couldn't. Every once in a while someone went upstairs and asked Bruno through the door if he was alright and if he needed anything, but all he kept saying was that he wanted to be left alone.

Finally at around 4:00 AM we heard Bruno's door open, and moments later he slowly descended the stairs with a duffel bag. He was clearly still in shock and didn't say anything when he saw us. He put the bag on the dining room table and we lined up to give him our condolences and a sympathetic hug. We made a spot for him on the couch and he joined us in front of the television staring blankly at the screen. He looked similar to what he looked like the night of the bad acid trip when he was staring at the television thinking he was dead, only this time part of him really did die.

His brother showed up at six. He looked just like Bruno except a little shorter and without a beard. Each of us shook his hand and expressed our sympathy and then hugged Bruno again on his way out. He thanked us and said he appreciated us staying up with him.

We watched from the porch as they pulled away. The sun had not yet risen, but the sky was light with predawn blue. It was extremely cold, the lawns covered with a stiff frost and the cracks in the street and sidewalks filled with patches of ice. After the car disappeared down the block we finally got to crawl into our nice warm beds, but as tired as we were, sleep did not come easy.

A couple of days later Ed went home to attend Mr. Sebastian's funeral. In the interim before he left he hardly said a word to any of us, but as he was leaving he remarked to Teke how he couldn't believe that we weren't going too and how he could no longer look at us the same way. While he was down there he and Bruno made amends, and Ed's parents even showed up at the wake. The rest of us had a $50 bouquet of flowers sent to the funeral home.

I was livid when Teke mentioned what Ed had said, but I didn't say anything when he returned a few days later. That night we went downtown and he told us about the funeral and how Bruno was holding up, but when we got back to the house and he started talking about what an "impressive show of respect for Mr. Sebastian's life" it was with all the people who showed up, I couldn't hold it in any longer.

"What are you getting at?" I asked.

"I'm talking about respect."

"What do you know about respect?"

"I know that if one of my friend's father dies, I show up at the funeral."

"Didn't you say that you no longer considered Bruno a friend?"

"I was there. You guys weren't."

"We couldn't just drop everything and go down to Brooklyn! We all have finals to study for and don't have the money to go down there! Bruno understands this. I don't think he expected us to be there. Besides, none of us except you ever even met his father."

"It's a show of respect," Ed said. "You're a friend of Bruno's and you should have been there. By not showing up, it shows that you don't respect Bruno."

"That's bullshit, Ed," Russ said. "I am going to stay out of the rest of this conversation, but I just wanted to point out that that was a bullshit comment."

"How can you say that?" I said to Ed. "We couldn't go! We personally offered our condolences to him the night it happened, and then we all pitched in and sent flowers to the funeral home. Just because we didn't express our sympathy the same way you did doesn't give you the right to say we don't respect him!"

"Well, ah, I think that a death in the family is a private matter anyway," Teke said. "If we knew the man or even just met him, maybe it would be different. But we never met him and we don't know Bruno's family."

"I can't believe what I'm, hearing!" Ed said. "If you guys had gone down there it would have meant a lot to them, especially Bruno.

Don't you realize that if a lot of people show up at a man's funeral, it shows the family that he was a well-loved or at least a well-respected man and actually helps them accept their loss since he was not only a loss to them but to many others? How do you think they would feel if nobody showed up?"

"Well, ah, let's suppose you're right," Teke said. "Suppose I did decide to go down there. How was I supposed to get there? My car couldn't make it all the way to Brooklyn, and I can't afford a bus ticket right now. And even if I did make it down there, where would I stay? I don't think Bruno would have room at his house with all of his family there."

"You could have stayed at my house," Ed said.

"You never offered!"

"If you had thought to ask, do you really think I would have said no?"

"But why would he even think to ask?" I said. "If you just assumed all of us were going, you should have automatically asked where him and Winston would be staying! But this is besides the point. Ed, you showed your condolences your way, and we showed it our way. You can't hold it against us that we look at it differently than you."

"I'm not holding it against you! All I said was that I couldn't look at you guys the same way anymore."

"You are holding it against us when you say that you thought we should have been there," Russ said.

"Well, I still think you guys should have been there."

"Then you're holding it against us."

"Alright, maybe I am."

"You know, Ed," I said, "I'm beginning to think that the real reason you went down there was that you were feeling guilty and wanted to prove to Bruno that you're still his friend."

"You take that back!" Ed yelled. "Right now!"

"You said right here in this very living room said that you no longer considered him a friend."

"That was said in the heat of the moment!"

"Heat of the moment? You guys didn't say a word to each other for weeks!"

"It happens, alright? Even the best of friends get into fights sometimes. Just because you and Russ are so warm and cuddly and never get into fights doesn't mean that it's like that for everybody!"

"That's the stupidest fucking thing you've said all night," Russ said.

"Maybe not!" I said. "Maybe not. He just acknowledged that all friendships are not the same. Sometimes friends get into big fights, sometimes they don't. That's just the way it is. I consider all of you guys my best friends in the world, but I have a different relationship with each and every one of you. On the one hand you're telling us that we all should have done what you did, and on the other you recognized the fact that all friendships are different."

"Well, fine then," Ed said. "I expressed my opinion. I feel you should have been there, and you feel otherwise."

"Don't get smug with me, Cafferty!" I yelled. "I know I didn't have to be there! I know that Bruno wasn't expecting us to be there, and I'm pretty sure that he wasn't expecting you to be there either!"

"I should hit you," Ed said with calm anger, his face and neck red and a vein visible on his forehead. He got up from the couch and slowly approached me sitting in one of the easy chairs. "I should hit you right now," he said, sticking his finger in my face.

"Get that fucking finger out of my face!" I yelled. When he didn't I suddenly exploded  out of the chair and shoved him across the room. He fell backwards over one of the plastic patio chairs, landing hard against the wall and yelling in pain before slumping to the floor.

"You deserved that, Ed," Russ said. "And I'm speaking objectively."

"I think my thumb is broken," Ed said from the floor, holding his left thumb. He also had a bloody lip. "But I don't give a shit! Gardner, you and I outside, right now!"

"Guys!" Teke yelled, leaping off the couch. "Enough already!"

"Let me tell you something," I said, standing over Ed. "If my father died, I wouldn't expect you to show up to his funeral."

"I would have," Ed said. "At least before you didn't show up to Mr. Sebastian's."

"No, you wouldn't have, and I wouldn't have wanted you there. Shows how much you know about me, you fucking prick. You would just blindly show up at my father's funeral out of some kind of bullshit respect. Well guess what? I wouldn't even show up to my own father's fucking funeral! I've barely to the drunk ass hole in five years! He doesn't give a shit about me and I don't give a shit about him, so why would I expect any of you guys to show up at his fucking funeral? I don't know what kind of relationship Bruno had with his father. He never really talked about the guy, just like I never talk about my own father. What if he had a strained relationship with his father, and by you showing up it only made it more of a burden for him?"

"But it wasn't like that with them!"

"I'm not saying it was! I'm only saying that I didn't know what kind of relationship they had and that I was looking at the situation from my own perspective. I know you have a good relationship with your father and I've heard you talk about him and that you would be devastated if you lost him, which is probably the real reason you feel the way you do, not because you were trying to prove to Bruno that you were still his friend. Fine, I take it back. But I think it's pretty selfish of you to criticize me and everyone else without even bothering to look at it from our point of view. Do you know what it's like to lose a father, Ed?"

"I can't say that I do."

"Well I do! And though the circumstances may be different, the fact remains that I do know what it's like and I can and truly sympathize with Bruno! So fuck you if you don't like the way I pay my respects, but don't you dare fucking say that I don't have any respect for Bruno and imply that I don't give a shit!"

My eyes were welling and I stormed out of the house before I started balling in front of the others. The cool air felt good and the late night quiet calmed my pounding heart. I went into the park and followed the asphalt path that led to the softball diamond, where I took a seat on the third base bench and sniffled as I wiped the tears from my face with my shirt sleeve. A couple of minutes later Teke came down the path and took a seat next to me. He too was sniffling.

"What are you crying about?" I asked.

"Well, ah, I don't know," he said. "I guess I had no idea that it was so bad between you and your dad. I knew your parents were divorced and I've heard you talk about your stepfather, but I didn't know it was so bad with your real father. Since you never talked about it, I guess we were just afraid to ask."

"It's not that I was trying to hide it from you guys. I just got tired of thinking about it a long time ago. They got divorced ten years ago, and now I hardly even remember what it was like having him around. It's gotten to the point where he just drops a child support check in the mail every month and that's all we ever hear from him. My brother and sister and I are nothing more than a financial obligation to him. At first he pretended to care, but when I got older it became obvious that he didn't. I had a hard time dealing with it for a while, but when I finally realized that it was him and not us, I was able to accept it and move on. I haven't really thought about it much since. I guess Ed hit a nerve and I just lost it."

"Ed deserved what he got. I'm surprised you were able to hold back as long as you did."

"I don't know. I don't want to think about it anymore. I feel stupid for crying."

"You shouldn't feel stupid. In fact, I'm glad that I got to see this side of you. I feel like I know you so much better now."

Ed and Russ came down the path. Ed's thumb was wrapped in several paper towels packed with ice.

"I'm sorry, man," Ed said. "I didn't know. And you know how I am when I'm drunk. Next time I start talking shit like that, feel free to break my thumb again."

"Is it really broken?" I asked.

"I don't know. It might just be a really bad sprain, but something's definitely not right and it hurts like hell."

"Sorry about that," I said. "Just don't go down to the police station and file a report on me."

# IV

# 1

I woke up feeling pretty damn good on the morning of my twenty-first birthday. The day I had been waiting for seemingly my whole life had finally arrived and the restraints of childhood had finally been broken. Though the only actual difference was that I no longer had to use my chalked license to buy beer and get into bars, for the first time in my life I truly felt free. I had this exhilarating feeling that I could do whatever I wanted and that nobody had any right to tell me what to do, and for as long as I was to remain oblivious to the fallacy of this sentiment, then, and only then, would I truly be free.

Going to class was not even a consideration. I slept in, bought myself a big lunch and ice cream sundae at Friendly's with some birthday money I had received, bought a new bong at Crazy Gifts with the rest of my birthday money, and spent the afternoon doing bong hits and taking a long nap. Later Ed and Bruno accompanied me to the Center Street Deli to pick up the keg for my party, which we had to wheel back to the house in a shopping cart because Teke's car wouldn't start.

By the time the guests started arriving for the party I was already bombed. I didn't invite anyone myself and had no idea who was going to show up, but there was a decent turnout, mostly people who hung out down at the Oak. The biggest surprise, however, was when Virginia arrived with her friend Barb and a couple of other girls I had never seen before. It was her first time back at the house since Ed's rampage, and she had apparently balked at first when Ed invited her until he told her that it would mean a lot to me if she was there. I didn't exactly know what to make of that, but I was glad she was there and too drunk to give it much thought.

The other surprise guest was a girl named Lucy Burns, who showed up with her short and stout roommate Olivia. A couple of weeks earlier Ed had met Lucy at the Dean's List buffet and later that night wound up in her bed. The following weekend they ran into each other downtown and Ed didn't want to deal with it, so he politely told her to get the fuck away from him. She promptly slapped him and the two got into a shouting match that got them both kicked out of the bar. Ed claimed that he didn't invite her to the party and vowed that if she came anywhere near him he was going to break out the fire extinguisher.

Lucy came from a tiny town named Deposit just outside of Binghamton, where she had been Valedictorian of her high school class. She could have easily gone to a more academically inclined school, but, more than a year shy of her twenty-first birthday, she was a full-blown alcoholic and wanted to go to a school where she could get good grades without having to give up drinking and where nobody would even notice that she had a problem. She looked years older than she actually was, her face hardened from alcohol and her blond hair frizzy as if it had been bleached and permed one too many times. She did, however, have a nice compact body and a decent pair of breasts that she wasn't afraid to show off, and she had a taste for leather and high-heeled boots that advertised her lust and made it difficult for any horny 21 year old man seeking an easy lay to resist—especially on a night such as this.

She was already drunk when she showed up. A couple of times while I was talking with some of the other guests I caught her looking at me. Then, after one of my many trips upstairs to use the facilities, I ran into her outside the bathroom door.

"Happy birthday, Hank," she said.

"Well thank you," I said. "Lucy—right?"

"Yep."

I thought she had been waiting to use the bathroom so I walked right by her, but she followed me down the hall to my room, where I was planning on doing a couple of quick bong hits before going back downstairs.

"This is a cool room," she said while looking around.

"Thanks. Do you want to smoke a little?"

"Sure."

"We have to make it quick, though. I only have a little left and I don't want everyone coming up here."

While I was hunched over my desk packing the bong, she came up from behind and reached up inside the front of my shirt with both hands. She started tweaking my nipples and I quickly became aroused. I took a hit and passed her the bong and we each got two hits before it was kicked.

"Where are you going to be later?" she asked.

"Oh, I don't know. I can go wherever I want now, but I'll probably wind up right back at the Oak. I'm sure I have a few free drinks coming to me."

"Well, if I don't see you downtown, you're more than welcome to stop by my room for some bong hits."

"Oh yeah? Where do you live?"

"Huntington. Room 319."

"I'll keep it in mind."

Before heading back downstairs, she ran her index finger down my chest and gave my crotch a light squeeze. I watched her tight leather ass walk down the hall and turn towards the staircase. After she disappeared I jotted her room number on a scrap of paper and stuffed it in my pocket before heading back down to the party.

Virginia greeted me at the bottom of the stairs.

"What is that slut Lucy doing here?" she asked.

"Lucy? I don't know. I didn't invite her."

"You should stay away from that girl."

"Why?"

"She's a whore."

"What are you talking about?"

"I mean it, Hank. Stay away. She's hooked up with half the guys in Oneonta."

"Including Ed?"

"Ed hooked up with her?"

"Yeah, a couple of weeks ago. I imagine that's why she's here."

"That's so fucking gross!"

"What makes you think I was going to hook up with her?"

"Because she's a whore and she followed you up the stairs."

"You sound jealous."

"I'm serious, Hank. That girl is the biggest slut in the school."

"Alright, I heard you. But I'm being serious too. You sound jealous."

"Maybe I am."

"Really?"

"Maybe."

"I'll have to take that under advisement then."

"Just promise me you'll stay away from her."

"Jeez!"

"Do you promise?"

"Alright! I promise!"

"Good."

"Listen, Virginia, I want to tell you something. I really appreciate you coming to my party."

"I wasn't going to miss your twenty-first birthday."

"I appreciate that. I know it's probably a little awkward for you to be here after what happened, but I want you to know that you are always welcome in my home and that it means a lot to me that you're here."

She looked like she was about to start crying and hugged me.

"You should visit more often," I said.

"You still haven't visited me."

"I know, I know. I promise I will soon."

We hugged again and over her shoulder I saw Lucy glaring at us from across the room. I pretended not to notice, but she knew that I had.

After the party everyone went down to the Oak and bought me drinks and shots ad nauseam, but the one that put me over the edge was the 'prairie fire' Russ bought me, a shot of tequila with Tabasco sauce in it. As soon as it went down, it started coming right back up like lava. I pushed my way through the crowd and cut the bathroom line amid several protests and projectile vomited into the sink, the only available drain in the facility.

Normally when I puke I'm done drinking for the night, but my mouth was burning so I grabbed somebody's pitcher of Michelob Dark off the table and poured myself a glass, filling it a little too high so that it went above the rim and spilled over the sides. I slammed the beer in one gulp and smashed the empty glass on the floor, attracting the attention of the bartender and bouncers. I didn't like the way they were looking at me, so I picked up another glass and smashed that one as well and somebody yelled "Mazeltov!" I managed to break two more before the bouncers hauled me out of the bar despite my protests that it was my birthday. After I was shoved out the door, one of them said, "Happy fucking birthday. Now don't let me catch you in here again."

I went from bar to bar looking for Lucy, and when I didn't find her I caught a bus up to campus. When I got up there I had to ask someone where Huntington Hall was because I was too drunk to remember, but even after being given very specific directions, it still took me half-hour staggering along the walks in the frigid cold to find it.

No one was in the lobby to let me in, so I had to call the campus directory operator from the call box outside and she was able to connect me. It rang about ten times before Olivia finally answered and told me to hold on a second before Lucy got on the phone.

"Who is this?" she asked sleepily.

"It's Hank! Let me in, it's fucking freezing out here!"

"Hank? What are you doing here?"

"You invited me for bong hits, remember?"

"It's three in the morning!"

"Please come down! It's fucking cold out here!"

There was a long pause before she finally said she would be down in a minute. I smoked a cigarette while I waited, and after ten minutes I began to think that she wasn't coming until I saw her finally emerge from the stairway.

"I was beginning to think you forgot about me," I said while she held open the door.

"I had to get dressed," she said.

"You were naked?"

"I was in my pajamas."

"Close enough."

I followed her up the stairs to the third floor. Along the way we passed a men's room and I told her I had to piss.

"I'll leave the door open for you," she said. "I'm right down the hall. 319."

I didn't really have to piss, but I had felt a puke coming on since smoking the cigarette downstairs. In the bathroom next to the regular sink there was a big wash sink that looked inviting, so I leaned over with hands clutching the sides and waited. It was slow in coming up, so I stuck my finger down my throat and started spitting. Moments later I puked so violently that some of the blood vessels on my eyes popped, part of the whites turning solid red and making me look a little Satanic.

"Fucking gross," I said, looking down at the pile of brown puke that looked more like diarrhea than vomit. I turned on the rubber hose connected to the faucet and ran it over my face and hands and rinsed my mouth before dropping it back in the sink. I left it running and headed down the hall to 319 feeling much better. Before going in I checked my wallet to make sure that I had a condom.

I went in without knocking and found Lucy on her knees swigging a bottle of vodka like it was spring water. She didn't seem to care that I was standing there watching in disbelief, and after she drained the bottle she looked up at me not like someone who had just been caught in the act, but someone who was ready to be challenged.

"Don't mind me," she said. "I'm an alcoholic."

"Aren't we all."

"No, really, I'm a clinical alcoholic. I should probably be in rehab, but up to this point I've managed to get by, so I'm holding it off as long as possible."

"Really?"

"Can't you tell?"

"Not really. I'm too drunk myself to tell the difference."

"Would you like some? I have another bottle in the other room."

"No, thanks. I think I've had enough alcohol for one night. I wouldn't mind doing some bong hits, though."

"I don't have any weed left."

"Isn't that what you invited me here for?"

"Olivia and I smoked the last of it when we got home. There wasn't much left."

"I see. It was just a ploy to get me to come up here, wasn't it?"

"Maybe."

"Ha! I'm on to you."

"You wish you were on to me."

"That's what I'm here for!"

She made a face and said she would be right back. She went into her bedroom and closed the door. I heard her say something to Olivia, but it was too muffled to understand. There was a copy of *369 Sexual Positions for the 90's* on the coffee table that I started flipping through, but after a couple of minutes I put it back and started looking around the room. On the desk in the corner there were several cheap plastic picture frames containing certificates with Lucy's name on them acknowledging that she had made the Dean's List. There was also her High School diploma and another one recognizing her achievement of representing the Valedictorian of the Deposit High School a couple of years earlier.

When she came back out she climbed on top of me and started kissing me wildly. The smell and taste of vodka on her breath made me gag a little, but I managed to fight it off. I fell back on the futon and put my hands on her ass while she kissed me and reached up my shirt. She started tweaking my nipples and it felt good until she tweaked a little too hard and I let out an "ouch."

"Sorry," she said between kisses.

"No, I like it," I said, sliding a hand inside the back of her panties and running it down her smooth warm cheek, but suddenly she stopped.

"We shouldn't do this," she said.

"Why not?"

"Ed."

"Ed?"

"Ed."

"What does Ed have to do with anything?"

"I hooked up with him a couple of weeks ago."

"So what."

"So, if you and I sleep together, your friends are going to think that I'm a whore."

"Who the hell cares what they think?"

"I do."

"Well, no one has to know about this. No one even knows I'm here."

"Olivia knows."

"Well, if we go somewhere else, she won't know that we did anything. We can make it a secret rendezvous. I have an idea." I picked up *369 Sexual Positions* and turned to the section entitled "Venues" and held it open for her.

"See?" I said.

"See what?"

"We don't have to do it here. We can go somewhere else and no one will ever know."

"Where?"

I grabbed her hand and pulled her out of the room without telling her where we were going. Out in the hall I picked her up and carried her like a honeymoon bride over the large puddle outside the men's room. When we got to the study lounge I was pleased to find that I was correct in assuming that it would be deserted at 4:00 AM on a Saturday morning.

"See?" I said, holding out my hand to show her that we were the only ones there. Unfortunately the door couldn't be locked without a key, so I pushed a table against the knob. Then I pushed two of the multi-colored dorm-issue love seats against one another to make a bed that somewhat resembled a crib.

"I don't like this," Lucy said.

"I didn't see a section in the book about study lounges, but I'm sure we can improvise."

"Hank, I don't know if I want to do this."

"Why not? Because of the study lounge or because of Ed?"

"Both. Hank, I'm tired. I want to go to bed. Come to bed with me."

"But Olivia's in there."

"Come to bed with me," she repeated with authority. She pulled me to her by my belt buckle and shoved her hand down my pants.

"Yes, ma'am," I said.

Back upstairs we stripped down to our underwear in the common room before quietly slipping into her bedroom trying not to wake Olivia. We slid under the covers and made out for a while before she reached into my boxers and started jerking me off. She was a yanker and not a slider, so I asked her if she had any Vaseline. She didn't, but instead she slid down under the covers and started blowing me. She was good, so good that it was on its way to becoming the best blow job I ever had until the light suddenly went on in the room and she stopped. Olivia had just gotten out of bed, so I rolled my head to the side pretending to be asleep and wished that Lucy would finish down there because I was so close, but she remained still. The clock radio said it was 5:00 AM. I thought Olivia was just going to go to the bathroom or something, but instead she pulled an ironing board out of the closet and started ironing a large pile of clothes that were already folded neatly in the laundry basket.

I eventually passed out. When I woke up several hours later the room was flooded with sunlight. It took me a couple of minutes to recall where I was and how I had gotten there, and as soon as I did I had this overwhelming urge to get the hell out of there. Lucy was still passed out under the covers with her head on my crotch and Olivia wasn't in the room. On the other side of the door the common room was quiet, so I jumped out of bed and went out there to get dressed. As I was doing so, Lucy groggily emerged from the bedroom in her bra and panties and asked where I was going.

"Home," I said.

"You don't have to leave."

"I know, but I have a lot of shit to do today."

"No," she said. I stopped for a moment and looked at her, not sure what she meant before continuing to dress.

"No!" she said again, leaping across the room and locking me in a bear hug. Suddenly she dropped to her knees, unzipped my pants, and started blowing me. Despite being right in front of the big common room window in full view of anyone who happened to be walking by below, after the unfinished business of the night before I wasn't about to stop her to pull down the blinds. It didn't take me long, and just before I came Lucy pulled her head away and yanked it out of me. My knees buckled and my wad sailed across the common room and through the open bedroom door, landing right on top of Olivia's ironing board.

"Oh my God!" Lucy cried. She frantically searched the room for something to wipe it with while I hastily put the rest of my clothes and boots on, and in her frenzy she didn't notice me leave. Out in the hallway a couple of janitors were mopping up the flood outside the men's room, and further down the hall Olivia was heading towards me with a fresh basket of laundry. She cheerfully said "Good morning!" and I grumbled hello without slowing down or even looking at her. I continued to hurriedly navigate the maze of hallways until I finally found the service entrance, where I threw my shoulder into the heavy door and fell out of the building into the bright Saturday sunshine, which immediately made my already bad headache even worse.

Despite stumbling repeatedly and being on the verge of either throwing up or passing out, I decided to walk home rather than take the bus to avoid a chance encounter with someone I knew. I was so out of it that down on Maple Street I walked into a mailbox, my knee hitting the obstruction hard and setting off a hollow metallic boom. Some kids playing in a yard across the street pointed at me and laughed, and I smiled and waved at them like the old town drunkard. They were the free ones, and they would remain so until the day they realized what I just had. And now, doddering back down the big hill towards a place I wasn't so sure I wanted to be, all I had left was the rest of my life. The exuberance of the prior day had merely been a cheap high produced by the last morsel of my youth fleeing towards oblivion, leaving behind a wheezing cavity that could never be filled and a nerve exposed that over time would only grow more sensitive until the body around it was numbed completely.

**2**

Frederick's of Oneonta Liquor & Wine Emporium was just a plain old liquor store with a fancy name, but to those undergrads who had yet to turn twenty-one, it's buzzing pink neon sign looked like a halo glowing in the Catskill night and the iron bars on the doors appeared as the gates of the promised land. It was well-known that if you tried to make a purchase at Frederick's using phony or altered identification, it would immediately be confiscated and turned over to the police; because of this, it had become a right of passage in Oneonta to make the pilgrimage upon reaching the magic age, and I made mine the weekend following my birthday.

When I went in I didn't know exactly what I was looking for. I started in the hard liquor aisle and looked at a few labels, checking the proof on each one, but nothing appealed to me. Next I went down the aisle with the piña colada and margarita mixes, and then the aisle with all the colorful liquors—blue curacao, crème de menthe, raspberry schnapps—and finally to the cooler at the back of the store that had the Mad Dog 20/20, the Boone's, and the $1.99 champagne. The only thing I hadn't looked at yet was the wine section, which took up nearly half the store.

I had always thought of wine as something old people drank with dinner or parishioners sipped at church, but lately I had been reading Kerouac and the idea of drinking some rotgut suddenly intrigued me. I didn't know where to begin and started randomly browsing the high-end section, which caught the attention of the guy behind the counter. He stopped playing with his receipts and hurried over, standing right behind me while I looked at the bottles. I did my best to ignore him, but finally after a minute or so I couldn't take it anymore and turned around.

"Can I help you, *sir*?" he asked with a snobby lisp. He was a short guy with a bad hairpiece and he was wearing an argyle sweater-vest over a pink dress shirt.

"I don't know," I said.

"Are you looking for a particular vintage?"

"Not really."

"What will you be serving with your wine?"

"Nothing. I'm just going to drink it."

"I see. You do realize that these are the dinner wines."

"Oh."

"Let me ask you this—how developed is your palette?"

"I don't have one."

"I wish I could be of more help, but you're not giving me much to work with."

"I'm just looking for something that'll get me drunk."

He looked aghast, and for a moment I thought he was going to throw me out, but he pointed me to the corner where they had the big jugs. After looking them over I picked out a gallon of Inglenook red sangria that looked cool in the store's fluorescent lighting and brought it over to the counter. The guy asked for my ID and scrutinized it as if really wanting to find some reason to reject me, but when he saw that my birthday was a week ago, he dejectedly said "happy birthday" and handed it back. He rang up $7.99 on the register, which I thought was a far better value than those dinky little bottles he was charging seventy-five bucks for.

We didn't have any wine glasses at the house, so on my way home I stopped at the Salvation Army and picked up a Pabst Blue Ribbon beer goblet for 50¢. When I got home I put the wine in the fridge and thoroughly washed the goblet in scalding water. After a bowl, a nap, and a shower, I threw a fish & chips TV dinner in the oven and poured my first glass of the evening. As I was doing so, Ed came in.

"That's a pretty big goblet you got there," he said.

"Want some?" I asked.

"No, thanks. Just be careful with that stuff, you can't drink it like beer. You have to ease into the buzz or else you'll drink too much and it'll suddenly nail you."

"I want to get nailed."

"Well, alright. But don't say I didn't warn you."

"Okay, pop."

I wasn't crazy about the taste or the nasty heartburn, but after finishing half the jug I left the house feeling gregariously flush. Down at the Oak I went up to the bar to order a beer and found a beautiful tall blonde sitting by herself a few feet away drinking a vodka tonic and smoking a long brown cigarette like *Kojak* used to smoke before he started sucking lollipops.

"Do you like *Kojak*?" I asked her.

"Do I like what?" she asked with a heavy European accent that sounded familiar, but I couldn't quite place it. She was intensely sexy in a James Bond chick kind of way, looking more like Roger Moore's type than Sean Connery's.

"*Kojak*—you know, the old 70's detective show with the bald guy who smoked the brown cigarettes like you're smoking?"

"I don't know American television. I'm from Sveden."

"Sveden, eh?" I said, imitating her accent. "Skål!"

She started laughing. "Talar ni Svenska?"

"I don't know what you just said, but it kind of turned me on."

"I ask if you speak Svedish?"

"No, not really. Varsågod! What did I just say?"

"You said, 'you're welcome.' How do you know that if you don't speak Svedish?"

"My grandmother grew up in Sweden and I remember those two phrases from the depths of my childhood. What was the first thing I said?"

"'Cheers'," she said raising her glass. I raised mine and we clinked glasses.

"Skål," I said.

After we introduced ourselves, I told her about my Swedish relatives and she gave me her impressions of America. She was an exchange student from Stockholm and would be going back there at the end of the semester. I started buying her drinks with my credit card and thought I was doing quite well despite being preoccupied with gawking at her body and hardly paying attention to a word she said.

"You are very handsome boy," she said, finally getting my attention. "You are rugged like Svedish boys, not like American boys. American boys are too skinny or overpumped muscleheads or fat pigs who eat too much at McDonald's."

"Why thank you," I said. "And I must say that you are very beautiful. I always wanted to meet a Swedish girl. American girls are all spoiled and stuck up."

"I have swinging bench on my front porch," she said. "I want you to come back to my house to sit with me and look up at the stars. When I was little girl I had telescope and my father taught me constellations. I still remember them by heart."

"I like stars and space and all that stuff," I said. "But don't you think it's a little cold to be sitting outside?"

"Not too cold if we hold each other." She leaned over and kissed me on the cheek. "I want you, Hank," she whispered in my ear.

"I want you too, —"

I tried to leave it at that, but she caught it.

"What is my name, Hank?"

"You already told me your name."

"Well, what is it?"

"I know it begins with an 'A'."

"Du drucken rövhål!"

I didn't know what she said, but it didn't sound very nice. She slid off her stool and stormed towards the exit, and I was too dumbfounded to try and stop her. After she was gone I pounded my fist on the bar and said, "Damn wine!" The bartender had seen the whole thing and offered me a shot of Jack Daniel's on the house.

"Her name is Ana," he said while pouring the shots, one for me and one for himself, "and she couldn't have gone far. After you finish this, go catch up to her and tell her what a beautiful name Ana is."

We raised our glasses and I said, "Skål." After downing the shots I thanked him and dropped a buck on the bar before heading out. I proceeded to look in every bar on Water Street and asked the bouncers and bartenders if they had seen a tall blonde with a heavy accent smoking brown cigarettes, but none of them had. I checked all the bars a second time just in case I missed her, but she was nowhere to be found. Finally I gave up and headed towards The Clinton.

As I neared the shopping center across Chestnut Street I encountered a grossly intoxicated chick with long red hair and freckles stumbling towards me. Her face was smeared with makeup as if she was loaded when she applied it, and all she needed was some striped socks pulled up to her knees and a pair of flapping braids to make her look like the grownup skid row version of Pippi Longstocking.

"You're drunk!" she said.

"So am I," I said.

"No, I said *you're* drunk!"

"Well so are you!"

"I know!"

"Then what are you making such a big fucking deal out of it for?"

"I'm not!"

"Well, it sure as hell sounds like you are!"

"Do you want to do some bong hits at my place?"

"Sure, baby. Why the fuck not."

She took my arm and led me towards Market Street.

"What's your name?" she asked.

"Anson. But you can call me Potsie."

"Anson? I don't think I've ever met an Anson before."

"Neither have I."

"I'm Phyllis, but you can call me Pinky."

"Alright, Phlinky. Just don't get all pissed off if I forget your name."

Her apartment was a big three bedroom place that was much nicer than most of the apartments in town. Both of her roommates had gone home for the weekend, so she had the place to herself.

"Do you want to see something?" she asked.

"I don't know," I said. She led me to the kitchen anyway and opened the refrigerator, pulling out one of the bottom drawers filled with rotting lettuce.

"I hate lettuce!" I said.

She moved the lettuce aside to reveal five sandwich bags stuffed with pot, each looking to be an ounce.

"I like that kind of lettuce," I said.

"It belongs to one of my roommate's boyfriend from back home. She's watching it for him because he thinks the cops are after him. It's really good stuff."

"Well, let's do some bong hits then."

"I have my own stash we could smoke from. I'm not even supposed to know about this stuff."

She went into her room and came back with a small bag of weed and a red three-foot Graffix bong. She packed it, took a couple of hits, and repacked it for me. I took a big hit and knew immediately that I was too drunk to be smoking. She took another hit and started packing it again, but I told her that I didn't want any more.

"Don't be such a wuss," she said.

"I'm gonna puke if I smoke any more."

"Well then fucking puke if you have to, wuss, but at least take a hit first."

I took a small hit and exhaled the smoke in her face. I tried to slide the bong back to her but instead knocked it over, spilling dirty bong water all over the coffee table that dripped over the edge and spotted the carpet.

"Fuck me, Potsie!" she said, ignoring the spill. She lunged over the table and pinned me down on the couch. We started kissing ferociously and she slid one of her hands down my pants while I slid both of mine up her shirt and under her bra. Her nipples were firm and she really seemed to enjoy my massaging and tweaking of them, moaning loudly like we were already fucking. It took me a couple of minutes to make the connection that while my left hand was massaging one nipple, my right hand was massaging two.

I yanked my hands out and said I had to puke. I tried to get up, but she pushed me back down and started unbuckling my pants. The room was spinning out of control.

"I'm gonna puke!" I cried and again unsuccessfully attempted to get up.

"And I'm gonna fuck you like a monkey," she said, which gave me enough of an adrenaline rush to push her off and roll off the couch. I ran for the bathroom but couldn't find it at first, and when I finally did I couldn't hold the vomit down long enough to make it into the bowl. I puked on everything—the floor, the sink, the counter, the shower curtain. Phyllis had followed me in and was standing in the doorway with arms folded.

"Do you think I'm a freak?" she asked. "Because I'm not, you know."

"No," I said and hurled again, this time able to project it into the toilet.

Suddenly she started gagging and puked in the sink. I ran out of the bathroom and went straight for the fridge, pulling out the bottom drawer and rifling through the lettuce. I took out one of the ounces and stuffed it in my pants before replacing the drawer and slipping out of the apartment.

I sprinted down the hall and found a side door that led to an alley. I went around to the back of the building and followed a gravel path that ran behind several other buildings until I hit the far end of Main Street. I casually walked past the police station and made the first turn onto a sidestreet and walked in a zig-zag pattern all the way back to the house. When I got there I went right up to the bathroom and dry-heaved a couple of times before stumbling down the hall and passing out with my clothes on, the bag of weed still stuffed inside my boxer shorts.

For the next week I was afraid to leave the house. Whenever I smoked from the looted bag I became extremely paranoid, and up on campus I darted from class to class wearing a hooded sweatshirt and sunglasses. Every redhead chick I saw made me nervous. I tried to rationalize my fear by reminding myself that she didn't know my real name, didn't know where I lived, and was so drunk that she probably didn't remember what I looked like, but the thought that somewhere out there a really pissed off drug dealer was probably looking for me brought it right back.

During the week I generously shared the weed with the other guys, but by Friday I still had well over an eighth left. I was still a little wary of leaving the house, so that night while everyone else went downtown, I decided to stay in and see how high I could get by smoking the rest of it in one sitting. I did bong hits for two straight hours expecting to come close to tripping, but I had built a tolerance for the stuff and after the first few rounds reached a plateau where I couldn't get any higher. Regardless, I finished the bag and spent the next morning coughing up something awful, but the spell had been broken and I was no longer afraid to leave the house.

Later that afternoon I got a little stir crazy and went for a walk. I walked through the park and then downtown and eventually found myself in the beer aisle at the P&C. It was a rare Saturday afternoon in that I was not hung over, and after the stress of the past week I was ready to do some drinking. For old times sake I picked up a 12 pack of Beast and finished it off before heading down to the Oak with the other guys later that night. I was hoping to find Ana down there and kept repeating her name in my head just in case, but by last call I finally gave up hope. At that point all I wanted was a slice of Gambaro's with cold cheese before going home and passing out.

Gambaro's was crowded and there were no seats available, so after I got my slice I took it outside. I sat on the curb watching the drunks stumble down Water Street while I ate, and after I was finished I got up to throw away my paper plate and napkin in the nearest trash receptacle. As I was doing so I heard some chick yell, "That's him!" Not thinking that the voice could possibly be referring to me, I hardly paid any attention. Moments later a stocky guy with a goatee appeared in front of me. I tried to walk around him, but suddenly he spun around with a roundhouse kick that connected with my chin. A sheet of lightning flashed in the sky and I started reeling backwards. My momentum was stopped by some other guy behind me who spun me around and punched me in the face. I fell hard, twisting my ankle on the way down and landing awkwardly on my wrist. I tried to get up, but I was knocked right back down. I rolled over into a ball and covered my head with my arms while my assailants repeatedly kicked me.

For the first time in my life I wished the cops were around. Some girl screamed "Oh my God! Somebody help him!" but no one came. I kept my face covered as they pummeled my body with their boots. It was only a couple of minutes, but it felt like an eternity. Finally there was a siren and a car screeched to a halt. The pummeling stopped and I heard footsteps running off in different directions, but nobody gave chase or yelled at them to stop.

I remained in a ball until someone said it was alright to get up. I tried to stand but was only able to rise to a kneeling position. Two Oneonta Police officers yanked me up by my underarms, and at first I was unable to maintain my balance, so they held me up until I was able to stand under my own power.

"Are you alright?" one of them asked. "Do you need to go to the hospital?"

"No, I'm alright," I said. I was dizzy and tasted blood. My entire body was in pain. Nothing seemed to be broken, but my wrist and ankle felt like they had been sprained and there was a long streak of blood on my shirt.

"Are you sure you're alright?" the other one asked. "It looks like you took a beating."

"Yeah, I'm fine," I said.

"Alright then, turn around, put your hands on the car, and spread your legs."

I looked at him with disbelief.

"Turn around and put your hands on the car!" he said loudly. I complied and he proceeded to pat me down. After he didn't find anything, he slapped the cuffs on.

"Why are you arresting *me*?" I asked. "I got attacked! I didn't even throw a punch!"

"Feet first get in the car," he said, directing me to the open back door of the cruiser.

"Seriously," I said. "I was just minding my own business and all of a sudden these guys attacked me for no reason!"

"I'm sure they had a reason," he said as I stepped into the vehicle.

There was hardly any leg room in the back seat so I had to sit sideways. The door was slammed shut and the noise on the street became muffled. After they got in and we were slowly rolling down Water Street, I looked out the window but didn't see anyone I recognized. When we turned onto Main Street it started to sink in that I was really being arrested, and though it didn't seem possible that I could be in any serious trouble for what had just happened, the thought crossed my mind that this wasn't just some plain old drug dealer I had swiped that bag from.

"I was attacked," I said calmly, realizing that I was still pretty drunk. "I'm the victim. I don't see how you guys can arrest me and let the guys who attacked me get away."

"Do you know who they were?" the one in the passenger seat asked.

"No! I've never seen them before in my life!"

"Then why did they attack you?"

"I have no idea! One minute I'm sitting there eating a slice of pizza, and the next I'm getting the crap kicked out of me until you guys showed up."

"So they attacked you for no reason."

"Yes!"

"Sure they did," the driver said and the two of them laughed. "But don't worry. We'll get them the next time they attack someone they don't know for no apparent reason."

Somewhere from behind the wall of sobriety a voice was telling me that for my own good I had better shut the hell up. I heeded the advice for a moment, but I couldn't help asking what I was being charged with.

"Disorderly conduct," the driver said. "And if you don't shut your trap, we'll tack on resisting arrest."

I didn't say anything for the rest of the ride. My entire body was throbbing and the cuffs were really tight on my wrists. Something Ed had said a while back ran through my mind about how everyone should get arrested at least once in their lives so they could experience firsthand what a farce the American justice system is. Having been arrested as many times as he has, he should know. He once got arrested for newspapering an NYPD cruiser parked right in front of a police station. Picturing this in my head I was able to relax a little and even enjoy the ride until we pulled into the garage at the station a few minutes later.

When they opened the door to let me out I was struck by a new wave of panic. Several surveillance cameras on the walls were pointed directly at me. When I got out of the car I became lightheaded and nearly fell over, but both officers roughly grabbed me and stood me up straight.

I was led inside to a brightly lit hallway that looked similar to the one the Merry Woodsman led me down the night I lost my mind. The lights were so bright that my eyes started to hurt, but I was already in so much pain that I hardly noticed. Cell doors were intermittently slamming in distant parts of the building and I thought I heard someone screaming. The officer who had been sitting in the passenger seat uncuffed me.

"Drop all of your possessions on the floor and take your belt off," he said.

I reached into my pockets and dropped my cigarettes, lighter, house keys, and wallet on the floor. I took off my jacket and pulled the belt out of the loops, dropping both on top of my other possessions.

I was led down another hall with a steel door at the end of it. Behind the door there were four empty cells on the left side, each with a wooden bench, stainless steel toilet, and a sink. He slid the first one open and pointed me inside.

"If you get some sleep you'll be out of here before you know it," he said before sliding the door shut and locking it.

"Do you know how long I'm going to be in here?" I asked.

"At least until the Sarge gets here in the morning, so you might as well get comfortable. Sweet dreams."

On the other side of the bars a surveillance camera mounted high on the opposite wall was pointed at my cell. Echoes of shouting and doors slamming resonated from other parts of the building. I took a leak and read some of the scratchings on the wall:

*Welcome to the Oneonta drunk tank! Enjoy your stay, and may it be a brief one...*

*Save the Teflon Don! John Gotti, good luck in court!* — *Skull, Bronx, NY*

*Fuck the Police!* — *NWA*

*The Honorable Judge Maurice J. Vander IV takes it up the ass.*

I really could have used a cigarette, but I happened to be incarcerated in a non-smoking jail. I tried to sleep on the bench, but given my predicament I probably couldn't have slept if my own bed was in the cell. I got up and made faces at the camera for a while until it occurred to me that they might keep me detained longer if they thought I was still drunk, so I sat back down on the bench and waited. Every so often the same officer came in and checked on me, and every time I asked him when they were going to let me out.

"When the Sarge gets here," he would say, sounding more annoyed every time I asked.

Without any windows I eventually lost track of time. I started feeling delirious from the combination of sleep deprivation, a hangover, and the stiff pain my entire body was in. When the officer came in the last time I didn't even bother to ask, but he looked in and said, "I can't believe you're still awake."

"I can't sleep in here," I said.

"This ain't exactly the Howard Johnson's," he said while fumbling through his keys. "But the Sarge is here. You should be on your way shortly."

He led me back down the hall where my belongings were still on the floor. He told me to pick them up and afterwards led me to a room where an overweight balding man with a mustache and stripes on his sleeves was seated behind a small metal cage that looked like one of the betting windows at Belmont. He was preoccupied with hunting and pecking at a computer keyboard and didn't seem to notice us, every so often muttering "I hate these goddamn things." Finally he got so frustrated that he turned around to the old woman sitting at the desk behind him and said, "Gladys, do you know how to use this fucking machine?" Gladys came over and made a couple of keystrokes to correct the problem.

"God damn," he said and turned to me, which is when I recognized him as the cop from the first night of college who caught Russ and I just about to smoke up with the Doobie Brothers. Fortunately, he didn't seem to recognize me.

"Have a seat," he said.

I did so and he looked at some papers attached to a clipboard.

"So, Mr. Gardner, I see you got into a little trouble last night."

"I got beat up," I said.

"I'll say you did. You look like hell."

"Thanks."

"Do you know why you got beat up?"

"No, sir."

"Random attack, eh? Don't you hate it when that happens?"

"Yeah. Especially when I'm arrested for it without even throwing a punch."

"Had you been drinking?"

"Yeah, but I was eating pizza at the time and was just about to go home."

"Well, that's what you get for being down there in the first place."

"I'm twenty-one years old. I have every right to be down there."

"You're asking for nothing but trouble whenever you go down there. If you really felt like you had to drink, you should have bought some beer from the store and invited a couple of friends over for a nice quiet evening at home."

"You probably would have arrested me for that too."

"Pardon?"

"Nothing."

"Are you being a wise ass?"

"No sir."

He gave me a long look before collecting information on me that I imagined would be forwarded to the FBI and the CIA. Between each question I had to wait for him to enter it into the computer, and a couple of times he needed Gladys' assistance. He asked for my height, weight, hair color, eye color, school address, home address, where I was born, social security number, ethnicity, marital status, religious affiliation (he gave me a funny look when I told him I was a Mormon), if I had ever been arrested, if I had a lawyer, if I had any tattoos or distinguishing birthmarks, if I had ever engaged in homosexual activity, if I had any diseases, if I had ever been hospitalized, if I had any nicknames, my mother's maiden name, if I had any outstanding debts, and, finally, if I had any pets. After an hour of this he finally explained that I was being charged with disorderly conduct, which was a violation that if I plead guilty to I would have to pay a small fine determined by the judge plus a $45 court surcharge. If I pleaded not guilty, I would be tried in court and run the risk of being found guilty of misdemeanor disorderly conduct, which was considered a crime, and if I chose this option he strongly suggested I get a lawyer. He then had me sign something acknowledging that he explained the charges to me and that I understood what he told me. After I signed, he pointed to a wall calendar hanging next to him and set a court date for 9:00 AM a week from the upcoming Wednesday.

"If you don't show up," he said. "A warrant will be issued for your arrest and you'll be in a world of shit. Got that?"

"Yes sir."

The courthouse was in the same building as the police station. There were long sheets of computer paper taped to the walls with hand-drawn arrows on them pointing the way to the courtroom. A sign just outside the courtroom said that you had to sign in at the window to the right before entering. An old lady seated behind bulletproof glass asked my name and found me on the list. She slid the clipboard under the glass in a drive-thru bank teller drawer and instructed me to sign next to my name. After I had done so, she told me to wait inside the courtroom until my name was called.

The courtroom was large and had high ceilings, red carpeting, and wood-paneled walls similar to the paneling in our living room. The windows and skylights were clouded so that you couldn't see outside and gave the room a chalky natural light. The judge's bench and leather swivel chair were on a platform at the front with a large City of Oneonta seal on the wall behind it. Several people were already seated in the last two rows of pews as far away from the front as possible, most of them townie vagrants except for a group of four frat boys wearing suits seated between an entourage of parents and lawyers. Seeing the lawyers made me wonder if I should have consulted one considering that I had no idea what was about to happen. The room was quiet except for the parents and lawyers speaking in whispers while the frat boys stared straight ahead.

At nine the lady from the sign-in window came in and sat down at the stenographer's desk. A few minutes later the bailiff appeared wearing a flannel shirt, jeans, and muddy workboots. For fifteen minutes he stood near the door looking over the crowd with arms folded until the judge finally came in.

"All rise for the Honorable Maurice J. Vander the Fourth," he said.

Judge Vander was a large, angry-looking man in his sixties or seventies with stark white hair and matching mustache that starkly contrasted his pink face. He instructed everyone to be seated as he got comfortable in his chair and looked over some papers. He called out four names and the frat boys got up with their lawyers and went up front.

The microphones didn't work very well and it was difficult to hear. The judge said something about breaking and entering, trespassing, and fourth degree criminal mischief, and from what little I could hear, I gathered that these guys were being accused of breaking into someone's apartment and trashing the place. The judge, lawyers, and District Attorney went back and forth for fifteen minutes before the judge called the lawyers and D.A. to the bench. They had a discussion that lasted several minutes until Judge Vander announced that they would reconvene in a month to set a trial date and hammered down the gavel.

The other cases went more swiftly. Most of the other defendants were represented by a public defender who had a pony-tail and a big cast on his leg that excused him from rising when he addressed the bench. Most were being charged with trespassing, though one had been caught shoplifting at Wal-Mart and another had stolen the District Attorney's sign from the wall outside his Main Street office.

Finally after an hour-and-a-half my name was called. As I walked down the aisle I felt many eyes on me trying to guess what I had done, just as mine had been doing to those who went before me. When I went through the little gate I started trembling. The bailiff greeted me with a Bible and told me to place my left hand on it and raise my right hand. He asked me if I swore to "tell the whole truth and nothing but the truth so help me God?" I said yes. I couldn't believe they did that in real life.

Though his platform was only a couple of feet high, Judge Vander looked like a giant pink-faced monster and I felt like I was two feet tall. I stood there shaking for several minutes while he looked over the report. When he was finished, he removed his reading glasses and stared me down for thirty seconds that seemed like a lifetime.

"Henry Gardner," he finally said, his voice booming. "Are you defending yourself?"

"Yes sir."

"You are aware that if you can't afford counsel, the court can appoint a lawyer for you."

"Yes sir."

"To the violation of disorderly conduct, how do you plead?"

I hesitated before answering.

"Guilty, sir."

"Do you understand the charge you are pleading guilty to?"

I thought about it for a second. "No, not really, sir."

"Then allow me to give you a brief explanation. You are being charged with a violation and not a crime, which means that if you plead guilty you will not have a criminal record, and if you clear the probationary period without further incident, the violation will be removed from your record. If you plead not guilty, you will be tried and you run the risk of being found guilty of misdemeanor disorderly conduct, which is considered a crime. If you are found guilty of a crime, you will have a permanent criminal record, so if you do choose to plead not guilty, I would strongly recommend that you hire legal counsel or allow the court to appoint you an attorney. Do you understand this, Mr. Gardner?"

"Yes sir."

"I will ask you again, Mr. Gardner, to the violation of disorderly conduct, how do you plead?"

"Guilty, sir."

"Are you a student, Mr. Gardner?"

"Yes sir."

"Why don't you tell me what happened that night."

"I was down on Water Street eating a slice of pizza."

"Were you intoxicated, Mr. Gardner?"

"A little bit, but not too much."

"You were intoxicated, then."

"Well, yes. Sir."

"Proceed."

"I was eating a slice of pizza when a fight broke out, so I went over and tried to break it up, but the combatants started kickboxing me in the face. The next thing I knew I was on the ground in a ball being kicked and punched. I didn't throw a punch or anything. Then the cops showed up and the guys who were beating me ran off while I was still on the ground. The officers helped me up and asked me if I was hurt and were all nice about it, but then they suddenly arrested me."

"You were trying to break up the fight?" the judge asked, hastily flipping through the police report.

"Yes sir."

"How many people were fighting?"

"Two."

"I don't see anything about breaking up the fight in the report," Vander said. "It says here that you were engaged in a brawl when the police arrived and that you later claimed that you didn't know why you were attacked."

"That's correct, sir."

"But you just said that you were attacked because you were trying to break up the fight."

"That's right, sir. I was only trying to break up the fight. I don't know why they attacked me."

"Did you know either of the participants of the fight?"

"No sir."

"Then why did you try to break it up?"

"It seemed like the right thing to do, sir. I abhor violence."

"Abhor?"

"Yes, sir."

"You could have gotten yourself hurt."

"I did get hurt, sir."

He looked at me for a long time without saying anything.

"I admire your courage, Mr. Gardner," he finally said. "But let me give you a little piece of advice. The next time you see a fight break out, call the police and let them handle it. There are a lot of sick wackos out there, and believe me, I've had a good number of them appear before me right in that very spot you're standing now. You could have gotten yourself seriously hurt or even killed. Do you understand what I'm trying to say, Mr. Gardner?"

"Yes sir."

"Good."

"Thank you, sir."

The judge gave me a look and then wrote something down. When he was finished he stared me down for another eternity before finally speaking.

"This court finds you guilty of the violation of disorderly conduct. Fifty dollar fine plus forty-five dollar court surcharge and one year probation as of this date within the city limits of Oneonta. Can you pay that fine now, Mr. Gardner?"

"Yes sir. I brought my checkbook."

"We don't accept checks, Mr. Gardner."

"Do you take credit cards?"

The judge looked like he was about to find me in contempt before suddenly exploding into a maniacal belly laugh. After twenty seconds or so his laughter subsided just enough for him to crack, "And we don't take green stamps either!" before breaking into another fit even more intense than the first. Everyone else in the room including the bailiff looked frightened.

"That's rich," the judge said when he finally caught his breath. I couldn't tell, but it almost looked like tears were running down his face. "I needed a good laugh. We only accept cash as a form of payment, Mr. Gardner. Do you have the cash on you now?"

"No sir."

He suddenly looked pissed again.

"You have until 5:00 PM tomorrow to pay the fine at the window where you signed in earlier. If the fine is not paid by then, a warrant will be issued for your arrest. Is that understood, Mr. Gardner?"

"Yes sir."

**3**

There were several places in town besides Frederick's of Oneonta Liquor & Wine Emporium that were none too kind to minors, and these, I thought, would be the true reward for surviving twenty-one years on planet Earth. Places such as Kitty Gordon's, the Blind Pig, Red's Filling Station, the Copper Fox, the Silver Wolf — each in itself a whole new world and a sanctuary from rotting away at the Oak night after night or any of the cheeseball frat bars on Water Street. These were the exclusive bars, adults only, that wouldn't be too crowded to breathe and where the surrounding faces would be as unfamiliar to me as mine was to theirs. Here I would find the older, experienced women I had been lusting for since puberty, like my eighth grade English teacher Ms. Wilcox who wore the leather mini-skirts and high heels to school every day or those of my mother's friends who had me running up to my room with a wad of tissues when they came over.

As badly as I wanted to check out these new bars, however, I didn't feel comfortable going into any of them alone, so I waited until after Russ' birthday a few weeks later before making the rounds. Our first stop was the Silver Wolf, a little dive two blocks south of Water Street near the railroad tracks. When we went in the main part of the bar was empty except for the bartender, a white-haired old lady wearing a fringed leather halter top that exposed a little too much wrinkled skin, but there was a sign with an arrow pointing down a flight of stairs to a pool room where we heard music and people. A chalkboard behind the bar advertised $1.00 Rob Roys, and after the lady scrutinized our licenses, we ordered two of them and toasted to "uncharted territory."

The Rob Roys were the foulest concoction of liquor either of us had after tasted, both of us gagging on our first sips. After recovering from the initial revulsion, we drank the rest quickly to get to the cherry at the bottom of the glass, the reward for finishing such a hideous drink. As soon as we were done, we splurged on two bottles of St. Pauli Girl to get the dirty old man liquor taste out of our mouths.

We decided to see what was going on down in the pool room, but as we headed towards the stairs the bartender lady stopped us and asked if we were serious players.

"Not really," I said.

"I just wanted to warn you that the people down there are pretty serious players."

"We're probably just going to hang out and watch," Russ said.

"Well, alright. But don't say I didn't warn you."

There was a pool table down there, but no one was playing pool. An old guy wearing leather chaps was bent over the table having his bare ass flogged with a cat-o-nine-tails by an old lady in a Catwoman outfit. On the couch another bare-assed old guy was sprawled face down across the lap of an elderly nun who was spanking him with a ruler. Another fat old guy wearing a diaper and a cowboy hat was sitting on a barstool in the corner with Rob Roy in hand.

"Whaddaya say, boys!" he called across the room. "Care to join the fun?"

We were halfway up the stairs before he finished the question. On our way out the bartender lady tried to tell us that we couldn't take the beers with us, but we paid no attention.

Our next stop was Red's Filling Station, which on the inside was easily the coolest bar in Oneonta. Many years earlier it had been a corner service station, a theme that had been retained by whoever bought it and turned it into a bar. The walls were covered with road signs and old license plates, the benches in the booths were springy old school bus seats, and in the middle of the huge floor were the two original gas pumps left over from the service station days. Because it was right across the street from the police station, however, the only few people who ever went there were cops. It was a letdown that the place was so dead, but I thought maybe it could at least serve as an alternative to The Clinton when an escape from the crowds was needed and some serious drinking had to be done.

I hadn't noticed until we ordered our beers that one of the three customers sitting at the bar was "The Sarge." There was a shot of whiskey and a glass of beer on the bar in front of him. He gave me a long look as if daring me to say something, but I pretended not to notice. Finally he threw back his shot and sipped his beer before he resumed staring at the bottles behind the bar. I told Russ that we had better finish our beers pronto and get the hell out of there.

Russ had a joint in his cigarette pack, so we went up to the top of the parking garage and smoked it before heading off to our next destination. Having had no luck so far in our quest for horny older women (not counting the kinky dames at the Silver Wolf), we pinned our hopes on Kitty Gordon's, the upscale tavern on Main Street. As soon as we walked in, however, one of Russ' professors spotted him and invited us to sit and have a drink with him and several of his colleagues. Professor Wixom was Russ' favorite professor, having been a city planner in Rochester for twenty years before going into teaching, and Russ was Wixom's prize planning pupil, but we were so blatantly stoned that everyone at the table felt uncomfortable. After a couple of minutes I got up and went to the bathroom with my beer and hung out in there until I finished it. When I went back to the table I told Russ that it was time to go meet the girls, and at first he gave me a confused look, but after he caught on he excused himself and we left.

Next we headed back in the direction of the Silver Wolf, staying on the other side of the street as we passed by. We crossed the railroad tracks and several blocks later arrived at the Blind Pig, an aptly named dive as only a blind pig would feel comfortable in there. The place was so filthy and run down that it made The Clinton look like a cozy little cocktail lounge.

Russ said he wanted to try a salty dog, an homage to the Artie character on The Larry Sanders Show, which we had watched earlier in the day. The bartender, a tall skinny guy with greasy disheveled hair wearing a stained wifebeater tank top that showed off the tattoos that completely covered his arms from wrists to shoulders, scoffed at our order, saying that this was a beer and whiskey joint and that he didn't know how to make fancy-ass drinks. Russ explained that it was simply a double shot of vodka with salt in it, not realizing that it was not a shot but actually a drink in which grapefruit juice was the mixer and that the salt was supposed to rim the glass like a margarita. The bartender smiled, exposing a large gap in the upper left side of his mouth where several teeth used to be, and said he could handle that. He put two rock glasses on the bar and poured what looked like three or four shots into each and then sprinkled them with a salt shaker.

"Am I s'posed to stir it?"

"I don't think so," Russ said.

"I'll make a deal with you fellers," the bartender said. "If both of you can finish these in one shot, I won't charge ya for 'em. If not, then I'll charge ya five bucks a piece."

"How much do they usually cost?"

"Normally I'd charge three bucks each for such a concoction."

"I don't know," I said, staring at the vodka in the glasses that looked harmless as spring water. "That's a lot of vodka, and I really don't like vodka."

"I'll tell you what," he said. "Same bet, only I'll only charge regular price if ya can't do it."

"What's in it for you then?" Russ asked.

"Entertainment. Look at this place, fellers—does it look like I get this type of excitement in here every night?"

The only other person in the place was a fat old man passed out with his head on the bar.

"Alright," Russ said.

I was hoping that the liquor would be watered down, but it wasn't. The salt gave the vodka a bite and I gagged a little after the first ounce went down, and when I caught a glimpse of the large quantity still in the glass I thought there was no way in hell I was going to be able to finish it. Russ had already finished his, but he was clinging to the bar in the midst of a violent coughing fit. Instead of gulping the rest in one shot, I let in a small but steady stream for the next ounce, but this method was torturous. Finally, when there was about a shot left, I brought it all in my mouth, gulped it down, and slammed the glass down on the bar.

"Pretty impressive," the bartender said. "You boys alright?"

Both of us were coughing and gagging as we headed towards the door and it took us several minutes walking in the cold air before we finally recovered. By now we were in an unfamiliar part of town and we continued our journey off the beaten path until we encountered a small brick building with a neon Genesee Beer sign in the window. There was nothing on the outside of the building to indicate the name of the place, which seemed a little suspicious, but it was really cold so we decided to go in.

"Howdy, boys!" the bartender asked jovially. He was an older guy, probably in his sixties, wearing red suspenders over a flannel shirt and looked like someone to whom owning and running a bar was the only way of life. It was a nice little place, clean, well kept, and quiet. There were a few locals at the end of the bar drinking and talking who paid no attention to us.

"Howdy," I said, realizing that this may have been the first time I ever said "howdy" to someone. "Is this a private bar?"

"Not at all," he laughed.

"What's the name of this place?" Russ asked.

"Well, my name's Sparky, so everybody usually just calls it 'Sparky's.' Most folks around here know who I am, so I never bothered to put up a sign."

He asked us what we wanted without asking to see our ID.

"How about a prairie fire?" I suggested to Russ, who was taken aback until I explained that one way or another I was going to puke in the very near future, and this would be easier than sticking a finger down my throat.

The bartender had never heard of a prairie fire and chuckled when we told him what it was. After they were ready and paid for, we took them along with a pitcher of Genny to the table closest to the men's room. I took a sip of beer to cool my mouth beforehand and we toasted to "Sparky's." Without hesitating I downed the liquid fire and immediately leaped to my feet, knocking my chair over in the process, and stormed into the bathroom with shot glass in hand. Russ was close behind, and since the bathroom was only meant for one at a time, he puked in the sink while I puked in the toilet. Because the liquor in our guts hadn't been down there long it came back up rather easily, and afterwards both of us felt much better.

"You boys alright?" the bartender asked when we came back out.

"Couldn't be better," I said.

We sat back down at the table.

"I like this place," I said and sipped of my beer.

"Me too," Russ said. "It's relaxing. But it's a bit out of the way."

"That's part of it's charm."

"I think we've reached the end of the road."

"So do I, and I can't say that I'm not disappointed. I really thought there would be something more."

"There is, just not here."

"I feel hollow. And I'm not talking about puking."

"I know what you mean. This whole night has been a letdown. We'd been looking forward to this for so long and it turned out to be nothing like we thought it would be. Not only that, now we don't have anything more to look forward to. Here we are, still a year-and-a-half to go, with hardly any prospect of experiencing anything new."

"I think that's what made the first couple of years so cool. Everything was new to us back then, and now it's just the same old shit. It's depressing."

"Get used to it."

After finishing the pitcher we headed back into town and Russ suggested that we stop at the Oak. I didn't want to at first, but he said that we should in order to set the wheels of acceptance into motion. He wanted to do a shot, not a prairie fire, but just some plain old Cuervo Gold. I could have done without it, but at that point it didn't matter so I agreed. The bartender asked if we wanted salt and lime and I said yes to the lime but declined the salt while

Russ wanted neither. As the shots were being poured I spotted Lucy and Olivia at the door coming in. Russ and I toasted to "the same old shit" and downed the shots, and afterwards I gently placed my glass down on the bar and said "see you later" to Russ. I made my way through the dense crowd and met Lucy in the middle. She was drunk and threw her arms around me, asking where I had been all night, and I told her "nowhere" before picking her up and carrying her out of the bar.

**4**

"I can't believe you hooked up with that little whore!" Virginia said, sounding rather intoxicated. We were at the Oak and it was St. Patrick's Day, one year to the day since she and Ed first hooked up, an anniversary that as much as I would have liked to have forgotten probably remembered better than they. "I'm surprised at you!"

"Ed hooked up with her first," I said.

"Shame on both of you!"

"Who cares. I sure as hell don't."

"What has gotten into you lately?"

"A hell of a lot of alcohol."

"I'm worried about you, Hank."

"Why?"

"Because you seem to be driving really fast down a dead end road."

"What?" I laughed. "Did you get that from an A.A. poster at the infirmary?"

"No, you just seem out of control lately. Whenever I see you you're not just drunk, you're like, really wasted. I'm worried because I care about you."

"No you don't."

"Yes I do, Hank! It hurts me that you would even say that!"

"You say that you care, but you don't mean it."

"Why are you being like this?"

"Like what?"

"You're being mean."

"I'm not being—*you're* being mean! You're standing there calling a girl I hooked up with a whore and you're lying right to my face saying that you care about me like a fucking cocktease!"

She looked like she was about to start crying. "I thought you were my friend," she said.

"I'm sorry," I said. "I didn't mean that. We are friends, but what I'm trying to say is that I think about you as more than just a friend. After that night last year when we smoked the joint and kissed I thought that something was going to happen between us, and I guess I'm just frustrated that it hasn't."

"What are you getting at, Hank?"

"Have you ever thought about you and me?"

"You and me what?"

"You and me going out."

"I don't know about that, Hank."

"You must have thought about it after that kiss."

"I thought about it before that kiss, the day we tripped up in the fields. That was the best day I've had since I've been here. I wanted you to kiss me that day, but then you suddenly disappeared and later I found you fucking that hippie-freak roommate of mine in my own bedroom!"

"We've already discussed this."

"I know, but now you go around hooking up with that whore Lucy—how am I supposed to think about going out with you when you're running around totally wasted and hooking up with whores?"

"If it wasn't for the whore and the hippie-freak I wouldn't have gotten laid in college."

"That wouldn't be such a bad thing."

"Then how do you explain hooking up with Ed? He's just as much a whore as Lucy! How is that different than me hooking up with Lucy?"

"It's different with Ed."

"How?"

"It just is."

"That's bullshit! Tell me, how?"

"I don't want to talk about this anymore."

"You're a hypocrite."

"I am not!" she said loudly. A few people near us turned around. "Alright, I'll tell you," she said more quietly, "if you promise not to tell anyone else and that afterwards we won't talk about it anymore."

"I'm listening."

She took a deep breath and leaned over to tell me in my ear, but she hesitated before speaking and her warm breath sent a chill through my body. "Ed was my first and only," she finally said.

"You're kidding," I said as she pulled her head away.

"It's true."

"A beautiful girl like you has only—with one? Ed?"

"Yeah."

"Wow. Why?"

"I don't know. I just never did it until I met him. Do you really think I'm beautiful?"

"Of course I do! You're the most beautiful girl I've ever seen. That's why it seems so shocking."

"That's sweet, Hank."

"I'm glad that we're finally starting to open up a little, but I still think we should talk about us, though. I mean, I see what you're saying about the drinking and whoring, but I think that's a direct result of my frustration of not being with you. That would, of course, change if our relationship changed."

She looked away for a moment and then back at me.

"Seriously, I think we should talk about this. Tomorrow. When we're sober."

"Okay."

"Seriously."

"Okay!"

"Do you want to call me or should I call you?"

"Either way. No, I'll call you."

"You have my number?"

"Yes. I've tried calling you before, but you never pick up the phone."

"I'll pick it up this time. I promise."

"Okay."

I spent the entire next day sitting next to the phone, but she didn't call. That probably wasn't such a bad thing considering that I was too stoned and hung over to have a meaningful conversation anyway, but I was disappointed nonetheless. It occurred to me that she might be in the same sorry condition as I was and would call on Sunday instead, so the next day after getting up and eating lunch I resumed my position in front of the television with the phone by my side and waited.

I held off smoking a bowl as long as I could, but again the phone didn't ring. I gave her until three before finally taking a couple of hits to calm my nerves. After my little buzz wore off I got restless and picked up the phone. I dialed the first six digits of her number but hung up before punching the last one.

I caught the next bus to campus. I didn't exactly know what I was going to say to her, but whatever it was needed to be said immediately. My determination was steady up until the moment I was standing outside her suite with my hand poised to knock on the door when the butterflies turned to bats. This seemed all too familiar.

After hesitating briefly I knocked and a couple of Virginia's suitemates called through the door to come in. They were in the common room watching *Moonstruck* and looked disappointed when they saw me. I asked if Virginia was home and they glanced at each other before one of them said she was in her room. One of the rooms had its door closed and I asked if that one was hers, and both nodded with expressions like they were about to say something, but neither did before I knocked.

It seemed like a long time before Virginia said "just a minute." Then some guy in the room asked her if she wanted him to get it. A moment later the door opened and Ed was looking back at me.

"Hank!" he said loudly and laughed. He was wearing only a pair of jeans. "Fancy meeting you here, m'boy! Looking for drugs?"

"Uh, yeah," I said, relieved that Ed had supplied me with an excuse for being there even though I hadn't bought a bag through Virginia in several months, not since before she was chased out of our house with a fire extinguisher and called a "five-cent whore." My relief was short-lived, however, when I realized that I only had a couple of dollars on me.

"Hi, Hank," Virginia said without the slightest hint of awkwardness as if the conversation we had two nights earlier hadn't even taken place. She looked really good, wearing a pair of cutoff jean shorts and a T-shirt that said *Dharma Bum*. "He's out until next week."

"Oh," I said. "Well, that's alright. I can wait."

"Are you heading back down to the house now?" Ed asked, putting on his T-shirt.

"Yeah."

"Wait up a second and I'll ride down with you."

None of us said anything while Ed put on his purple Chuck Taylors. On our way out I gave Virginia a cold good-bye and Ed said "See ya later," and though at that point it didn't matter, I was glad they didn't kiss.

"I thought you were through with her," I said to Ed when we were outside.

"You know me. I just can't stay away."

"How long has this been going on?"

"Since your party."

"Am I the first to know about this?"

"I guess so. She still doesn't feel comfortable coming down to the house, so I usually come up here."

"She feels uncomfortable about what *you* did."

"I know. Go figure."

**5**

It wasn't long before Lucy became a habit, and, like nicotine, she was a tough habit to break. It was extremely difficult, if not impossible, especially under the spell of alcohol, to resist free sex that involved virtually no effort whatsoever to get—no cheesy pickup lines, no buying drinks, hardly any conversation—and had no strings attached or emotional bullshit. We wanted the same thing from each other, so it was easy to take it and go our separate ways until next time. It got to where the receptionists at the Health Center knew my face from my constant raiding of the complimentary condom basket and I had to start going at all different hours to avoid the furrowed brows that accompanied the inevitable *Weren't you just here?* Finally it got to be too much, so I went down to the pharmacy and splurged on a value pack of Trojan ribbed and lubricated condoms.

In the back of my head I knew that Virginia was probably right, but I didn't care. This was the lifestyle I had fantasized about in high school, the only difference being that back then I had pictured more than just one girl. I hadn't daydreamed of love or relationships or feelings; there weren't supposed to be any feelings.

After about a month, however, when I would wake up next to Lucy in the morning, I started feeling like a fallen log all rotted out on the inside and a faint voice inside my head was saying, *You can't keep doing this.* The voice grew increasingly stronger until the words finally formed on my lips and I heard myself whispering them out loud. At that point I started halfheartedly promising myself that this would be the last time, but it would quickly be forgotten as soon as I saw her again downtown.

One morning, however, after waking up in her bed and getting dressed, I caught a glimpse of her as she slept. Normally in my haste to leave I wouldn't even notice her, and the night before I was usually so drunk that I didn't know what she really looked like, but for the first time through fairly sober eyes I caught myself thinking that she looked pretty. Just before leaving I leaned over and kissed her good-bye, something I had never done before, and on the way home I couldn't shake the vision of her sleeping beauty out of my head.

This was a serious breach, and I knew that now it had to end for real—no more phony promises or hangover declarations. I was well aware of my lack of willpower and my inclination while under the influence to give in to temptation without a second thought, so rather than confronting her and telling her that we had to stop seeing each other, I decided it would be easier to avoid her altogether, which actually wouldn't be so easy since we both hung out at the same place and rarely went elsewhere. Nevertheless, I successfully managed to avoid her for two whole weeks until one night I got careless and she spotted me at the Oak. As soon as I saw her I ran for the door and bounced from bar to bar desperately trying to latch on to any chick who wasn't talking to another guy, but she wouldn't let up. After passing through several bars I wound up back at the Oak with her still on my heels and invited myself to sit at a booth with several Asian exchange students. Despite the sudden silence that fell over the table as soon as I sat down, the girls hanging their heads in what may have been fear and the guys staring at me as if attempting to will me into leaving, I tried to make it look like I was talking and laughing with them and having a grand old time. Out of the corner of my eye I noticed Lucy watching from the bar with double vodka in hand. When I asked the girl sitting next to me if she had a boyfriend, one of the guys finally asked me to leave them alone and go away. I laughed it off like I thought he was kidding, but when he got up and approached one of the bouncers I left.

I went next door to Sports On Tap figuring that she would never look for me in there since it was frat central. I fought my way through the crowd and ordered a rum & Coke at the bar and started talking to a cute girl wearing a Chi Beta Psi sweatshirt. I told her that I was the president of the Intra-Fraternity Council and her face lit up as if in the presence of a god. She listened in awe as I told her how the job wasn't as glorious as it sounded and how most of the time I was sitting in boring meetings and putting out little fires. I thought I had her in the bag until I noticed Lucy pushing her way through the crowd. I pretended not to notice and told the sorority girl that I had to leave, but if she was interested in a drink or something later I would be at the Oak, where I liked to go every so often to get away from the ho-hum of Greek life and enjoy a drink without being hounded, and she said she might stop by. By then Lucy was only a few yards away, but she wasn't tall enough to see me cut around a group of bulky Omega Chi guys standing between us, so that by the time she got to the bar I was already halfway out the door.

I headed up to Main Street and went into Kitty Gordon's thinking that even if she did see me go in there, she wouldn't be able to get in. Sure enough, as soon as my beer was paid for, there she was at the door. There were no bouncers, so the bartender greeted her at the end of the bar near the door and asked to see her ID I watched with great anticipation of seeing her get the boot, but to my dismay the bartender nodded and asked what she would like.

A few stools down towards the other end of the bar was a woman sitting by herself. Being distracted I hadn't even noticed her at first, but here was the kind of woman Russ and I had in mind the first time we came here—mid-to-late thirties and very sexy, long curly blond hair, a little black cocktail dress revealing some nice cleavage, a pair of gams crossed like Sharon Stone's in *Basic Instinct*, and high heels that reminded me of slutty old Ms. Wilcox. I offered to buy her a drink and she accepted, so I moved over to the stool next to her. She ordered a $5.00 glass of cabernet, and while the bartender was pouring the wine she asked who the girl was at the other end of the bar angrily staring at us.

"I don't know," I said. "She's been stalking me all night. I can't get rid of her."

"So you thought you'd pretend to be with me so she would stay away from you."

"No, no, not at all. I would have offered to buy you a drink whether she came in or not. In fact, I didn't know she would even get in here because *I don't think she's twenty-one*," I said loudly enough for the bartender to hear.

"What makes you say that? Do you know her?"

"No. I was at the Oak before and out of nowhere she just starts talking to me and hasn't left me alone since. I tried to be nice at first, but now it's pretty obvious that she can't take a hint."

The bartender gave the woman her glass of wine and I paid for it with my credit card. I proposed a toast "to possibilities" and she smiled as we tinked our glasses. I started sipping my beer but cut it short when I noticed that she wasn't sipping her wine, and just as I was about to ask her if something was wrong, she threw the contents of her glass in my face.

"Cabernet stains nicely," she said and slid off the stool. She picked up her purse and headed towards the door, and on her way out she stopped and spoke to Lucy for a minute or so, occasionally glancing over at me as she did so.

I asked the bartender for something to wipe my face with and he handed me a roll of paper towels. Afterwards my face was sticky and I stared at myself in the mirror behind the bar until Lucy's reflection appeared next to mine. I lit a cigarette smoked the whole thing before finally turning and looking directly at her. As soon as I did she slapped me hard across the face.

"Alright, I deserved that," I said, rubbing my cheek. In the mirror I could see the red on my face and the cabernet stains on my shirt. When I stopped rubbing she slapped me again. There were ten or so people in the bar and they were all staring.

"Alright, once was enough," I said. "Physical violence isn't going to solve anything."

"Go to hell!"

"What do you want?"

"I want you to go to hell!"

"I'm already there."

"That woman told me what you said. She said you were an immature pig and that for my own good I should stay away from you."

"Then what are you doing here?"

She didn't answer, but her eyes started welling. She fought to control herself, and in doing so a wave of anger flashed across her face before she slapped me again.

"That's it," I said, getting off the stool and finishing the rest of my beer in a single gulp. I slammed the glass down on the bar and headed towards the door without looking back, trying to avoid the staring eyes of the other patrons and hoping that none of them belonged to any of my professors.

I knew she would follow, so I tried to lose her by taking a circuitous route to Gambaro's. While I was at the counter, however, she came in and sat at one of the booths next to the big window overlooking Main Street. After I paid for my slice I took the seat opposite her in the booth and started eating as if she wasn't there. She stared out the window with a scowl and refused to look at me until Ed and Teke walked by outside. They saw us and came in.

"Hank!" Ed said loudly and laughed. "Some sorority chick who thinks you're the president of the IFC is looking for you!"

"Well, ah, she was pretty hot," Teke said.

"A little too Long Island for my taste, but I'd stick her," Ed said.

I nibbled my crust without looking up at them and picked at the strands of cold cheese that had been warmed by the slice and melted to the paper plate. Lucy continued staring out at Main Street. Ed and Teke looked at each other before Ed finally said,

"Well, we're heading back to the Oak. Enjoy the rest of your evening."

After they were gone I disposed of my plate and left. Lucy waited a moment before getting up and following a short distance behind like a stray cat. I walked casually and pretended she wasn't there all the way up to Center Street, but a block away from the house she stopped at the corner and started crying. I was already halfway up the walk and tried not to look, but I couldn't help it. I got worried that she was just going to stand there crying all night, so finally I went over and asked if she wanted to come inside.

"You're such a pig!" she cried and started pounding my chest before breaking down and wailing into my shoulder. I put my arm around her and led her to the house, helping her along after she paused a couple of times as if her will was trying to stop her from going inside. After I unlocked the door she suddenly became quiet, holding on tight as I led her through the dark living room and up the creaky stairs.

In my room we lay in bed staring up at the blue Christmas lights I had swiped from somebody's hedges a couple of months earlier and strung across the ceiling. After several minutes I rolled over to kiss her, but she turned away. I rolled back over and resumed staring at the ceiling until she sat up and started staring at me. I didn't know what she wanted and her staring irritated me, and when she noticed this she started crying into the pillow until a few minutes later she said she felt sick. When she didn't get up I was afraid she was going to puke in my bed, so I helped her up and led her down the hall to the bathroom. After closing the door I lifted the toilet seat and she fell to her knees, wrapping her arms around the rim of the bowl while I held her hair back, and her body started shuddering for several minutes before finally going limp.

Back in my room we fell asleep in each other's arms. We woke up in the daylight and she had heavy bags under her eyes and dried mascara streaks running down her cheeks. She was beautifully ugly. She sat up and looked at me for a moment before turning away.

"I have to go," she said.

"You don't have to."

"Yes I do."

"Do you want to go have breakfast somewhere?"

"No. I have to go."

She sat up and I watched her put her shoes on. She was about to leave when I told her to wait so I could walk her to the bus stop.

"Were you really going to leave without saying good-bye?" I asked with mock lightheartedness, but she ignored me and left.

She refused to look at me while I followed her to the bus stop.

When we got there we waited silently until the bus appeared a few blocks away, and just before it pulled up I hugged her and kissed the top of her head. When she didn't hug back I looked in her eyes and saw that she was crying. I asked her if she was alright but she looked away, and without a word she boarded the bus. I lit a cigarette and watched it pull away and turn on East Street as it began its ascent up the hill before eventually disappearing.

**6**

No longer did I try to avoid Lucy, but she started avoiding me. Over the next couple of weeks I hardly ever saw her, and whenever I did she would either turn and leave as soon as she saw me if we were down at the bars or veer off in a different direction if we were approaching each other on campus. One night, however, after finishing off a jug of white zinfandel, I spotted her at the Oak and managed to confront her before she noticed me.

"Hey," I said.

"Hey yourself."

"How are you?"

"Terrible."

"Sorry to hear it."

"You should be."

"Why are you avoiding me?"

"So you know how it feels."

"What are you talking about?"

"Give me a fucking break."

"I haven't been avoiding you lately."

"What do you want, Hank?"

"I want to talk to you."

"Is that all?"

"For starters."

"You're a loser."

"Yeah, so, what about it?"

She started to walk away, but I grabbed her arm.

"Let go of me," she said angrily.

"I want you, Lucy."

"You want to fuck me."

"I want to make love to you."

"You're a jerk."

"Lucy, I like you."

"You like fucking me."

"But I also *like* you."

"You're full of shit."

"No, really."

"You're full of shit."

"Alright, fine. If you're gonna be that way, then I guess I don't want you."

"Good."

I watched her leave, and after she was gone I planted my ass on a barstool and drank Jack & Cokes until last call. When I got up to leave I turned around and there she was, standing with arms folded and looking considerably drunker than she had earlier.

Up in her room after making love, she sat up in bed and started staring off at nothing in particular. Olivia had gone home for the weekend, so we had the place to ourselves. I sat up and massaged her shoulders and kissed her neck and asked if she was alright, and she nodded. She turned and gently pulled me down on top of her so that my head was resting on her breasts.

"You're my baby," she said in something just above a whisper. She stroked my hair and kissed my forehead, and for a moment my perpetual feeling of wanting to be somewhere other than where I was had vanished. Eventually I drifted off to sleep, and as if not a moment had passed, I opened my eyes to the bright morning sunlight filtering through the blinds. My head was still resting on her breasts and she was already awake slowly stroking my face with the back of her index finger.

"Good morning, sleepyhead," she said and kissed me.

"Hi," I said in a drowsy haze. My initial impulse was to flee, but I realized I was comfortable where I was and didn't move.

"I was starting to wonder if you'd ever wake up," she said.

"How long have you been awake?"

"A couple of hours."

"You could have woke me up."

"You looked so peaceful. Besides, if I did you'd probably just get up and leave."

"I won't leave." I rolled over and she started stroking the other side of my face and adjusted my arm so that my hand was on her muff. I massaged her until she came to a shuddering orgasm, and afterwards she slid beneath the covers.

I could have stayed in bed all day, but a little while later Lucy said she was hungry and ordered me to get up and get dressed. On our way to the dining hall I noticed that for the first time since I had met her she was in a good mood. There was a spring in her step and a smile on her face, and rather than the prowling downtown tramp, she looked like the haggard little angel.

While we were on line we showed each other our student IDs and driver's licenses. I was shocked to see on her license the picture of a young high school girl who bore almost no resemblance to the girl standing next to me. The girl in the picture was cute and innocent and looked ten years younger.

"This isn't you," I said.

"What do you mean it's not me?"

As I handed back the license I tried to find the girl from the picture in Lucy's face, but she wasn't there. I wondered if she was still alive, perhaps trapped beneath the surface of what was there now and struggling to break out, but my reverie was interrupted by a cranky old lady wielding a spatula. I ordered a grilled cheese sandwich and French fries. Lucy ordered a reuben with sauerkraut.

"No salad?" I asked after we sat down.

"I hate salad."

"Me too. You're the first chick I ever met who doesn't eat salad."

She kicked my shin under the table.

"What was that for?"

"No reason. I just felt like it."

After lunch we went back to her room and she put on *The Baddest of George Thorogood & The Destroyers* CD. We lay down in bed holding one another.

"I know this is going to crush you, but I'm so in love with George Thorogood," she said.

"You're *in love* with George Thorogood?"

"You got a problem with that?"

"No. He's swell."

"You're just jealous."

"Damn right I am. I can't compete with George Thorogood."

She punched me in the arm.

"Who is your celebrity love?" she asked.

"I hate celebrities."

"Come on, everybody has one."

"Alright. I kind of have a thing for Kennedy on MTV. I even wrote her a love letter once. Twice actually."

"She's a bitch."

"Isn't she, though? And beautiful."

"How can you like her? Everyone hates her."

"Maybe that's what I like about her."

"Hey, do you want to see my cow collection?"

Without waiting for an answer, she got up and started tossing the little plastic cows displayed on her dresser onto the bed. They were like the old Smurf figures except they were cows, and each had it's own distinguishing characteristic—one was playing an electric guitar, one was wearing Hawaiian shorts and holding a surfboard, another was wearing a wedding gown, etc. Then she reached under the bed and pulled out a stuffed cow and threw it at me.

"Squeeze his stomach," she said.

I squeezed and it made a long slow moo sound.

"How clever," I said. She punched me in the leg.

After she put the cows away she got back into bed and we made love again. Afterwards we started falling asleep until I noticed that it was after three.

"I think I'd better be going," I said.

"You don't want to stay and come to the library with me later?"

"I think I'll pass on that. I'm not a big fan of the library."

"Well, alright. I guess I'll let you go. For now."

I was exhausted, but I had just missed the bus and didn't feel like waiting for the next one so I walked home. As I neared the house I took the sidestreets that led to the small lane adjacent to the our side so I could go in through our seldom-used back kitchen door because the other guys had been hanging out on the front porch during the recent spell of nice weather and I was in no mood to explain where I had been. I just wanted to go in, smoke a bowl, and sleep until it was time to start drinking again.

Sure enough, as I approached the house, I heard voices coming from the front porch, including Virginia's. I quietly unlocked the kitchen door and tiptoed through the daytime-dark living room and up the stairs to my room. I opened the window and packed a bowl, and while I smoked I listened to them talk about nothing in particular until Virginia asked, "Is Hank still sleeping?"

"Well, ah, I don't think he came home last night," Teke said.

"He's probably up at Lucy's," Ed said.

"Eww, I hope not," Virginia said. "Why does he keep hooking up with that little whore?"

"Look who's talking," I said to myself.

"I think the boy's in love," Ed said. "I only hope that nine months from now little Hank Junior doesn't pop out and her *pa* comes chasing after him with a shotgun."

"That girl is such a loser," Virginia said. "Why does he keep hooking up with her?"

"Because higher class whores such as yourself don't want anything to do with me," I said out the window. Ed let out a loud laugh, and Virginia stepped out onto the lawn so she could see me in the window.

"Hank, we're sorry," she said. "We were only kidding."

"Go to hell," I said and slammed the window shut. A couple of minutes later I heard them go into the other side of the house and close the door.

7

I kept telling myself that it would never work, that no good could come of it, that the very loneliness that was driving it could never be appeased by her. But I couldn't stop thinking about the cows. And the girl in the driver's license photo. And what a waste it would be to wait for something better when she was the only girl in Oneonta who wanted anything to do with me.

The battle between my heart and head became so fierce that I would spend days at a time locked in my room staring up at the Christmas lights on the ceiling. Finally one Thursday evening I couldn't take it anymore and the next thing I knew I was in the liquor store paying for a jug of burgundy. When I got home I didn't even bother to chill it, I just filled my Pabst goblet to the brim and plunked in a couple of ice cubes. I took a long slow sip and drained most of the glass, the dark wine bleeding down my chin and streaking my T-shirt. Someone had left a blister pack of decongestant pills on the counter, and for no reason other than that they were pills, I popped several out and washed them down with the wine. I refilled the goblet and went into the living room, where I planted myself in front of the television and smoked a cigarette. I was calm for about fifteen minutes or so before I started getting restless.

Not fully conscious of what I was doing, I went down to the basement and picked up Ed's empty fire extinguisher and struck a can of dark gray paint with it that the landlord had stored down there. It felt so good that I struck it again and worked myself into a frenzy, yelling obscenities at the can until the lid popped off and paint splattered everywhere. I tossed the extinguisher aside and kicked the can against the wall. Winston and Russ heard the commotion all the way up in their rooms and came thumping down the stairs. When I noticed them on the stairs I gave them a psychotic smile.

"Just letting off a little steam," I said to them.

"Jesus fucking Christ, Gardner," Winston said. "There goes our security deposit."

"I don't think we were getting that back anyway," Russ said.

Back upstairs I downed a couple of more goblets before storming out of the house. I went down the block to the overpass that spanned the open drainage sewer and climbed over the railing. The sewer was a concrete-walled canal about ten feet wide designed to help prevent the spring snowmelt on top of the big hill from flooding downtown below that originated up on campus and ran down through town all the way to the reservoir on the other side of the valley. During the fall and winter months when it was a trickling stream we had used it as a shortcut to and from downtown since it went straight to Main Street, but at this time of year it was a raging river and the only way to navigate it was to walk along the narrow ledge inside the chain link fence five feet above the water that separated the sewer from the backyards it cut through.

Normally I wouldn't have tried it, but I was out of my mind. I managed to make it halfway to Main Street by holding onto the crossbar of the fence until the last two goblets kicked in. Suddenly I became very lightheaded and missed the next section of crossbar I was reaching for. I started falling backwards, and in a desperate attempt to hang on I cut my right palm on a broken fence link. Seconds later I was hit with a cold shock and blacked out until I woke up coughing and gagging in the water just before the Main Street overpass. I struggled to stay afloat as the current pulled me under Main and clear across town until I was finally able to grab hold of a rusty shopping cart wedged against the wall. I pulled myself up to the ledge and spent the next several minutes coughing up water and trying to catch my breath. A chill shuddered through my body and I got scared that I was going to die of hypothermia. In a panic I struggled over the fence into someone's backyard and had to rest again before heading back towards town.

At first I jogged to warm myself up, but my wet clothes were too heavy and I was too out of shape to run more than a couple of blocks. As I limped back through town I pressed my wounded palm against my thigh to stop the bleeding. My skin was pale and shriveled and I was shivering badly. All I could think about was the nice hot shower I was going to take when I got home until someone started calling my name behind me on Main Street. I turned around and saw Lucy and Olivia walking towards me.

"Hank! What happened?" Lucy said.

"I was looking for you," I said.

"Where the hell were you looking?" Olivia asked, looking me over.

"I have to go home," I said.

"Are you alright?" Lucy asked. "Do you have to go to the hospital?"

"No. I have to get in a hot shower. Now."

"Let me take you back to campus. You can shower up there."

"I need dry clothes."

"You're coming with me. You won't need clothes."

Olivia continued on to the Oak, where they had originally planned on meeting their quadmates, while Lucy led me by my good hand to the bus stop. As we were boarding the driver gave me a look but didn't say anything. We took a seat towards the back, and after telling her what happened, she asked to see my hand.

"It looks like the bleeding has pretty much stopped," she said, inspecting it closely. "But when we get to my room I'm going to clean it and wrap it. Have you had a tetanus shot?"

"I think so."

By the time we got to her room I had warmed up enough for my teeth to stop chattering. Lucy sat me down in her desk chair and retrieved a first-aid kit and an economy-size plastic jug of Barton's vodka from her closet and a bottle of rubbing alcohol from her dresser, accidentally knocking over a couple of the cows in the process. She put all but the vodka down on the desk and took a long swig before opening the first-aid kit and removing a ball of cotton that she soaked with rubbing alcohol by pressing it against the open mouth of the bottle and turning it upside down.

"This is going to sting a little," she said.

"Good."

It stung a little more than I was expecting and I pulled my hand away.

"You're such a baby," she laughed.

After the wound was cleaned she covered it with a gauze pad from the kit and secured it by wrapping my hand with white medical tape.

"All better," she said.

"You're a regular Florence Nightingale," I said and kissed her.

She escorted me down the hall to the girls bathroom with a couple of towels and her bathing basket. After undressing me in one of the shower stalls and then removing her own clothes, she turned on the hot water and washed my entire body with a soapy loofah and shampooed my hair while I tried to keep the bandage dry by holding on to the curtain rod with the fingers of my bad hand. She then got down on her knees and put my balls in her mouth, which at first seemed a bit precarious, but she was gentle and it really turned me on. When I was fully aroused she started licking my erection long and slow from the base up before kissing the tip and putting her mouth around it.

She was a master. I was in all the way to her tonsils and it wasn't long before my come was shooting all over the stall. Afterwards she washed my groin with the loofah and turned off the water. She dried me off with one of the towels and wrapped it around my waist and I watched her dry off and get dressed. She escorted me back to her bed and put me under the covers before taking her clothes off again and slipping in with me, massaging my body and balls until I fell into a warm, comfortable sleep.

The next thing I knew a clock radio was buzzing and the room was flooded with sunlight. The clock said 7:15 and my head was throbbing.

Lucy rolled over and kissed me before sitting up. The sunlight on her face gave her a slight resemblance to the girl on the driver's license. Across the room Olivia was sitting on her bed in a pair of pink silk pajamas with an open textbook in front of her. I hadn't even heard her come in during the night.

"I have an eight o'clock class," Lucy said. "Do you have any today?"

"I have an eleven that I'm not going to," I said.

"Hank!" she said and slapped the covers.

"How's your hand?" Olivia asked.

"Alright," I said, holding it up for her to see. The tape was unraveling.

"That's quite a tape job," she said.

"I'm not a registered nurse," Lucy said. "I did the best I could."

"You did fine," I said and kissed her.

While the girls were getting ready for class I stayed in bed, but my headache kept me from falling back asleep. After they were gone I went out to the common room and watched an episode of *Happy Days* on their little television. It was the one when Fonzie tells Richie that he is in love with Pinky Tuscadero and wants to marry her and buy her a house with a white picket fence, but at the end of the episode he comes to realize that he couldn't go through life as Mr. Pinky Tuscadero and tells Richie that they had broken up.

After it was over I crawled back into Lucy's bed. I fell asleep until she came back and climbed in with me. She said she was going to make me go to my eleven o'clock, and again I told her that I wasn't until she started blowing me. Just before I was about to come she stopped and said she wouldn't finish until I promised to go.

Since I didn't have my books or anything with me, she supplied me with a pencil and several sheets of loose leaf paper. She said she was going to follow me to make sure that I really went and not just head home right after leaving the dorm.

Wearing damp, reeking clothes crusted with dried blood, mud, mountain runoff, and wine stains, and with a hand wrapped with medical tape hanging in strips, I staggered through the quad with my pencil and paper. I badly needed a cigarette, but mine had been ruined during the sewer run and I was too embarrassed to ask anybody for one. As luck would have it, a few of the other guys spotted me and started calling my name and laughing, but I ignored them. When I arrived at class I took a seat in the back corner hoping that no one would notice me, but nearly everyone did. After a while I no longer cared.

8

Several days passed before I saw Lucy again, during which time the pang of uncertainty I initially felt after leaving her room Friday morning had become a jackhammer of dread. Together we had staggered over a boundary to an unfamiliar place neither of us were sure we wanted to be, not with each other anyway, and now had no idea what we were supposed to do now that we were there. The only comforting thought was that the next time we saw each other we would probably be drunk.

On Wednesday evening, however, while waiting at the campus bus stop after my Restoration Literature class, I spotted Lucy heading towards me on her way to the library. For a moment I considered an evasive maneuver such as ducking behind the crowd or taking off before she noticed me, and perhaps a couple of weeks earlier I would have attempted it, but now I couldn't. She may have had the same initial impulse, for when she saw me she took a stutter step and slowed her pace.

"Hi Lucy," I said unenthusiastically as she approached.

"Hi Hank," she said, stopping in front of me but avoiding eye contact. She looked kind of cute with her bookbag and casual clothes, which only made her seem all the more a stranger.

"How are you?" I asked.

"Fine. And you?"

"Fine."

"On your way to the library?"

"Yep. On your way home?"

"Yeah."

There was a long lull.

"Are you going out tonight?" I finally asked.

"No, I have to study. Are you?"

"I don't know. Probably not."

She looked over in the direction of the library and then down at her sneakers. This lull turned into a prolonged silence that became increasingly uncomfortable until I could stand it no longer and blurted out the first thing that came to mind.

"Why don't you give me a call later."

She looked up at me like she didn't know why I would even suggest such a thing. I didn't know either.

"I don't have your number," she said.

"I'll give it to you," I said, playing it cool as if I had meant to suggest it all along. I opened my bookbag and tore out a piece of notebook paper, wrote down the number, and handed it to her. She looked at it like she didn't know what to do with it before stuffing it into her bookbag.

"How late are you going to be up?" she asked. "I'm probably going to stay at the library pretty late."

"I'll be up," I said.

"Alright then. Maybe I'll talk to you later."

"Maybe."

While we were trying to decide if we should kiss, the bus pulled up. Finally I leaned over and gave her a quick peck on the lips, one of those routine kisses that couples who have been dating for a while have prior to a brief departure. On the bus as I watched her disappear around the corner of the library building I tried to determine whether or not she was now my girlfriend, and as much as I attempted to deny it, I repeatedly arrived at the indubitable conclusion that the kiss indicated she was.

The phone rang just before midnight. I raced down to the living room before Russ or Winston had a chance to answer it. She returned my hello as if unsure as to why she was calling. I had smoked several bowls since I got home and had forgotten what I had prepared on the bus to say to her when she called.

"How was the library?" I asked.

"Alright."

"Get a lot of studying done?"

"Yeah."

"That's good."

Lull.

"What are you going to do for the rest of the night?"

"I'm going to bed now."

"Are you tired?"

"Yeah."

Another lull, this one really long. While I was trying to figure out what to say next, I became self-conscious of each breath I made into the phone.

"Do you want to come over this weekend?" I finally asked, wincing a little after I had done so.

"Come over?"

"Yeah."

"When?"

"I don't know. Friday night."

The connection became muffled on the other end and I thought I heard her take a swig.

"Friday night?"

"Yeah."

"And do what?"

"I don't know. Hang out."

"Hang out?"

Another muffled pause; this time I was sure I heard her take a swig.

"Yeah, I guess," she said.

"Unless you have other plans."

"No."

"What time do you want to come over?"

"I don't know."

"How does nine sound? Or ten?"

"Alright, I guess."

Lull.

"Well alright," I finally said. "I guess I'll see you then."

She said good-bye and hung up. I held the receiver to my ear until a mechanical female voice told me that if I would like to make a call I should please hang up and dial again.

When I got home from class Friday afternoon I locked myself in my room and did some bong hits to Pearl Jam's *Vs.* CD. Afterwards I lay on the floor and stared up at the dust particles floating in the beams of sunlight slicing through the blinds. *I'd rather be with an animal...* Eventually I dozed off and for the next several hours drifted in and out of consciousness, dreaming that I was asleep on the floor in my bedroom and waking up to find myself in another dream doing the same thing until I finally woke up for real in the dark.

I went downstairs and made a couple of grilled cheese sandwiches before taking a shower. Afterwards I did some more bong hits and played *Vs.* again, resuming my position on the floor, only now I was staring up at the Christmas lights. I was so burnt out from smoking earlier that I couldn't get high.

By ten I began to think she might not show, which at that point was what I was hoping for. At 10:15, however, there was a knock on the door. I grudgingly got up and went downstairs, took a deep breath, and opened the door to see Lucy standing there all dolled up in a leather miniskirt and high heels. Her hair was teased a little higher than usual and she was wearing an extra layer of makeup that made her look old. She reeked of vodka.

"Sorry I'm late," she said less than enthusiastically.

"That's alright," I said, thinking that this felt more like an appointment with a call girl than a girlfriend showing up for a date. "How are you?"

"Alright."

I invited her upstairs. I had some leftover burgundy and we swigged it straight from the jug until it was gone. We did some bong hits, but after that neither of us knew what to say. I looked around and spotted my sketchbook on the desk.

"Have I ever showed you my drawings?" I asked.

"No."

She sat next to me on the bed while I flipped through the pages, but she didn't seem very interested. My personal favorite was one of a giant strawberry surrounded by a circular field of zebra stripes and I asked her what she thought of that one.

"It's nice," she said.

"Do you think so?"

"Yeah."

"As a psych major are you able to read anything into them?"

"Yeah," she said. "In just about every one of these drawings there's a centered object surrounded by a force that it's trying to break free from."

"Really?" I said, looking at the strawberry. "Yeah, I guess you're right. Sometimes I do feel like that. Usually I only draw when I'm stoned and I never really give much thought to what I'm doing, but yeah, you're right."

I closed the book and put it back on the desk. I didn't know what else to do, so I started massaging her neck and then kissed her. She kissed me back and the tension broke as we rode into familiar territory, tearing each other's clothes off and fucking each other like *animals*. My stamina was much better than usual because this time I wasn't piss drunk and we both had intense climaxes. Afterwards we stared up at the Christmas lights while the CD player shuffled to "Indifference." It wasn't even midnight.

For more than half-hour we didn't move or say anything until Lucy rolled over and looked at me. I pretended not to notice, but after a while I gave in and looked back at her. As soon as we made eye contact she kissed me and climbed on top of me.

"No," I said, my voice garbled in phlegm.
"Are you out of condoms?"
"No," I said. "No more."
"No more?"
"No."
"Why not?"
"I can't."
"Are you feeling alright?"
"No."
"What's the matter?"
"This isn't going to work."
"What isn't?"
"Do you love me?"
"What?"
"Do you love me?"
"What are you talking about?"
"You know what I'm talking about."
She took a deep breath. "Can't we just go back to the way we were?"
"No."
"Why not?"
"We just can't."
"Why? Because I don't love you?"
"I don't love you either."
"Well then fine. Since we don't love each other, let's just go back to the way we were."
"I need more than this."
"What is wrong with you?"
"Nothing."
"All we've ever had was sex! Now all of a sudden you want something else, and if you can't have it you're willing to throw away what we do have?"
"I can't keep doing this."
"Then why did you fuck me first?"
"Because I didn't realize until just now."
"Fucking liar!"
"Fuck you."
She slapped me hard across the face then buried her head in the sheets and started crying. I stared up at the lights waiting for her to stop, and when she finally did she sat up and looked at me hatefully. I looked out the window at the dark street wishing that I had never met her and hoping she would just leave.

Suddenly she stopped crying and started blowing me. It felt good, but I carefully pushed her head away, a little worried that she would get mad and sink her teeth in. She resisted and I pushed her head away again, but she was persistent. Finally I said "No!" as if admonishing a dog with it's head in the kitchen trash can.

"I want you to leave," I said. She started wailing like a siren but then suddenly stopped, which made me nervous. I got up and sat at my desk, where I lit a cigarette and stared at the ashtray full of butts and the cover of my *Oxford Anthology of Restoration and Eighteenth Century Literature*. As I was stubbing out the butt she suddenly sprang off the bed and started dressing so hastily that she nearly fell over while putting on her skirt. She was sniffling and wouldn't look at me, and when she was dressed she grabbed her keys and ID off the dresser and pulled the door open with such force that the hinges loosened. She gave me one last hateful look before her lips started quivering and she exploded down the hall in a fresh burst of tears. She thumped down the stairs and across the living room floor. The front door opened but didn't close. I waited until I could no longer hear her heels clacking on the concrete outside before going downstairs and locking the door.

V

# 1

Perhaps for the first time in my life, I was glad to be home on Long Island, though it was actually being anywhere other than Oneonta and not waking up with a grueling hangover that was making me feel good during that first morning of what would likely be my last summer vacation ever. The first few days of a vacation were usually good—I could sleep as late as I wanted, Mom would cook my favorite meals, nothing was expected of me but rest and relaxation after the rigors of scholarly life—but then one night I'm asked to take out the garbage. Then mow the lawn. Then clean the upstairs bathroom. And then I'm asked when I'm going to start looking for a summer job, which, by then, despite the disruption it would cause to my nightly routine of smoking bowls with David Letterman and scribbling in my journal until three in the morning, doesn't sound like such a bad idea.

I got my job back at the camera warehouse, which was kind of fun the previous two years because there had been other college students working there for the summer, but this year the place was filled with ex-cons fresh out of prison and retirees who hadn't saved enough money for retirement. After a couple of weeks I started feeling the grind for the first time in my working life, getting up early every morning and wasting eight hours a day packing cameras and styrofoam peanuts into boxes for the financial benefit of a faceless Japanese corporation. During the long mindless hours it began to dawn on me that if I didn't figure out really soon what I was going to do after graduation in a year, I was going to wind up right back in this warehouse, only next time I wouldn't have college to go back to at the end of the summer, just the vast expanse of nothing ahead of me that was the rest of my life.

I started sending résumés to publishing houses in the city inquiring about internships and entry level positions after college. I applied for scholarships to graduate creative writing programs all over the country, sent writing samples to newspapers ranging from the local *Pennysaver* to *The New York Times*, submitted book proposals for books I had not yet written to the same publishing houses I sent the résumés to offering them the golden opportunity to publish my first novel in exchange for a generous advance, but I didn't hear back from any of them. By the end of the summer my frustration had boiled over and I didn't want to think about it anymore. I just wanted to go back to the place where three months earlier I couldn't wait to get away from, and, despite having to take 39 credits in order to graduate on time, 33 of which were upper division, and having no prospects whatsoever to look forward to after graduation, I was going to have the greatest year of my life.

Though Bruno and Ed had made amends, they had no intention of living together senior year. There was gossip that, despite all outward appearances, the two hadn't really forgiven each other and that Bruno was still secretly in love with Zoë and thought that not living with Ed would improve his chances of finally winning her over. The real reasons, however, were probably exactly what each said they were, that Bruno wanted peace and quiet while Ed wanted a party pad on Main Street right upstairs from the bars where he could truly experience the life of a senior at Oneonta State College.

Winston, meanwhile, did not want to live with Russ and I again, nor anyone else for that matter. In order to complete his botany/organic chemistry double major, he needed a quiet place to study and go to bed early without being woken up at all hours of the night. After looking for his own place, however, he quickly realized that he could not afford to live alone and approached Bruno. In a single afternoon the two found a tiny apartment near the armory on the other side of town. It was cheap and quiet, the bills were paid on time, the dishes were done on a regular basis, and, since they rarely had visitors, Bruno had the TV all to himself and didn't have to share his weed with anyone while Winston was able to study without being disturbed and be in bed by 9:00.

The rest of us found a decrepit four bedroom apartment on Main Street three floors above Crazy Gifts. We could have moved into a much nicer place for the same price somewhere else, but Ed was insistent on living on Main Street and the rest of us didn't really care as long as we were getting away from Center Street. The living room had crumbling brick walls, splintered hardwood floors, and high ceilings with dirty skylights that hardly let in light. The bedrooms were tiny, there was no dining room, and the kitchen was so small that we had to push Ed's oak table against the wall and could only sit around half of it. The bathroom hardly had enough leg room to sit on the toilet, and the walk up to the apartment was a grueling four flights of stairs.

Yet it might as well have been paradise. The four of us were finally going to experience off-campus life the way we thought it would be before Center Street happened. It would feel like freshman year again, that uninhibited freedom of being out from under the roof of our parents' home for the first time, and we figured that if we did the same things we used to do when we were freshmen, we would be able to recapture the magic of our youth once more before being thrust out into the cold cruel world.

During the first weekend of the semester the Teeks hosted an open house party on Center Street at the very same house we had been headed towards the first night of college before Fred and his Phi Ep buddies talked us into going to their party instead. We were anticipating a grand return to our roots and being surrounded by a brand new crop of naïve freshman girls who would be awed by our status as seniors, but when we got there the house was so packed that we couldn't even move, much less get a beer, and it was unbearably hot. After unsuccessfully battling the freshmen on the keg line for twenty minutes, we, for the first time ever, broke the cardinal rule and left a party before the kegs were kicked.

A few nights later we decided that instead of just sitting in front of the television and smoking up as had become the habit, we should go up to the woods on campus like we did in the good old days. With the bus and the walking, however, it took us nearly an hour to get to our old fallen tree near Golding Path, and when we finally did, the skies opened and it started pouring before we could even light up. We had to make a run for it down to the bus stop on Maple Street only to watch the bus go by just before we got there. Since the next one wouldn't be by for another half-hour we had little choice but to walk all the way back down to Main Street with skin pale and wrinkled under the heavily drenched clothes our bodies had to lug up four flights of stairs before we finally got to smoke.

The following weekend Russ said that some guy he knew from one of his classes had some mild acid he was trying to unload. It sounded like a good idea at first, the four of us who tripped together at the end of freshman year taking one last walk down the hall before closing *The Doors of Perception* for good, and sounded even better when Ed suggested that while we were tripping we could make piña coladas with the blender he bought from the Salvation Army store a few days earlier. The blender, however, burned out after the first round, so we did whip-its with the leftover Redi Whip cans, made rum & Cokes with the leftover rum, and sat in front of the television laughing uncontrollably when the Interstate highways on the Weather Channel satellite maps started tying themselves in knots while the pregnant weather lady droned on oblivious to what was happening on the screen behind her.

Since the trip was initially mild as advertised, we decided to go down to the Oak just before the peak. We did not realize, however, that the alcohol had been masking the true strength of the acid, so that by the time we got down there we were a collective mess and everyone in the place knew it. It was so bad that we were unable to coordinate a simple trip to the bar to buy a pitcher of beer, and after several minutes of utter confusion we had to abort and go back to the apartment.

When we got back upstairs we went off in our own directions. I took a seat at the kitchen table and stared out the window sipping the last of the rum straight from the bottle. The normal view of charred brick and power lines had been replaced by an endless prairie of weeds visible only to where the land divided the sky. Despite the apparent hopelessness of the landscape it was beautiful, and I couldn't help feeling that somewhere beyond the curvature of the earth awaited a place I wouldn't want to leave, a place where I could be free and start living for real, a place, the only place in the world, that I could call *home*.

My reverie was interrupted when Teke started chanting something that sounded like Latin in his room. Russ and Ed emerged from their rooms and the three of us crowded around his closed door and listened as he started repeatedly humming "A-ummmm" with a deep voice. After a couple of minutes he stopped and was silent for a moment before reciting in his normal twang:

> *Well, ah, Divine Goddess,*
> *Mother of Night,*
> *Queen of Cannabis,*
> *Lady of Lysergic,*
> *My journey down the path*
> *has led me to your Pentacle,*
> *where I now stand ready*
> *to sacrifice all to your grace.*
> *By the power of the Earth, Fire, Water, Air, and Spirit,*
> *I offer the blood of my being to you*
> *as I leave the labyrinth and step*

*onto the Plain of Fire—*

"Jesus Christ!" Ed yelled and stormed into the room. Teke was standing inside a circle of candles wearing only a pair of tightie-whities and holding a shot glass filled with dark fluid.

"What the fuck are you doing?" Ed asked.

"Well, ah, I was just working out the kinks of a ceremony for my novel."

"Tell me that's not real blood in that glass," Russ said.

"It's real," Teke said. "I pricked it from my middle finger."

"Why don't you just slit your wrists and get it over with?" Ed said.

"Well, ah, drinking blood enhances a trip a hell of lot more than your vitamin C."

"I'm sure it does! My only concern is coming in here and finding your dead fucking body!"

"I wasn't really going to do it. This is for a character in my novel."

A little while later Ed suggested that we go up to campus and watch the sunrise from the fields, but the rest of us weren't up for it.

"Don't you guys realize that this is probably the last time we'll ever see a sunrise from up there?" he said. "Don't you remember how amazing that was?"

"Well, ah, we have a whole year left," Teke said. "Some of us longer."

"But how many times have we been up there since the last time? Even when we lived on campus? And who's going to get up before dawn in the dead of winter after a night of drinking to go up there? Come on, this is probably the last time in our lives we'll ever have a chance to see a sunrise after tripping all night—do you really want to waste it by staying cooped up in this fucking hole?"

The nicest time of year in the Catskills is the period of early autumn when the summer heat finally subsides and the hills turn their deepest shade of green before changing colors and attracting the bed & breakfast crowd from the city and suburbs. It was a beautiful morning, the kind that invigorates while at the same time makes you regretful about how many such mornings you have missed by sleeping your life away in the bowels of a nasty hangover. The grass was moist with dew, the air was cool and clear, and there wasn't a cloud in the sky. The hills surrounding the valley looked close enough to touch, and it was so quiet that you could follow the whir of an unseen car on a hillside road miles away.

We sat Indian-style on the edge of the third tier and passed a joint while waiting for the sun. For a moment the anticipation did make it feel like freshman year again, but that quickly evaporated when the first rays of light shot out from behind the hills. Like last time everything in the universe became perfectly clear, only now instead of being infused with hope, I was injected with despair. Things don't get better—they don't change at all. There is no *in* or *out*, just birth and death. I had been free all along, yet I knew nothing of freedom. There is no such place as *there*; no matter where I was, I would always be *here*.

On our way back downtown we walked down Golding Path, and while we were passing Fred's old house on Maple we had a few laughs speculating what he might be doing now, the most likely scenarios being stockbroker or gay porn director. I recalled what Teke had said when we made this walk freshman year about how it must be awesome to be a senior in this place and it seemed ridiculous now how naïve we were back then. Down on Main Street we sat on a bench and watched the old people for a while, this time with the understanding that someday we would be one of them if we were unlucky enough to live that long. After a while Russ and Teke started crashing and went back up to the apartment, but Ed and I had one more stop to make.

The front doors of the old church were still locked, so again we went around back. Like regulars we made our way through the corridors to the clergyman's entrance and without hesitating stepped into the main cathedral. Everything looked the same except smaller. Ed went up front and said a quick prayer at the altar, kneeling on the padded bar and crossing himself before getting up and giving the Crucifix a long look.

"Just in case," he said to me.

It wasn't until we were halfway down the aisle heading towards the back of the cathedral that I noticed a bald old man wearing a white frock and wire-framed glasses sitting in the last row of pews. He looked like Gandhi. His head was bowed in prayer and his eyes were wincing behind his glasses. I slowed down, but Ed kept his pace and went right by as if he didn't notice him. I tried not to look as I approached, but I couldn't help it. Suddenly the man looked up at me with wild bug eyes and hissed, "I'm here now!" My muscles stiffened and for a moment I thought I was going to drop dead, but I managed to stagger into the lobby where Ed was flipping through the guest register.

"Jesus Christ, man, are you alright?" he said when he saw me.

"Did you see that?"

"See what?"

"The old guy."

"What old guy?"

Ed looked into the cathedral and said no one was in there. I peeked as well and *HE* was gone.

As we headed out the door, my eyes fell on the guest register. I stopped and turned back a couple of pages and found our entry from the end of freshman year:

*19 May — I can't see HIM, but I can feel HIM. -Ed*
*May 19 — Hank was here. God wasn't.*

Back at the apartment I was still too wired to sleep, so I sprawled out on the couch and smoked a bowl in front of the television. After flipping through the channels I stopped at an old black & white movie about the loinclothed natives of a tiny island attempting to flee a smoking volcano that was about to destroy their homes. There was no dialogue, only an incessant bongo beat set to the pace of the natives frantically building canoes and rafts on the beach. As the smoke thickened atop the volcano and lava started oozing down the sides, the beat got faster until the low rumbling of a kettle drum signaled the eruption. The natives threw their unfinished crafts into the water and desperately rowed against the waves as the volcano exploded. Many were left behind and the lava set fire to their grass huts, and just when those who had managed to get their canoes and rafts out past the breakers felt safe and stopped rowing to witness the destruction, they started sinking as the sharks started circling. After a minute or two of wild splashing the waters became calm and the sharks left, leaving behind broken pieces of wood floating in the waves. The camera panned back across the smoldering remains of the now uninhabited island, and the bongo beat slowed until the picture faded black.

**2**

"Would you ever try heroin?" Russ asked me one evening while we were in his room smoking a bowl.

"Heroin?"

"Yes. Heroin."

"Are you serious?"

"Just curious."

"You are serious."

"Yes."

"Honestly, I never really thought about it until I read *Junky*, but that was more of a curiosity about what it was like because of what I was reading. It seems so completely out of my league, and I've never known anyone who's actually done it and wouldn't have the slightest clue where to get it. What about you?"

"I think I've always been curious to try it, at least ever since I've used drugs. It's considered one of the best highs you can get besides crack. I would be extremely careful with it, though, and once I got a sense of what the high is like, I wouldn't do it again."

"You have that same fucking look you had about the acid freshman year."

Russ smiled. "That guy Josh who got us the acid a couple of weeks ago said he can get if we're interested. He says it's pretty good stuff."

"Holy fuck," I said, shaking my head. "Are you out of your mind?"

"Maybe."

"You're gonna stick a fucking needle in your arm?"

"It's powder. You snort it."

"Oh."

"So, do you want to try it?"

"Try it? I can't believe we're even having this conversation!"

"This is an opportunity to experience something most people never will."

"I'd try coke, maybe, but heroin is pretty serious shit."

"Coke is a fucking waste. You do coke so you have the energy to keep doing other stuff. Heroin is an experience in itself."

"Opium, maybe."

"They both come from the same plant."

"I don't know. I don't like the idea of taking something that you can overdose on."

"You drink alcohol."

"It's nearly impossible to OD on alcohol."

"Haven't you almost done it?"

"Twice. But it wasn't easy."

"You can choke on your own vomit and die of asphyxiation."

"I'm careful not to pass out on my back."

"But you're willing to try coke, which you can also OD on, not to mention the substantial risk of permanent brain damage that acid can cause, which you've done how many times now?"

"Well, I also don't like the idea of becoming a junky."

"It takes about six months of constant use to become fully addicted. I only want to try it."

"But that's how it starts."

"We'll just have to be careful."

"You've really given this some thought."

"It's all I've been thinking about the last couple of days."

"So you definitely want to do it."

"Yes. But only if you do."

"If *I* do? What about the other guys?"

"I would rather them not know. If it's just you and I we can do it quietly and discreetly, but if everyone else knew they would either try to stop us or, if they wanted to do it, it would turn into a circus. I don't want the whole world to know about this."

On Friday evening when Russ finally got home I was watching TV with Ed and Teke, who were drinking goblets of burgundy. I could tell by his nonchalant expression that he had it, but I waited for a commercial before getting up and casually wandering into his room. I found him sitting at his desk carefully unwrapping a small package of blue crepe paper with white dragons printed on it that reminded me of a design on a pack of firecrackers, and inside was a very small quantity of fine off-white powder that didn't look like it would be anywhere near enough to get both of us high.

"Don't sneeze," Russ said quietly.

"We paid sixty bucks for that?"

"This is supposedly a lot."

"If that's a lot, I'm only doing a tiny line."

"Bumps. With coke you do lines, but with this stuff you do bumps."

We decided to wait for Ed and Teke to leave for the bars, so I grabbed a beer and went back into the living room. When they finished their jug of wine, Ed asked if I was going with them and I said we would meet them down there later. After they left I waited a couple of minutes before going back into Russ' room.

"They're gone," I said to Russ, who already had the stuff laid out on top of the storage trunk he used as a coffee table. "Are you ready?"

"I've been ready for hours."

"I'll let you go first," I said. "I've never snorted anything in my life."

"Neither have I."

Russ took out a razor blade and poured a small amount of the powder onto his Beastie Boys *Paul's Boutique* CD case. I put on Pearl Jam's *Vitalogy* CD and "Last Exit" started playing while Russ built two small mounds that looked like anthills. He removed a crisp ten-dollar bill from his wallet and rolled it into a tight tube. It took him a while to work up the nerve, and as he was doing so I stared at the bump thinking that I was going to royally fuck up the snorting part. Finally he lowered his head with one end of the bill in his left nostril, and just before he was about to snort, he exhaled a little puff of air that scattered the powder all over the CD case.

"That's exactly what I thought I was going to do!" I laughed, and Russ started laughing too. Fortunately most of the powder had remained on the surface of the CD case, so he was able to easily reconstruct the bump. I suggested that instead of waiting until he was right on top of the bump to start inhaling, he should start when he began lowering his head. Russ took my advice and this time, just before the bill was going to make contact with the powder, the bump disappeared as if it had been sucked into a vacuum hose.

"Did you get it?" I asked.

"Oh yeah," Russ said, sniffing repeatedly as if trying to make sure it wouldn't fall out of his nose. He handed me the razor and I made a smaller pile than his had been and stared at it.

"I can't believe I'm really doing this," I said before re-tightening the bill and sticking it in my right nostril. I slowly lowered my head, immediately forgetting the advice I had just given Russ, and exhaled, demolishing my tiny hill. We laughed for a couple of minutes before I rebuilt the pile and tried again. This time I did it right and the powder shot up my nose with an itchy tingle.

Since we had no idea how much would get us high and how much would kill us, we had been extra cautious about how much we snorted the first time. After an hour or so, however, it was apparent that we had not done enough, so Russ made two more bumps that were noticeably larger than the first ones. Neither of us had difficulty snorting this time, and while we were waiting for it to kick in, I went into the kitchen and did a shot of blue curacao from the bottle Ed had brought up at the beginning of the semester that had been sitting untouched in the fridge ever since. The shot went down easy and tasted good, so I did a couple more before heading into the living room and lighting a cigarette.

It was raining hard outside. We shut the lights and listened to the heavy drops hit the roof and after a while started to feel a numbness similar to the effect of valium or quaaludes. Russ said he couldn't stop scratching his nose and that his entire body felt itchy. I kept expecting my mind to start playing tricks on me, but instead my body became perfectly relaxed to the point where I wasn't sure if I had any control over it while my head remained clear.

"I don't see the big deal about this stuff," I said, sitting up. Suddenly I felt nauseous and ran to the bathroom. I ejected the blue curacao into the bowl, the vomit all liquid and turning the toilet water turquoise.

Puking on heroin wasn't nearly as violent as puking when drunk, and afterwards I felt much better. I resumed my seat on the couch and listened to the rain until I got hungry a little while later and went into the kitchen to make myself a baloney sandwich. Fifteen minutes later I was back in the bathroom puking it up, the sandwich coming up in pretty much the same form as it had gone down. Half-hour later I was hungry again, but this time I stayed on the couch and fought it off.

The rain continued to fall and eventually I drifted off to sleep, as did Russ in the easy chair. I had a dream that the two of us were in an old castle sitting at a long dining room table covered with fancy food and a huge candelabra in the middle. There were many other people at the table we didn't recognize who seemed to know each other but who didn't seem to notice us. We didn't know where we were or what we were doing there and, while everyone else was devouring their food and commenting how good it was, we could hardly look at what was on the plates in front of us, which appeared to be fried brains covered with a thick Worcestershire sauce. A little while later the little old man sitting at the head of the table stood up and started tinking his glass with a spoon. Everyone quieted down, but instead of making a toast, he suddenly turned into a giant dragon and exhaled a stream of flame right at Russ and I. As the flame shot towards us we both screamed, which back in our living room woke both of us up.

It took a few moments for us to gather our senses.

"I just had the most fucked up dream," Russ finally said.

"So did I."

"You and I, sitting at this big table with a bunch of people we didn't know—"

"That's fucked up," I said.

"We were sitting there and then this old guy at the end of the table stood up—"

"And started tinking his glass, and then he turned into a dragon and sprayed us with fire."

Russ thought about it for a moment. "How is that even possible?"

"I don't know. We must be on the same wavelength."

"Yeah, but still, that's *too* fucked up."

"Maybe we're still dreaming now. One of us, anyway."

I pinched my arm.

"Nothing," I said.

"Me neither," Russ said after pinching his.

"We could be dead," Russ said.

"I don't know. Maybe."

"Alright, I'm going to bed. I guess we'll find out tomorrow, *if* we wake up."

The next day Ed asked why we hadn't gone out and I told him that we smoked too much dope and couldn't get off the couch. Later that evening, he and Teke started drinking beers after dinner while Russ and I smoked in Russ' room, both of us anxious for them to leave so we could start snorting the remainder of our stash. We probably could have done it without them knowing, but we didn't want to take the chance of being caught in the act or look suspicious by closing the door, so we waited. Finally at around ten they got up to leave and shouted down the hall to ask if we were coming, and I shouted back that we would be down in a little while.

"That's what you said last night," Ed said.

"Leave already," Russ said under his breath.

"We'll be down there in an hour or so," I said. "You know I don't like those early crowds."

Russ already had the bumps set up on the *Paul's Boutique* case hidden behind a pile of textbooks on his desk. The apartment door had barely been shut before his head was buried in the first bump. We used the same ten-dollar bill as the night before, and this time neither of us hesitated. There was a considerable amount more left than what we had done the night before and we did it all in one shot and then headed down to Water Street.

By the time we got down to the Oak we were fucked up but still functional. I started drinking Michelob Dark, a heavy beer that usually didn't go down very easily but was now going down like water. After several glasses I realized that the alcohol was having no effect on me whatsoever, but I kept drinking anyway until I suddenly found myself standing next to the pinball machine in the corner unable to move. The noise in the bar faded as I hypnotically stared at the blinking lights on the machine in a wave of euphoria far more intense than I ever experienced on acid or pot. I'm not sure how long I was there before Bruno wandered over and asked if I was alright.

"Dude, you look so fucked up," he laughed.

"Can you feel it?" I asked him.

"Feel what?"

"That," I said, limply pointing at the machine.

Ed came over and Bruno told him I was gone. Ed started looking at me suspiciously and was about to say something until some girl he had recently hooked up with came over and distracted him. I told Bruno that I was fine and he eventually went away thinking that I was just stupid drunk or stoned, once again leaving me alone with my blinking lights. People were staring at me, but unlike the self-conscious nature of pot and acid, I didn't care. The lights were pulsing through every pleasure sensor in my body, and every so often I got a warm-cold shiver that felt like a full body orgasm ten times over. The angst I usually felt at the Oak was absent now that I was experiencing something far better than sex and not frustrating myself by trying to hook up with every girl in the bar.

A little while later Virginia showed up. Ed was still talking to his other girl, so she came over and said hello to me.

"Hello," I said with shit-eating grin.

"Are you alright?" she asked.

"Never better."

"You look really fucked up. Are you tripping?"

"No—maybe—yes. Feeling fine."

She looked at me for what seemed like an eternity while I stared over her right shoulder.

"Hank, are you mad at me?"

"Mad? Nope. Feeling good, feeling fine. You should come visit my world sometime and check it out."

"Maybe I will."

"Good. I'll take note of that."

She looked at me with an expression of befuddlement until Ed came over.

"Is Hank alright?" she asked him.

Ed looked at me suspiciously again, this time leaning over and looking closely into my eyes. I tried not to make eye contact with him but couldn't help doing so.

"I think he's tripping," Virginia said.

"No," Ed said. "He doesn't have acid eyes." He moved in a little closer. "What the hell are you on?"

"I'm high on life, man! We smoked a lot of dope before we came out. I think it was laced." I started looking around for Russ, but he was nowhere in sight. Finally I said I had to take a piss and headed for the bathroom. I really didn't have to go, but I went inside anyway to make it look good and waited on line. When it was my turn I unzipped in front of the urinal and stared at the wall tiles pretending to piss before flushing and heading out, going straight for the door without looking in the direction of the pinball machine.

I went up to the Red Barrel on Chestnut Street and wandered through the store unsure of what I was looking for until I spotted a pack of sour apple gum in the candy aisle. Without realizing what I was doing, I picked it up, looked at it for a moment, and casually slipped it into my pants pocket. I think the cashier saw me do it, but he didn't try to stop me as I walked out the door. Out in the lot I unwrapped all the pieces and put them in my mouth at the same time, and a few moments later I felt like I was about to swallow my face before experiencing a facial orgasm that paralyzed my jaw and made my knees buckle so badly that I nearly fell over.

Back at the apartment I went straight to my room and locked the door. I fell back on the bed and stared at the old blue Christmas lights on the ceiling, drowning in one last euphoric wave thinking that although I might actually die tonight, this was surely the way to go. I recalled having heard somewhere that drowning was the most peaceful way to go because you are consciously brought back to the serenity of the womb once you let go of the struggle to save yourself, and now that I knew how beautiful death was, my previous fear of it seemed unwarranted. I also knew that those who were going to mourn over my stiff body wouldn't understand— they would whine and cry about how shocked they were that I was a *'drug addict,'* and I would lay there in my casket with clenched teeth wishing there was some way to make them understand, but I would soon realize that they never could because their nearsightedness prevented them from seeing beyond their prejudices.

The next morning I woke up in hell. For a moment I wasn't sure if I was even still alive, and, after realizing that I was, thought that I would probably be better off if I wasn't. I reeked of something awful, and even after a nice hot shower and a few extra coats of Speed Stick, I still smelled. I had two huge papers due Monday and Tuesday respectively that I hadn't started writing and two tests later in the week that I hadn't started the reading for, and later that afternoon I tried working on the papers, but I couldn't concentrate at all. I finally wrote them hastily before class on Monday and Tuesday just to have something to hand in, but I didn't care. All I could think about was Friday night when Russ was going to pick up another package that his connection said was far better than the first stuff we bought.

On Friday morning I woke up and for the first time all week felt good. After my morning classes I had lunch at the Downtown Deli Company and then stopped at the cash machine. On my way back to the apartment I passed a *Oneonta Star* vending machine and the front page headline in the little window caught my eye: **Student Found Dead from Heroin Overdose**. I pulled 35¢ out of my pocket and plugged it into the machine.

> *Joshua J. Lieberman, age 20, was found dead in his apartment Thursday evening by his girlfriend Jennifer Cohen, age 19, from an apparent heroin overdose. A subsequent search of the apartment by the Oneonta Police Department revealed that Lieberman had as much as a kilo of the substance hidden on the premises. Lieutenant Halsey Barnes stated that "Mr. Lieberman was a significant player in the city's current heroin boom. It is unfortunate that we had to catch him in this manner, but this is the nature of the drug trade, and we are pleased that this particular supply line is now severed." [Lieberman's girlfriend] Cohen contends that Lieberman had only "experimented with it a couple of times and was not a [drug] dealer."*

Back at the apartment I handed the paper to Russ.
"Holy shit," he said repeatedly as he read the article.
"I take it he was your connection," I said.
"Yeah," he said, still reading. "Holy shit, holy fucking shit, that's him! I was just about to call him—I can't believe this! Holy fucking shit!"
Over the next couple of weeks there were several more articles in the *Star* and the school papers about how the local cops were working with the DEA and the FBI to crack down on the Oneonta heroin trade. During that time even pot was difficult to find, but

after that it was pretty much forgotten about and things went back to normal. Russ and I never mentioned it again, not even to each other. Even so, I couldn't help thinking that if ever again presented with the opportunity, I wasn't convinced that I would say no. It was somewhat despairing to think about how unlikely it was that I would ever experience anything that good again, but, if I did, at least next time I probably wouldn't have to tolerate the nuisance of waking up.

3

Since freshmen year we had talked of going to Jamaica for spring break when we were seniors, and when Ed started coordinating the trip just prior to the start of our final semester at Oneonta, I was all for it. A couple of weeks later, however, to the surprise of everyone in my family, my mother began a new career as a flight attendant on a major U.S. airline, and that changed everything. One of the perks of this new job was that she was issued a number of non-revenue passes for her immediate family wherever the airline flew within the continental United States, which meant that I could now go pretty much wherever I wanted for free as long as I didn't leave the country. Suddenly the spring break package deal to Jamaica that Ed had found advertised on a tenth-generation photocopy tacked to the Hunt Union bulletin board didn't seem quite as alluring.

At the time I had been thinking about moving to the West Coast after graduation, and having read *The Electric Kool-Aid Acid Test*, *Tales of the City*, and the entire Kerouac catalogue, I had an itch that a week of snorkeling and smoking cheap pot on the beach couldn't scratch. I wanted to walk across the Golden Gate Bridge, stand on the corner of Haight-Ashbury, and perhaps catch a glimpse of my future in a place several thousand miles away from everything I have ever known. I had never been west of Pittsburgh, and even when I was there all I saw was the airport. Everyone else except Winston, who didn't have as strong an interest in Jamaican culture as the rest of us and was not willing to part with the money to get there, went on to fulfill their spring break fantasies, and I would have loved to have been there with them; but I was determined not to start my life as a Bachelor of Arts rotting away in a 10 x 8

Oneonta: The Novel

bedroom on Long Island that didn't even belong to me, and this was my first opportunity to do something that might help prevent that from happening.

On the afternoon before my flight I took a Greyhound bus to Binghamton and spent the night at a Days Inn near Edwin A. Link Field. I had to catch a flight to Pittsburgh at 7:00 AM and from there catch a connecting flight to San Francisco, so I woke up at 5:30 the next morning and took the complimentary hotel shuttle van to the airport. I was a little nervous about going through security with an eighth of weed and my ceramic hash pipe stashed in my cigarette pack, but I made it by without a hassle. It seemed funny how much nicer people had been treating me since I had my long hair cut off a couple of months earlier.

The catch of using my mother's airline passes was that I had to fly standby, and since she had just started the job and had no seniority, I was at the very bottom of the list. As a relative of the employee I also had to follow a dress code—shoes, slacks, collared button-down shirt, suit jacket or sportcoat. I had everything but the jacket, so I had to borrow the sportcoat Ed's father had passed down to him, an old tweed thing with elbow patches that was a couple of sizes too small on me but good enough to get me on the plane. There were only a few other people going to Pittsburgh so I had no trouble getting there, but when I arrived at the gate for the San Francisco flight there was a large crowd. While I was checking in, the lady behind the counter said that it didn't look too good for me getting on this flight but to stay nearby.

Thirty minutes prior to the scheduled departure time, an announcement was made that there was a mechanical problem with the plane that would delay the flight about an hour. There was a collective groan, but I didn't mind so much when I noticed a little bar called Alberto's across the way that was packed with people drinking Bloody Marys. I headed over there and ordered a 'tall' beer that turned out to be the largest glass of brew I ever had, and it went down so easily that I had another before heading back over to the gate. There was no update on the departure time, so I went back to Alberto's and had a couple more that gave me a good buzz.

When boarding finally started, the confirmed passengers were called up by rows, and after they were on the plane there were ten standby passengers left including myself. I overheard one of the ladies behind the counter say that she doubted they would be able to get all the standbys on, which, though I was anxious to get out there, didn't sound so bad because I was having a good time at Alberto's watching the planes roll by on the tarmac. Several minutes later they started calling the standbys up to the counter, where they

248

were given a boarding pass and instructed to get on the plane immediately. The first eight got on, leaving only me and one other guy who looked like he was ready to blow his top if he didn't get on. They closed the door to the boarding hallway and several minutes went by before it opened again and a flight attendant said that there was room for one more. The other guy was called and the door closed for another five minutes. Finally I was called up to the counter and the lady was about to list me on the next flight when the door opened again and the flight attendant said there was one more seat left.

I spent the flight sandwiched between a fat guy, who was sitting in the aisle seat across from his wife and two kids, and a teenager in the window seat who slept the whole time with Smashing Pumpkins blasting in his Walkman headphones. As soon as we reached cruising altitude I ordered my first $3.00 can of Miller Genuine Draft, the only non-light beer they had, and by the time we were over Pike's Peak I was bombed. Somewhere above Utah the flight attendant informed me that I had single-handedly wiped out their entire supply of MGD, which by then was fine with me because I needed a breather anyway. When the captain announced that we had just flown over the California border, however, I ordered a little bottle of red wine to mark the occasion, and the flight attendant gave it to me on the house "for being such a good customer." The fat guy, who, after having done his best not to look at me during the ten or fifteen occasions I asked him to get up so I could go take a leak, gave her a sharp look like he was not only shocked that she was giving me a buyback, but that she was still serving me at all. When we were getting off the plane in San Francisco I tried to tip her $5.00, but she said that while she appreciated the gesture, they weren't allowed to accept gratuities.

I was in dire need of a cigarette, but there didn't seem to be any smoking areas in the immediate vicinity. Like a guy who had to take a really bad shit I walked as fast as I could through the terminal without actually running until a pair of glass doors slid open in front of me and I was greeted by the golden California sun. I was shaking when I lit up, and as the nicotine and warm air started mixing with the alcohol in my system I became so lightheaded that I nearly fell over. One wasn't enough, so I lit another with the butt of the first, and only after finishing that one did my attention shift to trying to find out how to get to the hotel.

I had no idea where I was in relation to the city or how I was going to get there, only that my reservation was at the Days Inn on Grove Street, which was somewhere near the Civic Center. I went up to the cab stand and asked one of the drivers how much it would cost to get to the Civic Center and he said $42, so I thanked him and started looking at the bus stop signs. I asked some lady waiting for a bus and she said I should get on one of the 'B' buses, of which there were several. When one of them pulled up I asked the driver if he went by the Civic Center and he said he did, so I got on.

It was an interminably long ride through the bowels of South San Francisco, and after the first hour I thought I was going to die. The driver had failed to mention that this was not the express and was actually the local bus that made every stop on the route until finally, more than two hours after leaving the airport, he announced that we had arrived at the Civic Center.

I was dizzy and exhausted and had no idea which way to go. I consulted the map at the bus stop and walked up several blocks until I hit Grove, then followed the address numbers until I arrived at the Days Inn. After checking in I went up to my room and smoked my first California bowl before passing out in front of the television.

I slept soundly for twelve hours and woke up the next morning at seven local time. After showering and smoking a bowl I felt much better and was surprisingly not too hung over. I packed my bookbag with my notebook, camera, *San Francisco Access Guide,* bag of weed, bowl, and a can of Mr. Pibb that I bought from the vending machine down in the parking lot before heading out in the general direction of the yet-to-be-seen Golden Gate Bridge.

The sky was overcast and in some areas foggy, but the warm Pacific air felt good after the spring freeze I had left back East. It was a quiet Sunday morning, and once I got out of the Civic Center area the city began to look more like the San Francisco I had imagined—steep hills, sidewalk cafes, old Volkswagen Beetles, and glimpses of the bay between the buildings and townhouses. After nearly two hours of walking and consulting my maps, I finally caught my first glimpse of the bridge between two buildings. Only a tiny section was visible from where I stood, but even so, it was a magnificent sight.

I stopped for an early lunch at a place called New York Buffalo Wings and from there continued up Lombard. I wound up at the Presidio, where the bridge looked big and close, but I had no idea how to get to it. I walked straight towards it hoping there would be a pedestrian tunnel that crossed under Highway 101, but all I found was a large chain-link fence that was too high to climb, not that I would have been able to cross 101 there anyway. I backtracked through the park and asked some guy wearing a teal designer sweatsuit how to get to the entrance to walk across the bridge, and he effeminately sneered, "Now why would you want to do that?" and continued on his way.

After backtracking through the Presidio, I passed through an upscale neighborhood that led to a public beach crowded with joggers and dogs. There were several people constructing towers of rocks by balancing them on top of one another that I thought might be an example of local earthquake detection art. I stuck my hand in the gentle waves of the frigid bay and picked up a souvenir rock that I put in my bookbag. After walking along the shore for several minutes, I spotted a somewhat secluded picnic table in a wooded section about thirty yards from the water that had a nice view of Alcatraz. I discreetly packed a bowl, taking a few small hits while writing in my damp journal, and couldn't have been in a more peaceful frame of mind until a pickup truck with a flashing yellow light on top pulled up. I covered the bowl with my hand and continued writing as if I hadn't noticed the truck, but my train of thought had been derailed: *...Alcatraz spotlight, Clint Eastwood swimming towards Angel Island trying to get away from the warden but one of the rock towers just toppled over, is that an earthquake? no, just my heartbeat and Ti-Jean drinking rotgut down at Big Sur planning his next jaunt up to the big city to eat chop suey and visit a couple of whores before freaking out and going back down the coast to do it all over again, trying not to freak out, that is the key—* The driver jumped out and emptied a nearby trash can, tossing the full garbage bag in the truck bed and lining the can with a new one before climbing back in and driving away. When he was gone I hastily packed up, stuffing the unfinished bowl into my cigarette pack and the journal into my bookbag, and headed back over towards the water, continuing along the shore towards the bridge feeling high from the weed and the bugout and the pleasant skepticism of not truly believing where I really was yet knowing it was real.

As I neared the bridge I still didn't know how to get up there. At Fort Point directly beneath it I followed a family of tourists around hoping they would lead me to a staircase or a shuttle bus that would take me up, but they only seemed interested posing for pictures in front of the old cannons. I was too stoned to ask anyone for directions, so I backtracked to the beach and noticed people emerging from a wooded trail. I went up through the woods and several minutes later found myself in a parking lot that had food stands, a bus stop, a gift shop, and the sidewalk entrance to the bridge.

After walking on concrete for nearly four hours, several painful blisters had developed on my feet and I was now limping. I stopped to rest at the first tower and watched the surfers in wetsuits down below catching waves in the little nook next to Fort Point. Two overweight women wearing Oklahoma Sooners sweatshirts came by and asked me to take their picture, and after doing so I asked them to take mine in front of one of the suicide crisis phones that were all over the bridge. As I continued onward I had to stop every few minutes because my feet felt like they were on fire, but I was too close to turn back now and convinced that I was going to find something on the other side that would inspire me, something I could use as motivation during the period of hell I was about to enter back home after graduation.

What I found, however, was a rest stop, one that didn't have a soda machine or even a water fountain, just a small white building with restrooms and a few parked cars belonging to people who had to go to the bathroom. There was also a sign that pointed to a tunnel that crossed under the highway to the big hill that on a clear day provides the famous view of the bridge and the skyline across the bay, but the fog was so thick that none of it was visible. I took a seat on the curb outside the men's room and sat there for about fifteen minutes before heading back over the bridge, which took twice as long since my feet were now so bad I could only walk on my toes. When I finally got back to the other side I caught the first in a string of several buses that took me back to the hotel, where I spent the rest of the evening soaking my feet in Days Inn ice buckets filled with hot water and a six pack of Bud tallboys soaking in the trash can filled with ice water beside me.

I envisioned my visit to Haight-Ashbury as a pilgrimage to a place where thirty years earlier the ideal of freedom was exercised to the extent that it changed the world, a place where the pioneers of the counterculture crammed into Victorian-style homes under the influence of an excessive amount of drugs and lived in a way that now in the age of AIDS and crack could only be imagined, a place where even today the energy that once radiated from this intersection and called to the youth of the planet to live and be free could still be felt. When I got there, however, and looked up at the signs that said 'Haight' and 'Ashbury' and the Ben & Jerry's ice cream store behind me, I didn't feel anything. I closed my eyes and touched the pole that the street signs were attached to, and after a couple of minutes I finally did start to feel something, which, after opening my eyes again, I recognized as a close relation to idiocy. All I saw were cars and buses and people going by just like in every other intersection in the city. If I hadn't already known, I never would have realized where I was; there was nothing to be seen, heard, or felt to indicate the significance of the place. I was just another guy in a big city standing on a street corner touching a pole.

Behind me an attractive girl about my age was sitting on the steps of Ben & Jerry's and I asked her to take my picture in front of the Haight-Ashbury signs. She seemed baffled by my request and looked like she was about to ask why but then thought the better of it, sparing me the embarrassment of having to explain that I was a tourist who traveled 3,000 miles to stand on this very corner. She grudgingly snatched the camera from my hand and snapped the picture, and as she was handing the camera back I thanked her, but she didn't so much as even look at me while she was handing it back.

The rest of the neighborhood looked a little like what I had pictured. There was some tie-dye, a few peace symbols, and homeless teenage hippies all over the place with dirty feet and hands out begging for spare change. Seeing them reminded me of Sandy, and I wondered if she was still in Colorado, if she ever made it there at all, or if she had found her way here and started knocking on the front door of the old Grateful Dead house down the block to see if Jerry was home. Maybe she had eventually realized since I saw her last that she was clinging to something that wasn't really there and changed her direction, but that somehow didn't seem as likely as her having taken so much acid by now that she was locked up in a mental ward somewhere, or that she had graduated psychedelics and was now living as a whore in a heroin den or a crackhouse, or, perhaps, not anywhere at all. I didn't want to think about it.

I ducked into a head shop named 'Peace, Love, & Bongos' that I thought would be the real deal, a museum of psychedelic treasures right in the heart of where it all started, but inside it looked more like the gift shop of a deceased generation: tie-dyed Haight-Ashbury T-shirts, coffee mugs, keychains, beer cozies, stickers, postcards, and under a glass counter in the back a small collection of pipes and bongs that was even less of a selection than the one at Crazy Gifts in Oneonta. The shop was a microcosm of the neighborhood's deterioration from cultural Mecca to tourist trap complete with coffee-serving gift shops every ten yards to accommodate the mindless droves wandering the streets in khaki shorts with socks pulled up to their knees and cameras hanging from their necks. Nobody even offered me any drugs.

My feet were too swollen and sore to do anything else, so I spent the rest of the afternoon in my hotel room smoking bowls, drinking beer, and writing postcards. I told everyone I was having a great time visiting parking lots and intersections. After catching a nice buzz, I attempted to find a bar in the neighborhood but only made as far as the bodega on the corner, where I picked up another six of Bud tallboys and hobbled back up to the room.

The next morning my feet were still so swollen I could barely put my shoes on, but it was my last full day in San Francisco so I had to go out and do something, preferably that which involved little or no walking. After eating lunch at a diner down the block, I went down to the BART station and jumped on a train headed towards Oakland just to see what was there.

The train crossed under the bay and emerged from the tunnel where the tracks became elevated, but even so I couldn't see what was out there. I got off a few stops later and from the station platform I could see Oakland in all her glory—factories, smog, urban plight as far as the eye could see. The station looked like the nicest part of the neighborhood, so I went downstairs and crossed under the tracks and caught the next train back to San Francisco.

I got off near the TransAmerica Pyramid and limped around until I found a cable car stop. I climbed aboard the first one that came by and rode up to a quiet residential neighborhood on top of Nob Hill. Across the street from the stop was a bar called 'Company' with a neon Bass Ale sign in the window that gave me a hankering for a beer, so I went inside.

By the name alone it should have been obvious, but even the plush carpeting and Elton John on the stereo didn't clue me in. Not that I would be receiving any unwanted solicitations because the place had just opened and the only other person there besides the older gentleman behind the bar was a woman about the same age wearing a pink sweatsuit. I ordered a beer and took a seat at a candlelit table next to the crackling fireplace, and after I sat down I couldn't help but think that this was the nicest goddamn bar I had ever been to.

I sat at my fireside table scribbling in my journal for over an hour until I caught a snippet of the conversation over at the bar regarding someone they knew who had just 'come out.' I looked around again, noticing now that Elton John had been on the whole time I had been there, and only then did I finally realize. On my way out I dropped a couple of singles on the bar and thanked the bartender, who gave me a look as if he knew why I was leaving but told me to enjoy the rest of my vacation.

I caught the next cable car back down the hill. I was a bit buzzed, and this in conjunction with my swollen feet made it difficult to maintain my balance down the steep grade. At one point I fell backwards into a little old lady who may have fallen off the thing if the brakeman hadn't been there to catch her. Fortunately she was alright and I apologized profusely, which she accepted, but several other people were giving me dirty looks, so I got off at the next stop.

There was an entrance to a BART station on the corner, so I went down the stairs and jumped on a train without knowing where it was going. Since this part of the line was underground, I had no idea until I stepped off the escalator at 24th & Mission that I had landed in a Hispanic neighborhood and was the only white person in sight. I was about to turn around and head back down to the train until an enormous sign that said 'EL FAROLITO BAR' with soccer and billiard balls on it caught my eye.

Not surprisingly, every person in the place looked at me when I walked in. I was probably the first blond-haired/blue-eyed person who had ever stepped foot in El Farolito. I gave my audience a sheepish smile and took a seat at the bar close to the door and ordered a shot of tequila and a bottle of Sol cervesa from the short chubby woman behind the bar.

The place was dark and full of soccer memorabilia. There were Mexican flags all over and Latino music playing loudly on the jukebox. The barmaid spoke some broken English so we were able to communicate a little, but she didn't seem as curious about me as some of the other people looking in my direction. Some guy sitting at the other end of the bar moved over and sat in the stool right next to mine. I became a little nervous and threw back the most watered-down shot of tequila I ever had and sipped my beer pretending not to notice him until he started speaking to me in Español. My high school Spanish was a little rusty and it took me a couple of minutes to realize that he was asking me where I was from.

"New York," I said, catching the barmaid's attention.

"Nueva York?" she repeated, but then went off to serve another customer.

Through a combination of broken English, broken Spanish, and hand gestures, I explained that I had flown to San Francisco on a plane (this part involved flapping my arms like wings) and was on vacation for a few days before going back to Nueva York. After this was straightened out I asked him, "Que nombre es El Farolito?" When he figured out that I was trying to ask him what the name of the bar meant, I interpreted from his answer that it was just a name and didn't have any particular meaning.

I enjoyed talking to this friendly fellow, so I ordered another shot and a beer. While we were talking, Santana's "Oye Como Va" came on the jukebox and some of the guys playing pool in the back started cheering and waving to get my attention. I waved back to let them know I was familiar with Santana, which I thought would be enough to satisfy them, but then one of them came over with his pool cue and got in my face.

"You like Santana?" he asked hoarsely. He was covered with tattoos and missing a couple of teeth. The guy I had been talking to slid two stools over.

"Yes, si," I said. "Santana muy bueno."

He leaned in closer and I could smell the beer and menthol cigarettes on his breath. I subtly gripped one of the straps on my bookbag and was ready to bolt. Out of the corner of my eye I noticed the lady behind the bar wiping a glass with a cautious eye on us.

"Are you worried, man?" the guy finally asked me.

"Excuse me?" I asked.

"Are you worried, man?"

"Am I worried? About what?"

"You worried?"

"I'm worried that I'm almost out of beer!" I picked up my beer and finished it, putting the empty bottle on the bar and saying "Gracias" to the bartender. I slid off the stool and said "Adios," afraid that the Santana guy was going to try and stop me, but fortunately he didn't. I waved to the guy I had been talking to earlier and said, "Adios, amigo!" and he nodded. After making it safely outside, I took my beat up old New York Mets cap out of the bookbag and put it on while hurriedly limping towards the BART station, continually looking over my shoulder until I boarded a waiting train that took me back up to the Civic Center.

After limping around the financial district for a while, I stumbled upon an upscale topless joint called 'Stocks & Blondes'. The place was dark and nearly empty, only a few guys in suits sitting around the stage watching a topless Asian dancer swing around a brass pole. I was greeted at the door by a tall redhead woman wearing spiked heels and a fluorescent green bikini that glowed in the blacklight, and a few feet away a beefy black guy was sitting on a stool staring straight ahead with arms folded. The redhead told me that I would have to take my hat off, and after doing so I seated myself at a booth in the back. I was pretty drunk by now and almost immediately forgot the hat rule and unconsciously put it back on. Moments later the redhead came right over and said, "I'm serious, sir, if you don't take your hat off, I'm going to have to ask you to leave." I gave her a look and tossed the hat on the table and ordered a $6.00 bottle of Bud.

After the Asian dancer finished her routine, a black chick got up on stage. These dancers were far better than anything you would ever see at the Novelty, but even so, they still had some skanky quality about them that was perhaps a sign of experience in the profession. Several minutes into her act, the dancer pointed at me and mouthed the words, "Come here, baby," indicating that she wanted me to sit at one of the stools surrounding the stage, but I just shook my head and mouthed back "No thanks" and tried not to look at her again.

By the time I finished my beer I had had enough of California. I put my hat back on and the redhead scurried over, but before she had a chance to say anything I got up and said, "Don't worry, I'm leaving. But I wanted to let you know that it's a little disturbing to come to a place called 'Stocks & Blondes' and be the only blonde there. Six dollar Budweisers my ass..."

Later that night at the hotel, I was watching TV in bed with a cigarette burning in my hand when I drifted off to sleep. I was out for several minutes before being jolted awake by a stinging sensation on the back of my right thigh. I jumped up and discovered that the cigarette had fallen out of my hand and had somehow become trapped beneath my leg, burning a hole through the comforter, sheets, and mattress. Smoke was streaming up through the hole and I couldn't see the cigarette, and in a panic I ran into the bathroom and filled one of the ice buckets with cold water. I dumped the water on the bed and waited, and after I was sure that the hole was no longer smoking, I was eventually able to fish out the soggy butt with my fingers. Afterwards I flipped the mattress over, remade the bed, and had another cigarette, this time sitting wide awake at the table over near the window and grounding the butt hard into the ashtray before flushing it down the toilet and passing out.

**4**

For three whole days I had the apartment to myself before the other guys returned from Jamaica, during which time I had the opportunity to experience exactly what I wanted my daily routine to be like after graduation: wake up at one or two in the afternoon, eat lunch, read for a little while, sit in front of the word processor and work on some short stories, smoke a bowl, eat dinner, pick up a six pack and watch TV, and finally smoke a nightcap bowl while scribbling away in my journal before passing out at three or four in the morning. It would have been even better if, instead of watching TV, a submissive non-English speaking woman could come over for an hour or so and then go away, but such a luxury would have to wait at least until I was a published author.

As ideal as this routine was, on Saturday evening I got a little stir crazy and called Winston to see if he wanted to go down to the Oak. I was expecting him to say no as usual, which was usually the case these days since he had so much schoolwork to do, but to my surprise he said he would and agreed to meet me there in half-hour.

I hardly ever saw Winston anymore, not that I ever saw much of him even when we lived in the same house. When I got there I found him sitting at a window booth overlooking Water Street with a pitcher of Genny and two glasses on the table in front of him. He was in good spirits and seemed more relaxed than he had been the last few times he came out drinking with us when he would just sit there staring at the suds in his beer before suddenly getting up and leaving without a word. Some of that had to do with his dislike of the Oak, but on more than one occasion he mentioned that he didn't have time to drink anymore because he had too much to do, so even on those nights when he wanted to drink and managed to make it to the bar, he would spend the evening battling his conscience about wasting valuable time getting drunk instead of studying or drawing or playing guitar or doing whatever else he did in his lair. But tonight he was loose, and a couple of hours and several pitchers of Genny later both of us were feeling pretty good. At one point Winston asked the bartender to play some Skynyrd, a request that on a normal Saturday night probably would have been denied, but since most of the spring break crowd hadn't returned yet and the place was nearly empty, he agreed to put on the first disc of *Gold & Platinum* but said that he would absolutely not play "Free Bird."

It had been so long that I had forgotten about the good times we used to have and the old stories were flying across the table like a ping pong rally—*Remember when we broke into Littell and lit off the smoke bomb?... Remember the time we showed up piss drunk at the service fraternity ice cream rush and said we were Bruno and Ed? And then three days later they showed up at their room and gave them bids!... Remember the time we found Teke's address book and wrote that letter to his friend from home? And then the guy wrote back to Teke and said he felt the same way but had always been too shy to act on his feelings!...Remember Eliot and the Big Guy's party—J.F.P.!...Remember when Zoë was having her period on our couch during the World Series?...*

After we ran out of *remember when's*, however, we didn't know what to say to each other. We had halfhearted discussions about baseball and music, and after a while it started to feel like I was talking to a stranger. One particularly long gap in the conversation became uncomfortable to the point that I asked him what his plans were after graduation, a question I didn't like to ask since it seemed like everyone else had their act together or at least had some idea of what they were going to do when they got out.

"Blow stuff up," he said seriously.

"For a job, I mean, not a hobby."

"I'm serious. I applied for a job at this company in Binghamton that tests product durability. Manufacturers send their products to them to see how much stress they can withstand and how they hold up under extreme circumstances. They said they've recently blown up mailboxes, toilet bowls, urinals, refrigerators—shit like that."

"It sounds like your dream job."

"It is! If I get it, which I think I will because I already interviewed with one of the managers and he said it looked good, they also have a tuition assistance program that would pay for most of my grad school, and by the time I get my Masters I'm hoping to have enough money saved to start working on my Doctorate. I know this job isn't directly related to what I majored in, but it'll eventually all tie together for my *master project*."

"What's your *master project*?"

"I can't really tell you right now, but it will involve everything I've ever done in my life and will be bigger than anything in the universe."

"It sounds nuts, but I believe you."

"You'll see. What about you?"

"I don't know. I'm thinking about moving West."

"San Francisco?"

"Nah, probably not. I'm thinking more towards the Northwest actually."

"Don't tell me you're moving to Seattle."

"Maybe. I know it sounds kind of played because half the country is moving there, but I'm also considering Portland and Vancouver. Or maybe Denver."

"What are you going to do out there?"

"Write. Read. Get drunk."

"What about a job?"

"Yeah, I guess I'll have to find some cheesy job until my book is published."

"What if you don't get published?"

"That's fine, as long as I'm not living on Long Island."

"Or Downsville."

"Or Oneonta."

Suddenly out of the corner of my eye I noticed Maria Viola walk in. I hadn't seen her since we were sophomores two years prior, and in that time I hadn't as much as given her a second thought. She looked good, and different, but I wasn't able to pinpoint exactly what it was. When she saw me she smiled and came over, and I got up and hugged her. She sat down on the other side of me and said hello to Winston, but he was already staring at his suds and gave her a nod without looking up. Moments later he raised his glass to his lips, threw his head back, and suddenly the beer was gone. He put the glass down on the table, gave us a farewell nod, and slid out of the booth before heading for the door.

"What's his problem?" she asked, getting up and sliding into Winston's vacated seat so that we were now facing each other.

"It's nothing personal. He just gets that way around people."

"*O*-kay," she said, exaggerating the 'o' as she often did when she didn't understand something but didn't really want to know. "So, how are you, Hank?"

"Alright, I guess. I'm just trying not to go crazy before I get out of here."

"I know what you mean. I spent junior year over in London, so I guess I'm not as sick of this place as you are, but I'm definitely ready to get out."

"What were you doing in London?"

"I signed up for the student exchange program. I needed to get away for a while."

"When did you get back?"

"Last semester."

"You were here last semester and I didn't even see you?"

"I don't get out much anymore. When did you cut your hair off?"

"A couple of months ago."

"Any particular reason?"

"I got tired of waking up in the middle of the night choking on a mouthful of hair."

"You look good."

"Thanks. So do you."

I went on to tell her about my trip to San Francisco and she told me about her year abroad. It was easy to talk about what we had been doing since we last saw each other, but when we were done catching up we ran out of things to say. During the lull we stared out the window at lonely Water Street and I tried to think of how to get out of there without making it look bad.

"I should really be in bed right now," she finally said, and I was relieved. "I have to get up early for work tomorrow."

"Where do you work?"

"Damascene Bookstore. We're doing inventory tomorrow, so I have to be there by seven."

"What are you doing out drinking then?"

"I was actually hoping I would find you."

"*Really,*" I said, letting out a nervous little laugh. "Well, that shouldn't have been too difficult."

"I have something to tell you."

"What's that?"

"Come back to the house with me. I don't want to tell you here."

"Why not?"

"Please Hank, just humor me. It's important."

I looked at my watch.

"That won't work," she said. "I'm the one who has to get up early tomorrow."

It was a clear night but chilly, and since she was living up at the Philanthan house I thought she might want to take the bus, but she said she would rather walk under the stars. Along the way neither of us said anything, but it wasn't an uncomfortable silence and about halfway there she took my hand and held it until we reached the corner of Center and Maple. I stopped and looked up at the giant house of which most of the upstairs windows were dark, but the tower closest to us had a light on inside shining like a beacon over the lifeless neighborhood.

"That's my room," she said.

"I bet you get a nice view from up there," I said.

"Of the intersection, yeah."

She started towards the front walk but stopped when she realized that I hadn't followed.

"Come on," she said.

The living room looked pretty much the same as what little of it I remembered from St. Patrick's Day three years earlier, only smaller. I sat next to Maria on one of the couches and started looking around at the many framed sorority composite pictures hanging all over the walls. In the center of each one there was a picture of the same elderly woman.

"Who's the old lady?" I asked.

"The Philanthan Mother. She's the oldest living member of the sorority."

"How old is she?"

"I think she's over a hundred. She still lives in town. They send a photographer over to her house every year and take her picture."

She started running her fingers through my hair.

"Your hair looks good," she said. "I like it better short."

"I liked it better long, but it was too much of a pain in the ass to deal with."

The front door opened and two Philanthan sisters came in. They both looked surprised to see us and said hello before heading up the stairs. One of them said "Oh my God!" and they both giggled just prior to a door closing.

"This is going to cause an uproar," Maria said, suddenly embarrassed.

"What is?"

"You being here."

"Why?"

She let out a deep breath before pulling a diamond ring out of her front jeans pocket and displaying it in her open palm.

"I'm engaged."

"Engaged? Really?"

She nodded.

"Well, congratulations! Why didn't you say anything?"

"I felt kind of awkward telling you."

"There's no reason to feel awkward—this is good news. I'm happy for you. Really, I am."

"Don't be too happy about it."

"Why not? Aren't you?"

"I don't know."

"Why not? Do you love him?"

She turned away. "Yes. I don't know."

"That wasn't very convincing."

"That's just it. Rick's a great guy and he probably deserves better than me, but I don't love him the way I loved you."

"But I was your first crush—you can't love someone the way you did your first crush. His name is *Rick*?" At that moment I pictured some older guy with a porn mustache.

"It's more than that, Hank. When you gave me that Valentine's card, you totally caught me off guard. I've been kicking myself ever since. I let you get away because of that loser Dale, and now I'm engaged to someone I don't love." Her eyes started to well until they could no longer hold the tears that started streaking down her cheeks.

"How long have you been with this guy?"

"About a year. I met him over in London."

"He's English?"

"No, he goes to school here. We were in the same program and we started hanging out over there and that's how it happened. But ever since we got back here it hasn't been the same. Hank, I still love you. I know you've probably moved on and forgot all about me, but I still love you. Part of the reason I went to London was to get away from here hoping I would forget about you, and for a while I did. But now that I'm back and you're sitting here next to me, I love you more than ever!"

She buried her head in my chest and started crying. I started smoothing a section of hair on the back of her head with one hand and with the other clasped both of her hands while unconsciously rubbing the ring with my thumb.

"I don't even know why I love you so much!" she cried. "I'm so sorry for putting you through this! I know it's not fair to you, but I just don't know what else to do!"

I stared at the carpet searching for something to say.

"Hank, I don't want you to leave."

"I don't want to be responsible for breaking up an engagement."

"You won't be! Even if I hadn't seen you tonight, this marriage probably wasn't going to happen. I'm not asking you for a commitment—I just want to hold you. I want you to spend the night here with me and then tomorrow you can leave and never think about me again. But please, Hank, you have no idea how much this would mean to me."

"I don't know, Maria. Maybe if you weren't engaged, but—"

"It's going to be daylight in a few hours. You can sleep and then wake up and go. All I want to do is hold you. Don't worry about my fiancé, he's out of town and I don't love him anyway. But please, please, *please* spend the night here. I'm begging you!"

I followed her up four flights of stairs, the last of which was a narrow circular staircase of which I was barely able to fit. Her bedroom was a tiny round chamber with a twin bed in the middle that took up most of the floor space. We took off our shoes and positioned ourselves on the mattress, me on my back and Maria on her side crying softly with her head on my chest. I stared up at the dark spot inside the tip of the cone-shaped ceiling twenty feet above that in my exhaustion I imagined to be the black hole that had sucked in everything that ever existed between us. Two years earlier I thought I loved this girl, but at this point in my life I wasn't sure that anything I felt prior to Virginia Duvall was really love. Looking back it seemed like Maria was the one who just happened to be there to fill the void until the real thing came knocking, and what I thought was love was merely a salve to remedy my loneliness. Now all I felt was sorry for her.

Not long after I had finally fallen asleep, the sharp buzz of the clock radio jolted me awake. Maria slammed the snooze button and we both sat up.

"I have to get ready for work," she said without looking at me.

"Yeah," I said, staring at the clock.

"Hank, I'm really sorry about this."

"There's nothing to be sorry about."

"My whole life is something to be sorry about."

"Don't say that."

"It's true. But thank you so much for staying. I know it was totally selfish and you probably have no idea how much it meant to me, but thank you so much."

"You're welcome."

She leaned over and kissed me on the cheek.

"So, now what?" I asked.

"What do you mean?"

"Oh."

"I'm sorry, Hank."

"That's alright."

"No, it's probably not, and I would understand if you don't forgive me."

"It's alright, really."

There was a long lull.

"So, are you going to marry this guy?" I finally said.

"I don't know. But seeing you has kind of brought me back to reality."

"Is that what you wanted?"

She looked towards the window. "Not really."

"If I asked you to run away with me right now, would you do it?"

"Are you asking?"
"Maybe."
"Where would we go?"
"I don't know. Somewhere out West. Seattle, Portland, Vancouver. Maybe Denver."
"Yes."
"You would?"
"I love you, Hank."

The sky was gray and a light rain was falling. Walking towards Main Street, I took out the piece of paper on which she had written her name and phone number and stared at it for several blocks until it all came back. I had loved her. It wasn't the same love I had for Virginia, nor could it have been. All love is different, but love is still love. I started thinking about how she probably loved me all these years and would probably love me in some way for the rest of her life, and that she may have really been willing to run away with me to a place where it would be just the two of us and nobody would know or care who we were and we would both probably be very happy. I stopped on the corner of Main Street and considered it for a moment, but after the moment passed I crumpled the paper into a ball and tossed it in the sewer.

**5**

Walking down the big hill from campus after my last final felt like just being released from prison. For the first time since age three I was not enrolled in some type of school, and the thought that I would never have to step foot in a classroom again momentarily allowed me to enjoy the notion that now that I had not a single commitment in the world, I was free to do as I pleased. Buried beneath this blissful cloud, however, was the reality that I still had no idea what I was going to do when I was back on Long Island in two days. My mother was not going to tolerate a 'starving artist' living rent-free in her home and sleeping until noon every day, and she most certainly was not going to accept any rants about the greed of our money-driven society when she asks how the job search is going. *Writing is a nice hobby, but you can't make a living from it... Why did you declare your major in English if you don't want to be a teacher?... Is that what you're wearing to your job interview?... Have you considered the military? They might need writers...*

I spent the rest of the afternoon working on a 12-pack of Beast and later went with the other guys down to the Oak for the free buffet they were hosting for graduating seniors. At the door one of the bouncers was checking IDs against a list of names and everyone else got in ahead of me, but when it was my turn he couldn't find my name on the list. I suggested that he try looking under my first name even though it had been alphabetized by last names, but still he couldn't find me. I asked him where he got the list and he flipped back to the first page to show that it had been photocopied from the Office of Student Affairs, which made me a little nervous until I noticed that this was a list of students participating in the graduation ceremony and not a list of those who were actually graduating. Since I had chosen not to take part in commencement, my name was not on this list. I had wanted out of Oneonta so bad that I didn't want to hang around a few extra days coordinating visiting relatives for the sake of sitting through a three-hour ceremony just to have my name announced and my college receipt handed to me. My mother was upset over my decision and I tried to explain that she should be proud of the actual accomplishment of successfully completing my course of study and not the ceremonial bullshit that went along with it, but that only seemed to upset her even more.

I thought that after explaining to the bouncer why my name was not on the list he would let me in, especially since he knew me from all the time and money I had spent in this bar over the last couple of years, but he was a prick about it and wouldn't let me in. A head of steam started building inside me, but just before I was about to explode into a drunken tirade against this son of a bitch, a chill passed through me and suddenly I didn't care. I was done with this fucking place and it didn't matter. Without another word I went back outside figuring that the other guys would come out to see why I hadn't gone in and then we could all go somewhere else, but after waiting ten minutes and smoking two cigarettes, no one came. Finally I said fuck it and went to The Clinton.

I sat at the bar drinking whiskey & Cokes that I paid for with my nearly maxed-out credit card and stared blankly at a playoff basketball game on the TV behind the bar. When the game was over I left and passed through the Alley, the Sip & Sail, and even ducked into the Aquarium for the first time since freshman year thinking that maybe I could find some freshman chick to hook up with, but since the dorms close on the same day as finals end, the freshmen were already gone and the place was empty except for a handful of townie high school kids.

Eventually I wound up back at the Oak. The buffet was over by now and this time they let me in. Ed and Bruno were at the bar, and as I was walking by they asked what happened to me earlier, but I ignored them and kept walking. I took a seat at the far end of the bar and ordered a whiskey & Coke that I told the bartender to make strong. While I was on my third one, someone tapped me on the shoulder and I turned around to see Virginia standing there.

"Congratulations, Hank!" she said.

"Thanks."

"How does it feel?"

"How does what feel?"

"Being finished with school?"

"I'm done with this fucking place and I don't have to be here anymore. I don't even know what the fuck I'm doing here now."

"Are you mad at me?"

"No."

"You seem mad."

"I'm not mad."

"Well, it seems like something is bothering you."

"Maybe something is bothering me. Maybe something has been bothering me for the last two years."

"Like what?"

"You see, that's exactly it right there. You act like you don't know what the fuck I'm talking about when you know very well."

Virginia looked frightened. I finished my drink and slid the glass across the bar. The bartender gave me a look.

"Do you remember St. Patrick's Day last year?" I asked.

"*Last* year? I hardly remember it from this year!"

"That little talk we had, right over there at the other end of the bar?"

"What talk?"

"Oh, come on, Virginia. I know we were both a little loaded, but you must remember some of it, or at least that it happened."

"Hank, I really don't know what you're talking about."

"We were talking about starting a relationship, and you told me that Ed was your one and only—"

"Okay, I kind of remember that."

"And you promised to call me the next day so we could talk about it when we were sober."

"I don't remember that part."

"Well, you did, and I sat next to the phone all day, but you didn't call."

"I'm sorry, Hank. I really don't remember that."

"That's alright. It happened, but it was no big deal. I was pretty hung over anyway and not in much of a condition to talk, and I figured you were too, so I waited again the following day, but still you didn't call. Finally I was going to call you, but then I had another idea. I figured it would be better to talk to you about it in person rather than on the phone, so I decided to pay you a surprise visit. I jumped on the next bus and went up to your room and knocked on your door, but *whoa*, do you remember the look on my face when Ed answered the door half-naked? Is any of this ringing a bell?"

"You were looking for drugs."

"Ah, not true, not true. I only said that because I felt like an idiot showing up at your room to tell you that I loved you and wanted to start a relationship with you only to have Ed answer the door moments after he banged you!"

"I should slap you for that."

"I'm sorry, Virginia. I don't mean to be crude."

"Yeah, well, I had no idea that's how you felt, Hank."

"How could you have no idea? Even before then we talked about it. Like at my party—why did you make me promise to stay away from Lucy?"

"Because the girl is a whore!"

"But what does that matter if you weren't interested in me?"

"Because I didn't want to see you hook up with a whore!"

"Then why did you say you would be jealous if I did?"

"I don't remember saying that."

"But you did!"

"I don't remember."

"Do you remember anything? Do you remember when we kissed after we smoked that joint on the bridge?"

"Yeah."

"What did that mean to you?"

"It was just a kiss."

"So it didn't mean anything to you."

"I'm not saying that it didn't mean anything. I'm only saying that it was just something that happened at the spur of the moment. The only reason it happened at all was because Zoë and Hannah sent me to find out what was going on with you and Sandy. How do you think I felt out in the common room listening to the bedsprings squeak while you were in my room fucking that freak all night?"

"I thought you understood after I explained it to you that hooking up with Sandy was a freak occurrence, pardon the pun. We were both under the influence of a powerful drug and she wandered out of our suite, so I followed her to make sure she was alright. Then I wound up in her bed and we had sex. Since you were with Ed at the time, it didn't even occur to me that it would bother you. How do you think you hooking up with Ed every other night made *me* feel? I liked you the very first moment I saw you. Hell, at that moment I fell in love with you, and up until then I didn't even believe there was such a thing as love at first sight. And then after the bridge I thought you understood that Sandy meant nothing to me, which should have been obvious by how I handled that whole thing, and that when you and I kissed it was the start of something. I spent the whole summer thinking about that kiss. I was in love with you. I thought that when we got back to school something was finally going to happen between us, but then right off the bat you started hooking up with Ed again."

"I didn't realize, Hank."

"That's a load of crap, Virginia. I remember how you used to look at me and how you used to talk to me. You knew I liked you. And maybe it was the drugs, but I thought you kind of liked me too."

"To be honest, I did like you at first. I still do in a way. But you changed. You used to be nice and mellow and funny, and since what I had with Ed wasn't serious, I didn't think it was out of the realm of possibility that someday we would be more than just friends. But I was a freshman! I wasn't looking to get into a serious relationship. And then when you guys moved downtown, you became this insane drunk."

"That's because you were hooking up with Ed again! And then when he started hooking up with Hannah, I thought maybe you'd finally had enough of him, but instead you got insanely jealous. I couldn't take it anymore! That's why I started drinking so much!"

"I wasn't jealous of that slut!"

"And if that wasn't enough, after Ed called you a 'five cent whore' and chased you out of the house with a fire extinguisher, I thought for sure you were done with him, especially when you finally came back to the house for my party and made me promise to stay away from Lucy. But then that very night you wound up right back in bed with him, which of course I didn't find out about until I showed up at your room and Ed answered the door."

"Are you finished?"

"I'm sorry, Virginia. I'm not trying to embarrass you or anything, I'm just trying to figure it out. I apologize if I'm being rude, but I'm just hurt and disappointed and frustrated that nothing ever happened between us despite the fact that I spent half of my college career thinking that something eventually would."

"You really loved me, Hank?"

"Honestly, I still do. And I still don't think it's too late for you and I."

"What do you mean?"

"We still have the whole night ahead of us."

"I don't think that's such a good idea."

"I'm not necessarily talking about sleeping with you, though I certainly wouldn't object to it. But I am talking about you and I starting a relationship."

"Hank, you're graduating. And I'm leaving tomorrow."

"I know."

"It would never work. We can't have a long-distance relationship if we haven't already had a relationship to begin with."

"I'm not talking about a long-distance relationship."

"Then what are you talking about?"

"A short-term relationship."

"A what?"

"In four years of college, I never had anything close to a meaningful relationship. All I've had was letdowns and heartbreaks. But it's not too late. All I want is one night. Not a one night stand, a one night *relationship*."

"I don't understand."

"I'm talking about either walking away from this place that has been my life for the last four years with nothing but bad memories of the girls I was involved with here, or walking away with one good relationship that would make me forget all the rest. It doesn't matter how long the relationship lasts, I just want a memory to take with me that I can hold onto for the rest of my life. I know I'm young and I still have my whole life ahead of me, but you never know, I may never again have a chance to spend the night with someone I truly love. I want to know what that's like at least once in my life."

Virginia looked around the bar and then turned back to me.

"I'm supposed to meet my roommates at the Sip in a couple of minutes," she said. "It's Barb's birthday."

"If you don't want to, just say so. I'll understand. But don't resort to lame excuses."

"No, Hank. I have to buy her a drink. I promised."

"Do what you gotta do then."

"I'll run over there and buy her a drink and come right back. I'll be back in a few minutes and then we can start our relationship."

"Do you mean it?"

"Yes."

"Do you promise?"

"I promise."

Well over an hour later she hadn't returned. I took a piss and then walked around the entire bar looking in every dark corner to see if she had come back while I was in the bathroom, but she was nowhere to be found. The high that I had been riding for the past hour or so broke and I started kicking myself for believing that she would actually come back. I went up to the bar and ordered a 151 & Coke and brought it to a booth that had just opened up near the door.

I sat there with a look on my face that made every person who happened to make eye contact with me turn away. Again I reminded myself that it was over, that in 48 hours I would be far from this place and would never have to think about it again, and that none of this meant mean anything, but this offered little solace. I didn't even want to go to the senior picnic the next day despite having been looking forward to it as the last big bash of my college career and having already blown twenty bucks on a ticket when they were on sale several weeks earlier. Instead I would finish packing and smoke the rest of my stash and forget that this night ever happened, and then the next morning I would be gone.

Shortly before last call, two heavily made up women in their mid-to-late 30's wearing leather miniskirts, fishnet stockings, and high-heeled boots came in. They were almost identical except one was a blonde and the other a brunette, both with hair teased high like they had just come from an 80's party. I wondered if they were somehow related to Lucy. The bouncer let them in without checking their ID, and when they noticed me sitting alone they sauntered over.

"Excuse me, hon, is this a gay bar?" the brunette asked with a heavy upstate twang.

"Sometimes, I guess," I said, taking a sip of the melted ice in my glass. "But tonight it looks pretty straight."

"Well, we heard somewhere that this was a gay bar, but we weren't sure and wanted to check it out. We don't want to be hangin' out in no gay bar, if you know what I mean."

"Well, I'm not gay," I said.

"You most certainly are not, sugar," the blonde said.

"Mind if we join you, sweet-cheeks?" the brunette asked. "You look like you could use a little cheerin' up."

"Go ahead," I said.

"I'll go get some wine," the blonde said and went up to the bar.

"So, what's your name, sunshine?" the brunette asked after sitting down across from me.

"Hank."

"My, that is a manly name. My name is Brandy, and that over there is my sister Bonnie."

"Are you ladies from around here?"

"We're from Fishs Eddy. There ain't nothin' to do down there, so every once in a while we come up here for a good time."

"Do you always have a good time here?"

"Without fail, honey-lips."

Bonnie came back to the table with three glasses of white wine and took a seat next to me.

"His name is Hank," Brandy said to Bonnie.

"Ooh, I like that name," she said.

"Bonnie's a pretty name," I said. "And so is Brandy."

"Why thank you, teddy bear."

I had never knowingly seen any prostitutes in Oneonta, but these two made me suspicious. "What do you ladies do for a living, if you don't mind my asking?"

"We run a beauty salon down in the Eddy," Bonnie said. "Brandy does hair and I do nails. Do you like my nails?"

"They're nice," I said, looking at her long red claws.

"So what do you do?" Brandy asked.

"Nothing now," I said, sipping my wine. "I just graduated."

"Well congratulations, scholar buns!" Bonnie said.

"Thanks."

"Would you like to celebrate with a dance, jelly bean?"

Without waiting for an answer, Bonnie took me by the hand and we danced to "Son of a Preacher Man" from the *Pulp Fiction* soundtrack they played night after night. She pressed her crotch against mine and slipped her hands into my back pockets as we swayed our hips to the music. While we were dancing, Virginia walked in. She stopped dead in her tracks and gave us an astonished look before continuing on her way to the bar.

"Who was that, your kid sister?" Bonnie asked, removing her hands from my pockets and putting her arms around my neck.

"Nobody," I said, watching Virginia order a drink. I looked back at Bonnie and she put her hand on my crotch and kissed me. I suggested that we sit back down.

"I was starting to get jealous," Brandy said as I slid back into the booth followed by Bonnie. Brandy started playing footsies with me under the table.

"He's a wonderful dancer," Bonnie said and started rubbing my erection. "Don't worry, gum-drop, I'll take care of you're little friend there."

"Do you need some more wine, Hankums?" Brandy asked.

"Sure," I said.

"We have some Boone's chilling in our hotel room," Bonnie said.

"Boone's, you say?"

"That's right, candy cane! Would you like to come back with us for a drink and maybe a little hanky-panky, Hankie?"

Virginia was sitting at the bar with her back to us. The last vestige of sobriety in my otherwise absolute state of intoxication felt bad, but the rest wanted her to see me walk triumphantly out of the bar with a skank in each arm. As we were going out the door I was tempted to turn and see if she was looking, but I wanted her to know that she no longer meant anything to me, so I resisted.

I was escorted to a little red pickup truck in the parking garage. Bonnie climbed into the driver's seat and I got in through the passenger door followed by Brandy so that I was sitting between them. The cab reeked of perfume and cigarettes. Bonnie pulled out of the space with a screech and Brandy gave me a kiss on the cheek while rubbing my crotch, letting out a little laugh at my boner that caused Bonnie to laugh, and the two of them got me going and we laughed all the way to the Howard Johnson's.

Bonnie parked around the back of the hotel and we went in one of the side doors. Their room was on the second floor and had a king size bed and a recliner in the corner. An unopened bottle of Boone's strawberry wine was soaking in an ice bucket full of water with the Howard Johnson's logo on the side. Brandy hung the "DO NOT

DISTURB" sign outside the door and locked it with the chain while Bonnie dug through one of the suitcases on the floor. She took something out and went into the bathroom while Brandy opened the bottle of Boone's and poured the contents into three plastic cups. Bonnie yelled through the bathroom door not to start without her.

"Come, sit down," Brandy said to me, sitting on the edge of the bed. I took a sip of the Boone's and sat where her hand was smoothing the comforter. She ran her fingers through my hair and said it was nice.

"Thanks," I said and took another long sip of the Boone's.

"Relax, Hankie-pooh," she said and started massaging my shoulders. "We're gonna take good care of you."

Bonnie emerged from the bathroom wearing a vinyl bustier and appeared to have put on a fresh coat of makeup. Brandy removed my shirt and Bonnie came over and took off my shoes and pants.

"Is this your first time with two women?" Brandy asked.

"Yeah."

"Well, don't you worry about a thing, porkpie."

"Have you ever heard of Steve Perry?" Bonnie asked.

"Steve Perry?"

"Lead singer of Journey," Brandy said.

"Yeah, I guess. Why?"

"We used to be band-aids for them. Stevie used to invite us up to his room all the time. He would specifically ask his roadies to come get us and send us up to his room."

"I miss Stevie," Bonnie said.

"So do I," Brandy said, easing me down so that my back was between her legs and my head between her breasts. She started tweaking my nipples while Bonnie started blowing me.

"This should get you nice and warmed up," Brandy said. "You're gonna fuck me hard and long, aren't you, Hankwich?"

"Sure," I said.

Brandy slid out from underneath me and pulled a handful of extra-sensation lambskin condoms out of the open suitcase. She unwrapped one and handed it to Bonnie. As drunk as I was, Bonnie had given me a sporting boner that she covered with the condom while Brandy removed all of her clothes except stockings and boots. She bent herself over one of the arms of the recliner, looked over her shoulder, and told me to come here. Bonnie pulled me off the bed with surprising strength and playfully pushed me towards her.

"In the ass?" I said.

"You should be so lucky," Brandy laughed. "I want that hard cock of yours in my wet spot."

"Just save some of that for me, sausage man," Bonnie said and laughed.

I stood there undecidedly until Bonnie reached around and guided me into Brandy. She pressed her crotch against my ass to get me going, thrusting slowly at first, but after a while I got into it. I started thinking about Virginia and Maria and all the other girls who ever made a fool of me and started fucking harder. Brandy said, "Now you're gettin' it!" and moaned while Bonnie began pleasuring herself with the empty bottle of Boone's. Moments later my frustration exploded into a knee-buckling climax that made even a seasoned whore like Brandy scream with delight. Bonnie cheered and tossed the bottle across the room, and the three of us watched it sail through the air in slow motion until it crashed through the television screen with a spark and a puff of smoke.

"Whoops!" Bonnie laughed.

"I'm glad we didn't use real names when we checked in!" Brandy laughed before heading into the bathroom.

Bonnie peeled the loaded condom off my pulsing erection and flung it against the mirror above the dresser. It slapped against the glass and stuck, my juice slowly streaking down the surface in several long thin lines. She unwrapped a fresh one and put it on me. I didn't want any more, but I was too weak to resist. She pushed me down on the bed and jumped on top of me, sliding me inside her with the ease of expertise, and rode me like a bronco, one hand waving wildly in the air and the bed squeaking so loud that it nearly drowned out her hooting and hollering. My balls started hurting and I wanted her to stop, but my voice had deserted me and I no longer had any control over my body.

Brandy emerged from the bathroom and climbed on the bed. She positioned her hole right over my face, and the smell was so foul that I immediately started feeling dizzy and nauseas. Moments later I blacked out.

The next thing I knew a phone was ringing. It was one of those old bell ringers that was so loud you could still hear it long after it stopped ringing. I almost picked it up before I realized that I didn't know where I was. My head was throbbing and I was dehydrated, my mouth so pasty that my tongue was stuck to the back of my teeth. The curtains were drawn and the room was daytime dark, but after my eyes adjusted and I saw the bottle of Boone's sticking out of the television, it all came back. The condom was still stuck to the mirror, and on the wall next to it a giant message had been written with bright red lipstick: *HANK BABY, THANKS FOR A GREAT NIGHT!* ♥ *B&B*. I was naked and a condom was caked to my penis. I looked at my watch—11:15—past checkout time.

I carefully peeled the condom off and tossed it aside. After hastily getting dressed, I checked my back pocket to make sure my wallet was still there and was a little surprised that it was, not that there had been any money in it. I took a quick look around to make sure that I wasn't leaving any incriminating evidence behind before putting an eye to the peephole on the door. It looked like the coast was clear and I didn't hear anything, so I quietly pulled the door open. The "DO NOT DISTURB" sign was still hanging from the knob. I peeked out into the hallway and saw a maid's pushcart in front of an open door two rooms down, but there was no one in sight.

I slipped out of the room and gently closed the door. Just as it clicked shut, the phone started ringing again inside. I calmly walked down the hallway like I belonged there, and when I reached the stairwell I leaped down the stairs four at a time until I was out the door.

Out in the parking lot there was a pair of tire marks in the space where the pickup had been parked. I was relieved that no one else was in the lot at the moment and hoped that I wouldn't run into Valentino, our old drug dealer who a couple of years ago took a front desk job here after he retired from dealing and had worked his way up to assistant manager. He had always been a good businessman.

The hotel was located on a county road just outside of town and there were no sidewalks, so I had to walk along the shoulder. I was worried that a cop was going to pull over and ask where I was coming from, but fortunately none went by. When I got back to Main Street half-hour later my legs were so tired and my feet so sore that I was barely able to make it up the stairs to the apartment.

As soon as I stepped inside, I encountered Oneonta State College senior class president Monica Wadsworth emerging from our bathroom wearing nothing more than a bra and panties. She had been in one of my classes and we gave each other an embarrassed hello before she continued down the hall and disappeared into Ed's room.

I went into my room and collapsed on my bed without removing my clothes or shoes. An hour later someone started pounding on my door. Suddenly I was wide awake, but I remained completely still.

"C'mon, let's go!" Bruno yelled through the door.

"What the hell is the matter with you guys?" Winston yelled, pounding on a door down the hall.

When it hadn't stopped several minutes later, I finally got out of bed and opened the door.

"Jeez," Bruno said when he saw me. "What the hell happened to you?"

"Rough night."

Ed's door was already open and the room was vacant. Russ' door opened and he stood in the threshold in his boxer shorts. "I'm not going," he said.

"I'm not either," I said.

"What the fuck?" Bruno said. "You guys already paid twenty bucks for the ticket and just yesterday you said you were going—"

"That was before last night happened," I said.

"What the hell happened last night?" Winston asked. "You guys look like a train wreck."

"Listen, I can't do it," I said. "I'm out of gas. I feel like death. I can't even think about drinking."

"Well, at least ride over with us and get some food," Bruno said.

I couldn't remember the last time I ate. There was no food in the house and I was dead broke.

"Alright, give me a few minutes," I said.

I closed the door and smoked a quick bowl. Russ had also decided to go just for the food and said he was coming back right after he ate. Teke hadn't bought a ticket but said he would walk down to the bus depot with us because Monica had mentioned the night before that they would be selling some tickets that had suddenly become available.

The senior picnic used to be an official school event held at nearby Oquaga State Park, but in recent years the alcohol consumption had gotten out of hand and the State Park administrators started issuing fines to the school. The final straw came a year earlier when 47 graduates were arrested for a laundry list of reasons ranging from public drunkenness to grand theft auto after one of the Park Ranger Broncos was stolen and later recovered in downtown Cleveland. The next day Oneonta State College president Thaddius Lockwood announced that the school was withdrawing it's sponsorship from the event due to "illegal, irresponsible, and grotesque behavior."

Having one of the biggest events of our career at Oneonta State pulled out from underneath our feet generated a lot of anger amongst our class. The issue was a hot topic during student elections, and Monica Wadsworth used it to her full advantage. She vowed that if she was elected, we would not be the first graduating class in 35 years not to have a senior picnic and that she would do whatever it took to have it whether she had the school's cooperation or not. She won in a landslide. When she started organizing the event, the school had not changed its stance and the State Park people didn't want anything to do with it, so she had to scramble. She eventually found a roadhouse on Route 206 called Husky's with a large field behind it that they were willing to rent out for the afternoon.

Several school buses had been chartered to shuttle people back and forth between the bus depot downtown and Husky's. Monica was at the depot selling the last of the extra tickets and Teke haggled one from her for thirteen bucks and some spare change. Ed, having walked down with Monica earlier to help sell tickets, was already waiting on the bus that we boarded. He laughed when he saw me and asked if I had gotten any last night, but I didn't feel like talking and gave him a blunt no.

The arriving buses were greeted by twenty or so bikers wearing red Husky's Security T-shirts under leather jackets. They were all big bearded biker guys who seemed giddy at the prospect of an afternoon of keeping college students in line like the Hell's Angels did at Altamont. In exchange for our tickets, plastic bracelets were wrapped around our wrists and we were directed past a chicken wire fence across an open field with a softball diamond in one corner and a Busch beer truck with taps sticking out of the side of it in another. A canopy for the grills was being set up next to the truck, but we were told that the food wouldn't be ready for at least an hour.

With time to kill, I grabbed a beer. I wasn't in much of a condition to be drinking and had to fight it down, but I drank quickly and by the time the burgers were finally being flipped, I had four in me with a good buzz going. A band named Extinction had been setting up at home plate and opened their set with the Stones' "Gimme Shelter."

A couple of hours later there were hundreds of people packed into the field, people we hadn't seen since the open house frat parties freshman year, people who lived down the hall from us in Golding and Matteson, people we had chance encounters with over the past four years and had forgotten about. We didn't talk to any of them. Just like in the old days, we had our own little huddle near the beer truck and stood there drinking and making fun of people. Now that it was over, everything that had been wedged between us over the past couple of years suddenly vanished. For one day we were closer than we had been since we lived in Matteson Hall and it felt good, but this clearly wouldn't have been the case if it wasn't the very end.

The afternoon flew by. At around 5:30 Ed and I were on the beer line when the taps were suddenly shut off. Confusion rippled through the crowd from the truck on back. Up on stage the lead singer of Extinction said that one of the beer guys had an announcement.

"Can I have your attention," the beer guy shouted into the mike. He was wearing an official pinstriped Anheuser-Busch button down shirt and matching baseball cap. The lead singer told him he didn't have to shout.

"Can I have your attention," he said again, this time without shouting, and the crowd quieted down.

"We need beer out here!" someone from the crowd yelled.

"It seems that we have encountered a disturbing situation," the beer guy continued. "Apparently, some of your own classmates have abused your privileges by printing up over 100 counterfeit tickets, so as of this point the beer and catering services have been used up."

"That's bullshit!" someone yelled, and the crowd started chanting "Bull-shit!"

"Unfortunately, this is not bullshit. This is the work of your fellow classmates. You have no one to blame but yourselves."

The "Bull-shit!" chant got louder and the beer guy looked over at someone off-stage with an *I've done all I can do* shrug. The bikers started getting restless as if they knew that something was about to go down and were awaiting a signal to start busting heads. The fervor of the crowd continued to escalate until somebody yelled "There's still beer in the truck!" and that was it. The crowd surged forward and started rocking the truck as if trying to tip it over and break it open. The bikers jumped into the fray and started tossing people aside like they were nothing, and though heavily outmanned, they were extremely efficient fighters, knocking out college students with one punch and quickly moving on to the next one without losing any of their own.

Meanwhile, those who decided to flee the beer truck riot ran to the waiting school buses and started a riot of their own. I was amongst these rioters and managed to squeeze into the first bus before the driver whipped out a bullhorn and threatened to radio the state police if those still trying to get on didn't back off. After he had some clearance, he slid the doors closed and pulled away.

The bus was packed but quiet. During the chaos just about everyone had been split apart from whoever they were with, so most of us on the bus didn't know each other and almost everyone was out of breath. It was only a fifteen minute ride, but I was so exhausted that I slept through most of it and the guy sitting next to me on the inside of the seat had to wake me up when we got back into town.

Downtown Oneonta was deserted. The bars were open but nobody was in them, and the bartenders hardly took notice of me wandering in and out. When I reached the end of Water Street I turned onto Chestnut, crossed Main, and passed by the big church. I kept going until I reached West Street, where I made a right and headed all the way up to Center Street. I made another right and passed Eliot and the Big Guy's old house and a little while later crossed Maple, where I caught a peripheral view of the Philanthan house but didn't look directly at it. I had been walking close to an hour now, yet I had not encountered another soul and not a single car had driven by. At the other end of Center I stopped at a vacant and recently remodeled house and looked in the first floor windows to see that it looked nothing like it did when we lived there. I continued up East Street for a few blocks and then turned back over to Maple, where I passed Fred's old house before heading up Golding Path. I went by Golding Hall, Matteson Hall, the dining halls, the lecture halls, the administration building, the Hunt Union, and finally up the three tiers of fields. In the distance a motionless cloud of smoke clung by a thread to the smokestack on top of the campus power station, and to the west a smear of hazy orange light slowly descended until it was no longer there, leaving me as naked as I was when I first got to this place with only the surrounding sky to protect and confine me.

Made in the USA
Lexington, KY
13 December 2014